HOT SHOT

ALSO BY SHELDON SIEGEL

Mike Daley/Rosie Fernandez Novels

Special Circumstances
Incriminating Evidence
Criminal Intent
Final Verdict
The Confession
Judgment Day
Perfect Alibi
Felony Murder Rule
Serve and Protect
Hot Shot
The Dreamer

David Gold/A.C. Battle Novels

The Terrorist Next Door

HOT SHOT

A Mike Daley/Rosie Fernandez Thriller

Sheldon Siegel

This is a work of fiction. Names, characters, places, and incidents either are the product of the author's imagination or are used fictitiously, and any resemblance to actual persons, living or dead, businesses, companies, events, or locales is entirely coincidental.

Sheldon M. Siegel, Inc.

Copyright © 2019 Sheldon M. Siegel, Inc.
ALL RIGHTS RESERVED

No part of this book may be reproduced, scanned, or printed or electronic form without permission. Please do not participate in or encourage piracy of copyrighted materials in violation of the author's rights. Purchase only authorized editions.

ISBN: 978-0-9996747-2-7 E-Book
ISBN: 978-0-9996747-3-4 Print

In loving memory of

Jan Harris (1934-2018)
Matz Sandler (1925-2014)

"Move fast and break things."
— Mark Zuckerberg

"Don't be evil."
— Original Google Code of Conduct

1
"WE HAVE A NEW CLIENT"

The twinkling Christmas lights strung along the pinewood bar reflected in the gregarious barkeep's eyes. My uncle, Big John Dunleavy, spoke to me in a well-practiced brogue—even though he'd never set foot on the Emerald Isle. "What'll it be, lad?"

"You're off duty, Big John."

"I've been running this dive for almost sixty years, Mikey. I'm *always* on duty."

"Not tonight." Although his grandson, Joey, had taken over the day-to-day operations a couple of years earlier, Big John still showed up every morning and stayed until last call. "Dunleavy's isn't a dive. It's a neighborhood institution."

"Give your favorite uncle a break."

"I'm trying." I leaned forward and shouted above the roar in the crowded saloon on Irving Street on the west side of San Francisco where the sun rarely peeked through the fog. Big John's body and mind were as sound as ever, but his ears required a little boost from his hearing aids. "It's your eighty-fifth birthday party. You get the night off."

"Fine." His jowls wiggled as he poured himself a pint of Guinness using the immense right hand that once hauled in passes when he was an all-city tight end at our alma mater, St. Ignatius. "I'll be back at work first thing in the morning."

"I wouldn't expect otherwise."

At ten-thirty p.m. on Sunday, December twenty-third, Big John's pasty face rearranged itself into a satisfied smile as he tossed a dishtowel over his shoulder and scanned the festive room packed with well-wishers—many of whom had been regulars for decades. Over the years, he had adapted to changing times and tastes as his Irish and Italian customers moved to the suburbs and were replaced by second- and third-generation families from Chinatown. During the day, Dunleavy's was now a gathering spot for the neighborhood's seniors who sipped tea from white mugs and consumed Big John's "Special Noodles," a concoction he'd based on a family recipe provided by

Mayor Ed Lee, who used to stop by a couple of times a week before he died of a heart attack at the Diamond Heights Safeway. The local cops and fire fighters still came in for Big John's fish and chips.

I spoke directly into his better ear. "A lot of young people here tonight."

"Millennials. Business went up almost thirty percent when I put in free WiFi. The tech kids love it. I have my own Facebook page and Twitter handle."

You can't stay in business for more than a half-century unless you're adaptable. "There are trendier places."

"We have a five-star rating on Yelp. Seems we're viewed as one of the last 'authentic' pubs in the City."

That's true. "The kids come all the way out here for authenticity?"

"I don't question their motives before I accept their cash, lad."

Neither would I. "Where do they park?"

"They don't. Driving is so last millennium. They take Uber and Lyft. Sometimes they even take the N-Judah. Public transit is hip again, too."

The streetcar stopped a block from Dunleavy's. "You okay with a younger crowd?"

"Absolutely. They're well-behaved. They're good tippers. And they spend most of their time texting. Besides, I have a long-standing policy of treating all paying customers equally. Money is money, Mikey."

Yes, it is. "Your regulars don't mind?"

"They like being around the kids, too. It makes them feel young again."

It had become fashionable for Baby Boomers like me to bash Millennials like my kids, but I enjoyed their company—especially since my daughter and son were members of their tribe.

I walked around to the business side of the bar and put on a well-used apron. I had taken the helm of the watering hole countless times. So had my dad, a San Francisco cop who was married to Big John's sister. And my older brother, Tommy, who was a star quarterback at St. Ignatius and Cal before he died in Vietnam. And my younger brother, Pete, who became a cop, and then a P.I. Pop had helped Big John build the bar three years before I was born. Thomas James Charles Daley, Sr.—who was Big John's best friend—had been gone for twenty years. My mom had been gone almost ten. They would have enjoyed the party. Although he wouldn't say it aloud, I knew that Big John missed them. And I did, too.

I took a moment to savor the ambiance. The mismatched tables were adorned with balloons. Behind the pool table, a Christmas tree stood between a Hanukkah menorah and a Kwanzaa kinara. For patrons of more secular and whimsical persuasions, Big John had situated a Festivus pole near the big-screen TV. Everybody was welcome at Dunleavy's.

Big John smiled broadly as my twenty-year-old daughter, Grace, approached us. His phony Irish lilt became more pronounced. "Hello, darlin'. How's my favorite great-niece?"

"Fine. Happy Birthday, Big John."

"Thank you. I wasn't sure that you would make it tonight."

"Wouldn't have missed it. I just drove up from L.A. Came straight here."

"You still seeing that boy?"

"No."

"Boys are like the N-Judah, honey. If you miss one, another one will come along soon enough."

"May I use that line?"

"Absolutely."

Grace Fernandez Daley was halfway through her senior year at USC. She was a dead ringer in appearance and temperament for her mother, who was sitting in a booth near the back door. Rosita Carmela Fernandez was my ex-wife and San Francisco's Public Defender. She was also my boss. Grace was a film major who had lined up a post-graduation job at Pixar. In her spare time, she was running a wildly successful dating and sex-advice app for college students that she had modestly christened the 'Love Goddess.'"

"How's business?" Big John asked her.

"Excellent."

"Everybody here reads your stuff."

"Glad to hear it."

He finally dropped the brogue. "What can we get you to drink, young lady?"

"Just water, Big John."

"Can we offer you a beer?"

"I won't turn twenty-one until next month."

"As if you've never ordered a beer in a bar."

"I don't want you to get into trouble on your birthday."

My uncle let out a throaty laugh. "You think somebody is going to arrest me? This room is full of cops and their spouses, kids, grandkids, and great-grandkids. And, in a few cases, their mistresses. A couple of assistant chiefs are shooting pool. Your Grandpa Tom used to come here after work. Your Grandma Margaret wasn't crazy about it, but at least she knew where he was. I served your father his first adult beverage at this very establishment—when he was fourteen."

"Fifteen," I interjected.

"I stand corrected. I taught him how to tend bar when he was seventeen. It wasn't entirely legal, but the customers liked him, and it put a few bucks in his pocket to pay for college. Your dad is the head of the Felony Division of the P.D.'s Office. Your mom is the P.D. If I get arrested, my crackerjack legal team will take good care of me."

Grace's hoop-style earrings shimmered as she flashed a smile that looked just like her mother's. "Do you have a Grapefruit Saison?"

I looked over at my daughter. "A what?"

Big John spoke up before she could answer. "She's testing me, Mikey. It's a pilsner made by Holy Mountain Brewing in Seattle. It's all the rage with my younger customers." He turned to Grace. "I'm out of the Grapefruit, but I have a Hart and an Ox. Which would you prefer?"

Her smile became broader. "You're good, Big John."

"You think you're the first person who's asked for a craft brew?"

"Guess not. I'd like a Hart, please."

"May I see your ID, please?"

Her grin disappeared. "Really?"

"I run a business, young lady."

She pulled out her driver's license and placed it on the bar.

Big John pretended to study it. "Not your *real* ID, Grace. Your *fake* ID."

Her smile reappeared. She handed a second license to Big John.

"Nice work." He showed it to me. "The technology has gotten better, Mikey. This looks very authentic." He gave it back to Grace. "How much did it set you back?"

"Seventy-five bucks."

"Things have gotten cheaper, too." He reached below the bar, pulled out a bottle of Hart, and instructed me to pour it into a glass for my underage daughter. Then he turned to Grace. "Would you go out in the back and see if anybody needs anything?"

"Will do."

"Thanks, darlin'."

As I watched her head out to the patio, I spoke to my uncle. "You know that you're the only person on Planet Earth who can get away with calling her 'darlin.'"

"There are still a few privileges at my advanced age." He gave me a knowing smile. "She's a beauty, Mikey." He caught himself. "Am I still allowed to say that?"

"Yes."

"Looks just like Rosie. And every bit as smart."

"Indeed."

"So, how does my favorite nephew—the ex-priest—feel about his daughter's business?"

I was afraid you might ask. "I've been a lawyer a lot longer than I was a priest."

"You going to answer my question?"

Eventually. "I take it this means that you know about her little side hustle?"

"Everybody does, Mikey. Why do you think all the young people come to my homely little watering hole out here in the fog? I'm a D-List celebrity. Around here, I'm known as the Love Goddess's great-uncle."

"You're kidding."

"I'm not."

"How did they find out?"

"I might have let it slip."

"My eighty-five-year-old uncle is cashing in on the popularity of my twenty-year-old daughter's sex-advice app?"

"Don't be such a prude, Mikey. It's good for business. If I play my cards properly, this humble tavern is going to put another generation of Dunleavys through college. So, how does an ex-priest-turned-lawyer feel about his daughter running an app called the Love Goddess?"

"I'm conflicted. It wouldn't have been my first choice for a career path. Then again, it's paying for her senior year at USC, a nice apartment, and that new car parked outside." *And if the number of her followers continues to grow, it may be enough for a down payment on a house.*

He arched a bushy eyebrow. "You don't sound *that* conflicted."

I'm not. "I've become more open-minded as I've gotten older." *And I'm not a priest anymore.* "Besides, she isn't hurting anybody, and she's doing something she enjoys." *And she's hauling in a boatload of cash.*

"How does her mother feel about it?"

Not great. "She's become more open-minded, too."

Big John's smile broadened. "Is Grace still going to take the job at Pixar?"

"I think so." *If she decides that she can afford the pay cut.* "They've agreed to let her continue to run the app on her own time. They like to encourage their employees to develop their, uh, creativity."

"Gotta admire her entrepreneurial spirit."

"Just like you, Big John."

"And her tenacity."

"Just like her mother."

His voice filled with pride. "Don't let this go to your head, Mikey, but you and Rosie have done a nice job with your kids."

Especially since we got divorced eighteen years ago. "Thanks, Big John."

"Is little Tommy here?"

"He's out in the back." *And he isn't little anymore.* Our fourteen-year-old son, Thomas James Charles Daley, was taller than I was. "You aren't going to offer him a beer, too, are you?"

"Absolutely not. The drinking age for family is fifteen."

"Happy birthday, Big John."

"Thanks, Mikey. I'm going to take a lap and visit with my guests. Mind keeping an eye on the bar?"

"My pleasure."

* * *

At one o'clock the following morning, the Public Defender of the City and County of San Francisco was sitting next to the ex-cop-turned-private-investigator in a weathered booth beneath a faded autographed photo of Juan Marichal in the back of Dunleavy's. The most decorated homicide inspector in SFPD history sat across from them. The P.D., Rosie Fernandez, was my ex-wife. The P.I., Pete Daley, was my younger brother. The retired detective, Roosevelt Johnson, was my father's first partner. Rosie was looking at the big-screen TV, her ever-present iPhone pressed to her ear. Between scowls, she was drinking a Bud straight from the bottle. Pete nursed a cup of coffee. Roosevelt sipped a club soda.

I slid into the seat next to Roosevelt and put my bottle of Anchor Steam on the table. Roosevelt and my dad had spent countless nights in this booth after their shifts had ended.

Rosie lowered the phone. "The kids took my mom home."

"Good."

Rosie's eighty-four-year-old mother, Sylvia Fernandez, still lived in a two-bedroom, one-bath bungalow in the Mission that she and her late husband had purchased in 1962. Rosie's occasional suggestions that her mother cash in her chips and move into a condo requiring less day-to-day maintenance had not been well received.

I turned to Roosevelt, who was wearing his usual charcoal suit and understated necktie. "Janet okay?"

He responded in the familiar baritone that still had a hint of his native Texas. "So-so."

His wife had been waging a heroic fight against multiple forms of cancer for almost a decade. "You working on any cold cases?"

"Not at the moment. I'm trying to focus on my grandchildren."

"Sounds good." I looked at my brother. "Nice party."

Pete's brown hair and mustache used to be a half-shade darker than mine. Now they were a distinguished shade of gray. His pockmarked face bore the scars of a decade as a cop and almost twenty years as a P.I. He adjusted the sleeve of his bomber jacket and spoke in a Clint Eastwood rasp. "Yup."

This represented chattiness for him. "You okay?"

"Fine, Mick."

"I saw Donna."

"Margaret wasn't feeling well. Donna took her home."

Margaret—named after our mom—was Pete's twelve-year-old daughter and my niece. Pete's wife, Donna, was a patient soul who had the profoundly thankless job as the chief financial officer of a big law firm downtown. Donna had adapted—at times grudgingly—to

Pete's unpredictable hours.

"You and Donna okay?" I asked.

"Fine."

"'Fine' as in 'good,' or 'not so good, but we're dealing with it'?"

"We always work it out, Mick." He changed the subject. "Could you believe all the tech kids here tonight? Big John is going to have to hire another bartender."

"Maybe we could take a couple of shifts."

"I got more work than I can handle."

"I was kidding. You working tonight?"

"Later."

"Cheating wife?"

"Cheating husband. Everything you've heard about sex, drugs, and misogyny in the tech world is true—only worse."

"I assumed that much of it has been exaggerated."

"You'd be amazed."

Rosie finally ended her call. "We need to get down to the office."

"It's one a.m. on Christmas Eve."

"We have a new client."

It wasn't unusual for defense attorneys—including the Public Defender—to get calls in the middle of the night—even on Christmas Eve. "What is it, Rosie?"

Her cobalt eyes gleamed as she played with the collar of her Armani Collezioni blouse. When we had met almost twenty-five years earlier in the file room of the old P.D.'s Office, her straight black hair had cascaded down to her waist, and her wardrobe consisted of jeans and denim work shirts. When she ran for Public Defender two years earlier, she had shortened and styled her hair and acquired a wardrobe more suitable for her occasional TV appearances.

She pointed at the TV. A reporter from Channel 2 was standing in front of a Victorian. Flashing red lights reflected off the house. The caption indicated that she was on Twenty-First Street, above Mission Dolores, where a bunch of tech moguls had refurbished several blocks of turn-of-the-century houses. "You see that?"

"Something happened on Billionaires Row?"

"One of the billionaires is dead. They're saying our new client killed him."

2
"THE PRINCE OF DISRUPTION"

"Which billionaire?" I asked.

Rosie was still looking at her iPhone. "The 'Prince of Disruption.'"

I was more familiar with the players on the Warriors than those in the tech industry. "Does he have a name?"

Pete answered. "Jeff King. Founder of Y5K Technologies. If you believe the hype, his company is going to make cloud computing obsolete."

I was fairly adept at using my iPhone and laptop, but I lacked the capacity and the interest to obsess about every incremental advance in technology. "Who gave him that nickname?"

"He did. At his Ted Talk a couple of years ago."

Why am I not surprised? "How much is he worth?"

"You mean 'How much *was* he worth?'"

"Uh, yes."

"Supposedly, about ten billion."

As a practical matter, that figure was incomprehensible to the son of a San Francisco cop who made ends meet on a P.D.'s salary and was hoping to retire someday on a civil servant's pension. In the Bay Area's tech Neverland, King was just another billionaire.

Pete was still talking. "In Silicon Valley, the scuttlebutt is that his company can compete with Amazon Web Services."

"Don't believe the hype."

"It's also an open secret that King was one of the biggest jerks in the tech space. That was quite an accomplishment—he had a lot of competition."

It wasn't a news flash that bad behavior was prevalent in the tech universe—along with every other industry, including the legal profession. I asked Rosie how he died.

"Looked like an overdose, but it's too soon to know."

He wasn't the first high-profile entrepreneur to OD, either. "It could have been an accident."

"The cops are saying our new client gave him a hot shot of

heroin."

"Who is he?"

"She. Her name is Alexa Low."

"Where is she?"

"Homicide. They took her in for questioning."

The Homicide Detail was housed in San Francisco's Hall of Justice at Seventh and Bryant, next to the I-80 Freeway.

She stood up. "I'll give you a lift downtown. We need to talk to her right away."

I turned to Pete, who was pulling on his jacket. "You want to tag along?"

"I'll head out to Billionaires Row and see what I can find out."

"I thought you were tailing a cheating husband."

"I'll get somebody to cover for me." He gave me a conspiratorial wink. "Betcha I'll have company. Half the P.I.s in town were watching the Prince of Disruption."

* * *

"What do you know about King?" I asked Rosie.

"Just what I've read in the papers." She gripped the wheel of her Prius as we drove east on Lincoln Way along the southern border of Golden Gate Park. A mist covered the windshield. "His company is supposed to go public next year. It's the hottest offering since Facebook."

I didn't pay close attention to such matters. "Is he really worth ten billion?"

"It's all funny money to me."

Me, too.

Her eyes were on the road, where traffic was light. "Late forties. Serial entrepreneur. Made money on a couple of startups, but had more failures than successes. This company was supposed to be his big payday."

She knew more than I expected. "Inconvenient time to OD."

"If he did, in fact, OD. For all we know, somebody could have given him rat poison. Either way, a lot of people may lose millions."

"You think somebody killed him to stop the IPO?"

"Don't know."

"Any chance our new client killed him?"

"No idea."

I asked her if King was married.

"The third time was the charm. A pretty wife and a baby daughter. If you believe the *Chronicle*, he was a dedicated family man."

"Who died of a heroin overdose administered by our new client."

"*Allegedly* administered. And we don't know for sure that it was heroin or an overdose."

"Right. Am I correct in assuming that our new client is not King's wife?"

"You are."

"What was her relationship to the deceased?"

"We'll find out when we talk to her."

3
"WE NEED TO SEE OUR NEW CLENT"

Four a.m. The veteran homicide cop fingered the lapel of his Men's Wearhouse suit jacket. Inspector Ken Lee leaned back in a rickety swivel chair behind his metal desk in the bullpen housing SFPD's Homicide Detail on the third floor of the Hall of Justice. He spoke to Rosie as if I wasn't there. "Kids okay?"

"Fine."

"Your mother?"

"All good."

"Glad to hear it."

After we made our initial request to see our new client, Lee had let us cool our heels for almost three hours in the otherwise-empty hallway in the drab fifties-era building squeezed between Bryant Street and the I-80 Freeway in the South of Market neighborhood that was rapidly transforming from an industrial area into a tech hub. The fortress-like, asbestos-laden edifice had been declared unsafe from earthquakes, and many departments had moved to safer quarters in other buildings. The D.A.'s Office, Homicide, several courtrooms, and a few dozen jail cells were still housed in the old warhorse with leaky windows and spotty plumbing. Visiting the Hall was like going to a Giants' game during the last season at Candlestick. If anything broke, the City wasn't going to fix it.

Lee was still talking to Rosie. "You going to run for re-election?"

"That's the plan."

"You could take early retirement with a decent pension."

"We have another kid to put through college."

"I have two."

"Then I guess we'll just keep rolling."

Rosie and I feigned interest as Lee talked about the complications of sharing custody with his ex-wife. We understood the issues. Then again, Rosie and I were a permanent—albeit unmarried—couple, and we got along reasonably well most of the time. We also knew that it was essential to observe protocol when you're trolling for information from a homicide inspector in the wee hours on Christmas Eve. Never a chatty soul, Lee worked alone because he liked it that way. After two decades working undercover in Chinatown, he was rewarded with a promotion to Homicide. His boyish good looks had given way to a leathery complexion, and a scar ran across his right cheek. His hair was more gray than black, and he walked with a limp.

Rosie tried to ease him into the matters at hand. "We didn't expect to find you here."

"Criminals don't keep regular hours."

"We figured you'd still be up on Billionaires Row."

"I'll be heading back shortly. Looks like I'll be working today and tomorrow."

So will we.

Rosie's tone remained even. "We need to see our new client."

"Which one?"

As if you don't know.

Rosie held up a hand. "Alexa Low."

"I didn't realize the P.D.'s Office was representing her."

"That's not your concern."

"You're sure that she'll qualify? Her LinkedIn page says that she's a programmer for a FinTech startup, so she must be pulling down some coin. Her driver's license indicates that she lives in one of those new loft buildings near the ballpark. And she was at a party at the house of the founder of a hot startup."

Rosie folded her arms. "We'll ask her about it. I presume that she's still here?"

"She's still down in intake."

"You shouldn't have questioned her outside our presence. You've already violated her right to remain silent."

"I advised her of her rights. She spoke to me voluntarily."

"Anything she told you is inadmissible."

"Other than her name and date of birth, she didn't say a word."

"We need to see her *now*."

"*After* she's processed."

"You are denying us the opportunity to talk to our client."

"No, I'm not. I'm simply informing you of her whereabouts. You're free to talk to her after she's completed intake."

Rosie kept pushing. "We understand that the decedent was Jeff

King."

"I cannot confirm or deny that information at this time."

"It was on the news."

"I cannot officially release the name of the victim pending notification of family."

"Have you decided on a charge?"

"We booked her on murder-one. We will, of course, forward everything to the D.A., who will decide on the formal charge in court."

The D.A. could hold our client for up to seventy-two hours (not including weekends and holidays). It was likely that she would be held until after Christmas.

"Has a time been set for the arraignment?"

"Not yet."

Rosie glanced my way, and I took the cue. "Would you mind telling us what happened?"

"I can't talk about it now."

You mean you won't talk about it. "Just a few highlights?"

"Off the record, there was a gathering at King's house to celebrate his company's forthcoming IPO. Your client was there."

"Was King's wife at the party?"

"As far as we know, she was at their house in Palo Alto."

"They have places in Palo Alto and San Francisco?"

"And a co-op on Central Park West, a townhouse in La Jolla, a bungalow in Malibu, a beach house in Maui, a chalet in Lake Tahoe, a cabin in Aspen, and a pied-à-terre in Paris."

Nice life. "Was anybody at the party mad at him?"

"No comment."

"He must have ruffled a few feathers."

"No comment."

"It's too early to rule out the possibility that somebody killed him because they were unhappy about a business or personal matter."

"That's something to discuss with your client."

We will. "King was divorced twice. He had a reputation for treating people poorly—especially women."

"All I know is what I've seen in the papers."

"What makes you think our client was involved?"

"She injected King."

"How do you know?"

His eyes narrowed. "We know."

"Heroin?"

"No comment."

"Are you suggesting our client supplied it and injected King with intent to kill?"

"No comment."

"Had they met before last night?"

"Yes." He didn't elaborate.

"Is she a hooker?"

"She's definitely a looker."

"You think King was paying her for sex?"

"We found five grand in unmarked bills in her purse."

That would fall squarely into the category of bad optics. "Who found the body?"

"The victim's security chief. He called 9-1-1. Your new client tried to flee, but he stopped her. She made no effort to help King."

Not good. "We'll need a list of everybody who was there last night."

"It will be in my report."

I tried again. "How can you be so sure that our client injected the decedent?"

"We have it on video."

4
"SEXY LEXY"

The petite young woman with straight black hair, chiseled cheekbones, and delicate features stared at us through glassy brown eyes and spoke in a hoarse whisper. "Are you my lawyers?"

Rosie answered her. "At the moment, yes. We'll make a final determination after you complete our intake procedures."

At four-thirty a.m., Alexa Low had just finished a brief intake interview, been showered with disinfectant, and completed a perfunctory medical exam. Her fair skin had a pale cast from a light bulb dangling from the ceiling of a windowless eight-by-ten-foot consultation room on the fourth floor of County Jail #2, the Costco-like structure jammed between the Hall of Justice and I-80 in the nineties. The cops had dubbed it the "Glamour Slammer."

Our new client's voice filled with desperation. "I need you to get me out of here."

Rosie invoked the maternal tone that I had heard for the first time when I was a rookie public defender. "We'll do everything that we can, Ms. Low."

"Lexy."

"Rosie Fernandez. I'm the Public Defender. This is Mike Daley. He's the head of our Felony Division."

"I didn't expect to see the Public Defender at this hour."

"It's Christmas Eve. We gave our deputies the night off."

"Will you be handling my case?"

"We'll decide on staffing in due course."

Lexy cut to the chase. "I didn't kill Jeff."

"We'll talk about what happened in a few minutes."

Rosie was being coy for strategic reasons. Neither of us wanted to ask Lexy flat-out if she'd killed King. If we knew that the answer was yes, we couldn't let her lie about it in court. We defense lawyers find creative ways to dance around this rule, but it's better to avoid the issue altogether.

Rosie started with the basics. "What is your full name?"

"Alexa Susan Low." She said that she was twenty-five.

"Are you hurt or sick?"

"No."

"Did they give you something to eat?"

She took a sip of water from a paper cup. "A tuna sandwich." She declined Rosie's offer of additional food.

"What have you told the police?"

"Just my name and date of birth."

"Good. Have you talked to anybody else?"

"No."

"Even better. Rule Number One: You don't talk to anybody except Mike and me. Not the cops. Or Inspector Lee. Or the press. Or anybody in the hallway. And especially none of the other detainees. Not tonight. Not tomorrow. Not ever. Understood?"

"Yes."

"Do you have a cell phone or laptop?"

"Both. The police took them."

"Did you give them your passwords?"

"No."

"Is there anything that might be problematic if they manage to crack your passwords?"

She thought about it for a moment. "I don't think so."

"Good." Rosie's voice softened. "Who can we call for you?"

"Nobody."

"Somebody must be worried about you."

"Nobody," she repeated.

"Are you married?"

"No."

"Divorced?"

"No."

"Boyfriend? Girlfriend?"

"No." She confirmed that she had no roommates, either.

"Parents?"

"Gone." Lexy explained that her mother had died in an auto accident two years earlier. She had never met her father. She had no siblings.

"Friends?"

"Not anymore."

How sad.

Rosie asked if she had ever been arrested.

"No."

"Where are you from?"

"Daly City." She said that she had graduated from Cal four years earlier.

Rosie pointed at me. "Mike's a Cal alum, too."

Go Bears. I asked, "What did you study?"

"Computer science." She said that her first job was as a programmer at Uber. Then she moved to a FinTech startup. "We competed with Bitcoin."

"You must have been well compensated," Rosie said.

"I was." Lexy's eyes turned down. "I lost my job about a year ago. I had a disagreement with my boss."

"About work?"

"About his hands. He couldn't keep them off me."

"Did you report him to HR?"

"Yes. The first time, they did nothing. The second time, they gave him a warning. The third time, they fired me. I looked for another job, but they blackballed me."

"That's illegal," I said.

"It was his word against mine. You know how it goes."

Unfortunately, I do. "Where do you live?"

"When they have room, in a shelter in the Mission. Some nights, on the street."

"Your driver's license lists an address in an apartment near the ballpark."

"I don't live there anymore. I ran out of money about six months ago. I had to move out of my apartment, sell my car, and default on my student loans."

She had covered a lot of territory in a short period.

Rosie kept her tone even. "What haven't you told us?"

Lexy pulled up her sleeve and showed us needle marks. "Heroin."

I wasn't surprised.

Rosie and I sat in silence as Lexy filled in details. Raised by a single mother in Daly City. Graduated at the top of her class from Jefferson High School and worked her way through Cal. A programmer at Uber for two years. Recruited to a FinTech startup. At first, she was well-respected, well-liked, and well-compensated. Then her supervisor started hitting on her. When she rebuffed his advances, she was fired. Around the same time, her mother died in an auto accident, and she started taking anti-depressants. Then she injured her knee while jogging. She got hooked on pain killers and medical marijuana. That led to stronger drugs and, ultimately, heroin. Her habit got more expensive as her income disappeared.

Her tone was somber. "I lost my job. I lost my mother. I lost my savings. I lost my apartment. I lost everything."

Rosie's lips turned down. "Are you getting treatment?"

"Sometimes."

Rosie and I exchanged a glance. In the best of circumstances, dealing with addiction was extraordinarily difficult. It was even harder for somebody who was unemployed and living in a shelter. It would be almost impossible for somebody in custody.

I told her that we would ask for a medical evaluation. "I'll need you to sign a HIPAA form and give us authorization to obtain your medical records. We'll make sure that you get treatment."

Her voice was flat. "Fine."

"Were you high last night?"

"I took a little smack to take off the edge."

"Drinking?"

"Just a glass of wine."

That would seem to rule out a "diminished mental capacity" defense. "Do you have any money in the bank?" I hated asking this question, but it was my job.

"A couple hundred dollars." She said that she owed ninety thousand on her student loans. "I thought about bankruptcy, but it wouldn't have gotten rid of them."

It wasn't a good time to ask why she hadn't paid off her loans while she was flush. "We'll need you to complete a financial declaration and a request for appointed counsel. If your financial story checks out, it's likely that you'll qualify for our services."

"Thank you." There was a hint of light in her eyes. "When can you get me out of here?"

That's always the top priority. "The earliest will be at an arraignment. Given the holiday, it's unlikely to happen before Wednesday."

"What can you do now?"

"First, you need to understand that you have to be completely honest with us. It's our only absolute rule. We can't be blindsided in court or when we talk to the D.A."

"Understood."

Here goes. "Tell us about your relationship with Jeff King."

"I've known him for about six months."

"You knew that he was married?"

"Yes. Unhappily."

"You were dating?"

"We were having sex and doing drugs. Crystal meth. Speed. Heroin. Designer stuff."

"Which you provided?"

"If you were a billionaire, would you accept drugs from somebody you met on the Internet?"

"Probably not." *Stranger things have happened.* "He paid you for sex?"

"I'm not a hooker, Mr. Daley. We had a sophisticated relationship."

At the risk of being judgmental, it doesn't seem sophisticated to me. "You met online?"

"Yes."

"Match? Tinder?"

"Mature Relations."

"I'm not familiar with that site." *Or any other hookup site, for that matter.*

"It's like Sugar Daddy with a more exclusive clientele."

"Sugar Daddy?"

"It's a site for affluent people seeking mature romantic relationships."

Call me old-fashioned, but I'm having trouble grasping how this arrangement could result in anything resembling romance.

Her voice remained even. "It's like every dating site. You set up a profile and post photos. You also specify how much you're willing to spend, and how much you expect your match to spend on you. You provide financial information. They plug it into the algorithm and send you a list of names."

Very romantic. "How did you qualify?

"Do you think they really check your assets?"

Guess not.

"Jeff liked my photo. He wanted to sleep with me. That's all that mattered."

"Did you have any other patrons from Mature Relations?"

"No."

"Is your listing still active?"

"Yes. My handle is 'Sexy Lexy.'"

Of course. "We'll need your login and password to take it down. It will not enhance your credibility with potential jurors if a screenshot appears on the front page of the *Chronicle*."

"Fine." Her tone turned pointed. "In a perfect world, I wouldn't be hooking up with rich old guys, but I'm not the only person doing it. People in tech work crazy hours. Nobody has time to meet people in bars. Jeff had an unhappy marriage and wanted something that I was able to provide. I liked him well enough, and I needed the money. It was working pretty well."

Until last night. "Did his wife know?"

"Probably. It isn't public, but they were separated. They are getting divorced."

According to Rosie, his marriage had been portrayed in a more idyllic light in the *Chronicle*. "You understand that once the press gets wind of this, it won't look good."

"Jeff and I didn't invent this stuff. Mature Relations has more than ten million subscribers. Everybody does it."

Well, not everybody. "Let's go back to the beginning. I want you to tell us everything that happened last night from the minute you arrived until the cops showed up."

5
"THERE WAS A 'CUDDLE PUDDLE'"

Lexy was drinking her third cup of water. "It was just business," she insisted.

"How many times had you seen King before last night?" I asked.

"About a dozen. Usually at the house here in San Francisco. A couple of times at the Four Seasons in Palo Alto. Once at a resort in Carmel Valley."

"What about his house in Palo Alto?"

"Never. His wife and baby lived there."

Kudos for discretion. "He invited you to his house knowing that others would be there?"

"Sometimes your urges trump your judgment."

"When did he invite you to the party?"

"I got a text from him around eight o'clock last night. He had just landed at SFO. He'd been travelling all week, and he wanted a little action."

"He didn't want to see his daughter?"

"He wanted to see me."

I was beginning to see why King and his wife had separated. Rosie and I got married after a brief romance while we were working at the P.D.'s Office. She had just spun out of a bad marriage. I had spent three unhappy years as a priest. We were young, stubborn, and incompatible. Nowadays, we're older, still stubborn, and more compatible. We've also learned that we need our own spaces. That's why we've maintained separate residences in Marin County, even though we spend many nights together. We weren't good at being married, but we never cheated.

Lexy was warming up. "Jeff invited some people to his house to thank them for their work on the IPO. He asked me to come over later. He said that I shouldn't talk to the guests. He told me to go upstairs and wait in his bedroom until everybody left."

Because a good family man didn't want his high-flying pals to meet the woman he had met on Mature Relations. "You were okay with it?"

"It was part of our deal. We were never seen together."

"He provided the heroin?"

"Always. Every time we met at his house, he left it in a drawer in the master bath."

"Some of the guests were still there when you arrived?"

"Yes. The party ran late."

"Did you talk to anybody?"

"No. I went straight upstairs."

Rosie reasserted herself. "Do you know the name of King's supplier?"

"No."

"How many people were at the party?"

"About a dozen." She said that there were about an equal number of men and women. "I presume that the men worked for the company or were involved in the IPO. The women were there to entertain them."

"Hookers?"

"That's not how it works in the Valley. You need an invitation. A lot of successful women would give anything to be invited to a party at Jeff's house. A few are gold diggers. Most are looking for business connections."

Or other connections.

She read my expression and asked, "Have you ever been to a Silicon Valley party?"

Do I look like a guy who hangs out with people like King? "Afraid not."

"A bunch of horny guys with money hit on pretty women invited to show up and flirt. They're expected to go home with the men. The sex is often supplemented by high-end pharmaceuticals. It's demeaning, but it's the way things work."

Yup, it's demeaning.

Rosie was a master at hiding her emotions, but I saw the disgust in her eyes. "What time did you get there?" she asked.

"Around eleven. The party was pretty tame. The houses on the hill are close together and everybody has security, so you need to keep it down or they'll call the cops."

"Did you see anything downstairs?"

"Not much. I looked into the living room as I headed upstairs. People were eating, drinking, vaping, smoking weed, and doing some harder stuff. There was a 'cuddle puddle.'"

During my three years as a priest and two decades as a lawyer, I had never encountered this term. "A 'cuddle puddle'?"

"People get high and make out in groups on the sofa and the floor."

Sounds like a party after a St. Ignatius football game. "What time did it end?"

"Midnight. Jeff came upstairs for our after-party."

"You had stayed upstairs the entire time?"

"Yes."

"You found the heroin in the bathroom?"

"Right where Jeff always left it. We always did it the same way. I cooked it and injected him. Then we had sex. He was pretty good in bed, and he wasn't into anything kinky."

More information than I needed. "He let you inject him?"

"He didn't like doing it himself. I prepared a second syringe for myself, but he started having convulsions. He threw up and collapsed."

"Had anything like this ever happened before?"

"No."

"What did you do with the second syringe?"

"I emptied it when Jeff collapsed."

"Did you try to help him?"

"Of course. Then I ran downstairs and found his security guy, who was still there. He knows CPR. He called 9-1-1."

"Inspector Lee told us that the security guard said that you tried to run. He also said that you made no effort to assist King."

"That's a lie."

Here goes. "They seem to be suggesting that you may have killed King on purpose."

"Not true. I don't know what happened. Maybe he had a bad reaction to some high-powered smack that *he* provided. Or maybe it was tainted. Either way, I didn't kill him. He was my source of support. I needed the money."

Rosie drummed her fingers on the arm of her plastic chair. "Did you see King put the heroin in the bathroom?"

"No. He could have left it there last night or last week. I don't know."

"Did anybody else use the bathroom while you were there?"

"Several people." She explained that the master bath had two entrances: one leading into the hallway, and the other leading into the bedroom.

"Did you see who else went into the bathroom?"

"No. I was trying to stay invisible. I closed the door between the bathroom and the bedroom."

"Did anybody say anything to you?"

"No."

"Is it possible that somebody else put the heroin in the bathroom or tampered with it?"

Work with us, Lexy. For our purposes, the correct answer is yes.

She thought about it for a long moment. "I guess."

Not forceful enough.

Rosie asked whether anybody was angry at King.

"Everybody hated him. He had a huge ego and he treated everybody like crap, but people at the party were going to make a fortune on the IPO."

"How were you and Jeff getting along?"

"Fine."

"Did you like him?"

"We had a business arrangement. I provided sex and companionship. He provided money and drugs. The sex was okay. The money was good. The drugs were better than the stuff I bought on the street. I was prepared to continue as long as I needed the money. I didn't have any choice."

Her lack of emotion was equal parts troubling and sad. I said, "Inspector Lee told us that they found five thousand dollars in your purse."

"Jeff always paid cash."

"He seems to think that you gave him a hot shot, took the money, and tried to run."

"It was consensual. He provided the smack."

"Why didn't you call 9-1-1 immediately?"

"I panicked."

"Were you and King fighting?"

"No."

"Did he threaten to tell the cops or his wife about you?"

"No."

"Did he threaten to end your relationship?"

"No." She clenched her fists. "Can you get me out of here?"

"Not today. We'll know more after we talk to the D.A."

"What about bail?"

"At the moment, you're being held on a 'no-bail hold,' which means that we won't be able to get bail until the arraignment."

"What are the chances then?"

"Not great—especially if they charge you with first-degree murder. And even if the judge sets bail, you have no money."

"I have five thousand dollars."

"It won't be enough, and you can't use it because it's evidence." *And, arguably, it was obtained illegally.*

"I'll wear an ankle monitor."

"You're still going to need money."

If you can't afford bail, you can buy a bail bond for a non-refundable fee equal to ten percent of the bail amount. The bond agent guarantees that the accused will show up in court. In many cases, it's the only way a defendant can get out of jail. California recently passed legislation to end the practice of requiring money bail, but the law hasn't taken effect.

"If you have enough for a bond," I said, "you won't qualify for our services."

Lexy closed her eyes as the reality set in. "What happens next?"

"There will be an arraignment in a couple of days. They'll read the charges. You'll plead not guilty. We'll ask for bail. We'll go from there."

"What happens between now and then?"

"You need to sit tight, stay calm, and avoid talking to anybody. I'll send over an intake attorney with some additional paperwork. We'll start making arrangements to get you treatment. I want to talk to my contacts at the D.A.'s Office. And I want to remove your listing on Mature Relations."

6
"THIS CASE IS GOING TO BE PROBLEMATIC"

Rosie took off the wire-framed glasses that replaced her contacts when she was tired. "I'm getting too old for all-nighters."

I took a sip of bitter coffee. "So am I."

Her eyes twinkled. "Had you ever heard of a 'cuddle puddle'?"

"Uh, no."

"Neither had I. Learn something new every day." Her tone turned serious. "This case is going to be problematic."

Yes, it is.

We were sitting in her office at six-thirty a.m. on Christmas Eve. The hallways were dark. The P.D.'s Office was uncharacteristically quiet.

She lowered her voice. "Murder cases are always difficult. They're almost impossible when the client has a substance problem."

"I'll request a medical exam and treatment options. It's all that we can do for now."

"You'll need to watch her closely, Mike."

"I will. In the meantime, I asked Pete to see if he can get any information about what's on Lexy's cell phone. And he's going to see what he can find out about King."

"He doesn't work for us."

"It's a Christmas present."

She pushed out a sigh. "Were you able to take down Lexy's listing on Mature Relations?"

"Yes."

"How degrading was it?"

"Very."

"Worse than our daughter's app?"

"Yes. Grace gives relationship advice to college kids. Mature Relations focuses on sex."

"I could make a credible argument that Grace does, too."

"So could I."

"You're okay with it?"

"I would have preferred something more suitable for a family audience, but I learned long ago that I have little control over our daughter."

Rosie's eyes gleamed. "Even less now that she's making more money than we are."

"Fortunately, she's much more grounded than I was at twenty. She's smart, responsible, ambitious, and very careful. Her moral compass is pointed in the right direction. If we're lucky, she might be supporting us in a few years."

"If people keep downloading her app, it may be sooner than you think." She scanned her e-mails. "Is Mature Relations like Ashley Madison for rich people?"

"Sort of." Ashley Madison caters to married people looking to cheat. It gained some notoriety when the former governor of South Carolina found an Argentine lover on the site. The tawdry episode had little impact on his political career—he was subsequently elected to the U.S. Congress. "Mature Relations is more tasteful than I expected. The clientele is well-heeled."

"It's a hookup site, Mike."

"It looks like high-end soft-core porn."

She arched an eyebrow. "How would you know?"

"Research."

"You expect me to believe that you've never looked at a porn site?"

"On occasion. You?"

"On occasion."

"I'm not satisfying your urges?"

"Most of them." She switched topics. "What did you think of Sexy Lexy?"

"She's bright and credible. She isn't the first person to get chewed up by the tech industry and hooked on opioids. People think the tech kids play foosball all day while they're raking in big bucks. In reality, it's like being a lawyer. They work ungodly hours. A few make a ton of money, but many don't. There's an insane amount of stress. You know how it goes when people get hooked on booze or drugs. There's a fine line between recreation and addiction."

Her expression turned somber. We'd seen the lives of many clients and several colleagues swirl down the drain after they got addicted. "Do you think she was telling the truth?"

"I think so."

"So do I. She admitted that she's an unemployed heroin addict. She told us that she met King on Mature Relations—not her proudest moment. Their relationship sounded purely transactional."

"He was also her source of income, and she needed the money to feed her habit."

"What's the narrative? Are you planning to argue that his death was accidental?"

"Ideally, no. That could still be manslaughter, which would be preferable to murder, but not great. I'd rather argue that somebody with a grudge against King planted some spiked heroin knowing that it was likely to kill him."

"Any evidence?"

"Not yet."

"Do you have any potential suspects in mind?"

"Everybody who was at King's house last night."

"A SODDI defense?"

It stood for "Some Other Dude Did It." "Why not? There were other people at the party. Some of them used the bathroom upstairs."

"You'll need to show motive."

"That may be the easiest part. Seems everybody in Silicon Valley—including many at the party—hated King."

"Then you shouldn't have any trouble proving it." Rosie's face rearranged itself into the million-dollar smile that adorned faded campaign posters nailed to power poles around the City. "And if you can't pin it on somebody else?"

"We'll argue that Lexy had no incentive to kill her sugar daddy. If that doesn't work, we'll say that it was an accident. If the jury buys it, we might get manslaughter instead of murder." I switched to logistics. "I take it that you'd like me to deal with this?"

"Yes."

"Can I do it myself?"

"If you have time."

"I do." As co-head of the Felony Division, I spent most of my time dealing with administrative and scheduling issues. On many days, I felt more like a traffic cop than a lawyer. Rosie and I had agreed that I could take on a couple of cases a year—if I stayed out of her hair. "I'd like to have Rolanda sit second chair."

"She's on her honeymoon, Mike. She won't be back for three weeks."

Rolanda Fernandez was one of the best attorneys in our office. She was also Rosie's niece. Rosie had promoted her to co-head of the Felony Division six months earlier after Rosie had concluded—correctly—that my laissez faire attitude toward bureaucratic formalities was setting a less-than-stellar example for our younger lawyers. For those who insist that irony is dead, I would note that the person that Rosie and I used to babysit and who once worked as our law clerk was now tasked with providing adult supervision to *me*.

Rosie invoked her cross-exam voice. "I am not going ask her to come back early from Fiji."

That's fair. "Neither am I."

Rolanda and her longtime boyfriend and newly minted husband, Zach, had postponed their honeymoon twice. It comes with the territory when one spouse is the co-head of the Felony Division of the P.D.'s Office, and the other is a baby partner at one of the big firms downtown. The first time, Zach had to drop everything to handle a series of hearings in Houston. The second time, Rolanda couldn't persuade one of San Francisco's least sentimental judges to delay the murder trial of a Hunters Point gangbanger. They had scheduled their current trip on the logical assumption that things would be quiet over the holidays. They couldn't have anticipated that we would be asked to represent a woman accused of killing a tech entrepreneur on Christmas Eve.

Rosie eyed me. "Are you sure that you want to deal with a murder case?"

We had been around the block enough times to know that Lexy's case would likely consume much of my time for months. Then again, for a trial lawyer, there was nothing more exhilarating than a murder case. It also beat reviewing calendars and court dockets.

"I'm in," I said.

"Good. You can decide who will sit second chair."

"I think it might be better if it's a female attorney."

"That's sexist."

Yes, it is. "It's in our client's best interest. And it wouldn't be the first time we've made a staffing decision for a similar reason."

"You can choose whomever you'd like."

"Any chance you might be available?"

"No."

It was worth a shot. I looked at my watch. Six-forty a.m. "You should go home. It's Christmas Eve. You have people coming over tomorrow."

"I will. You might want to head over to the Hall and see if you can talk to our D.A. about Lexy's case."

"What makes you think she'll be there at this hour?"

She pointed at her computer. "She's being interviewed on TV at her office right now. She just said that she has sufficient evidence to convict our client of murder."

7
"TELL YOUR CLIENT TO PLEAD GUILTY"

The District Attorney of the City and County of San Francisco flashed a politician's smile, extended a willowy hand, and spoke to me in a tone oozing fake sincerity. "Good to see you again, Mike."

"Good to see you, too, Nicole," I lied.

Nicole Ward was sitting behind a Lucite-topped desk in her immaculate corner office on the third floor of the Hall of Justice at seven a.m. As always, her makeup was perfect, her hair coiffed, and her Elie Tahari silk blouse looked as if she'd purchased it at Bloomingdale's earlier that morning.

My guess was that she had come to the office solely to appear on TV and expound upon Lexy's case. Christmas Eve was usually a slow news day, and the savvy operator knew that her interview would run on the morning, afternoon, and evening newscasts. Not surprisingly, she had proclaimed that SFPD had irrefutable evidence that Lexy had murdered King.

"I didn't expect to see you here on Christmas Eve," I said.

"I'm always working."

Your deputies are always working. You go on TV. I feigned admiration of the framed college graduation photos of her twin daughters. Jenna was a law student at Yale. Missy was in medical school at Northwestern. Already knowing the answer, I asked, "Going to court?"

"Not today."

Not ever. "Fundraiser?" The next election was almost a year away, but she was already testing the waters for a mayoral run.

"It's Christmas Eve, Mike."

"Were you on TV?"

"As a matter of fact, yes."

I'm shocked. "CNN?"

"Just local today." She was a master of the humble-brag. Her smile finally disappeared. She scrunched her prim nose as she looked me up and down. "Have you been up all night?"

Uh, yeah. "We picked up a new case."

"Which one?"

The one that you were pontificating about on TV twenty minutes ago. "Alexa Low."

"Sexy Lexy qualifies for a P.D.?"

"Yes."

"I was told that she isn't some small-time hooker from the Tenderloin. She's a Cal alum who works for a tech startup."

"Worked," I said. "She's unemployed."

"I understand that she and King hooked up on Mature Relations."

She knew more than she was letting on. "Millions of people are on Mature Relations. I suspect that their vetting process isn't terribly rigorous."

"It isn't."

I couldn't resist. "How do you know?"

"My office has made it a priority to investigate fraud in the online dating industry. You'd be surprised how many people get screwed."

I resisted the temptation to make a double entendre. "Do you know anybody on Mature Relations?"

"Not that I'm aware of." She pointed a slender finger at the somber African-American man sitting in the chair next to mine. "What about you, DeSean?"

"Not as far as I know."

DeSean Harper was the tight-lipped head of the Felony Division. About my age, the Bayview native had graduated at the top of his class at Cal and Harvard Law School. Smart, meticulous, and tenacious, he was among the most respected prosecutors in California. Unlike his boss, he was a straight shooter. Many of us were silently hoping that he would succeed Ward if she moved up the political ladder.

He touched the sleeve of his powder-blue oxford cloth shirt. "Ask your brother about it. The tech boom has been a bonanza for sex sites and P.I.s."

"So I understand. Will you be handling Ms. Low's case?"

"For now."

Ward glanced at her watch. "How can we help you?"

"I was hoping that you might provide information about my client's case."

"She was arrested six hours ago."

"I presume that Inspector Lee has consulted with you about the charges."

"We haven't decided."

"Come on, Nicole."

"She's already guilty of possession of a controlled substance."

"King provided the smack. She has no criminal record. It would be overkill to charge her with possession."

"She solicited sex."

"It was consensual. You can't charge everybody who hooks up on Match or Tinder."

"We found five grand in her purse. If she got it from King for sex, it's solicitation. If she stole it, it's theft. Either way, it's a bad look."

"You're seriously going to charge her for possession or for having consensual sex? That's a bad look, too, Nicole."

"There's also the fact that King is, for lack of a more discreet term, dead. As a result, we'll be charging her with murder. We'll make a final determination of the degree when we have more facts."

"It was an accident."

"She gave him a hot shot of heroin."

"Which *he* provided. And he asked her to inject him."

"Says your client."

"You think she jammed a needle into him without permission? King probably had a medical condition that was triggered by the smack. Either way, she didn't mean to kill him."

"She tried to flee."

"She went to get help. Besides, she had no motive. He was her source of income."

"Maybe they had a falling out."

We volleyed back and forth for another five minutes, but neither Ward nor Harper would give an inch or supply any additional information. Finally, I recited the standard defense-lawyer catechism. "You have a legal obligation to provide evidence that might exonerate our client. We'll also need copies of the police reports and the names of everybody who was at King's house last night."

Ward answered. "We'll get it to you as expeditiously as possible."

"Have you scheduled the arraignment?"

"No sooner than Wednesday. DeSean will be in touch." Ward stood up—a signal that our conversation was ending. "Are you going to handle this case yourself?"

Yes. "We'll decide on staffing in due course."

"You're hedging like a politician, Mike."

"I'm learning."

"Give my best to Rosie."

"I will." Rosie and Ward couldn't stand each other.

"Is Rosie going to run for another term?"

Absolutely. "She's going to make a decision in the next few months."

"You *are* learning."

I'd like to think so. "In the spirit of the holidays, is there anything else that you'd care to share with me about this case?"

"Tell your client to plead guilty to first-degree murder."

"You're overreaching."

"It will save everybody a lot of time and make our holidays more enjoyable."

* * *

My iPhone vibrated as I was sitting at my desk a couple of hours later. Pete's name appeared on the display.

"You got anything on Lexy's phone?" I asked.

"Not much, Mick. She got a text from King inviting her to the party. Just time and place. He told her not to talk to anybody. No other details."

"Where are you?"

"Billionaires Row. I may have some information for you."

"We haven't been approved to handle Lexy's case."

"You will."

"Even if we are, I can't hire you."

"You want the information or not, Mick?"

"I'll be right there."

8
BILLIONAIRES ROW

Pete pulled up the collar of his bomber jacket to block the gusty wind. "What took you so long?"

The sky was overcast. "Uber was slow."

At ten-thirty on Monday morning, we were standing on the sidewalk on Twenty-First Street, halfway up the steep hill between Church and Sanchez, two blocks above Dolores Park. When I was a kid living down the hill in the Mission, the peak between our neighborhood and the Castro was known as Liberty Hill. In the eighties, the real estate agents rechristened it as Dolores Heights. Nowadays, everybody called it Billionaires Row.

Century-old oak and pine trees formed a graceful canopy over refurbished pre-earthquake Victorians, Edwardians, and brown-shingles. The houses had survived the 1906 earthquake because water had miraculously continued to flow to a still-functional hydrant around the corner at Twentieth and Church. In commemoration of its historic significance, the neighbors give it a fresh coat of gold paint on April eighteenth of every year.

Although the homes had panoramic views from the Golden Gate Bridge to downtown, the neighborhood's origins were working class, so the houses were more modest than the mansions of Pacific Heights. To their credit, the tech honchos kept their security guards, limos, and surveillance cameras out of view. On the other hand, if Pete and I had accidentally encroached upon somebody's property, we would have received an instant response from a polite and well-armed guard. Billionaires Row was the safest street in San Francisco.

"You ever work security here?" I asked.

Pete's eyes were always moving. "Couple times."

"I understand that the head of Facebook lives down the street."

"I cannot confirm or deny."

"Did he make you sign a non-disclosure agreement?"

"That's confidential."

"You can't even tell me if you signed an NDA?"

"That's confidential, too." My brother gave me a wry grin. "In this neighborhood, you can't take out your trash without signing an NDA."

Welcome to my hometown in the new millennium. I pointed at a white frame house hidden behind a garish display of Christmas decorations. "Tom and Jerry are still here?"

"Yup."

The "Tom and Jerry House" had become a San Francisco holiday institution three decades earlier—long before the tech barons arrived. Two good-natured souls named Tom and Jerry started hanging lights on the pine tree in front of their house. The decorations became more elaborate as the tree got taller. They transformed the sidewalk and garage beneath the stately pine into a fantasyland of toys, trains, giftwrapped boxes as big as Priuses, and two huge stockings bearing their names. The gaudy exhibition looked out of place on the staid street, but the neighbors took it in stride. Over the years, it had become a tourist attraction rivaling the "Full House" house on Broderick.

"Why don't they sell?" I asked. "They could cash in for millions."

"They like it here, Mick."

So would I. I thought about the days when our parents scraped together a down payment for a modest house on Kirkham Street around the corner from Big John's saloon. According to family lore, Pop got the money during a brief stint in Chinatown, where "gratuities" to the cops were more lucrative than his usual beat in the Tenderloin. Pete and I finally sold it after our mom passed away—at a seven-figure profit.

I smiled. "Think Mom and Pop could have afforded a house on this street when we moved to Kirkham?"

"Probably. This neighborhood was pretty beat up in those days. If they had, we could have made a fortune by selling it to another tech honcho."

That would have pleased Tom and Margaret Daley. Our parents were children of the Depression who lived within their means, paid off their mortgage early, and put four kids through Catholic schools and state universities. They would have been appalled by the profligate spending and crass consumption of the tech titans living on Twenty-First Street.

Pete's tone turned philosophical. "We made out on the house, Mick. Pop would have said it was okay that we didn't extract every last penny from the family that bought it."

My younger brother had inherited our father's practical wisdom and generous spirit.

I looked up San Francisco's most exclusive block and saw a half-dozen black-and-whites parked at the crest of the hill in the intersection of Twenty-First and Sanchez. News vans were parked haphazardly below the police cars.

"Which one is King's house?" I asked.

"The big one at the top. Probably cost twenty million to buy it, gut it, and remodel it."

"That's insane."

"It was walking-around change for him. He tried to buy the house next door, too, but the owner wouldn't sell."

"Were you ever hired to tail him?"

"Nope."

"Do you know anybody who was?"

"Maybe."

"You ever work security for him?"

"I'm not qualified."

"You're an ex-cop."

"The head of King's security detail is a retired Israeli commando. He's very selective."

"Can you find out who was there last night?"

"I'll see what I can do." Pete's thin lips transformed into a half-smile. "Does this mean you plan to hire me?"

I hope so. "For now, this is just a brother-to-brother favor."

"What's in it for me if I do you a solid?"

"Dinner for you, Donna, and Margaret at the Gold Mirror." It was the old-school Italian restaurant at Eighteenth and Taraval where our parents took us for pasta on special occasions.

"Might work."

"You said you had some information for me."

"Ken Lee just left. They're almost finished processing the scene. King's widow showed up a little while ago. She was pretty upset."

"Understandable. Anybody else?"

"Blackjack Steele. He didn't look happy, either."

I recognized the name. Jack "Blackjack" Steele was the CEO of Y5K. The veteran "suit" had been brought in to provide adult supervision to the founders of a series of startups, including Y5K. Between gigs, he was a venture capitalist and a talking head on Fox Business.

I took a step toward King's house, but Pete stopped me.

"Not a good time," he said. "The cops won't let you inside. Besides, if you get any closer, one of King's security guys might shoot you."

"That would ruin my Christmas."

"Mine, too. Let's not take any unnecessary chances. You go back to the office and do lawyer stuff. I'll do some poking around."

I was about to start walking down the hill when I saw a commotion in front of King's house. A young woman dressed in an overpriced sweatshirt and high-end yoga leggings stormed out the metal gate and strode to a Tesla parked at the curb. She turned around to face a pudgy, balding man, whom I recognized as Steele. She pointed her finger at him and began gesticulating.

"King's widow?" I said.

Pete nodded. "Chloe was married to King for three years. She was the personnel director at his previous startup. She broke up his second marriage."

Awkward.

Chloe's high-pitched voice transformed in to a plaintive wail that carried down the street. "You killed my husband! You knew that he was doing smack, and you did nothing to stop him."

Steele held up his hands in a defensive posture.

She pointed at the house. "This house belongs to me." She got into her Tesla and slammed the door behind her. The status symbol barreled around the corner onto Sanchez and disappeared.

My brother took it in with his usual stoicism. "I'll call you, Mick."

"Pete?"

"Yes?"

"Thanks."

9
"I FIGURED YOU MIGHT NEED A HAND"

At eight-thirty on Monday night, the doorway of Rosie's office was filled by the six-foot-six-inch, three-hundred-pound presence of our secretary, process server, bodyguard, and onetime regular client, Terrence "The Terminator" Love. "Evening, Mike," he said.

"Evening, Terrence. You didn't have to come in tonight."

"I saw our D.A. on TV talking about Sexy Lexy. I figured you might need a hand."

"I do." *And I'm profoundly grateful.*

The former small-time heavyweight boxer and retired petty thief was dressed in a double-breasted suit and a maroon tie that he had purchased with his first paycheck after he had come to work for us at Fernandez and Daley. We hired him as part of a plea bargain that I worked out with a sympathetic judge after Terrence had gotten into a shoving match with a homeless guy over a stolen roast chicken in front of his favorite liquor store on Sixth Street. When Rosie and I moved to the P.D.'s Office, we insisted on bringing him with us. To his unending credit and our everlasting delight, he hadn't missed a day of work or consumed a drop of malt liquor in more than ten years.

The gentle giant's shaved head reflected the light as he handed me a printout and spoke in his high-pitched voice. "This is the financial report on Alexa Low."

"Thanks, T."

"Anything else today?"

"Yes. I want you to go home and celebrate Christmas Eve with your daughter. And tomorrow is a holiday, so you need to stay out of here. Understood?"

His smile exposed a gold front tooth—a souvenir of his last stay at San Francisco County Jail. "Yes."

"Thanks for coming in today. Merry Christmas, Terrence."

"Merry Christmas, Mike."

A decade ago, if you had told me that one of our most dedicated employees would have been a recovering alcoholic and former small-time crook who had lost more prizefights than he had won, I would have said that there was a better chance that I would be the starting point guard for the Warriors.

I turned to the last page of the report, which I read aloud. "Defendant has total assets of less than five hundred dollars and debts in excess of ninety thousand."

Rosie was scrolling through her e-mails. "Sounds like we have a new client. Lexy must have gone through a lot of money in a hurry."

"Heroin addiction is expensive."

I turned to face one of the newer additions to our team. Nadezhda "Nady" Nikonova was an intense woman in her mid-thirties whom Rosie and I had liberated from a well-connected firm downtown where she had spent mind-numbing hours poring over phonebook-length documents to help her clients buy and sell office buildings. Nowadays, she spent mind-numbing hours trying to keep criminals out of jail—which she found more to her liking. Nady liked to say that there was little substantive difference between the morals of her old and new clients—the former simply had the wherewithal to pay private lawyers.

I spoke to Rosie. "I'm going to take the lead. Nady will sit second chair."

"Excellent."

I turned to Nady. "The arraignment will probably be set for Wednesday. I'll need your help tomorrow preparing document requests."

"Already started."

She was painstakingly thorough. "I'm sorry that you'll need to work on Christmas."

"Hanukkah ended on Wednesday."

"I'll put in a good word for you with your rabbi."

"Thank you." Her expression turned serious. "Should we bring in backup?"

"You can handle it. This isn't like your old firm where matters were staffed with a dozen lawyers. It will be a good experience for you." *And trial by fire.*

"Great."

She was one of our most promising lawyers. She had graduated at the top of her class at UCLA and Boalt Law School and was a lightning-fast study. She was also fearless. It may have had something to do with the fact that she and her mother had been chased out of Uzbekistan when Nady was eleven, and eventually found their way to relatives in L.A.

I turned back to Rosie. “We’ll need an investigator.”

“You can pick anybody in the office.”

Here goes. “I’d like to use Pete.”

“He doesn’t work for us.”

“Our people are great, but Pete is better.”

Her hesitation indicated that she agreed. “We don’t have the budget for an outside P.I.”

“I’ll find the money in my discretionary fund.”

“No.”

“He has excellent contacts in Silicon Valley.”

“No.”

“I’ll pay him on my own nickel.”

“Let’s try it my way for now, Mike.”

“Fine.”

“Then we’re in agreement.”

Not exactly. I looked over at Nady. “I need you to find out everything you can about Jeff King. We need to know who had a grudge against him—the list could be long. See if you can figure out who was at his house last night.”

“Will do.”

“I want you to prepare paperwork to qualify us as attorneys-of-record.”

“Already done. I’ve also started putting together requests for police reports, security videos, cell phone logs, computer records, and everything else that I can think of.”

“Perfect.” She reminded me of Rosie—always thinking two steps ahead. “You can reach me on my cell if you need me.”

“Are you going home?”

“No, I’m going to church.”

10
"MERRY CHRISTMAS"

I closed my eyes and listened to the soaring tones of the organ and the choir. I opened them and looked up at the familiar statue of St. Anne comforting the Virgin Mary beneath the stained-glass window in St. Peter's Catholic Church, which had stood on Florida Street in the Mission since 1867. My parents were married here. So were Rosie and I. The modest frame structure where my siblings and children had been baptized lacked the majesty of St. Ignatius, but its understated dignity embodied the working-class neighborhood it had served for more than a hundred and fifty years.

I still loved sitting in church.

At one o'clock on Christmas morning, I was in the seat that I had occupied at midnight mass for fifty-four of my fifty-seven years. I had missed three years while serving as a junior priest at St. Anne's in the Sunset. I knew every word of the liturgy by heart.

My parents had grown up around the corner on opposite sides of Garfield Square Park, when the Mission was still home to Irish and Italian families. When I was little, we lived in a two-bedroom, one-bath apartment across the street from the Garfield Swimming Pool. We moved to the Sunset when I was seven, but we always came back to St. Peter's for Christmas Mass. When the Irish and Italians moved out of the neighborhood in the fifties and sixties, the Latino families moved in. Rosie's parents bought their bungalow on Harrison Street the same year that we moved to the Sunset. Swaths of the Mission had gentrified during the tech boom, but many Spanish-speaking families still lived in the two- and three-story apartments along its crowded streets and narrow alleys. Mass at St. Peter's was celebrated in Spanish and English.

When my parents were still alive, the seating arrangements in the ninth row on the left side were always the same. My dad sat on the aisle. My older brother, Tommy, sat next to him. I came next. Then Pete. Then our baby sister, Mary. My mom sat on the other end. We could get away with a little mischief at home, but never—ever—at church, where I was known as Officer Daley's second son and Tommy, Jr.'s younger brother.

Nowadays, our seating configuration was, of necessity, different. Rosie's mom, Sylvia, sat in my dad's old seat. Rosie was in Tommy's place. I still sat in my usual spot. Then came Grace and little Tommy. Pete and his family used to join us, but they now attended mass at St. Anselm's in Marin County. Mary lived in L.A. Times change.

Rosie's older brother (and Rolanda's father), Tony, sat with us. He ran a produce market around the corner on Twenty-Fourth. His wife had passed away a dozen years earlier and Rolanda was on her honeymoon, so we made sure that he wasn't alone during the holidays. Rosie's younger sister, Theresa, was conspicuously absent. She had married at eighteen and had two kids right away, one of whom died of lymphoma at the age of five. Shortly thereafter, her husband walked out, and she started drinking. Then she got addicted to painkillers and crack. She was in and out of treatment for years until her liver gave out the day after her fiftieth birthday.

I thought about my dad as I sat between my ex-wife and his grandchildren. He got to hold Grace when she was a baby. He never met Tommy. He would have feigned disappointment that Rosie and I had a baby after we got divorced, but he would have welcomed his second grandchild. Rosie and I never got a formal annulment, so in the eyes of the Church—and my father—we were still married. Thomas James Charles Daley, Sr. always described himself as a practical Catholic instead of an observant one, but he still went to mass every Sunday. I liked to think that he would have been proud of Rosie and me, notwithstanding our unconventional relationship. I suspect that he would have been more irritated that his one-time daughter-in-law was the Public Defender, and I was the co-head of the Felony Division. He wouldn't have been happy about his granddaughter's sex-advice business, either, but he wouldn't have said a word about it to her.

The choir concluded the final hymn and the majestic organ went silent. I reached over and squeezed Rosie's hand.

"Beautiful service," she said. She pecked me on the cheek. "Merry Christmas, Mike."

"Merry Christmas, Rosie."

As we made our way to the rear of the sanctuary, Rosie paused to greet friends, and Sylvia worked the aisle like an experienced politician. Rosie still knew many people in the neighborhood. Her mother knew everybody.

A few minutes later, I took a deep breath of the cool air as we strolled past St. Peter's School, where I attended kindergarten and first grade. We were in good spirits as we walked the two blocks to the house that Sylvia and her late husband had purchased six decades earlier for the princely sum of twenty-four thousand dollars. Nowadays, Sylvia could have sold it for almost two million—as if she ever would.

I waited in front of Sylvia's house as Rosie, her mother, Grace, and Tommy went upstairs to retrieve Sylvia's overnight bag and six tins of Christmas cookies. We would be spending Christmas in Marin, but Sylvia's house would always be Fernandez family headquarters. Technically, Rosie's official residence was a studio apartment across the street. While she spent most nights in Marin, the Public Defender was required to be a "resident" of San Francisco. Everybody knew about this sham; Rosie wasn't the only politician who engaged in a similar charade.

I was admiring the blinking lights on the Christmas tree in Sylvia's window when Pete's gravelly voice broke the silence.

"Hey, Mick."

"I thought you were at mass in San Anselmo."

"Margaret wasn't feeling well, so she and Donna stayed home."

"I take it this means that you didn't make it to mass?"

"Correct."

Pete had never been as enthusiastic about Catholicism as I had. "Will Margaret be okay for Christmas dinner?"

"If cookies and presents are involved, she'll be fine." He handed me a hand-written note. "These are the names of a couple of the people at King's house last night. It isn't everybody, and you didn't get it from me."

Excellent. "I take it that you didn't get it from the former Israeli commando who is the head of King's security detail?"

"If you want the skinny on what goes on behind closed doors, you never ask people who get paid to keep their mouths shut."

"Caterer? Bartender? Clean-up crew?"

"Get real, Mick. What's the hardest thing to do in this town?"

Of course. "The parking valet?"

"Possibly." His tone turned serious. "He's a nice kid. He didn't go inside the house, so you can rule him out as a suspect. More important, he parks cars for other people on Billionaires Row, which makes him a very useful source. I don't want him to lose his job."

Got it. "Can you make time to work on this case?"

"Yes."

"I still need to clear it with Rosie."

"Understood. I'll see you at Christmas dinner."

"Thanks, Pete."

"Merry Christmas, Mick."

11
"HE'S JUST DOING HIS JOB"

Sylvia Fernandez sat at the butcher block table in her daughter's postage-stamp-sized kitchen at ten-thirty on Christmas night. Except for her stockier frame, silver hair, and bifocals, she could have passed for Rosie's older sister. Her voice was filled with affection. "You made a wonderful dinner, Rosita."

"Thank you, Mama."

Rosie had taken over holiday duties after Sylvia's second hip replacement.

Sylvia added, "You're turning into a real pro."

"Not as good as you."

"I've had more practice."

Sylvia used to spend weeks preparing turkey, ham, salsa, soup, dressing, and a dazzling array of holiday cookies. Rosie took a more egalitarian approach. She and I cooked the turkey. Tony supplied fruit and veggies from his market and pastries from La Mexicana in the Mission, which became our go-to bakery after La Victoria closed after a sixty-year run. Grace and Tommy made cupcakes under their grandmother's supervision. What the younger generations lacked in skill, we made up for with enthusiasm.

The blinking lights of the Christmas tree spread holiday cheer, and the aroma of leftovers wafted through Rosie's post-earthquake bungalow across the street from the Little League field near downtown Larkspur, a leafy suburb about ten miles north of the Golden Gate Bridge. Rosie and I had rented the two-bedroom cottage after Grace was born. Nowadays, I spent three or four nights a week over here, but I still kept my apartment behind the Larkspur fire station that I had rented after our divorce. The three-block buffer zone was helpful for our sanity. Rosie and I hit the jackpot when a grateful client—a one-time mob lawyer—bought the house for us after we got his death penalty conviction overturned. In the Bay Area, this was like winning the lottery.

Rosie and I were putting away the dishes. The food had been

consumed, the presents had been opened, and the guests had gone home. Rolanda had joined us by Skype. So had my baby sister, Mary. It was a smaller gathering than when I was a kid, when forty of my aunts, uncles, and cousins squeezed into my parents' apartment.

My former mother-in-law informed me that Grace would be driving her home in the morning. "Tommy is coming with us. I'm taking them to lunch at the St. Francis."

As if we didn't get enough to eat today. "I'm jealous."

To tourists, the St. Francis referred to the historic five-star hotel on Union Square now run by Westin. To natives, it meant the St. Francis Fountain around the corner from St. Peter's, where they'd been serving burgers and shakes since 1918. When we got good report cards, my mom and dad used to take us there after church.

I pointed down the hallway. "Are the kids still up?"

"Grace is online giving advice. She says that she has to post at least a dozen times a day."

"Even on Christmas?"

"Just business, Michael. Tommy is downloading stuff onto his new iPhone."

Hopefully, not his sister's app. "You didn't need to get him such a fancy phone, Sylvia."

"Grandmother's privilege. I understand that your office is representing the young woman who killed that hot shot on Billionaires Row."

And here we go. "*Allegedly* killed him. I thought we agreed not to talk about work at Christmas dinner."

"Dinner ended three hours ago, Michael."

Yes, it did.

She was just getting started. "They said on the news that she worked for a tech firm. How did she qualify for a P.D.?"

"She doesn't work there anymore."

"She must have made a lot of money. How is it possible that she didn't save any of it?"

I loved Sylvia dearly, and she had many redeeming qualities. Being non-judgmental wasn't among them. Then again, her views were understandable. She grew up in profound poverty outside Monterrey, Mexico. She and her husband worked long hours to scrape together money to come to the U.S., where they worked even harder.

She was immensely proud that her family always had enough to eat and a roof over their heads even though they never took a penny from Uncle Sam. She had little tolerance for those who didn't live within their means, and she didn't hide her contempt for the affluent tech workers who were gentrifying the Mission—*her* neighborhood.

"She has a heroin addiction," I said. "We don't get to pick our clients like we did when we were in private practice."

"Maybe being a public defender isn't such a great deal after all."

Rosie finally interjected. "He's just doing his job, Mama."

Sylvia gave her the "Death Stare," which she had graciously passed down to her daughter and granddaughter. She turned back to me. "Have you assigned an attorney to this case?"

"Me."

"I thought you weren't doing trial work."

"Rosie and I agreed that I would do one or two a year. This is going to be a high-profile matter requiring somebody with experience. One of our younger attorneys will help me."

"Can't you assign it to somebody else?

Yes. "It would have been perfect for Rolanda, but I'm not going to ask her to come back from Fiji."

"Good."

I let her answer hang in anticipation of additional commentary, but none was forthcoming. This was the closest that I had ever come to winning an argument with Sylvia.

She pushed back her chair and stood up. "I'm going to help Grace."

Dear God. "You sure you want to do that?"

"Just because I'm eighty-four doesn't mean that I can't teach Millennials a thing or two, Michael."

As she walked down the hall, I had no doubt that she could—and would.

Rosie's eyes danced as she took a sip of Cab Franc. "If you poke the tiger, it'll bite you."

"I should have known better." I finished my Diet Dr Pepper. "She's feisty tonight."

"Nothing changes."

"She okay?"

"Same as always. She doesn't want to admit that she's slowing down."

"Neither do I." My mom was the same way until Alzheimer's took away her memories. "What does she think about Grace's business?"

"If I had done it, she would have been appalled."

"That's a double standard."

"Grandmother's privilege."

"Has your mother expressed her opinion to Grace?"

Rosie smiled. "No, she expressed it to me."

Figures.

Her smile broadened. "Her view of Grace's business changed dramatically after I told her how much money she's making."

"So did Big John's."

"They grew up during the Depression, Mike."

"Is Grace still planning to take the job at Pixar?"

"Absolutely. She understands that apps have a short lifespan. She's putting away most of the money to buy a house."

I squeezed her hand. "You must have done something right."

"*We* must have done something right."

I was happy to take credit—even if it wasn't entirely deserved. "You okay?"

"Tired. Christmas dinner is hard work. You ready to resume the battle for Sexy Lexy?"

"We're trial attorneys, Rosie. It's what we do."

"I do it because it's my job. You love it."

True. "Every once in a while, we actually find a little justice."

"Not very often."

"It doesn't mean that we stop trying."

"I spend most of my time raising money and preparing budgets."

"That's why you have me." I lowered my voice. "I need to talk to you about Lexy's case."

She finished her wine. "Do I need to pour myself another glass?"

"Maybe. I want to hire Pete."

"We discussed it. I want you to use one of our investigators."

"Pete has unique expertise. He's already given me the names of some people who were at King's house."

"We would have gotten that information from the D.A. sooner or later."

"It would have been later. I *want* to use Pete. He knows the players in Silicon Valley."

"He's almost as much of a Luddite as you are."

"Not true. Besides, he doesn't need to know how the technology works. He knows who's sleeping around."

She tried to freeze me with her version of Sylvia's "Death Stare," but I decided to do the unthinkable and fight back. "I *need* him, Rosie."

"You *want* him, Mike. We have very good investigators."

"Not as good as Pete. It would be in the best interests of our client."

"Are you prepared to pay him out of your own pocket?"

"If I have to."

"You do."

"Fine."

"You're the co-head of the Felony Division. Make the call."

"I want Pete."

"Then it's decided."

I stood up and put on my jacket.

"Where are you going?" she asked.

"To the office."

"It's Christmas."

"I have less than twelve hours to get ready for the arraignment."

* * *

A light rain danced across the windshield of my Corolla as I drove southbound on the Golden Gate Bridge at eleven p.m. I instructed my iPhone to call the second name on my "Favorites" list.

Pete answered on the first ring. "What is it, Mick?"

"You're in."

"Great. Are you in trouble with Rosie?"

"A little."

"Thought so. Standard rates?"

"Yeah. And it's coming out of my pocket. I might need a payment schedule."

"Margaret needs to eat."

"Understood. Where are you?"

"Billionaires Row."

"Are you in trouble with Donna?"

"A little."

"Thought so."
"What time is the arraignment?"
"Nine a.m."
"I'll see if I can come up with something useful before then."

12
"NOTHING YET"

"Have you been home since yesterday?" I asked.

Nady's shoulder-length blonde hair was pulled into a pony tail. "No."

Thought so.

We were sitting at the table in the corner of my office at eleven-thirty on Christmas night. There was no traffic outside my window on Seventh Street.

"You didn't need to pull an all-nighter," I said.

"The arraignment is tomorrow morning. Besides, Max had to work, too."

Her fiancé of almost eight years had just made partner at Story, Short & Thompson, a mega-firm at the top of Embarcadero Center that was the successor to Simpson & Gates, the mega-firm at the top of the Bank of America Building where I had spent five interminable years when I needed cash after Rosie and I got divorced. The Executive Committee escorted me out the door because I didn't bring in enough high-paying clients. White-shoe firms don't like representing guys like Terrence the Terminator. Max was learning that unlike the old days when making partner resulted in a substantial raise, the astronomical salaries paid to associates meant that new partners took a pay cut for a few years—along with a six-figure capital contribution and paying for their own health insurance.

"You and Max might want to try to set some boundaries."

"Says the guy who is working on Christmas night."

Guilty. "Any update on wedding plans?"

"Maybe in the summer."

"As soon as we're finished, I want you to go home. I need you to be well-rested and ready for battle. You're going to end up looking like me if you don't learn to pace yourself."

"Max and I will be retired and living on a beach before we're fifty."

Sounds pretty good to me. "Anything come over from the D.A. or Inspector Lee?"

"Nothing yet." She said that a preliminary autopsy report would be available in the next few days. "We received confirmation of our appointment as attorneys of record for Lexy."

We're in. "We're going to use Pete as our investigator."

"Fine. Where do you want to start?"

"With our client. Any additional details on her background?"

"Her story checked out. Her last residence was a shelter on Valencia. The cops impounded her belongings, including her cell phone and laptop."

"What about the names that Pete provided?"

"The head of security at Y5K is Yoav Ben-Shalom. Fifty-six. Educated at Technion University in Haifa. Graduate degree from Georgetown. Married to an American. Two college-age kids. Honorable discharge from the IDF. Ran a security firm in Tel Aviv. Came here when a client opened a facility in Palo Alto. Moved over to Y5K about eighteen months ago. No criminal record. Very little about him in the press."

He undoubtedly preferred it that way. "Any other security people at the house?"

"A couple of retired SFPD were outside. They left when the guests departed. David Dito was the first officer at the scene."

"I know him." He came from a family of cops. "Was there a caterer?"

"No. Pancho Villa delivered the food. The parking valet is Jay Flaherty. Twenty-five. No criminal record. He wasn't allowed inside. If he needed to take a leak, they told him to use the porta-potty at the construction site next door."

Nice. "Who was there from Y5K?"

She looked at Pete's list. "Jack Steele, sixty, is the CEO. Gopal Patel, forty-eight, is the lead venture capitalist. Tristan Moore, twenty-nine, is the head marketing guy." She studied her notes. "Steele was the subject of an SEC investigation at a previous company, which was settled. Patel was accused of sexual harassment by a former employee, which was resolved quietly. Moore is clean. I have copies of profiles from various tech publications. You can also see them on YouTube. I'll e-mail you with contact information."

They may not be willing to talk to us. "Anybody else?"

"Not yet. Still waiting for names of the women."

"Was anybody besides Ben-Shalom still there when King died?"

"No."

We spent another hour going over our requests for police reports, security videos, and other evidence. We would also ask for an on-site inspection of King's house.

"We should ask for King's medical records," I said. "Maybe he had a pre-existing condition that was triggered by heroin."

"An accidental death could still be manslaughter."

"It would be better than a murder conviction."

"How do you think the arraignment will play out?"

"Likely to be a non-event. They'll read the charges. Lexy will plead not guilty."

"Bail?"

"We'll ask, but it's unlikely if they charge her with first-degree murder. Even if the judge says yes, Lexy has no money."

"Maybe somebody will post it for her."

"As far as I know, King was her only sugar daddy."

"What about one of her drug dealers?"

"Seems unlikely." I'd seen stranger things. "I'll meet you in court in the morning. Go home and get some sleep."

* * *

I was walking out of my office when Pete's name appeared on my phone. "Good news or bad?" I asked.

"Not great. Have you looked at the *Chronicle*'s Twitter feed?"

"Not in the last five minutes."

"There's a screenshot of Lexy's home page on Mature Relations."

Crap. "We took it down."

"Once something's on the Internet, it's there forever."

"Nothing we can do about it."

"Still glad you picked up this case?"

My day is now complete. "Absolutely."

13
"NOT GUILTY"

In the spirit of peace on earth and goodwill toward men, you might think that criminals take a little break on Christmas from stealing stuff, breaking into cars, selling drugs, and assaulting people. If you did, you would be mistaken.

At eight-thirty in the morning on the day after Christmas, the Hall of Justice was open for business as usual, and the corridor outside Judge Elizabeth McDaniel's courtroom looked like the post-Christmas sale at Macy's. In addition to the usual array of family members, friends, courtroom junkies, and other hangers-on, a lot of kids were milling around because school was out. They weren't allowed in court, so they had to amuse themselves in the hall.

Nady and I marched single file into court. We had already walked a similar gauntlet on our way into the Hall, where we were accosted by reporters. King's death was the big story after a slow news day, and the networks were milking it for every last ratings point. The screenshot of Lexy's listing on Mature Relations had been retweeted over a quarter of a million times. The cable outlets were running wall-to-wall coverage until something more salacious came along. Social media was going wild.

Nady and I took our places among the attorneys lined up against the back wall of the windowless courtroom. I nodded at the clerk, Christa Carter, who held up four fingers, which meant that we were fourth in line. Not a bad draw. Most lawyers weren't afforded a similar courtesy, but Christa's father had gone to St. Ignatius with my dad, and I always made sure that she got a bottle of her favorite mid-priced Pinot Noir for Christmas.

The heavy air smelled of mildew. It was better than the days when the plumbing backed up. The five rows in the gallery were filled. Woody Allen once said that showing up is eighty percent of life. For defense attorneys, waiting in court is ninety percent. Local reporters had scored seats in the back row. The bailiff had given them priority over people from CNN, Fox News, and MSNBC. In San Francisco, connections still counted.

"This building should be condemned," Nady muttered.

"Already is," I replied.

An hour later, Christa finally called our case. "The People versus Alexa Low."

Nady and I pushed our way down the aisle and took our places at the defense table. DeSean Harper was standing at the prosecution table next to Inspector Lee. Nady and I stood at attention as a deputy led Lexy to the defense table. Her eyes were red, face puffy, cheeks hollow. In her orange jumpsuit, she looked like a criminal.

I leaned over and tried to sound reassuring. "We've got you covered. When the judge asks for your plea, say 'Not guilty' in a respectful tone."

"Okay."

Lights! Camera! Arraignment!

Judge McDaniel glanced at her computer. "The defendant is present?"

I was still standing. "Yes, Your Honor."

Betsy McDaniel was a thoughtful former prosecutor who ran a tight courtroom. Now in her mid-sixties, she had gone on senior status a few years earlier to spend more time with her grandchildren. Between attending pre-dawn Pilates classes with Rosie and travelling the world, she frequently pinch-hit for her colleagues when they were on vacation. She didn't suffer fools, never grandstanded, and wouldn't allow cameras in her courtroom.

She tapped her microphone. "Counsel will state their names for the record."

"DeSean Harper for the People."

"Michael Daley and Nadezhda Nikonova for the defense."

"Nice to see you, Mr. Daley. You, too, Ms. Nikonova. Which one of you will be speaking on behalf of the defendant?"

I answered her. "I will, Your Honor. Our office has been appointed. We will file a copy of the documentation with the court."

She looked over at Harper. "Any objection?"

"No, Your Honor."

"Good." Judge McDaniel looked at Lexy and spoke in a maternal tone that still bore a trace of her native Alabama. "You lack the resources to hire a private attorney?"

Lexy's voice was barely audible. "Yes."

"Okay." Judge McDaniel recited the usual admonishment that if it was later determined that Lexy had sufficient funds to hire a private attorney, she would have to reimburse the City for the cost of her representation. In my years as a P.D., I had never seen this happen.

The judge glanced at her computer. "This is an arraignment. We will have a recitation of the charges and the defendant will enter a plea." She looked at Lexy again. "Do you understand why we are here, Ms. Low?"

"Yes."

"Thank you." She turned to Harper. "Have you decided on charges?"

"First-degree murder under California Penal Code Section 187."

I wasn't surprised that Harper had chosen first-degree, which had a minimum sentence of twenty-five years. Prosecutors frequently up-charge to give them wiggle room to work down to something more reasonable.

I spoke in a respectful tone. "The facts do not warrant a murder charge, Your Honor."

"That's up to Mr. Harper." Judge McDaniel speed-read the complaint aloud—it was part of the process. Then she addressed Lexy. "Do you understand the charge, Ms. Low?"

Her eyes filled with panic. "Yes."

"Are you prepared to enter a plea at this time?"

"Not guilty."

"Thank you."

That takes care of today's business.

The judge looked at me. "I presume that you'll want to schedule a prelim?"

"Yes, Your Honor."

A preliminary hearing, or "prelim," is a mini-trial where the D.A. must present just enough evidence to demonstrate that there is a reasonable likelihood that the defendant has committed a crime. The prosecution starts with a substantial advantage because the judge is required to give the D.A. the benefit of the doubt on evidentiary questions.

By law, the defense can request a prelim within ten court days after the arraignment. In many cases, we "waive time," which means that we agree to proceed after the ten-day window. It is often advantageous to stall because it gives us more time to interview witnesses and look for exculpatory evidence. In this case, I saw no reason to ask for a delay.

The judge shifted her gaze to Harper. "How many court days for the prelim?"

"One."

That's quick.

She studied her calendar. "Judge Ignatius Tsang is available on Monday, January seventh."

That's really quick, and Judge Tsang isn't a great draw for us. The former prosecutor was smart and generally fair, but his rulings often tilted in favor of the D.A.

Harper didn't flinch. "Works for us."

The judge turned to me. "That will work for you, right, Mr. Daley?"

"Yes, Your Honor."

"Very good. You should plan to submit motions to Judge Tsang no later than a week in advance." She glanced at her computer. "If there's nothing else—,"

I interjected. "We have a couple items, Your Honor."

"I'm listening."

"First, given the tight timeframe, we ask that you order Mr. Harper to provide copies of the police reports, the autopsy report, security videos, witness lists, and other evidence that we've requested on an expedited basis." I decided to make a quick play to the reporters in the gallery. "In particular, we would like to see all surveillance footage from the decedent's house which we believe will provide evidence of Ms. Low's innocence."

She looked at Harper. "You won't have any problem complying with Mr. Daley's very reasonable request, will you?"

"Your Honor, Mr. Daley knows that we're only required to provide evidence that would tend to exonerate his client."

"And you know that I don't like attorneys who play games. You'll provide any required evidence to the defense as you receive it. Anything else, Mr. Daley?"

"We'd like you to issue a gag order and prohibit the media from taking pictures or video of these proceedings. We don't want this case played out in the press."

"So ordered."

Good. "Ms. Low has some medical issues as outlined in our papers. We'd like a full exam and treatment for the conditions described therein."

"Also ordered."

"And we'd like to discuss bail."

"Bail has not been set?"

As if you didn't know. "Correct. Ms. Low was detained on a no-bail hold."

Harper spoke from his seat. "Given the gravity of the crime, we oppose bail."

"*Alleged* crime," I said. "Ms. Low isn't a flight risk. She lacks wherewithal. She is willing to surrender her passport and wear a monitor."

Harper shot back. "It would be unusual to allow bail in a first-degree murder case."

Not necessarily. "Your Honor has discretion."

She nodded as if to say, "Yes, I do."

At the end of the day, this was probably an academic exercise. Unless the judge set bail at a preposterously low amount or a benefactor came forward, Lexy didn't have the money.

Judge McDaniel listened intently as Harper and I volleyed for another five minutes. Finally, she made the call. "Bail is set at one million dollars."

In other words, no bail. "With respect, Your Honor, given our client's financial circumstances, that's exorbitant."

"With respect, Mr. Daley, given the nature of the charge, it isn't."

Harper couldn't resist adding his two cents. "With respect, Your Honor, given the seriousness of the charge, bail is inappropriate."

"With respect, Mr. Harper, I believe that it is."

At least we're all pretending to be respectful. "Your Honor, Ms. Low does not have the resources to post bail or obtain a bond."

"Then she's remanded into custody. If there are no further issues, we're adjourned."

I could see terror in Lexy's eyes as a burly deputy came over to escort her from the courtroom. "What happens next?" she asked.

"We'll talk about it downstairs."

14
"THIS ISN'T HAPPENING"

Lexy's face was contorted, voice agitated. "This isn't happening."

She, Nady, and I were sitting around a metal table in a consultation room in the Glamour Slammer at eleven-thirty on Wednesday morning.

I kept my voice even. "Your best chance to get through this is to stay calm."

"I'm trying."

In the best of circumstances, this was going to be difficult. Given that she was going through withdrawal, this was likely to be substantially worse.

Nady leaned forward. "Did they give you your own cell?"

"I'm with another woman. She's coming down from a crystal meth high."

"How are you dealing with the fact that you don't have access to—"

"Smack?"

"Yes."

"Not great."

"We've requested a medical exam and treatment."

Lexy's voice filled with resignation. "Helluva way to kick my habit, eh?"

"You'll need to fight through it."

"I don't really have any choice, do I?"

Nady had no answer for her. Neither did I.

Lexy's lips turned down. "Now what?"

"We go to work." I explained that we had already submitted requests for the police reports, witness lists, etc. "Our investigator has given us the names of some people who were at King's house on Sunday night. We'll compare it with the police reports. Ideally, we'd like to find evidence that King left the heroin for you, or somebody planted it in King's bathroom."

"Can you get me out of here?"

"You'd need to get your hands on a million dollars or pay a bondsman a hundred grand."

"Not gonna happen."

Didn't think so. "Do you have any friends?"

"Not the kind with a hundred grand burning through their pockets."

"What about other sources? Maybe somebody you met on Mature Relations?"

"No."

"Anybody owe you a favor?"

"Are you asking me if one of my drug suppliers might be willing to post bail?"

"Yes."

"Is that even legal?"

Technically, no. I did the customary lawyerly tap dance. "Obviously, you aren't allowed to make bail using funds obtained illegally."

"Obviously."

"So?"

"I know some people who have the resources, but nobody would be willing to post bail."

"Perhaps they might if they understand that you could provide their name to the D.A."

"You want me to rat out a dealer?"

"It's not an ideal solution." *It may be better than spending the next year in the Glamour Slammer*. "Think of it as a business proposition."

"It isn't a viable option."

I told her the truth. "You're probably going to be here for a while, Lexy."

"Can you get the charges dropped at the prelim?"

"We'll try, but the odds aren't great."

"And if not?"

"We'll find evidence that somebody spiked the heroin and get a jury to reasonable doubt at trial."

"You can't prove it."

"We just need one juror."

"Either way, my life is over."

* * *

"That didn't go well," Nady observed.

"It never does," I said. "We need to make arrangements for Lexy to get treatment right away. It's going to be very hard on her."

The corridor outside the visitor area of the Glamour Slammer was bustling with the usual parade of prisoners, deputies, medical personnel, and social workers going about the day-to-day business of intaking, processing, and housing prisoners.

She asked, "Did you really think that one of her suppliers would post her bail?"

"Doubtful. I was hoping that one of her old friends might step up. I was also testing the waters to see if she might give up the name of her dealer. That might be of interest to the D.A. More realistically, I was hoping another sugar daddy might be willing to front money for the bond."

Nady shook her head. "Doubtful."

"In the long run, it may be better for her if she stays in. At least she'll get treatment."

"If she survives. You going back to the office?"

"I'll meet you there. I want to check in with Pete."

15
"SHE ISN'T GRIEVING"

I avoided the media crush in front of the Hall by taking the rear stairway to the back door and exiting into the Sheriff's Department parking lot. I stopped between police cruisers and punched in Pete's number. He answered on the first ring.

"Bail?" he asked.

"Still a million."

"So, no bail."

"Correct. You got anything?"

"One of my operatives spotted King's widow hitting tennis balls at her club."

"People deal with grief in different ways."

"Most don't drink Mimosas with the tennis pro."

True. "Seems a bit insensitive for a grieving widow."

"She may be a widow, Mick, but she isn't grieving."

* * *

I walked through the parking lot to Seventh Street, which was gridlocked by midday traffic. I looked over at the impound lot under the freeway where people make the trek of shame and fork over four big bills to ransom their towed cars. In a modest accommodation to modern commerce, the tattooed guy behind the bulletproof glass now accepts credit cards.

I started walking down Seventh toward the office. My master plan to ditch the press was scuttled when a stoop-shouldered man sporting a tan trench coat emerged from the bus stop near the bottom of the freeway exit ramp at the corner of Seventh and Bryant.

He puffed on his ever-present Camel, extended a hand, and spoke to me in a smoker's rasp. "Good to see you again, Mr. Daley."

"Good to see you, Jerry," I lied.

For three decades, Jerry Edwards had been the *Chronicle*'s lead investigative reporter and resident manure disturber. With his rumpled raincoat, forties-style fedora, and worn leather notebook, he was a throwback to the days when journalists phoned in stories to copy editors and burned shoe leather instead of smart phones. He had lost a step after three acrimonious divorces and an ongoing battle with bourbon. Nevertheless, when he was on his game, he was still a player. I had been on the business end of his barbs dozens of times, and it wasn't fun. In a world of decimated newsrooms and endless claims of fake news, Edwards had never backed away from speaking truth to power—or to anybody else, including defense attorneys.

His lips formed a wrinkled smile. "Thought you could avoid me, eh?"

I tried. "How did you know I'd come out the back door?"

"Reporter's intuition."

His was still finely tuned. "You didn't want to hang out with the guys from Fox News and CNN?"

"They're a bunch of blow-dried bloviators getting background shots before they issue their personal opinions that your client is guilty."

I had heard the expression "blow-dried bloviators" countless times on his daily TV diatribe on Channel 2. "I gotta get to the office, Jerry."

He opened his notebook. "You seem to have picked up another high-profile case. Care to comment?"

"The usual. My client is innocent. We're looking forward to her day in court to disprove these outrageous charges."

"She killed King with a hot shot of heroin."

"Ms. Low is a victim. King was a billionaire who exploited her."

"You're saying she didn't do it?"

"She's an addict who was victimized by a rich tech mogul."

He stubbed out his cigarette. "King wasn't a Boy Scout, but neither was your client. I saw her listing on Mature Relations. She's pretty."

"She is."

"What kind of person subjects themselves to something so demeaning?"

A desperate heroin addict. "King took advantage of her."

"How does she qualify for a P.D.? She works in tech. She must be making a lot of money."

"She's unemployed."

"She blew all of her money on drugs, didn't she?"

"No comment."

"What a waste."

Indeed.

The veteran scribe played with the sleeve of his overcoat. "I'll just go with the usual line about how she qualifies for a P.D. and that you are confident about her case."

"She's a victim, Jerry."

"Right." He tucked his notebook inside his coat. "Off the record, she strikes me as a bright young woman whose life went off the rails after she got into the Silicon Valley scene."

"Something like that."

"It *was* drugs, wasn't it?"

"And King. He was a sexual predator."

He pulled out his pack of Camels. "I have a granddaughter about her age. How would you feel if your daughter was so desperate that she was paying for drugs by hooking up with a sugar daddy?"

"Not great."

"Helluva world, Mike."

"Yes, it is, Jerry."

* * *

Terrence the Terminator's shaved dome reflected the light above his workstation in the hallway outside Rosie's office. "No bail for Lexy," he said.

I corrected him. "Yes, bail. No money. Anybody looking for me?"

"The autopsy report on King will be finished in the next few days. If you ask nicely, our Medical Examiner said that she might be willing to give you the highlights."

That would help. "Anything else?"

"Inspector Lee left a message. He said that you should meet him up on Billionaires Row tomorrow morning. He'll show you King's house."

16
"DON'T TOUCH ANYTHING"

Inspector Ken Lee's arms were folded, expression grim. "Don't touch anything. This is a private residence and crime scene. I'm doing you a favor."

Yes, you are, but I could do with a little less melodrama. "We appreciate your time."

A winter wind gusted through the trees on Billionaires Row. At nine-thirty the following morning, Pete and I were standing on the front porch of King's refurbished Victorian. Except for the rookie cop guarding the door, the police presence was gone. The media horde had moved on, and life had returned to normal on Mount Olympus.

I admired the intricate ornamentation of the graceful Queen Anne painted pale blue with cream trim. The gingerbread details included lacey spindle work and a front-facing gable topped by a turret. King had added a garage beneath the bay window.

"They did a nice job restoring this place," I observed.

Lee scowled. "The studs are original. Everything else is new. King brought in the carpenters that George Lucas used on Skywalker Ranch."

It must have cost a fortune. "Are you done processing the scene?"

"Yes."

"What's going to happen to the house?"

"That's up to Mrs. King."

Who was last seen playing tennis and drinking Mimosas.

He opened the door and led us into a two-story foyer highlighted by a polished redwood stairway. "Do exactly as I say."

Pete and I nodded obediently.

Lee's cell rang. He held up a finger. Then he turned around and answered it.

While he was on the phone, Pete and I scanned the living room filled with period pieces surrounding a marble fireplace. The house smelled of a cleaning solvent.

Pete used his thumb to gesture. "Did you see the security cameras outside?"

"I saw one above the door."

"There was one at the gate, another over the garage, a couple on the roof, one in the front window, and one in the gangway."

"We asked for video." I turned to Lee, who had ended his call. "Where was the body?"

"Upstairs in the master bedroom. We'll start down here."

He acted like a docent at a museum as he led us into the living room and through the formal dining room. The wallpaper was a reproduction of what I surmised was late nineteenth century work. The crown moldings were handcrafted.

"Looks like he tried to keep the look and feel of the original," I said.

"He did." He explained that the house had once belonged to Mayor James "Sunny Jim" Rolph, who made a fortune in banking and shipping, spent almost twenty years in the mayor's office, and later became governor of California. "King wanted it to look the same as it did after the 1906 earthquake—with some modern enhancements."

The ambiance changed dramatically as we walked through the butler's pantry into the kitchen, which had been completely redone with white cabinets, polished quartz countertops, a restaurant-quality Viking range, and two mega-sized Sub-Zero refrigerators.

"The appliances cost more than my college and law school educations," I said.

Lee nodded. "The wine cellar is bigger than my house."

I stood next to the custom-built kitchen table and admired the expansive family room with picture windows overlooking a multi-level deck. We took in the panorama extending from the Golden Gate Bridge to downtown.

"This view is worth twenty million," Lee said. "This kitchen and the family room were part of an addition that King had built onto the back of the original house." He pointed at the terraced yard extending down the hill. The second level had an infinity pool and in-law unit. "Do you have any idea how much it cost to build a pool into the side of a hill? The grading and retaining wall probably cost five million."

"Mayor Rolph would have been impressed."

"Mayor Rolph would have thought that King was out of his mind."

Pete finally made his presence felt. "King could have bought the biggest house in Pacific Heights and donated the rest to cancer research. These Silicon Valley guys talk about changing the world. At the end of the day, it's about buying expensive toys."

He had a way of putting things into perspective.

Pete reverted to his cop-voice. "The party was here on the first floor?"

Lee pointed at the windows. "And out on the deck."

"People were allowed upstairs?"

"Yes. There's only one bathroom down here."

Pete didn't say it aloud, but this was important. Everybody at the party had access to the bathroom where Lexy said she found the heroin.

Pete kept talking to Lee. "Everybody left before King died?"

"Except the security guy and your client."

"You'll provide a list of everybody who was here along with security videos?"

"In due course."

"When might 'due course' be?"

"Soon."

"How soon?"

"Soon," Lee repeated.

We retraced our steps and went upstairs, where we found three bedrooms and a bathroom in the original house. The new construction in the back included a media room, a gym overlooking the Bay, a master bath, and a master bedroom bigger than the conference room at my old downtown law firm.

Lee escorted us into the master bedroom, which showed no sign that it had been a crime scene four days earlier. The king-size bed was fitted with high-end sheets and a navy comforter. A sixty-inch flat-screen was mounted above the fireplace. There was a hand-carved chest of drawers beneath the TV. A Plexiglass desk with a leather chair was next to the window. If Mayor Rolph came back today, he would have liked what he saw.

I looked around for security cameras, but they were well-hidden. "He died on the bed?"

"On the floor," Lee said.

"And you claim that our client injected him?"

"We know that she did. We have it on video."

"Where's the camera?"

"Embedded in the crown molding above the TV."

"You can see her cook the heroin?"

"And inject him. King went limp. Then he collapsed." His tone turned pointed. "Instead of trying to help him, your client grabbed her belongings and ran."

"She went to get help."

"She tried to flee. She would have made it if the security guy hadn't stopped her."

"She panicked."

"She grabbed an envelope full of cash from King and ran. Either way, she gave him the hot shot that killed him."

"Why would she have killed her patron?" I didn't want to use the term "sugar daddy."

"She needed the money."

"She would have gotten a lot more if he was still alive."

"Maybe they had a falling out. You'll need to ask your client."

Pete spoke up again. "Where did she prepare the injection?"

"On the dresser."

"You're saying that she brought the smack with her?"

"Yes."

"How do you know that King didn't provide it?"

"We know."

"A billionaire got his heroin from a woman he met online?"

"I've seen stranger things."

"Would you take smack from someone you met on a hookup site?"

"I wouldn't accept it from anybody."

"Where was the heroin?"

"She brought it in from the bathroom."

"Is there a camera in there?"

"No."

I looked into the master bath, which had two doors: one leading into the master bedroom, and the other leading into the hallway. "Did anybody else come upstairs?"

"Yes." He said that there was a security camera in the hallway. "You'll be able to see everybody."

"King could have left the heroin in the master bath a week ago. Or somebody else could have planted it on the night that he died. Or somebody could have tampered with it."

Lee wasn't buying. "That's the best you've got?"

At the moment. "A lot of people disliked King."

"Everybody had a huge financial interest in the IPO."

"Maybe it was personal."

"Good luck selling it to a jury."

* * *

I inhaled the cool air as Pete and I walked down Twenty-First. "They have something," I said. "Definitely video. Maybe more."

He didn't look at me as he kept walking. "You have options."

I waited.

"First, you can argue that King left the heroin in the bathroom sometime before Sunday night. You won't be able to prove it, but there's no way for them to disprove it."

"True."

"Second, if I was a billionaire, I would buy heroin from a reputable dealer, not from somebody I met on a hookup site—no matter how upscale it purports to be. It's hard to believe that Sexy Lexy was providing him with smack, unless he was reckless."

"Agreed."

"Third, the video from the surveillance camera in the upstairs hallway should identify everybody who used the master bath. Anybody on the tape could have planted the heroin or tampered with it. That sets up your potential SODDI defense."

"I'll feel better if we had something more definitive."

"So would I, but you take your evidence as it comes. Fourth, we should talk to everybody in the video. They probably won't confess, but we'll find out if they'll be convincing in court. You'll want to try to pin this on somebody who will make a crappy witness."

Exactly. "I'd like to start with the security guy."

Pete smirked. "He gets paid *not* to talk to guys like us."

"I need you to work your magic."

"It may not work so well with a retired Israeli commando, but I'll see what I can do." He tugged at his sleeve. "I'm going down to Palo Alto to check on King's widow. Then I want to see what's going on over at Y5K. What about you, Mick?"

I glanced at my watch. "I have an appointment with our Medical Examiner."

17
"HE STOPPED BREATHING"

The Chief Medical Examiner of the City and County of San Francisco extended a hand and invoked a professional tone. "Good to see you again, Mr. Daley."

"Thanks for making the time, Dr. Siu."

Dr. Joy Siu and I had met at least a dozen times, but we'd never gotten comfortable using first names.

At one-thirty on Thursday afternoon, she was sitting in an ergonomic leather chair behind a glass-topped table covered with meticulously labeled folders in orderly piles. From her pressed white lab coat to her carefully applied makeup to her coiffed jet-black hair, she exuded precision. Now in her mid-forties, the Princeton and Johns Hopkins alum and one-time research scientist at UCSF had succeeded the legendary Dr. Roderick Beckert three years earlier. Building upon her reputation as a world-class academic and expert in anatomic pathology, the former Olympic figure skating hopeful was one of the most respected medical examiners in the U.S.

Her office was on the second floor of a sixty-five-million-dollar warehouse-like building on Newhall Street in the industrial India Basin neighborhood, about halfway between downtown and Hunters Point. The new facility opened in 2017, and it was a vast upgrade over the old Medical Examiner's bunker in the basement of the Hall of Justice. The state-of-the-art examination facilities and expanded morgue made up for her less-than-stellar view of bulldozers at the recycling center across the street on Pier 96.

"Rod Beckert would have loved your new digs," I said. "Too bad it took so long."

"Things take time. It took twenty years to build the new police headquarters."

Every cop in town wanted to work in the half-billion-dollar complex between the ballpark and the new UCSF medical campus. "They still haven't found a home for Homicide. I'll bet you a cup of coffee that it won't happen before I retire."

"You're on." Her eyes locked onto mine. "I take it that you aren't here just to admire my new office or discuss the City's infrastructure projects?"

Here we go. "I understand that you did the autopsy on Jeff King."

"I did."

"When?"

"Christmas Day."

She was one of San Francisco's hardest-working public servants. "Do you have results?"

"Very preliminary. I will issue a final report after we get full toxicology."

This case was on a fast track. Ordinarily, autopsy results take weeks or months. "Do you have a preliminary conclusion?"

"Mr. King died of a lethal overdose of heroin."

"Could you explain how you came to that conclusion?"

She cocked her head to the side. "Ever tried heroin?"

"Uh, no."

"Neither have I. But you understand how it works, right?"

Yes, I do, but I want to hear you explain it. "It's a downer."

"Yes, it is." Her tone turned clinical. "When heroin reaches the brain, it breaks down into morphine. That excites the opioid receptors, which causes dopamine to flood the brain. This gives rise to euphoria. Over time, it can impair natural dopamine regulation, which can lead to physical, psychological, and behavioral symptoms." She said that it calms people for short periods. "Then they become desperate to maintain their high. Addicts will do almost anything to find another hit. If you're a regular user, you develop a tolerance, so you crave bigger doses. People get irritable and angry. They act irrationally. It's horrible stuff."

She would be terrific explaining it to a jury.

She was still talking. "It's highly addictive, and the side effects are horrible." She rattled off a list: warm flushing on the skin, dry mouth, leaden feeling in the arms and legs, severe itching, nausea, vomiting, drowsiness, clouded mental health capacities, depressed heart rate, low blood pressure, and slowed breathing. "This can lead to brain damage, coma, or death."

"What happened to King?"

"He stopped breathing."

That will kill you every time. "How much heroin does it take to kill you?"

"Depends on your weight, health, and the amount and purity of the heroin. Seventy-five milligrams could have killed a man of King's size. He ingested about two hundred milligrams. It was enough to kill an antelope."

Yikes. "How did you determine how much he took?"

"A security video caught your client loading two syringes."

"And the purity?"

She glanced at her computer. "We found traces in the syringes and in a baggie in your client's purse. It was potent stuff. High-end white. Ninety-seven percent pure."

"Any evidence of poison or other drugs? Rat poison? Fentanyl?"

"Nothing so far, but we'll wait for final toxicology."

"You think an unemployed woman living in a shelter bought the good stuff?"

"That's a question for Inspector Lee and your client."

"If you were a billionaire, would you get your stuff from a woman you met on the Internet?"

"I'm not a billionaire, and I don't know where it came from."

"Was King a regular user?"

"Needle marks on his arm indicated a high likelihood."

"Do you have any other information about his overall health?"

"Generally good. He wasn't overweight. Records from his most recent physical indicated that his blood pressure was slightly elevated. His cholesterol and blood sugar were high, but not extreme. He wasn't taking any prescription medications."

"What about other recreational drugs?"

"Not as far as I could tell. I'll know for sure when we get the toxicology results."

"How was his heart?"

"He had a stress test last year. Nothing out of the ordinary."

"Completely normal?"

"He had a slightly irregular heartbeat."

Oh? "How irregular?"

"Within a normal range."

"Irregular enough to kill him?"

"No."

We would find an expert who would express a contrary conclusion. "I haven't seen anything about funeral plans."

"King didn't want one. The body was cremated. His ashes will be sent into space."

"Seriously?"

"Yes." Her mouth turned up. "A company called Elysium Space puts your ashes into a special box that they send up on one of Elon Musk's SpaceX Falcon 9 rockets."

"You're kidding."

"I'm not. The rocket orbits the earth for about two years, then it reenters the atmosphere as a shooting star. They call it a 'memorial spaceflight.' You can track its path on your iPhone."

"How much does this set you back?"

"A couple thousand bucks. I can get you the information if you're interested."

The world has changed since I was a priest. "No, thanks."

* * *

Rosie's voice was filled with bemusement. "They're sending King's ashes to the moon?"

I pressed my iPhone to my ear as I sat in traffic near the ballpark. "No, just into orbit."

"Would you like us to make similar arrangements for you?"

"A simple pine box will do."

"Having a good day?"

"Wonderful." I gave her the highlights of our visit to King's house and my discussion with Dr. Siu. "A lot of people were in the house that night, some of whom had access to the bathroom where our client says that King left the heroin."

"Inspector Lee said that Lexy brought the stuff. Who do you believe?"

"Until I have evidence to the contrary, our client. I want to see the video. If it turns out that she's lying, I'm going to be very unhappy."

"Either way, how are you planning to deal with it?"

My ever-practical ex-wife. "Ideally, we'll find evidence that somebody planted the heroin or tampered with it. If that isn't convincing enough, we'll argue that King left it there for Lexy."

"That could still result in a manslaughter conviction."

"It's better than murder. Dr. Siu also said that King had an irregular heartbeat."

"Enough to kill him?"

"I'm not sure. Hopefully, it will convince one juror that a little high-end heroin could have killed him accidentally."

"That also could result in a manslaughter conviction."

"It's still better than murder."

* * *

"Where are you, Mick?" Pete asked.

I gripped the steering wheel as I was driving toward the office. "Third and Bryant."

"How would you like to have dinner in Palo Alto with Blackjack Steele and me?"

"Sounds lovely. How did you get the CEO of Y5K to dine with us?"

"I'm very resourceful."

Yes, you are. "Does he know that we'll be joining him?"

"Not yet."

18
"PEOPLE WITH MONEY ALWAYS GET THE BENEFIT OF THE DOUBT"

Pete picked at his boneless fried chicken thigh in a green curry sauce. "What do you make of this place, Mick?"

I admired the presentation of my wagyu skirt steak garnished with baby carrots and fish sauce. "Lovely, but not my cup of tea."

Bird Dog was a hot spot for Silicon Valley foodies. Billed as a purveyor of a fusion between Northern California and Japanese cuisines, it was housed in a remodeled auto repair shop in downtown Palo Alto. Its industrial-chic décor featured exposed brick walls, wooden tables, and track lighting mounted on beams. The bar was stocked with high-end booze from which urbane bartenders prepared new-age versions of old-style cocktails. The clientele was well-heeled and well-dressed. For a guy who thought it was a treat to go out for burgers at the Red Chimney at Stonestown Mall when I was a kid, it struck me as pretentious.

Pete always sat with his back to the wall so he could see the room. He wasn't finished sharing his review of his chicken. "Twenty-seven bucks for fancy KFC? Seriously?"

"It's an expense-account restaurant." I took another bite of my steak. "You said Jack Steele would be here."

"He will."

I was looking forward to meeting the CEO of Y5K. "Did the parking valet tip you off?"

"The hostess."

I should have known. "How much did that set you back?"

"More than the price of your dinner. It'll be on your bill, Mick. In the meantime, eat your overpriced steak and follow my lead."

Sorry I asked.

Pete pointed at the doorway, where Steele entered the restaurant accompanied by a younger man. They sported navy blazers, powder-blue dress shirts, and khakis. "Right on time—with matching uniforms."

"Who is the other guy?"

"The venture capitalist, Gopal Patel. He was at King's house, too."

A young woman wearing a designer blouse and black slacks accompanied them to the maître d's podium.

"That's Steele's daughter, Debbie," Pete said. "She had an internship at Y5K last summer. She graduated early from Stanford a couple of weeks ago."

"What's she doing now?"

"Taking a little time off. We need to order more overpriced chicken. We may be here for a while. Act natural, be discreet, and let me do the talking."

The hostess escorted Steele, his daughter, and Patel to the table next to ours. I surmised that Pete had paid the woman at the podium a premium to seat us next to them.

The paunchy, balding Steele looked more like an insurance salesman than a master of Silicon Valley. His wire-framed glasses were overwhelmed by a jowly face. His phony grin reminded me of the power partners at my old law firm where they'd smile to your face as they knifed you in the back. His daughter's features were more delicate, complexion darker, manner dead serious. Patel's demeanor was studious, his movements precise. He put on his reading glasses, pursed his lips, and examined the cocktail list.

A waitress with multiple facial piercings brought them sparkling water and an order of kohlrabi, a cabbage-like vegetable prepared with an apple and macadamia nut topping. Perhaps it tasted better than it looked.

Pete and I chatted about our kids as we tried to eavesdrop. Steele and Patel exchanged small talk. Debbie ordered a cocktail called a "Leave Britney Alone," which the menu described as a combination of high-end rum, tepache, Meyer lemon, and amaro.

The tenor of the discussion became more serious when Steele and Patel turned to Y5K.

"Our investment bankers want to put the IPO on hold," Patel said.

Steele remained upbeat. "Y5K isn't one person, Gopal. We need to keep developing our product. There is demand for it—with or without Jeff."

Patel was less sanguine. "Maybe."

"It isn't about personality."

"It was for Apple."

"The iPhone would have succeeded with or without Jobs."

"It was his idea."

Pete and I ate our second dinners as Steele and Patel discussed scenarios. They were concerned about negative press, nervous investment bankers, and even more nervous lawyers. They said nothing about the events at King's house. They barely spoke to Steele's daughter, who nursed her drink in silence.

Pete repeatedly made eye contact with Steele, who kept looking away. Finally, as the waitress poured Steele a cup of organic free-trade coffee, Pete started working his magic. He extended a hand to Steele. "I'm Peter Daley. You probably don't remember me, but I was the assistant head of security when you were at TMA."

"Of course, Peter. It's very nice to see you again."

Especially since you've never met.

"This is my brother, Michael."

I was just a prop. I didn't mention that I was representing the woman accused of killing his meal ticket. Steele would figure it out soon enough. I smiled and shook his meaty hand. He graciously introduced us to his daughter and Patel, who were also polite.

Pete spoke in a respectful tone. "I'm sorry for interrupting your dinner."

"That's okay, Peter."

"I hope Mrs. Steele is doing well."

The phony grin disappeared. "Actually, we divorced about two years ago."

"I'm sorry to hear that."

I had no doubt that Pete was aware of Steele's divorce.

"It was for the best," Steele said.

"It's always difficult." Pete turned to Debbie. "You must be in college."

Steele answered for her. "She graduated from Stanford a couple of weeks ago." He quickly added, "A semester early."

Everybody with a kid at Stanford always manages to work that into the conversation.

Pete kept talking to Debbie. "Any idea what you might do next?"

"Looking at options."

"Maybe you could work for Y5K."

"I think it's better to work for somebody other than your father."

"Not a bad idea. I went into the family business. It didn't work out so well."

"Security?"

"Law enforcement. My dad was a cop. I lasted ten years, then I moved into private security."

There was more to the story. Pete and his partner were fired after they used a little too much force breaking up a fight in the Mission. They arrested a young man who happened to be the nephew of a member of the Board of Supervisors. The kid's family sued, the City caved, and Pete and his partner were tossed under a bus.

Debbie's father spoke up again. "She hasn't ruled out the possibility of coming to Y5K. She interned with us. At the moment, she's taking the opportunity to do a little travelling, and she's also taking a little time to deal with some, uh, health issues."

Pete feigned concern. "Nothing serious, I hope."

"She'll be fine."

His daughter didn't respond.

Pete looked directly at Steele. "I'm sorry about Jeff King."

"Thank you. He was a visionary."

"You must be under an ungodly amount of stress."

"We are."

"They said on the news that he got some bad drugs at a party."

"All I know is what I've read in the papers."

Pete feigned concern. "Were you there?"

Steele nodded.

Pete looked at Patel. "You, too?"

"Yes."

Steele's daughter quickly distanced herself. "I was skiing."

Pete was still looking at Steele. "I'm so sorry. That must have been awful."

"It was."

"Were other people from the company there?"

"A few."

"How horrible. You didn't see anything, did you?"

"I was gone before it happened."

Patel added, "So was I."

"That's good," Pete said. "I saw that they arrested a young woman.

They said that she gave him heroin."

Steele repeated his mantra. "All I know is what I've read in the papers."

"Do you have any idea who she was?"

"No."

"You didn't see her at the party, did you?"

"No."

Pete decided to leave it there. "I'm sorry for interrupting your dinner and talking about such a difficult subject."

"It is what it is, Peter."

* * *

"What did you think of Steele, Mick?"

"Excellent manners."

Pete's car was parked in front of the Apple Store on University Avenue. Pete was looking at his texts. I was checking e-mail.

Pete finally looked up. "Guys like Steele have nice clothes, firm handshakes, and fake smiles. They spew clichés about connecting the world. Then they cheat on their spouses, treat their employees like crap, and keep score by the size of their private jets."

I sensed hostility. "That might be a bit of an over-generalization. His daughter was nice."

"If she's smart, she'll stay away from Y5K and the insanity down here."

"And the venture capitalist?"

"He'd stick a shiv in your stomach for one-hundredth of a percentage point in a Series B financing." He put his phone into his pocket. "Don't underestimate them, Mick. These guys are smart, calculating, and ruthless. And the scariest part is that if you put them on the stand, the jury is going to believe them."

"I'm not so sure."

"People with money always get the benefit of the doubt."

* * *

The round-faced barkeep with the full head of bright red hair spoke to me in a familiar fake Irish brogue. "What'll it be, lad?"

"That shtick works better for your father than it does for you."

"What can I get you, Mike?"

"Anchor Steam."

"On the house."

My first cousin, Ryan Dunleavy, was the youngest of Big John's four sons. His wife's family owned Molloy's Tavern, a watering hole in Colma across Mission Street from Holy Cross Cemetery, where my parents were buried. Molloy's had been serving post-funeral libations for a hundred years. In the daytime, Ryan was the CFO of a payroll processing firm. A couple of nights a week, he worked the late shift at Molloy's. I always stopped by when I was in the neighborhood.

"How's business?" I asked him.

"Recession-proof."

After people paid their respects to the deceased, it was customary to pay their respects to the House of Molloy. "Jeannie and the kids okay?"

"Fine." We caught up for a few minutes. Then his expression turned serious. "I've been following your case. Did Sexy Lexy really give that guy a hot shot?"

"We think somebody else spiked the heroin."

"Jerry Edwards at the *Chronicle* disagrees with you."

"He always does."

My iPhone vibrated. Nady's name appeared on the display.

"How soon can you get back to the office?" she asked.

"Less than an hour."

"Good. Inspector Lee sent over a list of people who were at King's house. And he sent over some surveillance videos."

19
"TOXIC MASCULINITY"

At ten-thirty on Thursday night, the conference room at the P.D.'s Office smelled of leftover pizza and stale coffee. The fluorescent light made Nady's skin look pale as she sat on the opposite side of the table, eyes on her laptop. Pete was next to her, a cup of room-temperature coffee in his hand. Rosie sat next to me, her attention focused on her iPhone.

Nady handed me a sheet of paper. "Inspector Lee sent over a list of the people who were at King's house."

Progress. Rosie and I studied it. King and Lexy were the first two names. Then came Steele and Patel. The fifth person was the head of security, Yoav Ben-Shalom.

Nady noted that two off-duty cops were working security outside. "They left early. And Pete already gave us the name of Tristan Moore, the marketing guy. Twenty-nine. Princeton undergrad. Columbia MBA. He's bounced around a half-dozen startups."

I kept going down the list. "Alejandro Sanchez?"

"Y5K's Chief Technology Officer. Thirty. Stanford and MIT. He created the algorithm for their data storage upgrade."

Smart guy. "Drew Pitt?"

Pete spoke up. "King's best friend from high school in the New York suburbs. Forty-eight. Divorced. Lives in Atherton. Around the company, he's known as the 'Guy from Rye.'"

"What's his job?"

"Nobody knows. Has a degree in computer science, but he rarely comes to work. His primary function seemed to be partying with King."

"Did that include providing women?"

"Probably."

"And drugs?"

"Possibly."

The list also included the names of six women described as "invited guests." I asked whether any of them worked at Y5K.

Nady answered. "No. Christina Chu is an associate at Patel's venture firm. Lee thinks she invited the others."

"Seems Patel's firm may have been providing more than venture capital."

Rosie was still studying the list. "By my count, other than King and Lexy, there were six men and six women at the party, not including the off-duty cops, the parking valet, and the kid who delivered the food. That's at least a dozen potential suspects for a SODDI defense—if you're inclined to go that way. It would help if you could place them inside the master bath to make a credible argument that one of them planted the heroin."

Yup, that covers it.

She was still talking. "It would also be nice if you can demonstrate that somebody had a motive to kill King even though he or she stood to lose millions if the IPO was cancelled." She stood up. "I'll let you sort it out. I'm going home."

Without another word, she headed out the door.

I looked around the table: my brother, my associate, and me. Compared to the big law firms, we were the legal profession's counterpart to a garage band. "I'll make fresh coffee."

"Where do you want to start?" Nady asked.

Pete answered her. "As they say on ESPN, let's go to video."

* * *

Pete had commandeered Nady's laptop and connected it to the TV. We were watching footage from a security camera mounted outside King's front door. The parking valet was the first to arrive. He had taken his post at eight-thirty p.m. King and his security guy, Yoav Ben-Shalom, arrived in a town car at eight-forty. Steele and Patel showed up at nine-ten. Tristan Moore, the sales guy, Alejandro Sanchez, the programmer, and Drew Pitt, the "Guy from Rye," arrived shortly thereafter.

Pete pointed at a young man lugging a food delivery chest up the walkway. "He's from Pancho Villa."

It was a low-brow choice for a bunch of millionaires. Pancho Villa was a no-frills burrito shop down the block from the Sixteenth Street BART Station in the de-militarized zone separating the gentrified and non-gentrified sections of the Mission. Despite its lack of ambiance, it always made the *Chronicle*'s list of best burritos in town.

The delivery guy left a few minutes later. Pete fast-forwarded to ten o'clock, when the first of six young women showed up in an Uber.

"That's Christina Chu from Patel's VC firm," Nady said. "She's pretty."

The rest of the women arrived in separate Ubers. All were petite, pretty, and wearing black cocktail dresses and high heels.

Pete rolled his eyes. "The bros had a thing for young women."

Nady frowned. "Toxic masculinity. Am I the only person who thinks this is sick?"

Count me in. "This is appalling."

Nady wasn't finished. "My mother and I got chased out of Uzbekistan with the clothes on our backs. We came here and worked insanely hard. And now these assholes—who won the lottery with some over-hyped software—are using their winnings to exploit these women."

"It's twisted."

Her voice filled with disdain. "You know what else bothers me? These women aren't desperate or destitute. They aren't hookers or escorts or addicts. Chu works for a VC firm. I looked up the bios of the other women. They work in tech, too. They must have thought it was a good way to make business connections with King and some tech players and maybe get funding for their startups. Have a little self-respect, people."

Pete restarted the video. At eleven o'clock, the security guy came outside and waved to Lexy, who emerged from an Uber. She looked nothing like the somber woman we had met at the Hall. She was dressed for a hipster club South of Market. She was wearing a black cocktail dress with a high-cropped leather jacket and Prada boots. A Gucci bag was slung over her shoulder. Her makeup was perfect, not a strand of hair out of place.

"Hard to believe it's the same person," Nady said.

"King must have paid for the clothes."

The next flurry of activity came at eleven-forty-five, when people started leaving. Patel was the first out the door, hand-in-hand with his associate, Christina Chu. They got into an Uber.

"He's married," Nady observed.

"Maybe not much longer," Pete said.

Five minutes later, three more women left. Then Tristan Moore and Alejandro Sanchez got into an Uber with the last two women.

"Somebody's getting lucky," Pete said.

Nady was seething. "This is disgusting."

Yes, it is. The remaining revelers departed in the next fifteen minutes. The "Guy from Rye" sauntered to the curb and left in an Uber. Blackjack Steele claimed his Tesla. The valet closed up and headed down the street.

Pete scowled. "They hired the kid to stand out in the cold for three hours to park one car." He studied his notes. "By my count, the only people still inside were King, Lexy, and the security guy."

He fast-forwarded to twelve-forty-one a.m., when a police car pulled up in front of the house. Ben-Shalom rushed outside, and two cops followed him into the house. Two minutes later, an ambulance pulled up, and the two EMTs ran inside. Shortly thereafter, they returned and loaded a lifeless King into the ambulance.

"He was pronounced at Cal Pacific," Nady said.

"San Francisco General is closer," I observed.

Pete looked at me as if I had lost my mind. "SF General is fine for the unwashed masses like us, Mick. Guys like King don't go to public hospitals." He turned to Nady. "Did Lee send over any footage from inside?"

"Yes, he did."

20
"NOTHING CHANGES"

My stomach churned from my second cup of coffee as we watched footage from security cameras inside King's house. The partygoers were eating burritos and drinking microbrews in the living room, dining room, kitchen, and family room. A few vaped on the deck. The women went through the motions of flirting with the men. The "cuddle puddles" were little more than brief interludes of awkward groping. Except for the fancy house and the advanced ages of the men, we could have been watching a freshman dorm mixer at Cal.

"Kind of low energy," I observed.

Pete answered. "You were expecting a rager? No sign of our client."

"King told her not to talk to the guests and go straight upstairs."

Pete ran footage from the family room. King was holding court near the fireplace, using a beer to gesture. He was surrounded by three women, fake smiles plastered on their faces. The "Guy from Rye" was across the room, talking to a woman who smiled when he looked at her, and frowned when he didn't.

"Frat party," Pete muttered.

"Pathetic," Nady said. "Looks like Blackjack Steele made a friend."

We watched Steele make a clumsy attempt to put his arm around one of the women, who rebuffed his advances twice before finally relenting. Her phony smile transformed into a pained expression until she managed to force another grin. Across the room, Patel was feeling up a woman who looked disgusted.

Pete's voice filled with sarcasm. "Smooth."

Nady's tone was laced with contempt. "Suave. Very James Bond."

"This looks like something out of *Mad Men*," I said.

"Nothing changes," Nady said. "Patel was hitting on Chu, who works at his firm. He's a walking sexual harassment claim. This party is just a bunch of guys with raging hormones and lots of money hitting on young women."

That covers it.

Pete started the next video. "This is from a camera upstairs mounted above the door leading into the master bedroom. It's pointed down the hallway toward the front of the house. The first door on the right leads into the master bath, which has a second door opening directly into the master bedroom. Down the hall, there are three bedrooms and another bath." Nobody came upstairs until Lexy appeared at eleven o'clock. "Here she comes."

Lexy came up the stairs, stopped, looked around, then walked into the master bath. She didn't come back, which indicated that she had entered the master bedroom via the second door.

Pete's eyes were focused on the flat-screen. "Pay attention, kids."

I took notes as we watched people trudge upstairs, turn into the master bath, and reappear shortly thereafter.

Eleven-fifteen: King.

Eleven-eighteen: Patel.

Eleven-twenty: Ben-Shalom.

Eleven-twenty-five: Sanchez.

Eleven-forty-eight: The "Guy from Rye."

Eleven-fifty-two. Steele.

Eleven-fifty-five: Moore.

Midnight: Ben-Shalom for the second time.

At twelve-fourteen, King came upstairs again and walked into the master bath. He didn't come out, which indicated that he had gone directly into the master bedroom.

Nady studied her notes. "I count eight people—including Lexy and King—who used the master bath. As far as I can tell, none of the women other than our client came upstairs."

We now had visual evidence that Lexy, King, and six others had entered the bathroom, where they could have planted or spiked the heroin.

Pete restarted the video. At twelve-thirty-two a.m., Lexy darted under the camera and hustled down the stairs. Her clothing was disheveled, the expensive purse dangling on her shoulder. She returned a moment later followed by Ben-Shalom, who pushed her into the bedroom. Then he went downstairs and came back with two cops. The EMTs showed up a few minutes later. Shortly thereafter, they hauled an unconscious King down the steps. Then a cop escorted Lexy downstairs. By one-fifteen, the activity had stopped.

I looked at Pete. "No camera in the bathroom?"

"Afraid not."

Crap. "What about the bedroom?"

"Yes."

He cued the next video. It was almost midnight as Nady, Pete, and I studied footage from a camera mounted above the TV and pointed at the bed. I remembered the layout from our visit. There was a dresser next to the closet. King's desk was near the windows. A pair of wall sconces provided enough light so that we could see everything clearly.

"Sparse furnishings," Nady observed.

Lexy didn't leave the bedroom from the time she arrived until King showed up at twelve-fourteen. She had spent most of the time on the bed, looking at her phone. When King came upstairs, Lexy went into the bathroom, and re-emerged a moment later wearing a silk robe. She held a baggie, a spoon, a lighter, two syringes, and some rubber surgical hosing, which she carried to the dresser. Her demeanor was calm, her expression serious.

"She'd done this before," Pete said.

Lexy poured the powder into the spoon. She used the lighter to heat the heroin until it turned into amber liquid. She looked like a nurse as she prepared two syringes—presumably one for King and one for herself.

Pete zoomed in on the syringes. "They're full. It was a big dose."

King had removed his shirt and pants, but he was still wearing his underwear. He stood next to the bed and spoke to Lexy. "All set?"

"Be patient. Perfection takes time."

He came up behind Lexy and rubbed her shoulders. Then he grabbed her by the arms, spun her around, and kissed her.

Nady's reaction was succinct. "Asshole."

King went into the bathroom, then came back wearing a silk robe.

"This is gross," Nady said.

Yes, it is.

King forcibly kissed Lexy again. Her expression changed from feigned enjoyment to contempt. King ripped off her robe and pulled her toward him, exposing her bra and panties.

She held up a hand. "Aren't you forgetting something?"

He walked over to the dresser, opened the top drawer, removed an envelope, and handed it to Lexy. She stuffed it into her purse.

Lexy forced a smile. "Ready?"

"Yes."

King sat down on the bed. Lexy wrapped the surgical hose around his right arm above the bicep.

"All good?" she asked.

"All good."

King was still smiling as she inserted the needle into his arm.

Pete was staring at the TV. "That eliminates the possibility of arguing that somebody else gave him the injection."

Lexy went back to the dresser and retrieved the second syringe. She turned around and her eyes grew wide. She depressed the plunger and shot the heroin onto the floor. Then she put the syringe back on the dresser and rushed back to the bed, where a motionless King was lying on his back, eyes open. She slapped his face. She felt for a pulse. She slapped him again. He fell to the floor. She uttered a string of expletives. Then she gathered the drug paraphernalia and stuffed it into her purse. She put on her dress and jacket and headed into the hallway.

Pete stopped the video. "She didn't help him."

"She slapped him and checked for a pulse."

"That wasn't helping, Mick. She just left."

"She panicked."

"It's going to look terrible in court."

Yes, it would. Pete fast-forwarded through the footage. Lexy returned to the bedroom followed by Ben-Shalom. The cops arrived. Then the EMTs, who hauled King's body downstairs. One of the cops escorted Lexy out of the room. Eventually, Inspector Lee showed up. So did a representative from the medical examiner's office. Then the field evidence technicians.

The video ended. My mind raced as I tried to process what we had viewed. Bottom line: no matter what Lexy was thinking at the time, it appeared that she had given King a big dose of heroin and tried to flee without calling for help.

Nady turned up the lights. Her voice filled with resignation. "She injected him. She took the cash. She tried to run."

"We'll say it was consensual. He asked her to inject him."

"That's our defense? He asked for it?"

"Our defense is that somebody else planted some high-powered heroin. If that doesn't fly, we'll argue that it was an accident, and hope we can get a jury down to manslaughter."

"You think that will fly?"

I don't know. "We'll also argue that seven people other than Lexy—and including King—used the master bath. Any one of them could have planted the heroin or spiked it."

"But *she* injected him."

"She didn't intend to kill him."

"Says who?"

"Lexy." I turned to Pete. "We need you to get as much dirt as you can on everybody who was at King's house."

"We have a lot of work to do, Mick."

21
"CAN YOU PROVE IT?"

Rosie's full lips transformed into the seductive smile that I still found as captivating as the day we had met in the old P.D.'s Office almost twenty-five years earlier. She switched on the light next to the bed. "You're sure that Lexy gave him the injection?"

"You can see it in the video. Then she left without helping him or calling 9-1-1."

She leaned over and kissed me. "You're screwed, Mike."

At two-thirty on Friday morning, I was exhausted, but Rosie was wide awake. Before she was elected as P.D., she never had trouble sleeping. Nowadays, she woke up more frequently, concerned about a detail at work or a fundraising question. Conversely, I rarely got up at night anymore. Unlike our days running a small-time criminal defense practice where we scrambled to pay the rent, I had regular paychecks, decent medical benefits, and the anticipation of a modest pension. It also reflected the reality that I was closer to sixty than fifty, and I no longer had the energy to sweat the smaller stuff.

Rosie cupped my cheek. "How are you planning to deal with this?"

At two-thirty in the morning? "Do we need to talk about it now?"

"I'm just doing my job."

"You want a status report in the middle of the night?"

"That's when we've always done our best work." She smiled. "If I find your performance satisfactory, I'll give you a bonus."

My job has excellent fringe benefits. "Are you suggesting that you would trade sexual favors for satisfactory job performance?"

"Yes. My motivational methods are unconventional, but effective."

Uh, yes. "Are they legal?"

"No." Her grin broadened. "Are you planning to file a complaint with HR?"

"No."

"Good." She turned serious. "How is our client?"

"Not great. They moved her into her own cell, but withdrawal is always rough. They did a medical evaluation and started giving her

Suboxone."

It worked faster than Methadone.

Her lips turned down. "Helluva way to get clean. Is she capable of helping with her defense?"

"At times. Nady goes over to see her at least once a day to check on her."

"Nady is a good lawyer."

"And a good person." I waited a beat. "She reminds me of you."

"Maybe a little. Are Ward and Harper going to stick with the first-degree murder charge?"

"For now."

"There was no pre-meditation."

"They're saying it took time for Lexy to purchase the heroin and prepare the needle."

"Lexy told us that King provided the heroin."

"Evidently, the D.A. thinks otherwise."

"And the motive?"

"Money." I reminded Rosie that they found five thousand dollars in Lexy's purse.

"Why would she have killed her sugar daddy?"

"Ward and Harper must know something that we don't, or they're bluffing. Maybe King threatened to cut Lexy off, and she decided to grab what she could."

"You'll go with a SODDI defense?"

"That's my first choice. Anybody who entered the bathroom could have left the heroin there. Or they could have spiked it."

"And motive?"

"A lot of people disliked King."

"All of whom stood to get millions if he had lived a few months longer."

"Pete will get some dirt on everybody who was there."

"Can you prove it?"

"I don't know. If it looks like the SODDI defense won't fly, we'll have a medical expert testify that King's heart condition made him susceptible to an accidental death from what otherwise would have been a non-lethal dose of heroin. I've already talked to a couple of doctors who might be willing to testify."

Her expression was skeptical. "Sounds like you won't be able to get the charges dropped at the prelim. Are you planning to put Lexy on the stand?"

"No. I may reconsider if we go to trial."

"She's the only person who can describe what she was thinking when she gave King the heroin."

"She's in no condition to testify. And she may not be sympathetic. She lost her job, got hooked on heroin, blew her money on her habit, and found a sugar daddy. There's video of her putting five grand into her purse, giving King the shot, and trying to run. The optics are terrible."

"Maybe Ward and Harper would be willing to cut a deal for manslaughter."

"Voluntary would be pretty good. Involuntary would be great."

Rosie was silent for a long moment. "Did you eat?"

"A couple of energy bars."

"Anything nutritional?"

"I'm working on it, Rosie." *Just not as hard as I should.* "I weigh as much as I did when I was in college."

"You can't fool your body. Your blood pressure and cholesterol are still too high. In three years, you'll be eligible for a city pension. You'll enjoy it more if you're still alive."

I was in decent shape for a fifty-seven-year-old, but age, children, and Hershey bars had taken a toll. "I'm going to walk the steps in the morning."

"Give my best to Zvi."

"I still want to be just like him when I grow up."

I played football and baseball in high school, but my days as a gym rat were history. When my cholesterol and blood pressure spiked a couple of years earlier, my doctor insisted that I give up fried foods, chocolate chip cookies, and Diet Dr Pepper. She also suggested that I start exercising more regularly. In lieu of accompanying Rosie to Pilates classes or joining a health club, I decided to walk up and down the one hundred and thirty-nine steps connecting Magnolia Avenue to the hills above downtown Larkspur. I performed this ritual three times a week, after which I strolled over to St. Patrick's Church, where I confessed my sins to my old pal, Father Andy Shanahan. Most days, I was greeted at the steps by the cheerful presence of Zvi Danenberg, a ninety-three-year-old retired science teacher who walked more than a million steps a year. Zvi was my idol.

Rosie lowered her voice. “Are you going to be okay?”

“I’ll be fine. We’ve handled bigger messes.”

“Anything I can do?”

“I may want to consult with you on strategy from time to time.”

“I’ll be available.”

“Thanks.”

She leaned over, pulled me close, and kissed me.

“What’s that for?” I asked.

“I told you that if I liked your report, I would give you a bonus.”

* * *

At five-thirty on Friday morning, I was awakened from a restless sleep by my iPhone. I struggled to focus on the display in the darkness of Rosie’s bedroom. The call was from an unknown number.

“Michael Daley,” I said.

“This is Sergeant Chuck Koslosky of the San Francisco County Sheriff’s Department. Your client, Ms. Low, had convulsions and lost consciousness. We are transporting her to San Francisco General. You’ll want to meet us there.”

22
"THIS IS A DIFFICULT PROCESS"

The name embroidered in blue lettering on the resident's starched white coat was Dr. Alice Yee. Her expression was stern. "Ms. Low had a rough night."

"Is she conscious?" I asked.

"She just woke up."

Dr. Yee and I were standing outside Lexy's room in a bustling corridor at San Francisco General. A sheriff's deputy stood guard next to the door—as if Lexy was going to make a run for it. The huge public hospital never slept. At six-forty-five a.m., you couldn't tell whether it was day or night outside.

Dr. Yee's tone was clinical. "They gave her Suboxone to wean her from the heroin. She had a bad reaction, which isn't uncommon. This is a difficult process."

Yes, it is.

She fingered her stethoscope. "Realistically, she's going to be fighting addiction for the rest of her life. There will be ups and downs. It will take several weeks just to get the heroin out of her system and control her cravings. We're starting her on a limited dose of Methadone, which takes longer and has its own side effects."

"How long will she be here?"

"If things continue to progress, a few days."

"Do they have sufficient resources to continue her treatment at the jail?"

"Yes, but as you would surmise, the infirmary at the Glamour Slammer isn't an ideal environment for addiction treatment."

No, it isn't.

"The medical staff is excellent," she continued, "but they're overworked. They've assigned an addiction counselor to her case, but she has time to see patients only twice a week. Ideally, Ms. Low should be talking to a specialist every day—at least for the first few weeks."

"She doesn't have the money to pay for a private therapist."

"What about family or friends?"

"None."

"This isn't an ideal scenario to promote a full recovery, Mr. Daley."

That much was painfully apparent. "Other than withdrawal issues, how is she doing?"

"Her physical health is pretty good. She's young, reasonably strong, and in better shape than many addicts. Her blood pressure is high, but her heart is fine. The psychological issues are a bigger problem."

"Will she be able to help us with her defense?"

"At times."

"We have a preliminary hearing in less than two weeks."

"That isn't ideal, either."

I asked if I could see her.

"Yes, but please keep it short."

* * *

Lexy forced a weak smile. "I must look like hell."

Better than I expected. "You look fine."

"I'm sorry, Mike."

You didn't become a heroin addict to inconvenience me. "No reason to apologize. We need you to get healthy."

"Working on it."

She was lying in the center bed in a triple room in San Francisco General's oldest wing. The cramped space was jammed with IVs and monitors.

I nodded at Nady, who was standing next to Lexy's bed. "Thanks for coming over."

"No problem."

Lexy struggled to talk. "What happens now?"

First things first. "You need to get well enough to get out of here."

"They'll send me back to jail."

"It's better than the hospital."

"What can I do now?"

"We need to know more about Jeff King. Several people used the bathroom upstairs where you said King left the heroin. We want to argue that one of them put it there or spiked it."

"They were a few months from collecting a fortune on the IPO."

"A lot of people disliked King."

"Not enough to kill him."

"Work with me, Lexy. Maybe somebody was trying to scare him."

"Giving somebody high-octane heroin is a helluva way to do it."

"We don't need to prove it. We just need to give the jury a few plausible options to get to reasonable doubt."

She pushed out a sigh. "Can you get the charges dropped at the prelim?"

"That's going to be difficult."

Her somber expression indicated that the reality was sinking in.

I tried another angle. "Do you have information that might be of interest to the D.A.?"

"Why would I help the D.A.?"

"To minimize your potential exposure. If we can cut a deal for voluntary manslaughter, the minimum sentence is three years with a maximum of eleven. For involuntary, it's two to four, and the court might let you serve in county jail. Both options are a lot better than first-degree murder, where the minimum is twenty-five, or second-degree, where it's fifteen."

"I didn't kill Jeff."

"They have video of you injecting him."

"He asked me to do it. He provided the heroin. A jury will believe me."

"They're unpredictable."

"I'm not interested in a deal."

"I'm just explaining your options. Do you know where King bought the heroin?"

"No."

"Where did you buy *your* stuff, Lexy?"

"On the street near the Sixteenth Street BART Station. The cops know the dealers."

"I'll be back to check on you later today."

* * *

My iPhone vibrated as I was walking through the parking lot of San Francisco General. Pete's name appeared on the display.

"How soon can you get to Philz Coffee on Middlefield in Palo Alto?" he asked.

"About an hour. Why?"

"It's down the street from Samayama Yoga, the in-spot for hot yoga in the Valley."

He liked playing cat-and-mouse more than I did. "You've taken up hot yoga?"

"No, but King's widow did. And she always goes to Philz afterward."

23
"WE HAD AN UNDERSTANDING"

Pete gestured subtly with his index finger. "Here she comes, Mick. Behind you in the fancy top and the expensive yoga pants. Act natural."

We were sitting at a table on the covered patio outside Philz Coffee in one of Palo Alto's "modest" residential areas, where the fifties-era Eichler ranch houses on the leafy cul-de-sacs would set you back "only" about two and a half million dollars. At nine-thirty on Friday morning, Pete and I were the oldest people in the café. The patrons were a mix of grungy programmers bent over laptops, young mothers sitting next to children in two-thousand-dollar strollers, well-appointed venture capitalists studying term sheets, and parents of kindergarteners discussing the fundraiser for their kids' private school.

Pete took a sip of his Jacob's Wonderbar, described on the chalk board as "a dark blend with elements of chocolate, smoke, and nuts." According to the Philz mythology, it was named after the founder's son. "Not bad for a five-dollar cup of coffee," he said.

"It's fine." Since my college days in Berkeley, I had been loyal to Peet's. The individually brewed offerings at Philz were also very good, but the lengthy production process required you to develop a long-term relationship with your barista. I glanced inside, where Chloe King was standing in line. "How'd you know that she would be here?"

"You think I'm the only P.I. watching her?"

Guess not. "How many phone calls did it take?"

"One."

I should have known. "She's pretty."

"Yes, she is." He shot a subtle look at Chloe, a tiny woman with porcelain features and straight black hair. "She's also young with big eyes, a full mouth, and large breasts. Remind you of anybody?"

"Lexy."

"And probably many others that King slept with over the years. Maybe that's why Chloe is playing tennis and going to yoga a few days after her husband died."

"She was more upset when we saw her on Monday."

"Seems she's recovered from the initial shock. I presume that you'd like to talk to her?"

"Yes."

"Stay here, save two seats, and give me five minutes." He held out a hand. "I need cash to buy each of us another designer coffee. The Jacob's Wonderbar isn't bad."

I slipped him a twenty, and he headed inside. I tried to be patient as I checked my e-mails and texts and wondered whether one of the young guys at the next table was creating the next Facebook. Ten minutes later, Pete emerged with Chloe, chatting like old friends. He offered her the seat next to mine, and he sat down across from her. Her handshake was firm, her tone cordial. I had no idea what Pete had said to her inside, but she was willing to talk to us.

I invoked my priest-voice. "We appreciate your time, Ms. King."

"Chloe."

"Mike. And we're very sorry for your loss."

"Thank you. It's been a difficult week."

"Given the circumstances, I hope you're doing okay."

"I'll be fine."

"And your daughter?"

"She's with the nanny. Thankfully, she's too young to understand what's going on."

We exchanged stilted small talk for a moment before I turned to business. "We're representing Lexy Low."

"I know. I don't envy you."

And I don't envy you. "I'm just doing my job. I know that this is a hard time for you, but we'd like to ask you a few questions about your husband."

"I have nothing to hide. I've been cooperating with the police."

I waited a moment, hoping that she would feel compelled to fill the void. My patience was rewarded when she took a sip of her coffee and started talking.

"It's no secret that Jeff and I had a complicated relationship. We separated about six months ago, and I told him that I was going to file for divorce. He asked me to wait until the IPO was completed, and I agreed. It made sense from a business and a personal standpoint."

It sounded as if their relationship was purely transactional.

Her voice was controlled. "We were starting to work out an arrangement for custody of our daughter. I thought it was better if Julie lived with me, but Jeff wanted to share custody. Obviously, money wasn't an issue, but I didn't think it was workable given his schedule and his penchant for sleeping with other women."

Chilly. "How long were you married?"

"A little over three years."

"I'm sorry that it didn't work out."

"So am I. Then again, he had been cheating on me from the beginning. It got worse after Julie was born."

"That must have been hard."

Her voice filled with resignation. "It was, but I should have known better. We started dating while he was still married. It's an old story. He cheated with me. It was only a matter of time before he cheated on me. Jeff's issues were exacerbated by the toxic culture in the Valley."

"Where did you meet?" I already knew the answer.

"I was the personnel director at his last startup. Ironically, I was in charge of investigating sexual harassment claims against members of management."

"Including Jeff?"

"*Especially* Jeff. Theoretically, I was there to help our employees. In reality, it was my job to protect him and the company, and I was good at it."

"Were there a lot of sexual harassment claims against him at Y5K?"

"At least once a month. Sometimes more. Things got out of hand after he and several of the marketing people were detained at a brothel in Bangkok. The lawyers got the charges dropped and kept things quiet, but it cost a fortune. The board adopted a policy that the company wouldn't reimburse management for strippers and hookers."

Excellent corporate oversight. "Was it enforced?"

"Are you serious? He packed the board with his pals. They were terrified of him."

"What did you do when you suspected him of cheating?"

"I hired a private investigator. It took her just a couple of minutes to find his accounts on Ashley Madison and Mature Relations. I confronted him, and he admitted it. We tried therapy, but it didn't help. We even agreed to try an open relationship for a few months. This is touchy-feely Northern California, right? That didn't work, either. He was always more interested in women he met online and in clubs. You think you can change somebody, but it never happens."

No, it doesn't. "Getting divorced is hard. I have personal experience." *Although I still sleep with my ex-wife.* I pointed at Pete. "So does he."

Pete spoke up. "It must have been insanely difficult for you to have a new baby and a cheating husband. How did you deal with it?"

"We had an understanding. He lived in the City, and I stayed down here with our daughter. He went his way, and I went mine. It wasn't especially acrimonious."

"I trust that you'll be okay financially?"

"I'll be fine. We had a prenup, but I never needed his money. There isn't any life insurance. My family has lived in this area since it was apricot orchards. I own a lot of real estate in my own name—including the land on which the Y5K building sits. I'll be more than okay, but people at the company are going to lose a lot of money if they cancel the IPO."

I re-entered the discussion. "We understand that Jeff wasn't a popular guy."

"He wasn't, but people respected him. More important, everybody was afraid of him."

Here goes. "Is there any chance that somebody disliked him enough that they would have wanted to kill him?"

"That's not how things work in the Valley. People lie and cheat and sleep around, but they don't kill each other. They measure their worth in dollars and stock options. The person with the most private jets wins." She shrugged. "Besides, Inspector Lee told me that there's a video of your client giving Jeff a lethal shot of heroin."

"We believe that Jeff provided the heroin, or somebody else planted it."

"Good luck with that."

Thanks.

"Look," she said, "I'm sure that you're a good lawyer, but everybody at the party—other than your client and the young women who were invited as eye candy—was going to make millions on the IPO. Nobody in their right mind would have killed him—at least not now. And if the D.A. asks me to testify, I'm prepared to say that."

That wouldn't be helpful.

She added, "In case you're wondering, I wasn't in the City on the night that Jeff died. I was at home with the baby in Palo Alto."

This was consistent with the information provided by Inspector Lee.

She finished her coffee. "For what it's worth, I'd like to know what happened to Jeff just as much as you would—mostly out of morbid curiosity. On the other hand, this wasn't the first time he did smack with one of his sugar babies. Maybe karma finally caught up with him."

"Do you know where he bought the heroin?"

"No clue. You can ask his pal, Drew Pitt, but you'll never get a straight answer."

"Would you mind giving us the name of your private investigator?"

"Kaela Joy Gullion."

Pete and I knew her. Kaela Joy was a retired model and one-time Niners cheerleader who developed a following on YouTube after somebody posted a video of her knocking out her ex-husband—a Niners lineman—on Bourbon Street after she caught him with another woman in the Big Easy. Kaela Joy had parlayed the notoriety into a lucrative career as a private eye.

"Mind if we talk to her?" I asked.

"Be my guest."

"Thanks, Chloe. I know that this is a rough time for you."

"That's why I go to yoga, Mike."

* * *

I finished my coffee. "How'd you convince her to talk to us?"

Pete was looking at his iPhone. "People like talking about themselves."

"Not to strangers."

"To me."

It was true. He had a gift. "You should write a book."

"I don't want to give away the secrets of my craft."

"You think she had anything to do with her husband's death?"

"Doubtful. She wasn't at the party. She didn't strike me as somebody who would have arranged her husband's untimely demise. There wasn't any life insurance—I checked. And she didn't need the money, anyway."

"She doesn't seem especially broken up about it."

"She seemed more relieved than angry, Mick."

True. "You knew about Kaela Joy, didn't you?"

"Yes."

"Have you talked to her?"

"Yes."

"Were you planning to mention it to me?"

"In due course."

I reminded him that he was working for me.

"She asked me not to give you her name until she got Chloe's permission to talk to you."

"I'd like to talk to her."

"I'll set it up."

24
"IT WAS A LITTLE MORE COMPLICATED"

The statuesque blonde flashed a Julia Roberts smile as she nibbled a greasy French fry. "Good to see you, Pete."

"Good to see you, Kaela Joy."

A week had passed since Pete and I had met with Chloe. The New Year's champagne corks had popped, the bowl games were over, and the post-holiday sales were in full swing. Meanwhile, Lexy was back at the Glamour Slammer, Grace was on her way back to USC, and Pete and I were on the hunt for information.

At noon on Friday, January fourth, Chloe's P.I., Kaela Joy Gullion, was sitting across from us at a Formica table in the corner of Red's Java House, which the *Chronicle*'s legendary Carl Nolte once described as the "Chartres Cathedral of Cheap Eats." Housed in a shack on Pier 30 in the shadow of the Bay Bridge, Red's opened in 1930 as a dive called "Franco's Lunch," which catered to longshoremen. In 1955, Tom ("Red") McGarvey and his brother, Mike, bought it and rechristened it "Red's Java House." The longshoremen were a distant memory, and the adjoining neighborhood had gentrified with upscale condos, but you could still get a burger and a beer at Red's for less than ten bucks.

"How was Cabo?" Pete asked.

"Terrific." Kaela Joy took a draw from a bottle of Bud. Dressed down in a denim shirt and a Giants' cap, she still carried herself like a model. She looked out the window at the Bay Bridge, which was hard to see through the drizzle. "How are Donna and Margaret?"

"Fine. Your kids?"

"Grown up." They exchanged pleasantries for a few minutes before she finally turned to me. "Still busy keeping criminals out of jail, Mike?"

"Trying." Her dad was a retired cop. "Are you still working for Chloe King?"

"Occasionally. She gave me permission to talk to you. I hope you aren't going to suggest that she had anything to do with her husband's death."

Depends what you tell us. "I'm not."

"If you want my help, stay off her back."

"We will." *Well, we'll try.*

"From what I've read, your client gave Jeff King a shot of heroin and tried to run."

That covers it. "It was a little more complicated."

"I saw the video on TV."

Well, there's that. SFPD had released a brief clip showing Lexy administering the injection. "King had a heart condition making him susceptible to an accidental overdose."

"Then I'm sure you'll find an expert to convince a jury that it was an accident."

Hopefully. "Either way, it was consensual. And *he* provided the heroin."

"Says your client."

"He was a billionaire. He could afford his own smack."

"He was a reckless asshole who cheated on Chloe and did drugs with women he found on a sugar daddy site."

"Our client didn't intend to kill him."

"Why didn't she call the cops?"

"She panicked. Besides, he was her only source of income."

"Maybe he threatened to cut her off."

"We have no evidence that he did."

"Says your client. Next you'll say that he loved her."

"As far as we can tell, their relationship was purely transactional."

"That's just sad."

"It is. There were a dozen people at King's house. So far, we've identified seven people other than our client who went into the bathroom where Lexy found the heroin."

"Unless she brought it herself."

"That's not the way it went down."

She darted a glance at Pete, as if to say, "You're kidding, right?" Then she turned back to me. "You're going to argue that somebody planted some high-end smack?"

"Or King left it there himself. A lot of people disliked him."

Her voice filled with sarcasm. "That's not entirely true, Mike. Everybody hated him."

Notwithstanding the occasional barbs lobbed in my direction, I liked her. "My mistake."

She was now engaged. "Who else was there?"

I started at the top of the list. "Blackjack Steele."

"Asshole, but King was worth millions to him. Divorced three times. His kids hate him because he treated their mother like crap. His son works at Facebook. His daughter interned at Y5K and recently graduated from Stanford. Last I heard, she was taking some time off. Must be nice to have rich parents. In the meantime, Steele is having a fling with the head of business development at the company. It isn't his first."

"I presume he looked the other way when King was sleeping around?"

"He encouraged it. He's on Mature Relations, too. Y5K is a cesspool."

"Gopal Patel was at the party, too."

"Asshole, but King was worth millions to him, too."

I'm seeing a pattern.

She took a bite of her cheeseburger. "Patel looks dignified, but he can't keep his hands to himself, either. Married twice. About to get divorced again. For the last few months, he's been having a roll with his associate, Christina Chu."

Who will make millions when she files the inevitable lawsuit. "She was at the party."

"I'm not surprised. In addition to churning out cash flow projections, she was tasked with finding women to attend King's parties."

"She did this voluntarily?"

"If she wanted to keep her job. Welcome to Silicon Valley. It's equally appalling that many of these women are first-rate programmers, engineers, and managers. Yet they still think they have to attend make-out parties with the bros to make connections."

"Was Chu sleeping with King, too?"

"Not as far as I can tell."

"Is Patel on a sugar daddy website, too?"

"Yes."

I seem to be the only one who isn't. "How did he get along with King?"

"They detested each other, but King needed Patel's money, and Patel needed King's company to hit it big to make up for a string of misses."

I asked her about Tristan Moore, the sales guy.

"Tall. Handsome. Smooth. He can sell anything to anyone."

At least you didn't describe him as an "asshole."

She was still talking. "He was with a different woman every time I saw him. They all looked like super-models."

The only woman I ever dated who looked like a super-model was Rosie. "Was he on Mature Relations?"

"He's too young. Besides, he didn't need it. He had more action than he could handle. King tolerated Moore as long as he hit his sales quotas. Moore tolerated King because he had stock options. They had a falling out six months ago when they discovered that they were sleeping with the same woman."

"Awkward."

"Indeed. The scuttlebutt is that King gave the clap to the woman and, indirectly, Moore."

"They kept working together."

"Seems financial interdependence trumps an STD."

"And Alejandro Sanchez?"

"World-class programmer. Single. Smart. Interested in three things: code, women, and money. He felt underpaid and underappreciated. Otherwise, he and King barely communicated."

"The security guy, Yoav Ben-Shalom, was there."

"He went wherever King did. If you're looking for somebody who's actually killed someone, he's your guy. He took out a dozen Hezbollah fighters in Lebanon twenty years ago."

A smart prosecutor like Harper would never let me introduce that information into evidence. "How did he get along with King?"

"He did his job. He protected King, and the company paid him handsomely."

Until the night King died. "Drew Pitt?"

This elicited a throaty laugh. "The 'Guy from Rye.' The luckiest man on Planet Earth. His father runs a hedge fund. His mother is a partner at a New York law firm. They bought his way into Harvard. He lived down the street from King. Pitt has tagged along to every company that King started, and he's made a fortune."

"What does he do at the company?"

"Nothing."

"Come on, Kaela Joy."

"I'm serious, Mike. He has a nebulous title like 'Director of Quality and Development.' In reality, he played video games all day and partied with King all night."

This was consistent with Pete's information. "He gets paid for this?"

"Millions. Plus stock options. And he wanted a raise, too. Notwithstanding the self-righteous hyperbole of the tech community, Silicon Valley isn't always a meritocracy. Pitt is the poster child for the hangers-on who've made obscene amounts of money by latching onto others who hit it big. And he's also on Mature Relations."

No surprise. "I feel for Chloe. She has plenty of money, but she's been through a lot."

"Yes, she has, but she knew what she was getting into."

Her tone was sharper than I had anticipated.

Kaela Joy scowled. "She was the HR director at King's previous startup. She broke up his second marriage. She knew that he had hit on dozens of women at the company. She should have known that he would cheat on her, too."

"She said they tried counseling and even did the open-marriage thing."

"It was never going to work. And it was a little more complicated. Are you familiar with the term, 'polyfidelity'?"

"Poly-what?"

"Polyfidelity."

"Uh, no."

Pete started to laugh. "Seriously?"

"Yes." Kaela Joy grinned. "Ever seen it?"

"A couple of times."

I tossed my brown paper napkin into the trash. "What's 'polyfidelity'?"

Kaela Joy's smiled broadened. "A loving exclusive relationship with multiple partners."

"Swinging? Threesomes? Foursomes? More-somes?"

"Not exactly. People who practice polyfidelity believe love is infinite, and you can have feelings for more than one person at the same time."

Pete interjected, "Sometimes it's referred to as 'committed non-monogamy.' It's all consensual, and everybody in the group agrees to the ground rules."

Glad I'm no longer a priest. "Am I the only one who finds this unusual?"

Kaela Joy responded with a bemused expression. "It isn't my thing, but it's more common than you might think."

"So the fact that King was sleeping with other women didn't technically qualify as cheating because he and Chloe were in a polyfidelitous relationship?"

"No, it was still cheating."

Huh? "You just said it was okay to have multiple partners."

"It is, but you're supposed to be exclusive with only those people. If you sleep with anybody else, it's cheating."

Thanks for the clarification. "How long was this going on?"

"About three months."

"Was King the father of Chloe's baby?"

"As far as I know."

"Do you know the names of the people with whom King and Chloe were involved in a polyfidelitous relationship?"

"Yes. Patel and his wife. More accurately, Patel and his soon-to-be-ex-wife. Mrs. Patel was fine sleeping with King and Chloe because they were included in their polyfidelitous group. She wasn't okay with her husband sleeping with Christina Chu or the women he met on Mature Relations, which constituted cheating. And, of course, she was unhappy that King was sleeping with women he met on Mature Relations for the same reason."

If King was cheating on Patel under the terms of their polyfidelitous arrangement, Patel was probably unhappy about it. Then again, it sounded as if Patel hadn't been faithful to this convoluted agreement, either. Either way, it was tempting to bring it up at trial. Juries don't like cheaters.

Kaela Joy's face rearranged itself into a bemused expression. "This would make for great material on a Netflix series, but I don't see how it helps your client."

Neither do I. "Any chance Chloe was involved in her husband's death?"

"Nope. For one, she didn't need the money. For two, I was with her in Palo Alto on the night that he died. She hired me to provide security."

And perhaps an alibi.

* * *

Pete looked like one of the longshoremen who had worked on the docks eighty years earlier as he stared at the Bay Bridge from the deck behind Red's. "How do you think Rosie would react if you asked her if she was interested in a polyfidelitous relationship?"

"It would be a very short conversation."

"Same with Donna. We live in a strange world, Mick."

"We do. Do you think Chloe had anything to do with King's death?"

"Doubtful."

"Where are you off to now?"

"Palo Alto. You?"

"The Glamour Slammer. I want to talk to our client."

25
"THE SHAKES FINALLY STOPPED"

"You look better," I said.

Lexy nodded. "The shakes finally stopped."

It was the best news we'd had in a couple of weeks. Later the same afternoon, we were sitting in a consultation room in the women's wing of the Glamour Slammer. Although her complexion was pale and her eyes were red, Lexy did, in fact, look healthier than she did at San Francisco General a week earlier.

I asked if they had begun tapering her Methadone.

"They may start in a few weeks."

Or you may be on a full dosage for the rest of your life. Methadone is an effective, albeit imperfect treatment that comes with its own risks, including addiction to the Methadone itself. Unlike other drugs, it doesn't harm the body's organs, but the psychological effects are often long-lasting. In addition to drug cravings, recovering addicts suffer from depression, hypertension, rapid heart rate, and muscle spasms. Long-term success is defined modestly as living a reasonably healthy life while continuing to take maintenance dosages to reduce the possibility of relapse. Odds of success increase if you go through the process at a treatment center. That wasn't an option for Lexy, who would ride out her demons at the Glamour Slammer.

"Are you eating?" I asked.

"Yes."

"Has anybody come to see you?"

"Just you and Nady."

How sad. "Anybody we might call?"

Her eyes turned down. "No."

I told her about our conversation with Kaela Joy. "Did you know that King and his wife were involved in relationships with multiple partners?"

"Yes."

"Did that bother you?"

"No. They all got tested for AIDS, and he always wore a condom with me."

Her relationship with King sounded depressingly business-like.

She changed the subject. "Can you get me out of here?"

Not likely. "Our motion for reconsideration of bail was denied. We'll ask again at the prelim, where we can make our case to a different judge."

"That isn't until Tuesday. I'm going to be here forever."

"We need you to stay strong."

"Seems I have no choice."

* * *

"Ever heard the term, 'polyfidelity?'" I asked.

"Yes." Rosie was sitting at her desk at eight-thirty on Friday night. "Don't get any ideas, Mike. I sleep with only one man at a time."

"Kaela Joy told us that King and his wife were in a polyfidelitous relationship with Gopal Patel and his wife."

Rosie couldn't stop a smile. "Seems Patel was providing more than venture capital."

"Know anybody who's tried it?"

"Yes."

"Anybody I know?"

"Maybe."

"Care to reveal any names?"

"No."

"Did they like it?"

"Let's just say that it was very complicated." Rosie looked at Nady. "How about you?"

"Max and I are also very traditional. A couple of my law school classmates tried it for a short time. It didn't end well." She handed us copies of the final autopsy report. "Dr. Siu confirmed her original conclusion that King died of a heroin overdose. No evidence of poison or any foreign substances in the heroin."

Rosie studied the report. "On page two, it confirms that King had an irregular heartbeat. It opens up the possibility that the heroin set off a bad reaction that killed him."

"It might be enough to get us to reasonable doubt on a murder charge at trial," I said.

"It doesn't rule out the possibility of a conviction for manslaughter, and it isn't enough to get the charges dropped at the prelim."

Always the voice of cold, hard reality.

She eyed me. "Did Pete get anything on the people at the party?"

"Working on it. He'll find some dirt."

"There's a difference between dirt and exculpatory evidence."

True. "It'll give us ammunition to muddy the waters at trial."

"That's the whole idea, right?"

"Right." The first thing that Rosie taught me when I was a baby P.D. was that high-minded concepts like justice and fair play are for law professors and post-trial beers. It was our job to defend our clients to the best of our ability within the rules of professional conduct. If the prosecutors, cops, and judges also did their part, the system—embodied in the form of jurors—would make the final call. More often than not, a semblance of imperfect justice would emerge. Moreover, as a practical matter, our clients judged us by our results. If we got them off, we were good. If we didn't, we were bad.

"Are you still planning to do a full prelim?" Rosie asked.

"Yes."

"Cable news has been replaying the video showing Lexy administering heroin to King. Judge Tsang is generally prosecution-friendly. Based on that alone, he won't drop the charges."

"I want to see the D.A.'s evidence and get some insights into their trial strategy. We'll challenge everything, but we won't show our cards." I turned to Nady. "Where are we on motions?"

"Done. Judge Tsang already ruled that the D.A. can show the video that's been on TV. I'll file a motion to reconsider, but I don't like our odds."

Neither do I. "Can you do it without working all weekend?"

She smiled. "I think so."

Rosie spoke to her in a maternal voice. "You need to learn to pace yourself, Nady. Otherwise, you'll end up looking like Mike."

"We've already had that conversation."

Terrence the Terminator appeared in the doorway. "Sorry to interrupt."

"No problem. What is it, T?"

"Jerry Edwards left a message. The *Chronicle*'s finest has some information for you."

26
"IT'S JUST A COINCIDENCE"

Edwards answered on the first ring. "Good to hear from you again, Mr. Daley."

Right. "I understand you have some information for me."

"A confidential source told us that Ms. Low was involved in at least one other relationship through Mature Relations. Would you care to comment?"

The back of my neck started to burn. Lexy had told us that King was her only patron. "I'll need the name of your source."

"You know that I can't reveal it."

"You have an obligation to provide relevant information on an ongoing criminal case."

"I will be publishing the name of your client's lover tonight, but I won't give you the name of my source."

"Withholding evidence is obstruction of justice. I can send you a subpoena."

"The *Chronicle* has lawyers, too. It's a losing argument."

Yes, it is.

Edwards kept talking. "Your client's paramour is Paul Flynn. Seventy-two. Retired biochemist who was an early investor in Genentech and several other biotech firms. Divorced. Two grown children. No criminal record. Lived at Millennium Tower."

Nice digs. It was a high-rise across the street from the Salesforce Tower where the lower-priced units would set you back around two million dollars. Its residents included Joe Montana, several Giants, and multiple tech titans. The swanky building had gained national notoriety because the developer hadn't drilled down and secured the foundation into bedrock. As a result, it had sunk a foot and a half and tilted fifteen inches toward Mission Street. The estimate to shore it up ran about a hundred million, and, not surprisingly, the residents were suing the contractor, the architects, the structural engineers, the City, and anybody else remotely connected to the fiasco. Every law firm in town was representing somebody involved in the endless litigation.

Edwards cleared his throat. "Flynn was found dead in his condo on the twenty-fifth floor on November sixteenth of last year. He died of a heroin overdose."

"What makes you think my client had anything to do with it?"

"She saw him that night."

Uh-oh. "How do you know?"

"Texts from Flynn to Ms. Low and security videos from the lobby of Millennium Tower. No charges have been filed, but the investigation is still open."

"Who is handling the case for SFPD?"

"Ken Lee."

* * *

I looked across the table at Lexy. "Does the name Paul Flynn mean anything to you?"

She closed her eyes, and then reopened them slowly. "I met him on Mature Relations."

At least you didn't deny it.

Lexy, Nady, and I were in a consultation room in the Glamour Slammer at nine-forty-five on Friday night. My somber mood was exacerbated by a headache.

"You told us that you didn't have any other relationships from Mature Relations."

Her eyes turned down. "That wasn't entirely true."

It wasn't at all true. "Anybody else?"

"No."

Last chance. "Flynn was the only other one?"

"Yes."

"How many times did you see him?"

"Twice."

"According to Jerry Edwards, Flynn died of a heroin overdose in November."

No response.

"Do you know anything about it?"

Still no response.

"Edwards said that the police have security footage of you entering Millennium Tower on the night that he died. They found texts between you and Flynn."

She spoke in a whisper. "I saw him that night."

"Did you sleep with him?"

"Yes."

"Did you give him the heroin?"

"No."

"Lexy?"

Her tone became more emphatic. "I didn't bring the heroin, and I didn't inject him."

"If they found your prints on a syringe, this is going to be serious trouble."

"They won't."

"Were you there when he died?"

"No. He was fine when I left."

"Did the police contact you?"

"Yes. I talked to Inspector Lee. I told them what I told you. We had a date. We had consensual sex. He paid me. That was it."

"Why didn't you mention it to us?"

"It has nothing to do with my case."

It might. "I can't have any more surprises, Lexy."

"I'm telling the truth, Mike."

One more chance. "Did you give him some bad heroin?"

"No. He was an old guy with a bad heart who shouldn't have been taking smack."

"The D.A. might still file charges."

"It's just a coincidence."

"I don't like coincidences."

"I didn't bring him the smack. I didn't inject him. And I wasn't there when he died."

"I hate surprises even more than coincidences."

"I'm telling the truth, Mike."

I was skeptical. "If they raise it, we'll file a motion to exclude information about Flynn."

"What if the judge rules against us?"

"I guess we'll have to argue that it was just a coincidence."

* * *

Nady was sitting in the chair opposite my desk. "Should we try to get ahead of the story that Lexy could be connected to another death?"

"It's already on the *Chronicle*'s website. If anybody asks, I won't deny that she got together with Flynn, but I'll say that his death was a self-inflicted overdose."

"Why haven't they filed charges?"

"Lack of evidence, I presume. They have video of Lexy entering and exiting the building, but they have no proof that she brought the heroin or gave him the shot."

"Unless they find her fingerprints on a syringe."

"If they did, they would have charged her by now."

* * *

Rosie took a sip of Cabernet. "You look tired, Mike."

"Long week."

We were sitting on her sofa at eleven o'clock the same night. Tommy was asleep. The TV was tuned to the news.

The airbrushed anchor looked into the camera. "We have a new twist in the case involving the murder of Silicon Valley entrepreneur Jeff King."

"Alleged murder," I muttered out of habit.

A photo of King appeared above his shoulder. Lexy's mugshot was superimposed next to it. "We go to Rita Roberts at the Hall of Justice."

The veteran reporter's face was bleached by the TV lights. "We have a startling new revelation in the Jeff King case. Our viewers will recall that a woman named Alexa Low has been charged with murder for injecting Mr. King with a lethal dose of heroin. Mr. King and Ms. Low met on a dating app called Mature Relations, one of the so-called 'sugar daddy' sites. It turns out that a second wealthy man, Paul Flynn, recently died of a heroin overdose in his condo at Millennium Tower. Coincidentally, he had also met Ms. Low on Mature Relations. Sources familiar with the case tell us that Ms. Low is a person of interest in the death of Mr. Flynn. While no charges have been filed, the police are continuing their investigation."

Rosie finished her wine. "Who's the source?"

"Somebody at SFPD. Could be Ken Lee."

"They might charge Lexy with manslaughter for Flynn's death, or even murder."

"Lexy confirmed that she slept with Flynn. The fact that he died of a heroin overdose is just a coincidence."

"I don't like coincidences."

I might have said the same thing. "I'm going to ask Lee about it in the morning."

27
"I CAN'T TALK ABOUT AN ONGOING INVESTIGATION"

"Thanks for seeing me."

Lee's response was terse. "Sure."

He was at his desk in the otherwise-empty Homicide bullpen at nine-thirty on Saturday morning. He didn't have to talk to me, so I decided to tread gently.

"I talked to Jerry Edwards last night. You probably saw his piece in the *Chronicle*."

"I did."

"I understand that you're investigating Paul Flynn's death."

"I am."

"Edwards told me that the Medical Examiner concluded that Flynn died of an accidental heroin overdose."

"I can't talk about an ongoing investigation."

"Edwards said that he had seen a copy of the autopsy report." This was a bluff.

"He didn't get it from me."

I wasn't going to accuse him of leaking. "Can you confirm the cause of death?"

"Heroin overdose. Dr. Siu offered no opinion as to whether it was accidental. And even if she did, I can't talk about it."

Seems you just did. "Edwards said there's video of Lexy entering and exiting Flynn's building."

"There is."

"And text messages between them."

"There are."

"Is there video from inside Flynn's condo?"

"No comment."

"Is there evidence that Lexy handled the heroin or a syringe?"

"No comment."

"Was Flynn a regular heroin user?"

"No comment."

"Is the D.A. planning to file charges?"

"That's up to the D.A."

I waited a beat. "I understand that you talked to Lexy about it."

"I did. She admitted that she saw Flynn that night. She denied that she gave him heroin."

"The fact that she and Flynn had a relationship doesn't prove anything."

"True."

"Flynn's death is irrelevant to our case."

"I'll let you and the D.A. argue about it. If anybody else that she met on Mature Relations turns up dead, not even an excellent lawyer like you will be able to keep her out of trouble."

* * *

"Got a sec?" I asked.

DeSean Harper was sitting at his desk. "I'm late for a meeting."

There's nobody else here. "I need just a minute. I talked to Ken Lee about Paul Flynn."

"I can't talk about an ongoing investigation."

Sounds familiar. "Mr. Flynn also had a relationship with Ms. Low."

"And he died of a heroin overdose, too."

"I understand that the Medical Examiner ruled the death an accidental overdose."

"He died of an overdose. It remains to be seen whether it was accidental."

"Any evidence that the heroin was spiked with another substance?"

"No comment."

"Do you have any plans to file charges?"

"We'll make that determination after the investigation is complete."

It was the correct answer. "Any idea when that might happen?"

"After we have looked at all of the evidence."

"My client had a consensual encounter with Flynn, an older man with a bad heart. She didn't give him any heroin."

"Says your client. A jury will connect the dots."

Maybe. "Not beyond a reasonable doubt."

"Contrary to their portrayal on *Law and Order*, jurors are smarter than you think."

That much is true. "Either way, Flynn's death has nothing to do with our case. Judge McDaniel won't let you talk about it at our prelim."

"The Flynn investigation is separate and ongoing. We'll go where the facts lead us. We'll make a determination of charges, if any, in due course."

28
"YOU'RE TALKING LIKE A LAWYER"

Lexy pressed the handpiece of the phone tightly against her ear. "Why are you here?"

"I need to talk to you about the prelim." *And a few other things.*

"We're still moving forward on Monday morning, right?"

"Right."

At six o'clock on Saturday evening, we were sitting on opposite sides of a Plexiglas divider in the visitor area of the Glamour Slammer. The consultation rooms were occupied. Most days, I could sweet-talk the guards into finding us a more private spot, but the rookie manning the desk lacked the flexibility of his more experienced colleagues.

First things first. "I talked to Ken Lee and DeSean Harper about Paul Flynn. They haven't decided whether they'll file charges."

"We had consensual sex. That's it."

I left it there. "I wanted to talk to you about what to expect at the prelim. As I explained, the prosecution needs to show just enough evidence to demonstrate that there is a reasonable possibility that you committed a crime. Given the circumstances, there is a good chance that the judge will bind you over for trial. We will challenge the D.A's witnesses, but I would recommend that we not put on a lot of evidence to avoid tipping our hand."

"You're planning to roll over?"

"I'm suggesting that we hold our cards tightly until trial."

"You think I'm guilty?"

"No, but unless we find something truly exculpatory in the next twenty-four hours, I think it's better not to telegraph our strategy before trial."

"You told me that you would be able to get the charges dropped at the prelim."

No, I didn't. "I don't see that happening, Lexy. At trial, we only need to persuade one juror that the prosecution has not proved its case beyond a reasonable doubt."

"You're talking like a lawyer."

"It's my job to explain the legal ramifications and make strategy recommendations."

Her lips turned down. "I want to testify at the prelim."

No, you don't. "That's out of the question. I don't want the prosecution to lock you into a story." *And Harper will tie you in knots.* "We may reconsider for the trial."

"And bail?"

"We'll ask again, but it's unlikely that this judge will rule in our favor. Even if he does, the practical reality is that you don't have any money."

She took a moment to process my less-than-satisfying advice. "If you can't get the charges dropped at the prelim, how soon before the trial starts?"

"Six months to a year." *Maybe longer.*

"Is there any way to do it sooner?"

"Technically, you have the right to demand a trial within sixty days, but I would strongly recommend against it. That wouldn't give us enough time to prepare."

"I want to go to trial as soon as possible."

"It's a mistake. We'll need to interview witnesses. We have to line up a medical expert."

"I am not going to rot in here for another six months."

"A delay would give us a much better chance of success."

"If you can't get the charges dropped, I want you to ask for a trial within sixty days. If you won't do it, I want another lawyer."

* * *

The light was on as I walked by Nady's office at eight o'clock on Saturday night. As I reached for the switch to turn it off, her voice startled me.

"Leave that on, please."

"What are you doing here?"

"I was about to ask you the same question."

"I work here." I sat down on the desk of one of her officemates. "I wanted to do a little more prep work for the prelim. I talked to Lexy again. If we can't get the charges dropped, she wants a trial date within sixty days, sooner, if possible."

"That's a bad idea."

"Yes, it is, but put yourself in her shoes. You can't make bail, you're going through heroin withdrawal, and your lawyer just told you that the prosecution probably has enough to bind you over for trial. Wouldn't you want to move forward as soon as possible?"

"Not if it was a lousy strategy."

"You're thinking clearly, and you understand the system. By the way, what are you doing here?"

"Luna wanted to go for a walk."

"You couldn't find a park?"

"They're overrated."

Her well-trained Keeshond appeared from beneath her desk. Luna looked like a mix between a German Shepard and a husky, with enormous brown eyes and an engaging smile. I wasn't inclined to remind Nady that the P.D.'s Office had a policy against bringing pets to work. Besides, Luna didn't know that she was a dog, and I wasn't going to break the news to her.

I reached over and patted Luna's head. "I don't have anything for you today." Notwithstanding her disappointment, the over-sized puppy extended a big paw, which I shook. I turned back to Nady. "Why are you really here?"

"Harper sent over texts from Lexy's phone and some additional police reports."

"Let me guess: nothing useful."

"How did you know?"

"I've been to this movie. The D.A. is obligated to provide information that would tend to exonerate our client. More often than not, they send over a boatload of stuff at the last minute to give the impression that they're cooperating. They know that we'll waste time going through it."

"You said that Harper is a decent person."

"He is, but he works for Ward, who isn't. Any mention of heroin in the texts?"

"No."

"What about Flynn?"

"Two texts indicating that Lexy was going to see him the night that he died."

"Lexy already admitted that they got together. Any other sugar daddies?"

"Not as far as I can tell."

"Anything else from Harper?"

"He sent over a final witness list for the prelim. It's short: the first officer at the scene, the Medical Examiner, and Inspector Lee."

"That's all he'll need. The cop will confirm that there was a body, Dr. Siu will say that King died of a heroin overdose, and Lee will show just enough of the security video to prove that Lexy gave him the shot."

"How do you want to play it if we can't get the charges dropped?"

"Our client has instructed us to ask for a trial date as soon as possible. I've explained the risks to her. If that's what she wants, that's what we'll do."

* * *

"Any chance you can get the charges dropped at the prelim?" Rosie asked.

"There's always a chance. If we can't, our client has instructed us to demand a trial within sixty days."

"That's a bad idea."

"I know."

I inhaled the heavy air that smelled of stale popcorn and sweat. We were sitting in the bleachers in the barn-like gym at Marin Catholic High School, Marin County's perennial athletic powerhouse, and the alma mater of Rams quarterback Jared Goff. At four-thirty on Sunday afternoon, Rosie and I were watching Tommy's freshman basketball team beat an overmatched squad from Marin Catholic. It brought back memories of a few epic battles on the hallowed hardwood of St. Ignatius when I was growing up.

I looked on with pride as Tommy blocked a shot. He dove for the loose ball, won a battle for possession, and fired a crisp pass to a streaking teammate, who laid it into the basket. Rosie stood up and let out a cheer. I remained seated and clapped politely. Although there was an outside chance that Tommy would be the first person in Daley family history to dunk, the odds were greater that the other kids would be taller than he was in another year or two.

The consummate multi-tasker, Rosie was capable of watching the game, encouraging Tommy, baiting the refs, checking her texts, and offering suggestions to our beleaguered coach, a well-meaning real estate agent who was better at selling houses than drawing up plays. As a former coach of Grace's softball teams and Tommy's Little

League teams, I took pity on him and kept my mouth shut.

Eyes still fixed on the game, Rosie turned to business. "I take it this means that Pete hasn't found anything terribly useful for Lexy's case?"

"Not yet." I no longer took it personally that she assumed that my brother would solve my cases before I did. And I had learned to ignore her habit of talking to me while she was focused on something else. "He's still down in the Valley."

"And Nady?"

"She's going through Lexy's phone records."

The final buzzer sounded, and the kids lined up for handshakes. As we made our way out of the gym, Rosie touched my hand. "You're still coming over for dinner, right?"

"Yes, but I need to go back to the office later. I want to check in on Nady."

She grinned. "Always good that my subordinates are working hard."

"My boss is an excellent role model." My iPhone vibrated, and Harper's name appeared on the display. I scanned his text and turned to Rosie. "I need a raincheck on dinner. Harper wants to see me."

"When?"

"Now."

29
"WE HAVE A PROPOSITION"

Harper's voice was subdued. "Thank you for coming in on short notice."

I took a seat opposite his desk. "No problem."

The credenza, bookcase, and floor of his workmanlike office down the hall from Ward's were covered with file folders. Unlike his boss, Harper was a working trial lawyer—and a good one. Framed photos of his teenage children were lined up next to his computer. Long divorced, there were no pictures of his ex-wife, a federal judge.

"I thought Nicole might be here tonight."

"She's at a fundraiser."

"Any last-minute additions to your witness list?"

"No."

Enough. "Why did you want to see me?"

"Nicole asked me to talk to you. We have a proposition for you."

Let him talk.

He cleared his throat. "We are prepared to offer a deal for second-degree murder, with a recommendation of a sentence at the shorter end of the spectrum."

"How short?"

"Fifteen years."

Not bad. It was the minimum for second-degree in a case not involving a firearm. "You won't get twelve jurors to convict on murder."

"I disagree."

"If you want to discuss manslaughter, we may have something to consider."

"Can't do it, Mike."

It was worth asking. "Are you prepared to confirm that you won't file any other charges against my client, including drug and solicitation charges?"

"Yes."

"Are you also willing to confirm that you won't be filing charges in connection with the death of Paul Flynn?"

"You know that I can't make any promises."

"Sure you can."

"No, I can't."

"I'll take your offer to my client, but I won't recommend it."

"Suit yourself. It will remain open until nine a.m."

* * *

Lexy's response through the Plexiglas was unequivocal. "No."

"We don't have to respond until tomorrow morning. You should sleep on it."

"I'm not pleading guilty."

"Please think about it, Lexy."

"No."

"I will inform the D.A. I still recommend against asking for a trial within sixty days if we can't get the charges dropped."

"I want a trial date as soon as possible."

"That's a bad idea."

"You aren't sleeping on a cot in a windowless room. I want to resolve this. Understood?"

"Yes. I'll see you in court."

30
"SHE LEFT HIM THERE TO DIE"

Harper positioned himself a respectful distance from the witness box. "Inspector Lee, did you uncover video placing the defendant in the victim's bedroom on the morning that he died?"

Lee answered in his courtroom voice. "Yes, Mr. Harper."

I stood at the defense table and tried to sound reasonable. "Your Honor, we renew our objection to the introduction of this highly edited and misleading security video."

Harper's tone was dismissive. "Your Honor, Mr. Daley is well aware that you have already ruled on this issue."

Judge Ignatius Tsang was resting his chin in his palm. "Thanks for the reminder, Mr. Harper."

A slight man in his late fifties with a quiet, but authoritative voice and a scholarly demeanor, Judge Tsang could have passed for a physics professor. He had grown up in Chinatown, where his parents held multiple low-paying jobs to allow him to focus on his studies. A brilliant student with a photographic memory, he graduated at the top of his class at San Francisco's super-competitive Lowell High, raced through UC-Berkeley in three years, and was first in his class at Boalt Law School. He clerked for Justice Byron White before he took a position at the San Francisco DA's office, where he labored tirelessly for two decades while pursuing his academic interests by writing law review articles and teaching criminal procedure at Boalt. He has brought the same tenacity and intellectual rigor to the bench.

I tried again. "It is inflammatory to show this disturbing video in open court."

"And as I noted in my ruling, it has probative value and is relevant to our proceedings."

"But Your Honor—,"

"Your objection is overruled, Mr. Daley."

It had been that kind of morning. At ten-forty on Monday, January seventh, the gallery in the stuffy courtroom was filled with press, regulars, and gawkers. Unlike most proceedings, no family members or friends were present to provide moral support to Lexy. Likewise, members of King's family—including Chloe—were conspicuously absent. The only onlookers with a rooting interest for our team were Rosie and Pete, who were trying to remain inconspicuous in the back row.

Lexy was sitting between Nady and me, eyes focused on a blank legal pad in front of her. She had remained composed so far. I wasn't sure how much longer she would last.

The prelim had moved quickly. Judge Tsang ran an efficient courtroom, and Harper knew what he was doing. The system works more expediently when the prosecutor is competent, and the judge is smart.

In a murder case, you begin with the decedent, so Harper had started with the first officer at the scene. It took Officer David Dito less than a minute to confirm that he had found King's body in the master bedroom.

Harper then called Dr. Siu to confirm that the body was, in fact, King's. It checked another box—the deceased had a name. She was on the stand just long enough to introduce her autopsy report into evidence and recite her finding that King had died of a heroin overdose. On cross, I got her to acknowledge that King had an irregular heartbeat, but she held firm that it had no impact on her conclusion. At trial, I would make a bigger deal about this. At a prelim, it was just additional evidence that Judge Tsang was likely to disregard.

Lee was up next. Harper led him through a concise timeline of the events at King's house. There were murmurs in the gallery when Lee testified that Lexy had met King on Mature Relations—as if this was still news to anybody with a phone or a TV. Lee confirmed that he had found Lexy's prints on a baggie containing traces of heroin. Other prints were smudged. He also described the drug paraphernalia and cash found in Lexy's purse. I objected frequently, and, in all likelihood, inconsequentially. While I was probably doing little to convince the judge to drop the charges, I was hoping that Jerry Edwards—seated in the second row—would report that I was casting doubt on the strength of Harper's evidence. Potential jurors rarely showed up in court, but many still read the *Chronicle*.

Harper returned to the lectern and pressed a button on his laptop.

The flat-screen TV next to the witness box came to life. The white block lettering on the black background read, "Security Video. Bedroom. December 24."

Lexy leaned over and whispered, "Can you do anything to stop this?"

"At the moment, no."

Harper spoke to Lee. "Could you please describe what we are about to see?"

"A portion of a security video taken by a camera mounted inside Jeff King's bedroom early in the morning of December twenty-fourth of last year."

"The day that Jeff was murdered inside his house by the defendant?"

Nice try. "Move to strike Mr. Harper's characterization of the events at the decedent's house as 'murder.'"

"Withdrawn." Harper hadn't taken his eyes off Lee. "What time does the video start?"

"Twelve-eighteen a.m."

"Who was there?"

"The victim and the defendant."

Though his tone was conversational, Harper was choosing his language carefully. He would try to evoke sympathy for King by referring to him by name or calling him "the victim." Conversely, he would try to dehumanize Lexy by referring to her only as "the defendant."

Harper pointed at the TV. "Could you please describe what's happening as I run the video?"

"Of course." Lee left the box and moved over to the TV. Harper ran the video in slow motion. Lee pointed at the screen and narrated. "The defendant enters the room holding a spoon, a lighter, two syringes, some surgical hosing, and a baggie filled with heroin." He noted that Lexy cooked the heroin, filled the syringes, and accepted the money from King. King sat down on the bed, where Lexy wrapped his arm in the hosing.

Lee was methodical. "Here the defendant administers a lethal injection of almost-pure heroin. Within seconds, Mr. King overdoses, has convulsions, collapses, and stops breathing."

I wanted to break up his rhythm. "Move to strike. Inspector Lee is not a medical expert."

"Inspector Lee will limit his testimony as to what we can see on the screen."

It was a negligible victory.

Harper started the video again. "Can you please describe what happened next?"

Lee noted that Lexy shouted at King, slapped his face, felt for a pulse, gathered her belongings, and ran out of the room.

"Did she call 9-1-1?"

"No."

"Did she administer CPR?"

"No." Lee held up a hand for emphasis. "The defendant made no attempt to assist Jeff King. She left him there to die."

Harper paused the video. "Did the defendant make it out of the house?"

"No. The head of Mr. King's security detail stopped her at the door. He escorted her back upstairs, called 9-1-1, administered first aid, and awaited police and emergency medical personnel, who arrived within minutes. Unfortunately, it was too late to save Mr. King."

"Based upon this video, what did you conclude?"

"The defendant carefully prepared a syringe filled with heroin, intentionally administered it to Mr. King, stood by as he collapsed, and attempted to flee without calling for help, while keeping five thousand dollars that he had given to her."

"No further questions."

"Cross-exam, Mr. Daley?"

"Yes, Your Honor." I stood, buttoned my jacket, and moved in front of the box, where Lee had returned. "Inspector, did the decedent and the defendant know each other?"

"Yes. As I pointed out earlier, they had met on a site called Mature Relations."

"They had several previous encounters involving sex and heroin, hadn't they?"

"Yes."

"The decedent and Ms. Low acted as if they had been through this before, didn't they?"

"Objection," Harper said. "Calls for speculation."

"Your Honor," I said, "I'm simply asking him to describe what he observed in the video."

"I'll allow Inspector Lee to answer."

Lee nodded. "It appeared that the defendant was familiar with the processes for cooking heroin, preparing syringes, and injecting someone."

"Did the decedent put up any resistance when Ms. Low injected him?"

"Not as far as I could tell."

"In fact, Mr. King asked Ms. Low to inject him, didn't he?"

"Yes."

"So this encounter was completely consensual, wasn't it?"

"It appears that Mr. King agreed to be injected. However, for obvious reasons, I do not believe that he consented to being given a shot of almost-pure heroin potent enough to kill him."

Good answer. "You're saying that a billionaire who ran a successful tech firm didn't understand the risks associated with being injected with heroin?"

Harper was on his feet. "Objection. Calls for speculation."

"Overruled."

Lee held up a hand. "Obviously, I can't tell you what was going on inside his head, but I suspect that he did not think that Ms. Low was going to give him such a potent dose."

"Because they had such a close and loving relationship?"

"Because he was a smart businessman."

"Are you suggesting that Ms. Low provided the heroin?"

"Yes. As I testified earlier, we found her fingerprints on the baggie."

"You would concede that Ms. Low could have gotten her prints on a baggie provided by Mr. King or somebody else, wouldn't you?"

"Objection," Harper said. "Speculation."

"Overruled."

Lee frowned. "Yes, it's possible."

"You also testified that you found smudged prints, which could not be identified."

"True."

"Which could have been Mr. King's or somebody else's, right?"

"Right."

"Which suggests that the baggie could have been placed in the bathroom by Mr. King or somebody else, right?"

"We don't think that's what happened."

"But you don't know for sure, do you?"

"No."

"And you have not provided any evidence demonstrating that Ms. Low had the heroin in her possession when she entered Mr. King's house, have you?"

"Objection," Harper said. "Mr. Daley is testifying."

Yes, I am. "I'll rephrase." I moved in closer to Lee. "Did you find any evidence that Ms. Low had the baggie of heroin in her possession when she entered the house?"

"Yes. We interviewed a witness who confirmed that Ms. Low purchased heroin earlier that evening from a dealer near the Sixteenth Street BART Station."

What the hell? I turned around and glared at Lexy, whose eyes turned down. Then I turned back to the judge. "Your Honor, this evidence has not been provided to us."

Harper answered from his seat. "We are only obligated to provide evidence that might tend to be exculpatory. This clearly isn't. Moreover, we weren't planning to introduce this information today, but Mr. Daley's line of questioning has made it necessary."

There was irritation in Judge Tsang's voice. "I'm not happy about this, Mr. Harper."

Neither am I.

Harper feigned contrition. "My apologies, Your Honor. But Mr. Daley opened the door."

"Are you prepared to present this evidence now?"

"Yes, Your Honor."

"Mr. Daley, do you have any more questions for Inspector Lee?"

"Not at this time, but we reserve the right to recall him."

"Fine. Redirect, Mr. Harper?"

"No, Your Honor."

"I take it this means that you will call an additional witness to present this evidence?"

"Objection," I said. "There are no additional names on Mr. Harper's witness list."

Harper smiled triumphantly. "Actually, for this purpose, we'd like to recall Officer David Dito, who *is* on our witness list."

31
"HAVE YOU EXPLAINED THE RAMIFICATIONS TO YOUR CLIENT?"

Harper approached the box. "I would remind you that you're still under oath."

Officer David Dito's uniform was pressed, star polished. "Yes, sir."

The lanky kid with the baby face and the crew cut had been with SFPD for three years. David was the nephew of my S.I. classmate, Phil Dito, a third-generation cop from the Excelsior, who had worked with Pete at Mission Station. Four of Phil's brothers were cops. The other three were firefighters. SFPD had recruited David after he graduated from UC-Davis. He quickly developed a reputation as a solid cop with leadership potential.

Harper's tone was even. "You were on patrol in the Mission on the evening of December twenty-third of last year, weren't you?"

"Yes."

"You were in the plaza of the BART Station at Sixteenth and Mission at approximately ten-thirty that evening?"

"Yes."

"What did you observe?"

"I saw the defendant, Ms. Low, purchase heroin from a dealer named Khalil Jones."

Lexy tensed.

"Did you place the defendant under arrest?"

"No, I placed Mr. Jones under arrest. We focus more on sellers than buyers."

Enough. "Move to strike, Your Honor. The fact that Officer Dito arrested Mr. Jones has nothing to do with our case. Furthermore, Officer Dito has offered no corroboration that Ms. Low was involved in the alleged transaction."

Harper turned to the judge. "I was just getting to that, Your Honor. We would like to introduce video taken by Officer Dito's body cam on the night of December twenty-third."

Oh crap. "Objection. We had no advance notice."

Harper's tone turned patronizing. "Mr. Daley knows that we are only required to provide evidence that would tend to exonerate his client. This clearly does not."

The judge nodded in my direction, as if to say "Gotcha." "Overruled."

Harper introduced a brief video from Dito's bodycam, which showed Lexy accepting a baggie from a burly man in exchange for cash, after which they walked in opposite directions. Dito and his partner took off after Jones on foot. They arrested him without incident on Mission Street. Lexy disappeared into the night.

Dito pointed at Lexy. "It shows the defendant purchasing heroin from Mr. Jones."

Harper made no attempt to hide a satisfied grin. "No further questions, Your Honor."

"Cross-exam, Mr. Daley?"

"Yes, Your Honor." I walked across the courtroom and positioned myself in front of the box. "Officer Dito, you testified that you didn't detain Ms. Low, right?"

"Correct."

"Did you retrieve the baggie that she allegedly purchased and confiscate it as evidence?"

"No."

"Then how can you possibly know what was inside?"

"Because Mr. Jones had two other baggies containing heroin in his possession."

That doesn't help. "How can you possibly know that Mr. Jones didn't hand Ms. Low an empty baggie or one filled with another substance?"

"Objection," Harper said. "Called for speculation."

"Overruled."

"I can't. I did not handle that baggie, Mr. Daley. However, I handled two other baggies which had been in Mr. Jones's possession, both of which contained heroin. We had been watching Mr. Jones for several weeks. Heroin was his only product."

"Did you find the baggies in his pocket?"

"No. Mr. Jones opened them and dropped them into a puddle on Mission Street in an attempt to destroy the evidence as he attempted to flee. We were able to retrieve the baggies."

"So the substance in the baggies was exposed to water and other elements?"

"Yes, but our lab was able to test them and confirmed traces of heroin."

"But you couldn't have verified its quality or potency with any accuracy because it had been exposed to the water and other elements, right?"

"Right."

"So the lab could not possibly have determined conclusively whether the traces of heroin found in the baggie at Mr. King's house were the same as the heroin that Mr. Jones allegedly sold to Ms. Low, right?"

A hesitation. "Right."

"And you have no direct personal knowledge or corroborating evidence that Ms. Low had the same baggie in her possession when she entered Mr. King's house later that night, do you?"

"No."

"You would therefore acknowledge that even if Ms. Low allegedly bought heroin earlier that evening, it does not prove that she brought it to Mr. King's house later that night, right?"

"Right."

I appreciated his honesty. "No further questions."

"Redirect, Mr. Harper?"

"No, Your Honor."

"Any additional witnesses?"

"No, Your Honor. The prosecution rests."

The judge turned to me. "Anything further for the prosecution's witnesses, Mr. Daley?"

"No, Your Honor."

"Do you wish to call any defense witnesses at this time, Mr. Daley?"

"No, Your Honor."

"I take it that you would like to make a motion?"

"Yes, I would. We ask the court to dismiss the charges against Ms. Low because the prosecution has failed to provide sufficient evidence to bind her over for trial."

The judge took off his reading glasses. "Based upon the evidence and testimony presented today, I believe that there is sufficient evidence that the defendant committed the crime for which she is accused. I am entering an order that Ms. Low be bound over for trial."

"But Your Honor—,"

"I've ruled, Mr. Daley." He glanced at his laptop. "We should spend a moment on scheduling. Trial will be set in Department 22. I trust your client will waive time?"

"No, Your Honor."

His eyes shifted from his screen to me. "Excuse me?"

"My client has a right to a trial within sixty days. She will not be waiving time."

He looked at Harper. "I trust you'll be ready to go within that statutory timeframe?"

"Of course, Your Honor."

He turned back to me. "Have you explained the ramifications to your client?"

"Yes."

"If you are trying to set up an issue on appeal questioning the competence of her counsel, that isn't going to fly."

"We aren't. My client is being held on spurious charges. We want to deal with this as quickly as possible so that she can continue her treatments and move on with her life."

"Fine." Ignatius Tsang was too experienced to show any hint of irritation. "How many trial days for the prosecution, Mr. Harper?"

"No more than three."

It will take longer to pick a jury.

"And for the defense, Mr. Daley?"

"No more than five." *Probably fewer.*

He studied the calendar. "Your timing is fortuitous. Judge Elizabeth McDaniel will be sitting in for Judge Busch next month. She was supposed to start a trial on Monday, February fourth, but it was settled. I trust this works for you, Mr. Daley?"

It was only four weeks away. "Yes, Your Honor."

"Mr. Harper?"

"Yes, Your Honor."

His eyes shifted back to me. "Since you're driving the timing, I can assure you that neither Judge McDaniel nor I will be pleased if you come back and request an extension."

"Understood."

"Subject to confirmation by Judge McDaniel, I am ordering you to produce pre-trial motions and witness lists by the end of next week. I am ordering expedited discovery, so Mr. Harper must provide all relevant evidence as he receives it. The existing gag order stays in place along with standing limitations on media access. Are we all on the same page?"

Harper and I nodded.

"Good. I am sure that Judge McDaniel will look forward to seeing your papers. Anything else?"

I spoke up. "We renew our request for reduced bail. Ms. Low is not a flight risk. She will wear a monitoring device and be subject to regular check-ins."

"Where would she live in the interim?"

"The shelter where she has been living for the past six months."

"How would this impact her addiction treatments?"

It isn't ideal. "We will make arrangements to ensure an orderly transition."

"You're asking a lot."

"Nothing out of the ordinary." *Yes, it is.*

He turned to Harper. "How do you feel about this?"

"Given the gravity of the charge against her, reduced bail is inappropriate."

His objection was more tepid than I might have expected. Then again, he knew that unless the judge imposed an absurdly low bail, Lexy didn't have the money.

Judge Tsang pondered his options and made the call. "In my opinion, Ms. Low would have little to lose by attempting to flee. Bail remains at one million dollars."

I tried to sound reasonable. "She won't survive in jail, Your Honor."

"I've ruled, Mr. Daley. You can file a motion for reconsideration."

"We will." *And even if you change your mind, Lexy will remain in custody because she'll never be able to raise the money—and you know it.*

32
"FASTEN YOUR SEAT BELT"

"Did you buy smack from Jones on the evening that you went to King's house?" I asked.

Lexy was staring at the floor. "Yes."

"Had you ever bought heroin from him?"

"A couple of times."

"Did he sell the high-end stuff that King took?"

"No, he sold the cheap stuff that I took."

We were meeting in a consultation room at the Glamour Slammer at two o'clock on Monday afternoon. Even though Judge Tsang's courtroom was a five-minute walk from here, it had taken the deputies a couple of hours to round up the defendants who had court appearances and escort them back to their cells.

"How much did you buy?" I asked.

"About a quarter of a gram. It cost fifty bucks. I didn't have the money to buy more."

It isn't uncommon for heroin addicts to buy multiple hits a day—and do whatever it takes to get more money to pay for another one after they run out. "What did you do with it?"

She finally looked up. "I went into an alley, cooked it, and took it. I wanted to take the edge off before I went up to Jeff's house."

"What happened to the baggie?"

"I don't remember."

"Any chance somebody will find it?"

"No."

It ruled out the possibility that we could have an expert testify that the stuff she bought on the street was different from the stuff she injected into King. On the other hand, since Jones had tossed the baggies into a puddle and contaminated the evidence, it was unlikely that the D.A. would be able to prove that it was the same stuff, either.

She added, "Do you think I brought Jeff some crap that I picked up on the street?"

"I don't know, Lexy. Did you?"

"No. And even if I had, do you think Jeff would have taken it?"

Maybe. "The prosecution is going to say that you brought the smack to King's house."

"I didn't."

"Can you prove it?"

"No."

Hopefully, they can't either. "You appreciate how bad this looks."

"I do, but I'm giving it to you straight. I bought smack from Khalil, took it, and went up to Jeff's house, where I found a baggie of high-end stuff in the drawer in his bathroom—just like always."

"You'd better hope they didn't find Khalil's prints on that baggie."

"If they did, it's because Jeff bought the smack from Khalil, too."

* * *

Rosie sat at the table, fingers templed. "I take it that you were not aware that our client had purchased heroin from a known seller earlier that evening?"

"She didn't mention it."

"I trust that you asked her about it?"

"I did." I filled her in on the details of my conversation with Lexy. "She says that she bought about a quarter of a gram of cheap smack that she consumed herself."

"You're absolutely sure?"

"I'm not absolutely sure about anything, Rosie."

"That's the most honest thing I've heard today."

Rosie, Nady, Pete, and I were meeting in the conference room down the hall from my office. At four o'clock on Monday afternoon, the P.D.'s Office was buzzing. To the untrained eye, it appeared chaotic. To those of us who had lived in the hive for years, it was improvisational theater.

Nady looked up from her laptop. "Did you ask Lexy about postponing the trial?"

"Yes. The answer is no. Unless she has a change of heart, the trial will begin four weeks from today. We need to start on pre-trial motions, witness lists, and exhibits."

"Already working on them."

"Fasten your seatbelt. We'll need to put Jeff King and everybody who was at his house that night on trial. We have plenty of unlikeable people to choose from." I turned to Pete. "It won't be easy getting people from Y5K to talk to us. Nobody is returning my calls."

"They've undoubtedly been told not to talk, but I'll get something on everybody."

"That's why we're paying you the big bucks."

"This could be a disaster, Mick. We're going to have to wallow in the mud to get information from these people."

"Where are you going to start?"

"Palo Alto. You?"

"Daly City."

"What's there?"

"The headquarters of Mature Relations."

33
"I'M A HOPELESS ROMANTIC"

The wiry man with the shaved head and the bleach-blonde goatee extended a hand and spoke in a baritone. "Brian Holton."

"Mike Daley. I'm Lexy Low's lawyer."

"I was expecting you."

The founder, CEO, and majority stockholder of Mature Relations was sitting behind a second-hand desk in the corner of an unfinished space in a nondescript two-story building behind Serramonte Mall. His "office" was demarcated by moveable partitions separating him from three dozen programmers wearing noise-cancelling headphones. They were pounding on their laptops at long tables that looked as if they were borrowed from the lunch room at St. Ignatius. The gray walls were bare except for a few unframed posters of scantily attired women posing beneath the Mature Relations logo.

"When did you start this company?" I asked.

"Almost five years ago."

"You run the entire operation from here?"

"Over ten million members." He looked around at his empire—such as it was—with pride. "When you operate in the lower end of the Silicon Valley ecosystem, you have to watch your overhead."

"I take it this means that you didn't get venture funding?"

"Are you serious? Our business involves giving rich old guys an easy way to hook up with attractive young women. Ten million members didn't get me a cup of coffee with the players on Sand Hill Road like Blackjack Steele or Gopal Patel. Ironically, a guy like Jeff King who was banging every young woman in Silicon Valley got a hundred million in VC money. I got bupkis."

While I appreciated his forthrightness, at the end of the day, he was still a high-tech pimp. "Are you married?"

"Thirty years. Two kids and four grandkids."

Go figure. "Did you ever meet King?"

"Once at a cocktail party. He treated me like pond scum. Patel and Steele weren't any better."

"Where did you get your funding?"

"Initially, from me. Nowadays, from membership fees and advertising. We plow every penny back into the business to keep our subscriber base growing."

"Are you looking to go public?"

"No, I'm looking to get bought out by a player like Match, Tinder, or Ashley Madison, whereupon I will find a sunny beach and sip fruity drinks with umbrellas for the rest of my life."

"Sounds pretty good to me. How did you get started?"

"You remember Netscape?"

"Sure. It was Google before Google."

"I was one of their first employees after I got out of Stanford. Once upon a time, we were a big thing and a bunch of us made millions. Then Yahoo and Google came along. After AOL bought Netscape, I formed a couple of startups, which failed. I hiked in Tibet for a couple of years. Then I came back and got bored, so I started this company."

"How did you happen to decide on this particular industry?"

"I'm a hopeless romantic."

So am I.

He turned serious. "Actually, I went about it methodically. I identified an area of substantial consumer demand that we could scale up quickly. Everybody is looking for love. I had experience in the dating space. One of my startups was a service that went head-to-head against Tinder—and lost. Our algorithm was better, but we couldn't get to scale fast enough. The Netscape experience taught me that the first to market doesn't always win. If MySpace had been a little smarter, nobody would have heard of Facebook."

He had his eye on the ball.

He added, "The key is being greedy, but not too greedy. It's better to get out a little early than a little late. People have short attention spans. One of these days, people will get tired of our site and move onto something new."

"Not anytime soon, I hope."

"That's what we said about Netscape." He adjusted the stud in his ear. "I take it that you wanted to talk about Jeff King?"

"I do."

"I have a policy of cooperating with the authorities. I've already spoken to Inspector Lee. I told him that King connected with your client on our site about six months ago. I don't know how many times they saw each other. Once people hook up, they contact each other directly."

"Can you tell me anything about their communications?"

He handed me a printout showing messages between Lexy and King. "I gave this to Inspector Lee. If you're looking for something titillating, you're going to be disappointed."

I scanned the two pages. Lexy and King had exchanged contact information. "Did Ms. Low make any connections besides King?"

"Just one: Paul Flynn. Inspector Lee also contacted me when Flynn OD'd." He handed me another printout. "Your client had even less communication with him."

His privacy policy was more relaxed than I might have thought. "Any mention of heroin?"

"No."

Good. "Did King meet any other women on your site?"

He grinned. "About a dozen. He was a member of our Executive Club."

"And Flynn?"

"He was a member of our Premium Club."

"How did Ms. Low qualify for membership?"

"She paid our fee."

"Your site caters to individuals of substantial means."

"We do."

"Ms. Low was living in a shelter."

"Our subscribers provide financial information voluntarily. Our membership agreement clearly states that we do not guarantee its accuracy."

"Has anybody ever complained about somebody lying?"

"Rarely. If they do, we refer them to our membership agreement. Many of our members are wealthy people who are, for lack of a better term, cheating on their spouses. They include entrepreneurs, politicians, and athletes whose names you would recognize. As you might expect, they're embarrassed about complaining to us, and they're reluctant to go to the authorities. If they're dissatisfied, they usually cancel their memberships."

"You're okay with catering to this niche?"

"I'm just trying to make a living."

"Were any other people from Y5K's management team subscribers to your service?"

"I'd rather not reveal that information."

"I'd rather not send you a subpoena."

"I'd rather not receive one. Jack Steele, Gopal Patel, and Drew Pitt."

Perhaps they gave each other discount codes. It confirmed the information provided by Kaela Joy. I imagined King, Steele, Patel, and the "Guy from Rye" swapping stories about their respective sexual conquests. "Did any of them meet anybody?"

"All of them." He gave me the names of several women who were not at King's party. Then he flashed another grin. "Mind if I ask you something?"

"Sure."

"Are you married?"

"Divorced."

His eyes lit up. "You're a perfect demographic fit for membership."

I don't think so. "I'm not a millionaire."

"Doesn't matter."

"I'm seeing somebody."

"So are many of our members. I'd be happy to help you set up a profile. We're running a post-holiday special—three months free. No obligation. You can cancel any time."

And Jerry Edwards would post a screen shot of my listing on the front page of the Chronicle. "Uh, no thanks."

"Let me walk you through the setup process. If you decide to proceed, fine. If not, no worries. You'll have a chance to see our technology and look at photos of some pretty women."

"I appreciate the offer, Brian, but I'm going to pass."

* * *

"How did it go at Mature Relations?" Pete asked.

I was driving north on the 280 Freeway. "Ten million members."

"We're in the wrong line of work, Mick."

"I don't think so." I summarized my discussion with Holton. "Steele and Patel are signed up on the site. So is the 'Guy from Rye.'"

"We already knew that from Kaela Joy. Got time for lunch?"

"I'm working."

"So am I. This is a business lunch."

"Fine. Where?"

"The Gold Club."

"Seriously?"

"Yeah."

It was a high-end strip club on Howard Street a few blocks from Union Square. "I don't have time, Pete."

"This is strictly business, Mick. If you want to get dirt on the tech bros, you need to spend time where they hang out."

34
"CONFERENCE ROOM G"

"We won't be going hungry," I observed.

Pete's face was tinged in blue and purple from the neon lights as he piled chicken and ribs onto his plate. "Best lunch in town. And still only five bucks."

At eleven-thirty on Tuesday morning, we were the oldest guys in the buffet line snaking around a cavernous space packed with Millennials, the overwhelming majority of whom were male. Pulsating dance music blared and lights flashed in the Gold Club, an upscale strip joint in a nondescript two-story building on Howard between the swanky W Hotel, the Museum of Modern Art, and the sleek tower housing the world headquarters of LinkedIn and the San Francisco office of Y5K. Twenty years earlier, this area was home to light industry, auto repair shops, and skid row. Nowadays, the Gold Club was in the center of San Francisco's tech world.

As we pushed our way across the room, a young woman with a pixie haircut and sporting a black corset and short-shorts stopped us. "Haven't seen you in a while, Pete."

"Busy working, Bernie. Kids okay?"

"Fine. The twins are in second grade. Your wife still at that law firm around the corner?"

"Yup."

"Their attorneys come in all the time."

Pete subtly slid five twenties into her palm. "Bernadette Small, this is my big brother, Mike, the ex-priest and current public defender."

"I've heard a lot about you. You're representing Sexy Lexy."

"Yes, I am. Do you know her?"

"No."

"What about Jeff King?"

"He used to come in at least a couple of times a week. Garden-variety asshole whose bank account was exceeded only by his ego."

That covers it. "I take it that you weren't impressed?"

"A rich asshole is still an asshole. Very demanding. Crappy tipper.

Hit on everybody."

"You?"

"I'm not his type. He liked them younger with long hair and big breasts."

Just like Lexy. "Did he ever ask for special services?" It was the euphemism for activities provided in the back rooms for an extra charge.

"Every time."

"Anybody working here who knew him pretty well?"

"Not anymore. A woman named Jasmine was his favorite, but you'd have to go to Thailand to talk to her."

Never mind.

Pete discreetly handed her another twenty. "Is Nick here?"

"Usual table."

"Thanks, Bernie." He motioned me to follow him.

"Nick?" I said.

"Nick 'the Dick.'"

"He's here?"

"At least three times a week."

Nick "the Dick" Hanson was a ninety-four-year-old P.I. who had been running the Hanson Investigative Agency in North Beach for almost three-quarters of a century. He had started as a one-person shop in a room above what is now the Condor Club on Broadway. Nowadays, he headed a high-tech operation employing dozens of his children, grandchildren, and great-grandchildren. In his spare time, he wrote mystery novels that were thinly veiled embellishments of his more colorful cases.

I followed Pete to a table in a corner alcove where Nick was eating by himself. At barely five-feet tall and just over a hundred pounds, he was sporting his usual custom-tailored three-piece suit with a fresh rose in his lapel. He wasn't an imposing physical specimen, but he was a tenacious investigator and a savvy businessman. There were rumors that one of the national security firms had offered him more than twenty million dollars for the agency, which Nick turned down. Many of us believe that Nick started the rumor himself. Over the years, he had also acquired about a dozen apartment buildings in North Beach, which were worth north of fifty million dollars.

His rubbery face transformed into a broad smile as he extended a hand and spoke in a sing-song voice where he elongated his words. "Hello, Michael. Great to see you again."

"It's been a long time, Nick."

"Indeed it has."

"I thought you finally retired."

"I got bored after a few weeks. I like hanging out with my great-grandkids." He spent the next fifteen minutes devouring the contents of a plate piled high with chicken, ribs, tri-tip, shrimp, and pasta, along with two glasses of pinot noir, while regaling us with tales of the expansion of his agency, the value of his real estate portfolio, and the marketing plans for his latest novel. "Confidentially, we're in negotiations with Netflix about a TV series."

It wasn't *that* confidential. Nick had leaked the information to the gossip columnist at the *Chronicle*. "Are you going to play yourself?"

He beamed. "Indeed I am."

I silently chuckled at the possibility that millions of people around the world would be able to binge-watch Nick. "You come here often?"

"Indeed I do."

"To watch the show?"

"To work." He took another bite of chicken. "A company whose name you would recognize asked us to monitor how many of their employees come here for, uh, lunch. They finally realized that operating a business like a fraternity house doesn't enhance their brand."

"Aren't you being a little, uh, conspicuous?"

"That's why I sit here in the corner. Besides, people are more interested in what's happening onstage."

"How do you monitor the second floor from here?"

"I have a dozen operatives working the floor." He grabbed another shrimp. "Bernie works for me."

I wasn't surprised.

Nick was still talking. "She's a single mom who works three days a week as a dental hygienist, and three days here to pay for her health insurance. She supplements her income working for me. It's a win-win."

Welcome to the gig economy. "I could make a strong argument that this establishment is exploiting her. Doesn't it bother you?"

"Indeed it does. On the other hand, I didn't invent strip clubs. I'm helping Bernie save for college for her kids, and she's helping me get dirt."

Pete subtly held up a hand in a secret sign between P.I.s that it was time to stop the BS. "How often did you see King?" he asked.

"Three or four times a week. This is where the tech guys blow off steam. They call it 'Conference Room G.'"

"Anybody else from Y5K?"

"Blackjack Steele, Gopal Patel, and most of the upper management team. A sales guy named Tristan Moore who looks like a young Chris Pratt. A programmer named Alejandro Sanchez who looks like a ratty Benicio Del Toro. And King usually brought his pal, Drew Pitt."

I wasn't surprised to hear the name of the "Guy from Rye." "Ever see Sexy Lexy?"

"Afraid not. Too bad. She's a looker."

"Was anybody mad at King?"

"Everybody on Planet Earth. He treated everybody like crap—especially the women."

"Even his friend, Drew?"

"Yes. And Steele. And Patel. And Moore. And Sanchez. And everybody he met."

"Were you ever asked to tail him?"

"He's one of the few people in the Valley that we haven't been asked to tail."

"Who else should we talk to?"

"It's going to be tough to get people at Y5K to talk. The place is an armed fortress. You can try Patel and his associate, Christina Chu, but they invested a lot of money in the company."

"Ever see anything suspicious when King was here?"

"This is a strip club, Mike. Everything is sketchy."

True enough. "Anything come to mind?"

"King brought Steele's daughter here once when she was an intern at Y5K. It showed an astounding lack of judgment. To her credit, she walked out."

Good for her. "Was her father here at the time?"

"No."

"We may have a few more questions for you."

"Happy to help. Next time, it's standard rates." He excused himself and headed to the restroom.

I turned to Pete. "I need you to find Debbie Steele. I'm going back to the office and see if I can get an audience with Patel."

The lights flickered and the music got louder. Applause filled the cavernous space as a line of scantily dressed women—including Bernie—made their way to the stage.

Pete finished his beer. "You want to stick around for the show?"

"No, thanks."

"You were more fun when you were a priest."

35
"HIS BEHAVIOR WAS ERRATIC AT TIMES"

"Thank you for seeing me," I said.

Gopal Patel's expression was stern. "I appreciate the fact that you called for an appointment this time instead of ambushing me like you did at Bird Dog."

I didn't want to throw Pete's mole, the maître d', under the bus. "I'm sorry."

"Apology accepted."

I appreciated his graciousness, however grudging.

Two days had passed since Pete and I had dined at the Gold Club. I was pleased—and a bit surprised—that Patel had agreed to meet with me. Then again, he didn't want to appear uncooperative. I looked around at his modest office on the ground floor of a two-story, cookie-cutter complex on Sand Hill Road, adjacent to the ritzy Sharon Heights Country Club. The modular furniture looked as if it had come from Scandinavian Designs. His bookcase was jammed with three-ring binders with hand-written labels for venture capital investments.

"Something the matter?" he asked.

"I guess I was expecting a successful VC's office to be a little fancier." *Especially one who's supposedly worth a half a billion dollars.*

"We invest our partners' money in our portfolio companies, not our offices."

Good line. I wonder how many times you've repeated it. "That's admirable, Mr. Patel."

"Gopal."

"Mike."

In response to my inquiry about his background, he walked me through his C.V. Born to an affluent family in Delhi. Studied electrical engineering at the India Institute of Technology. MBA from Stanford. Worked at a couple of startups before landing as the forty-third employee at Google. Made enough in the IPO to buy houses for his children and grandchildren. Married his current wife twelve years earlier. Two college-age kids from a previous marriage. A mansion in Hillsborough. A cabin at Lake Tahoe. A condo in Maui. The American Dream.

I asked him why he decided to become a venture capitalist.

"I got tired of playing tennis. I'm competitive. I wanted to prove that I didn't make a fortune just by being at the right place at the right time."

But it sure helped.

His tone turned self-righteous. "My partners and I decided to invest in entrepreneurs who demonstrate a commitment to good moral values, community service, and philanthropy."

"Very commendable." *Especially coming from a guy who is cheating on his wife and meeting women on a sugar daddy site.* "What percentage of your investments are profitable?"

"One in ten sees positive cash flow. One in twenty turns a modest profit. One in a million hits it big like Google or Facebook."

Might as well play the lottery. "How do you decide whether to fund a company?"

"The first question is always whether the entrepreneur is trustworthy and of good moral character. That's also the second question."

It wasn't clear to me how King's proclivity for hooking up with young women on Mature Relations checked those boxes. "And the third?"

"Whether the new technology is delightful."

You're kidding. "Delightful?"

"Think of the first time you did a search on Google or watched a baseball game on an iPhone. You'd never seen anything like it, right?"

I played along. "Right."

"We're looking to fund companies with products that millions of people can't live without."

"You don't *need* Google or an iPhone."

"Or ninety-nine percent of the stuff that we buy, Mike. But we *think* we do. Technology allows us to do things faster and cheaper, but it hasn't fundamentally changed what we want—things that make our lives easier, enhance our productivity, and entertain us."

And make you a ton of money. "In other words, it delights us."

"Exactly."

I wanted to puke.

His tone turned serious. "You didn't come here to talk about venture capital."

"I wanted to ask you about Jeff King."

"He was a visionary."

So I've been told. "Why did you decide to invest in Y5K?"

"Jeff was a seasoned entrepreneur, and the technology is a game-changer."

At least he didn't try to sell me on King's morals again. I kept my eyes on his and nodded at appropriate times as he recited a canned sales pitch about the potential of the Y5K platform. His description included multiple mentions of "synergies," "dynamics," "analytics," "enhanced reality," and "empiricals." It took every ounce of my self-control to avoid laughing when he started talking about something called the "hockey stick profit curve."

Finally, he folded his arms and spoke with conviction. "This company will be a case study at Stanford Business School of a near-perfect venture investment."

What could possibly go wrong? "Is the company making money?" I asked.

"Not yet, but it will."

"When?"

"Eventually."

"You said that you place great importance in the trustworthiness and integrity of the founders."

"I do."

"You trusted Jeff King?"

"He was a person of integrity and character."

Who was cheating on his wife, going to the Gold Club multiple times a week, shooting heroin, and picking up young women on Mature Relations. At the same time, he was cheating on you and your soon-to-be-ex-wife under the terms of your polyamorous agreement. Yup. Integrity and character. "What about his judgment?"

"He was vetted by our investment committee. Our decision was unanimous."

You might want to consider adding some new people to your committee. "Mr. King was a married man who had entered into a relationship with my client through a sugar daddy app called Mature

Relations. Didn't that bother you?"

"It wasn't ideal, but it wasn't illegal."

You would know. "He was cheating on his wife." *And you*.

"At times, we find it necessary to distinguish between an individual's business and personal judgment."

How convenient. "Do you think it enhanced the stature of your firm by investing in a business run by a guy who preyed on young women?"

"With hindsight, it wasn't ideal from a marketing standpoint."

Or an ethical one. Although I'm sure seemed like a fine idea at the time.

He added, "I try to avoid making moral judgments on people's personal lives."

Especially when you're cheating on your wife, too. "Would you patronize a hookup site?"

"Absolutely not."

"Do you know anybody else at the company who was using it?" *Other than you, Steele, and the "Guy from Rye."*

"No."

"But you were willing to invest in somebody who did?"

"If I had known about it at the time, I might have reconsidered."

"When did you become aware of Mr. King's relationship with my client?"

"When I saw it on the news."

I find that hard to believe. "Were you surprised?"

"Not really, I suppose. Jeff and Chloe had separated. He was under intense pressure."

"We've been told that Mr. King was accused of sexual harassment at several companies, including Y5K."

"Those claims were exaggerated."

Not exactly a denial. "Did Y5K pay any settlements?"

"That's confidential."

"We can subpoena the company's records."

"You'll need to address it with the company's lawyers."

"I understand that he was difficult to work with."

"He was demanding, but fair."

"Did you notice anything unusual in his behavior recently?" *Other than cheating on you and his wife, picking up women on a sugar daddy site, and doing heroin?*

He measured his words. "His behavior was erratic at times."

"Did he have a substance problem?"

"With hindsight, probably."

"Did you ever see him take heroin or other drugs, or offer them to others?"

"No."

I wasn't convinced. "You were at his house on the night that he died along with members of Y5K's senior management."

"Jeff wanted to thank us for our work on the IPO."

"There were also several women, including your associate, Ms. Chu."

"Christina is a very talented analyst and an important member of our team."

"Did you invite the other women to the party?"

"Christina did—at my suggestion. We've made it a priority to support female entrepreneurs."

By inviting them to parties as eye candy for a bunch of horny guys?

He added, "It was an excellent opportunity to make connections."

Until King died. "Were they expected to provide entertainment as well?"

"That was up to them."

"Did that include sex?"

"We're all adults, Mike."

How enlightened. And, as you've already pointed out, it wasn't illegal. "Were people using drugs?"

"Absolutely not."

"Did you know that Mr. King had invited my client to his house?"

"No."

"Do you think that was a good idea?"

"Obviously not."

We finally agree about something. "Did he ever mention that he and Ms. Low were having sex and using heroin when they got together?"

"No."

"Did he ever tell you whether he or Ms. Low provided the heroin?"

"We never discussed it."

"We believe that Mr. King provided it."

"That's not what the police told me."

"We believe that someone other than my client may have spiked the heroin."

"It wasn't me."

I didn't expect you to admit it. "It was somebody else at the party."

"I find that hard to believe."

"But you wouldn't rule out the possibility."

"I find that hard to believe," he repeated.

"Have you ever used heroin?"

"Absolutely not."

"Never even smoked a little weed?"

"No."

Right. "Is the IPO still on?"

"Absolutely. Jack Steele has been appointed as chairman. Tristan Moore is going to become acting CEO. Alejandro Sanchez will be promoted to Senior Vice President and remain as Chief Technology Officer."

"Seems everybody got a promotion."

"If you're suggesting that somebody killed Jeff to move up the corporate ladder, you don't understand how business works."

Guess not. "Were you and Mr. King friends?"

"We spent most of our time talking about business."

"Did you ever get together outside the office?"

"From time to time."

"I understand that he and his wife had an open marriage."

"That was none of my business."

Actually, it was. "And they were involved with multiple partners at times." I was looking for a reaction.

His expression didn't change. "You know more than I do."

I doubt it. I didn't want to reveal that Kaela Joy had told us that Patel and his soon-to-be ex-wife had been involved in a multi-partner relationship with King and his wife. We would save that for trial.

I handed him a card. "I would appreciate your help in arranging meetings with Mr. Steele and other members of management."

"I'll see what I can do."

When hell freezes over. "And I would also like to chat with Ms. Chu for a few minutes."

"Unfortunately, she isn't here."

"I can wait."

"She won't be in today."

I heard a knock on the glass wall behind me. I turned around and saw Chu standing outside Patel's office, mouthing the words, "Call me."

I swung around and looked at Patel. "How fortuitous. Looks like she's here."

36
"OUR RELATIONSHIP IS PURELY PROFESSIONAL"

Christina Chu's office was half the size of Patel's, and she had a view of the courtyard where the smokers congregated. She was a slender woman in her early thirties whose brown eyes were hidden behind over-sized eyeglasses. Her straight black hair was pulled into a French twist, exposing pearl earrings.

I pointed at the only personal item on her desk: a framed photo of decked-out Chu standing next to a beaming young man sporting a tux. "Husband?"

"Fiancé. It was taken at the Y5K holiday party last year."

I glanced at the massive diamond ring on her finger. "Have you set a date?"

"Not yet. We just got engaged."

"Best wishes."

"Thank you." Her tone turned serious. "I'm under no obligation to talk to you. And I am limited in what I can say because of existing non-disclosure agreements."

"Understood." *Venture capitalists are as uptight as lawyers*. "Are you a partner here at the firm?"

"Gopal and I will have that discussion next year."

In her cutthroat world, she would need to hit a few grand slams between now and then. "How did you get into venture capital?"

"I took a seminar from Gopal at Stanford. He reached out when I was at Facebook."

"He must think very highly of you. I've read that this is a tough field for women."

"It's very competitive. Fortunately, Gopal has been an excellent mentor."

"How long did you know Jeff King?"

"About ten years. He was a gifted entrepreneur and a charismatic leader."

And a gifted philanderer and a charismatic misogynist.

She added, "I introduced him to Gopal and recommended that we invest in Y5K. Its technology is extraordinary."

How do I say this delicately? "Were you at all concerned about Mr. King's reputation for some less-than-stellar behavior at his prior startups?"

"Those allegations were overblown. We have very high standards."

Seriously? "No issues?"

"In the course of our due diligence, some concerns arose about Jeff's behavior at his previous company. As a result, we brought in Jack Steele."

That worked out great, didn't it? "To deal with management or character issues?"

"Both. Gopal and Jack informed Jeff that even the appearance of inappropriate behavior would have a serious adverse impact on the company's prospects and our investment. He promised to be more careful."

Before or after his visits to the Gold Club? "Did he take these warnings seriously?"

"Yes."

Before or after he started meeting women on Mature Relations? "Did you know that he met my client through a sugar daddy site?"

"I do now."

"Did that bother you?"

"Yes, but we can't monitor the private lives of the CEOs of the companies we fund."

"I take it that your firm will make millions if the IPO moves forward?"

"Yes."

And you'll be a hero. "Did you see Ms. Low at the party?"

"No."

"Did you know that she was going to be there?"

"No."

I showed her a list of the names of the other women at the party. "Mr. Patel said that you invited them."

"I did. They're some of the most talented entrepreneurs and engineers in the Valley."

They're also beautiful young women who were flirting with King, Steele, Patel, and their pals. "Were you concerned about Mr. King's reputation for treating women poorly?"

"Absolutely not. I invited them because they're successful people who wanted to meet Jeff and other A-List people. I think it's misogynistic of you to suggest that my friends can't take care of themselves."

"I'm sorry." *No, I'm not.* "Did you notice anything unusual about Mr. King's behavior at the party?"

"He was a gracious host and a perfect gentleman."

Until he went upstairs to shoot heroin and sleep with a woman he had met on a sugar daddy site. "Did you know that he had a substance problem?"

"It didn't come as a great surprise."

"Was anybody using drugs at the party?"

"No."

"Was anybody angry at Mr. King?"

"Not that I'm aware of."

"What time did you leave?"

"Eleven-forty-five."

"By yourself?"

"Gopal and I shared an Uber."

I wondered if that was the euphemism for "We were holding hands." "I understand that he and Mrs. Patel have separated."

"That's none of your business—or mine. Our relationship is purely professional."

A little too defensive. "I wasn't suggesting otherwise." *Except that I just did.*

She stood up. "Anything else?"

I glanced at the photo of her fiancé. "Not at the moment. In the spirit of full disclosure, we are planning to contact your friends who were at the party."

"They didn't ask to be involved in this mess, and they can't help you."

37
"I LIKE CHALLENGES"

Yoav Ben-Shalom slid into the chair on the opposite side of the table and spoke deliberately in unaccented American English. "How can I help you, Mr. Daley?"

"I understand that you're the head of security here at Y5K."

"I am."

"You were responsible for Mr. King's personal security?"

"I was."

"You must have spent a lot of time with him."

"I did."

We were sitting in a windowless room in Y5K's state-of-the-universe security suite. It had taken me almost a week to penetrate the outer walls of Y5K's defenses to get an audience with the one-time Israeli commando. On Tuesday, January fifteenth, we were less than three weeks from the start of jury selection, and the clock was ticking.

Of medium height and build, Ben-Shalom was not physically imposing, but his unblinking eyes and serious demeanor evoked a "don't-even-think-about-messing-with-me" vibe. Dressed in a power suit, a snow-white shirt, and a subdued tie, he could have passed for an investment banker. Upon closer look, his ear-piece, buzzcut, and pockmarked face evoked images of the Mossad. The only thing missing was a pair of mirrored sunglasses.

"What was Mr. King like?" I asked.

"Driven."

"How was he to work for?"

"Demanding."

"A profile in *TechCrunch* said he was difficult."

"At times."

"And petty."

"Occasionally."

"And vindictive."

"Never saw it."

And you wouldn't tell me if you did. "Did you like working for him?"

"Yes."

"Why?"

"I am well-compensated, and I like challenges."

I tried to get him to elaborate, but he wouldn't bite. "He had relationship issues."

"Everyone does."

"He was divorced twice."

"So was your ex-wife."

I wasn't surprised that he had checked me out. "He and Mrs. King had separated."

"It happens."

"She told us that he had cheated on her throughout their marriage."

"My job was to protect him, not provide relationship counseling."

"I trust that you were also aware that he and his wife were involved in a multi-party relationship for a while?"

"As long as it didn't impact the company, how they chose to spend their private time was of no concern to me."

"It must have complicated your life."

"At times."

"You were aware that Mr. King met my client on a hookup site?"

"Yes."

"And you knew that Ms. Low wasn't the only person he met on that site?"

"He made some less-than-ideal choices."

"You knew that he was doing drugs with my client and others, right?"

"No comment."

"Did it concern you that he might get some bad smack?"

"Yes."

"Did you or the board do anything about it?"

"We encouraged Mr. King to use better judgment."

They did nothing. "Mr. King was also accused of treating several female employees inappropriately at Y5K and prior companies."

"I can't discuss personnel matters."

"I can subpoena the company's records."

"We have lawyers, too."

I decided to move in another direction. "Would you mind describing what you saw at Mr. King's house on the night that he died?"

"I gave my statement to Inspector Lee. I presume that he will provide a copy to you if he hasn't already done so."

Thanks. "Had you ever met my client before the party at Mr. King's house?"

"No."

"But you knew about her?"

"Yes."

"Were you concerned that Mr. King was seeing someone who was addicted to heroin?"

"Yes."

"Were you present at any of her prior rendezvouses with Mr. King?"

"All of them."

"In the room?"

"Nearby."

"Did you ever speak to her?"

"Not until the morning that Mr. King died."

"Did you vet all of the invitees to the party?"

"Yes."

"Did you search them for weapons or drugs?"

"No."

"You weren't concerned that somebody may have been armed or brought drugs?"

"Except for your client, everybody worked for Y5K and its venture capital firm, or they were business associates or friends of Mr. Patel and Ms. Chu."

"Did you search Ms. Low?"

"Mr. King had instructed me not to do so."

"You didn't see her bring heroin into the house, right?"

"Her arrangement with Mr. King stipulated that she would bring controlled substances."

"Says who?"

"Mr. King."

Who is dead.

He added, "I am prepared to testify that Mr. King and Ms. Low had agreed that Ms. Low would provide recreational drugs."

That wouldn't help. "Are you also prepared to testify that you saw her bring heroin into Mr. King's house?"

"No."

That would help a little. "Ms. Low told us that Mr. King provided the heroin."

"She didn't tell you the truth."

"A billionaire agreed to be injected with smack that somebody bought on the street?"

"I don't know where she got it."

"That would have been reckless behavior by Mr. King."

"I agree."

"With all due respect, Mr. Ben-Shalom, I find it hard to believe that a rich man like Jeff King didn't provide his own high-end drugs."

"With all due respect, Mr. Daley, I can assure you that he did not."

With all due respect, you don't want to admit that your boss was guilty of multiple felonies by purchasing smack for himself. "How were Mr. King and Ms. Low getting along?"

"Poorly. Ms. Low's behavior had become erratic. As a result, Mr. King had threatened to terminate their relationship. Ms. Low was very upset about it."

"She still came to the party."

"They had agreed to a tentative reconciliation."

"What happened after the guests left?"

His description was consistent with the police report. An agitated Lexy came running downstairs, clothes disheveled. Ben-Shalom prevented her from leaving the house. He took her back upstairs, where he found a motionless King. He called nine-one-one and administered CPR. The police and EMTs arrived within minutes. They couldn't revive King.

"It must have been terrible," I said.

"It was." He said that he called Steele, Patel, and King's wife from the hospital. "Those were very difficult calls."

"Mr. King wasn't a popular guy in the Valley."

"Steve Jobs rubbed a lot of people the wrong way, too."

"Was anybody at the party upset with Mr. King?"

"Just your client." He stood up. "Anything else, Mr. Daley?"

"I'd like to talk to Mr. Steele."

"He's very busy."

"Please inform him that it will be easier to talk in his office than in court."

"I'll pass along the message." His steely eyes narrowed. "Just so we're clear, your client provided heroin to Mr. King on multiple occasions, including the morning that he died. She was very upset after he threatened to terminate their relationship. As a result, I believe that she decided to give him a lethal shot of heroin, take his money, and run. And if you put me on the stand, that's exactly what I intend to say."

* * *

"What are you reading?" I asked.

Nady was at her desk at seven-thirty the same evening. Luna was sleeping in the corner. "Jerry Edwards."

"What's on the mind of the *Chronicle*'s finest?"

"Us." She closed her laptop. "He thinks Lexy is going to be convicted."

"He always says that."

"Is he ever right?"

"Occasionally."

"Is he right this time?"

"No."

Luna sat up, yawned, and shook her head in disagreement.

Nady eyed me. "Did you get anything useful from Ben-Shalom?"

"Not much." I filled her in. "Were you able to reach any of the women from the party?"

"All of them." She confirmed that they were, in fact, a who's-who of female entrepreneurs and engineers in the Valley. "All very impressive."

"Why did they go to the party?"

"They were more interested in meeting Patel than King. A couple were looking for funding. They were unanimous that King was a pig."

"Sounds like they were looking to use King and Patel for their own purposes."

"Seems it's accepted practice for people in the Valley to use each other."

"Anything we can use at trial?"

"Doubtful. Nobody said anything bad about King. Supposedly, he was the perfect host."

"Put them on our witness list in case something comes up. How are you coming on pre-trial motions?"

"Almost done. I'm cautiously optimistic that Judge McDaniel won't allow any mention of Flynn's death. I don't think she'll exclude testimony from Khalil Jones about selling smack to Lexy. We should talk to him to see if he'll be credible."

"He's looking to cut a deal. He'll say whatever the D.A. wants him to say. Who else is on the prosecution's witness list?"

"Officer Dito, Ben-Shalom, Dr. Siu, and Inspector Lee. Ours will include everybody at the house that night, our medical expert, Chloe, and Kaela Joy."

"Add Nick the Dick," I said. "We may not call on him to testify, but it will get Harper's attention. And be sure to include Lexy."

She looked up. "Are you really going to have her testify?"

"Not unless we're desperate."

"And you're still planning to accuse everybody at the house of murder?"

"If I have to."

"Do you have anything resembling proof?"

"We still have three weeks."

She chuckled. "Maybe Edwards was right. Any good news?"

"I got a message from Ben-Shalom. Steele agreed to see me."

"Why the change of heart?"

I smiled. "I presume that he wants to apologize for avoiding me for three weeks."

In the corner, Luna shook her head.

38
"SENIOR VICE PRESIDENT OF CORPORATE MESSAGING"

The woman with the bottle-blonde hair and botoxed forehead greeted me at the security desk on the Page Mill Road side of the Y5K campus. She extended a hand and flashed a practiced smile. "Jennifer Castle. You can call me Jen."

"Michael Daley. You can call me Mike."

She was costumed as a Steve Jobs clone in jeans and a black top. Notwithstanding the efforts of a competent hair dresser and an artful plastic surgeon, I surmised that she was close to my age.

"I understand that you met with Mr. Ben-Shalom," she said.

"I did." *He told me nothing.* "I'm looking forward to meeting Mr. Steele."

The fake smile disappeared. "I'm afraid there has been a slight change of plans. Mr. Steele was called overseas on an emergency. I don't know when he'll be back, so he asked me to talk to you."

Not what I had in mind. "I still need to talk to him."

"I'll let him know." Her smile reappeared. "Please come with me."

She led me on a circuitous trek through three inter-connected buildings where hundreds of youthful programmers were hunched over laptops in hangar-like rooms adjacent to stocked kitchens, ping pong tables, and yoga rooms. A full ten minutes later, we arrived at her office overlooking the parking lot of the law firm next door. It was barely large enough to squeeze in a standing desk, a leather chair, and a file cabinet. If she wanted to meet with more than one person, she had to reserve one of the conference rooms named after the company's venture capitalists.

I took a seat in the chair opposite her desk and started with a softball. "I take it that you work with Mr. Steele?"

"Yes. My title is Senior Vice President of Corporate Messaging."

Does this make you a flack or a shill? "Thanks for taking the time to see me."

"My pleasure."

We'll see. "I'm very sorry about your loss."

"You mean Jeff King?"

"Yes."

"Oh. Thank you."

Not exactly overcome with grief. I pointed at the only personal item in her office: the framed high school graduation photo of a young woman. "Daughter?"

"Granddaughter."

Yup, you're definitely as old as I am. "How long have you worked here?"

"Since Jeff formed the company." She explained that she had worked Hewlett-Packard and Oracle. "I was getting burned out at big companies, so I decided to roll the dice at a startup."

Must have felt like you had won the lottery—until King turned up dead.

Her expression turned serious. "How can I help you, Mr. Daley?"

Well, you see, I really wanted to talk to your boss, who has been ignoring me for weeks. After he finally condescended to give me an audience, he fled the country before we could talk. So he sent you in his place. "I'm representing Alexa Low."

"I know."

"I'm looking for information about Jeff King. You must have known him pretty well."

"I did."

Did he ever hit on you? "There's been speculation in the press that the investment bankers may postpone the IPO."

"You shouldn't believe everything you read in the papers."

And I shouldn't believe everything I'm told by a corporate mouthpiece, either. "What was it like working for Mr. King?"

"Exhilarating. Honestly, I think he could see the future."

Oh, please. "I understand that he wasn't the most popular guy in Silicon Valley."

"Neither was Steve Jobs."

"And he wasn't the most popular guy here at Y5K."

"He was tough, but fair."

She spent the next ten minutes responding to my questions with overworked corporate clichés. King was on a mission to bring the world together. If everybody used Y5K's software, their lives would be not just meaningful, but fulfilling. There were the usual mentions of cutting-edge technology and fostering greater understanding among disparate cultures. She left out any mention of trying to make billions or getting their venture capitalists a whopping return.

I tried to segue into more relevant matters. "How did the board and other members of management get along with Mr. King?"

"Fine."

"I understand that he and Mr. Steele didn't always see eye-to-eye."

"It isn't unusual for brilliant people to disagree from time to time. They believed that a certain amount of conflict was healthy. They were always on the same page on major issues."

"Is Mr. Steele going to stay with the company?"

"Absolutely."

"I understand that his daughter worked here."

"She interned here last summer. She's very bright."

"Is she coming back for a permanent position?"

"Nobody's mentioned it to me."

"Mr. Patel told us that several women filed complaints against Mr. King for inappropriate behavior."

"Personnel matters are confidential, Mr. Daley."

"Not anymore, Ms. Castle. Mr. King's death means that we can look into such issues in connection with a criminal investigation." It was a stretch, but I wanted to see how she would react.

"I can't comment on personnel matters."

"It will be easier if you answer my questions now rather than at a deposition or in court."

"I am not aware of any official claims filed against Mr. King."

"Who would know for sure?"

"You'll have to discuss it with our lawyers."

Who would assert the attorney-client privilege. "Did you know that Mr. King met my client through a hookup site called Mature Relations?"

"So I've read."

"Did it bother you that he was pursuing young women online?"

"It was none of my business."

"What about Mr. Steele? Have any complaints been filed against him?"

"I just told you that I'm not allowed to discuss personnel matters."

"You just did."

"About Mr. King, who is deceased. Mr. Steele is alive."

And conveniently out of the country.

She added, "I hope you aren't suggesting that Mr. Steele had anything to do with Jeff's death. Mr. Steele is a man of great integrity and character."

You might have a different view when you find out that he was also hooking up with women through Mature Relations. "I still need to talk to him."

"I'll see what I can do."

"I'd also like to talk to your Chief Technology Officer, Alejandro Sanchez, your Marketing Director, Tristan Moore, and your Director of Quality Control, Drew Pitt."

"I'll see what I can do."

That seems to be your go-to non-answer. I handed her a card. "Please inform them that we have included their names on our witness list."

"I'll have my assistant escort you to reception." The phony grin made a final appearance. "Thank you very much for coming in, Mike."

"Thank you for your time, Jen." *And for wasting mine.*

* * *

"How did it go with Steele?" Pete asked.

"It didn't." I was sitting in my car in the Y5K parking lot, my phone pressed to my ear. "He had to leave the country, so he sent his PR person to give me a bunch of corporate doubletalk."

"Steele never had any intention of talking to you, Mick. He's trying to run out the clock, so you won't have a chance to interview him before trial."

"Then I'll have to interview him in court."

"How soon can you get over to Printers Café near the California Street train station?"

"Ten minutes."

"I found the sales guy, Tristan Moore."

39
"HE HAD A GIFT FOR GETTING PEOPLE TO PART WITH THEIR MONEY"

Pete was sitting at a table in the corner of the cheerful café with maple tables and chairs. I walked across the room filled with young people staring at their phones and took a seat next to him.

He pushed a cup of free-trade organic coffee to me and nodded at the meticulously groomed young man sitting across from us. "This is Tristan."

"Mike Daley." I knew better than to ask how my brother had managed to find the head of sales at Y5K at a local coffee shop. I also recognized him as Christina Chu's fiancé from the photo in her office. *Small world.*

He looked up from his iPhone. "Nice to meet you."

His clear blue eyes matched his designer polo shirt. His flaming red hair was cropped into a buzz cut accessorized by a tidy goatee. He looked to be about thirty, but his pronounced widow's peak suggested that he could have been older. We exchanged stilted introductions. He lived in Menlo Park, was addicted to cross-fit, and had worked at Y5K for two years after shorter stints at a half-dozen startups, the names of which I did not recognize. He didn't mention Chu's name. I listened intently as his eyes darted between his iPhone and me.

I played it straight. "I trust that Pete has explained that I'm representing Alexa Low?"

"He has. I have been instructed by our board and our lawyers not to talk about it."

"It'll be easier here than in court."

He glanced at his phone again. "I'm meeting somebody in a few minutes."

"This will take just a moment." *Or two.* "I just talked to Jennifer Castle."

"She's very good."

"Yes, she is." *We talked for almost an hour, and she said nothing.*

He repeatedly looked at the door—as if hoping that somebody

would rescue him. His demeanor was professional, his tone engaging, but there was a hint of nervousness in his voice. "Did she tell you anything?"

No. "I understand that you've been named acting CEO. Sounds like you're stepping into a lot of stress."

"It was stressful before the situation with Jeff. Now it's insane."

Maybe that's why you're hiding here. "How long did you know Mr. King?"

"About five years. He recruited me to Y5K about two years ago."

This calls for a little flattery. "He must have thought very highly of you."

"He did."

Seems you think even more highly of yourself. "You must have spent a lot of time with him."

"I did."

"He's been described as a visionary."

"He had a gift for getting people to part with their money."

A little chillier than I had anticipated. "Jennifer told me that your product is going to revolutionize e-commerce."

"It is."

"Is the IPO still on?"

"Absolutely. Our company is about our product, not one person."

Sure. "I saw your photo in Ms. Chu's office."

He looked up from his phone. "We're engaged."

"Best wishes."

"Thank you."

"Her firm will do well if the IPO moves forward. I presume she'll get a bonus?"

"Presumably."

"You, too?"

"Hopefully."

"You were at Mr. King's house on the night that he died."

"My lawyer said that I shouldn't talk about it."

I would have given you the same advice. "I can't imagine that you have anything to hide."

"I don't."

"Why did you hire a lawyer?"

"I use him for personal legal issues from time to time."

"Had you attended other parties at Mr. King's house?"

"A few. They were pretty tame."

"Drug use?"

"I never saw it."

"Was anybody using heroin or other drugs on the night that Mr. King died?"

"I didn't see anything."

Neither did anybody else. "Did you know about Mr. King's relationship with my client?"

"Yes."

"Did you know that it involved consensual sex and the use of heroin?"

"He didn't provide any details."

"Had you ever met her?"

"No."

"Did you know that she was coming to the party?"

"Yes. I saw her come in. I didn't see her again."

"We've been told that Mr. King provided the heroin."

"I wouldn't know."

"The cops think our client brought it."

"I wouldn't know."

"You think Mr. King accepted smack from a woman he met on a dating app?"

"He didn't always exercise outstanding judgment."

"Who else knew about his relationship with my client?"

"Everybody. He wasn't subtle. He had issues with sex."

Now that you mention it. "What kind?"

"He liked it—a lot. And he would do it with almost anybody—including women he met online. He was involved in a multi-partner relationship for a while. It didn't work out."

"You think he was a sex addict?"

"I'm a salesman, Mr. Daley, not a therapist."

"A lot has been written about the Valley's culture toward women."

"We don't have a monopoly on bad behavior. My dad is a partner at a big law firm in the City. They've had more sexual harassment claims than Y5K. I'm sure you've had issues at the P.D.'s Office from time to time."

We have. "Was anybody mad at King?"

"*Everybody* was mad at him. Jeff was my boss, my mentor, and, I guess, my friend. But he was also an egomaniac. If you want to work at a place like Y5K, you need to buy into the culture, or you'll get steamrolled. It isn't a good fit for everyone. And it isn't just Y5K. There are a lot of guys like Jeff in the Valley."

He was more forthcoming than I had anticipated. "Sounds like a tough place to work."

"It is. Everybody had problems with Jeff. Jack Steele couldn't stand him. Neither could Alejandro Sanchez. Gopal Patel barely spoke to him. Hell, his own security guy hated him. Even his pal, Drew Pitt, got tired of it. We put up with it for one reason: money. Everybody was going to make millions—and in Jeff's case, maybe billions. Bottom line: nobody was going to jeopardize the IPO."

"Other than your fiancée, the women at the party didn't have a financial interest in the IPO."

"You want to try to blame this on the other women? They aren't hookers, Mr. Daley. They're some of the most talented entrepreneurs in the Valley."

"Why did they go to a make-out party at King's house?"

"Because that's how you make contacts in the Valley."

"It's demeaning."

"It's the Valley."

"King was my client's only source of support. Why would she have killed him?"

"Maybe it was an accident. Maybe he threatened to dump her. Or maybe he said something offensive to her—it wouldn't have been out of character." He glanced at his watch. "I gotta run. I'm supposed to meet somebody."

* * *

Pete picked at a gluten-free blueberry muffin. "These things have no taste."

I took a sip of my second cup of coffee. "How did you find Moore?"

"It wasn't hard."

"Where did he go?"

"Maybe he's looking for a new job."

"Seriously?"

"The company is in play. So are the employees. Maybe he's

hedging his bets if the IPO doesn't happen."

"His fiancée would never let him leave."

"Unless she thinks the IPO is cratering. Moore would be worth a lot to one of Y5K's competitors."

"He's probably subject to an iron-clad non-compete and non-disclosure agreement."

"Grow up, Mick. People down here change jobs more often than I change socks. By the time the lawsuits are resolved, Moore will be working someplace else."

True enough. "What did you think of him?"

"He was more honest than I thought. And he wasn't shy about throwing everybody else on the management team under the bus."

"You think he spiked the heroin?"

"And risk giving up millions and destroying the IPO that's going to make his fiancée's career?" He pushed back his chair.

"Where you going?" I asked.

"To find the tech guy, Alejandro Sanchez."

40
"HE BARELY KNEW HOW TO TURN ON HIS COMPUTER"

I glanced at my watch. One-thirty a.m. "You think he's going to show?"

"Be patient," Pete said. "My sources tell me that he comes in at this time every night."

More accurately, every morning. "This place makes Big John's saloon look like the Top of the Mark."

Pete sipped his coffee. "I took Big John to Tony's funeral. Tony left instructions for his family not to change a thing."

They had honored his wishes. Antonio's Nut House was the last dive bar in Palo Alto. Antonio "Tony" Montooth had opened his saloon six decades earlier, and it was among the last places in Silicon Valley where tech titans, blue collar workers, and Stanford students gathered to watch sports, drink beer, and eat burritos, pizza, and burgers. The ceiling tiles were emblazoned with ads that Tony had sold for five bucks a pop to the proprietors of long-closed neighborhood businesses. A handful of bras hung from the ceiling—the history of which had been lost to posterity. Customers with early-morning munchies helped themselves to peanuts from a box inside a cage enclosing a stuffed gorilla sporting a Cheshire cat grin and sunglasses. Mark Zuckerberg used to be a regular. The guy sitting next to him at the bar could have been a plumber who had just fixed a toilet at Facebook.

My lungs filled with the aroma of the peanut shells as Pete and I sat at a wobbly table beneath a faded sign reading, "I gave up drinking, smoking, and sex. It was the worst fifteen minutes of my life."

Pete glanced over my shoulder. "Here we go, Mick."

I tried to appear nonchalant as Alejandro Sanchez walked by us, took a seat by himself at the bar, pulled out his iPhone, and began texting. With his shoulder-length hair, t-shirt bearing the image of a heavy-metal band, and faded camouflage pants, he could have passed for a member of a grunge band. Without a word, the bartender handed him a beer.

Pete's mouth turned up. "Let's go make a new friend. Follow my lead."

As always.

We walked over to the bar, where we took the stools next to Sanchez. Pete ordered beers for us, then he turned to Sanchez and extended a hand. "Pete Daley."

"Alejandro Sanchez."

My brother flashed a friendly smile that would have made Big John proud. "Let me buy you that beer."

Sanchez's eyes toggled between his iPhone and Pete. He was somewhere north of thirty, a lanky six-three, with a pasty complexion with bags extending halfway down his cheeks. "You don't have to do that."

"I'd like to." Pete's phony smile broadened. "Y5K, right?"

"Uh-huh."

"I saw you on CNBC."

Sanchez sat up taller. "That was a few months ago."

"I'm in security. You developed some software that might be useful in my line of work."

He was now looking at Pete. "We have."

Pete corrected him. "According to the guy on CNBC, *you* have."

Sanchez feigned modesty. "I guess."

Pete gestured at me. "This is my brother, Mike."

"Nice to meet you."

"Same here."

Pete spoke up again. "You're here late."

"Busy."

"I trust that the IPO is still on?"

"Yes."

Pete cocked his head to the side. "Is there any doubt?"

"I'm not allowed to talk about it."

"You come in every night?"

"I live around the corner. This is the only place that stays open late."

Somewhere up there in that great heavenly dive bar, Antonio is smiling.

Pete was still going. "Helluva thing about Jeff King. How long did you know him?"

"Couple years."

"Good guy?"

"Complicated guy." He took a draw of his Bud. "He was good at identifying technology trends, but he couldn't write code. He barely knew how to turn on his computer."

"You wrote the Y5K program?"

"Most of it."

"So the guy on CNBC was right: you're the genius."

"I won't disagree with you." There was more than a hint of bitterness in his voice.

Pete wanted to keep him talking. "Seems unfair that King got all the credit."

"Maybe a little."

"Did he acknowledge your value to the company?"

"I get paid reasonably well, but he wasn't big on positive reinforcement."

"Was he difficult to work with?"

"For."

"Excuse me?"

"Nobody worked 'with' Jeff. We all worked 'for' him. Either you made him look good, or you found another job."

We exchanged stilted small talk for a few minutes. At two a.m., the bartender announced last call. I bought another round. Then I decided to play it straight. I handed him a card. "I'm representing Lexy Low."

He tensed. "The company's lawyers told us not to talk to anybody."

"I'd like to ask you a few questions. I can't imagine that you have anything to hide."

"I don't."

"It'll be easier to do this over a beer than in court."

He fingered his mug. "You probably know more about what happened than I do."

That much could be true.

He took a gulp of beer. "Jeff threw a party for some of us who were working on the IPO. Christina Chu invited some women. We ate burritos, drank beer, and smoked some weed. Some people may have been doing other stuff. It broke up early."

"Did you see my client?"

"Might have. I don't even know what she looks like."

"Did you know that Mr. King and my client met on a sugar daddy site?"

"No, but it didn't surprise me. Except for Chloe, I never saw him with the same woman more than once."

I glanced at Pete, who took the cue.

"Alejandro, did you notice anything out of the ordinary that night?"

"No."

"Did you see our client go upstairs?"

"No."

"Did you go upstairs?"

"I don't remember. I might have."

Yes, you did.

Pete kept his tone even. "You'd been to other parties at King's house?"

"A few."

"Did you ever see anybody doing drugs?"

"Could have been."

"Did King provide the stuff?"

"I never asked."

I spoke up again. "The D.A. thinks our client provided the heroin. Do you think he would have taken drugs provided by a woman he met online?"

"Jeff did some reckless stuff."

"Was anybody angry at him?"

"He treated everybody like crap, including me. He was worse to Jack, Gopal, and Tristan."

"Is there anybody else who can tell us more about King?"

"Drew Pitt. He and Jeff were friends since they were kids."

The "Guy from Rye." "I understand that he works for the company."

He laughed. "He's more of a consultant."

Right. "What exactly does he do?"

"Nobody knows."

* * *

"Sanchez didn't say much," I observed.

Pete's eyes gleamed. "Enough for us to know that he's bitter, and he'll be a nervous witness. It doesn't guarantee an acquittal, but you can use it to your advantage."

We were sitting at a table under the battered awning outside the Nut House at two-fifteen a.m. A red light from a Budweiser sign in the window reflected in Pete's eyes.

"Did you find out where Moore went after he ditched us?" I asked.

"He met with a guy from another startup. Seems he's already looking for a new job in case the IPO craters."

"That won't sit well with his colleagues at Y5K or his fiancée."

"All's fair in Silicon Valley." He zipped up his bomber jacket. "Go home and get some rest, Mick."

"Where are you going?"

"To find the 'Guy from Rye.'"

41
THE "GUY FROM RYE"

"You sure it's Pitt?" I asked.

"Yeah." Pete looked out the picture window and pointed at the Olympic-size pool at the Bay Club in Redwood Shores, a ten-minute drive up 101 from Palo Alto. "He's swimming."

It had taken Pete four days to track down the elusive "Guy from Rye." At nine p.m. on Wednesday, January twenty-third, we were nursing coffees in the café in the high-end health club wedged between the 101 Freeway and the bay. Like its cousin at the foot of Telegraph Hill, it was a place where attractive people worked out, were seen, and made connections. Pete had slipped a hundred bucks to the kid at the front desk, and two guest passes had materialized. As a longtime member of the Embarcadero Y, the Bay Club was a little too upscale for my taste.

I looked at Pete, who was watching the Warriors' post-game show. "What's the plan?"

"We wait." He used his index finger to gesture. "The pool is there. The locker room is there. The door is there. The only way from Point A to Point B to Point C is walking past us."

We sat for fifteen minutes in the otherwise empty cafe. Silicon Valley has an early-to-bed, early-to-rise culture. Pete watched TV and checked his texts. I watched Pitt and checked my e-mails.

At ten o'clock, Pitt emerged from the pool and headed into the locker room. Twenty minutes later, he trudged through the café, a Nike bag in his hand, an iPhone pressed to his ear. He went to the fridge and took one of those ten-dollar-a-bottle detox juices that taste terrible.

Pete put his phone on the table. "We're on, Mick."

As Pitt approached us, I gave him a friendly wave. "Hi, Drew."

"Uh, hi."

He was late forties, stocky, tanned. His slick hair was jet black—with help from a bottle. Perspiration soaked through a lime polo shirt and khaki pants—not an especially flattering look.

I extended a hand. "Mike Daley. This is my brother, Pete."

"Uh, yeah." He ended his call and took a seat. "El Camino Software? Sprockets?"

"Afraid not, Drew. I work for the San Francisco Public Defender's Office. Pete works security. I'm representing Lexy Low. We'd like to ask you a few questions about Jeff King."

"I gave my statement to the police."

"I know." *That's true.* "I've read it." *That's false.*

"Then you know that I didn't see or hear anything that night."

"That's what we understand."

His voice filled with relief. "There's nothing else I can tell you."

Sure there is. "We're just trying to confirm what happened."

"My lawyer said that I shouldn't talk to anybody other than the cops."

That's good advice. "He also probably told you that we can send you a subpoena if your name appears on our witness list, which, by the way, it does."

His Adam's apple bobbed. "He didn't."

"If you can confirm a few items, we won't need to bother you again."

He waited a beat. "Okay."

I'm glad—because it's a lie. "What time did you arrive at King's house?"

"Around nine-twenty."

"Were you by yourself?"

"No, I was with Tristan Moore."

"We talked to him. Nice guy."

"Right."

His tone suggested that he and Moore weren't pals. "He told us that people were eating burritos and doing smack."

"The part about the burritos is true. I don't know anything about the rest of it."

I asked him who was there.

He rattled off the names that we already knew: King, Steele, Patel, Chu, Moore, Sanchez, Ben-Shalom, and, of course, Lexy. "There was a parking valet and a guy who delivered the food."

"I understand that there were also some other women."

"They were friends of Christina's."

"Did any of the women go home with the men?"

"I don't know."

"Did you know that Mr. King had met my client through an app called Mature Relations?"

"Yes. Jeff had an unhappy marriage. He didn't have time to go to bars or meet women at health clubs."

"You knew that they got together for sex?"

"Wouldn't surprise me."

"And to consume heroin?"

"I wasn't aware of that."

Of course not. "We understand that Mr. King always provided the heroin."

"That's impossible."

"You really think a billionaire took heroin that somebody bought on the street?"

"He made some bad decisions."

"Was anybody at the party behaving unusually?"

"No. It broke up early and everybody went home."

"Except our client."

"Right."

"We understand that Mr. King always left the heroin in the bathroom upstairs."

"Your client brought the heroin."

"Did you go upstairs?"

"Yes. And if you're suggesting that I planted it, this conversation is over."

"I'm not suggesting anything." *Well, maybe.*

Pete finally made his presence felt. "What do you do at Y5K?"

He grinned. "I make sure that our software does what it's supposed to do."

"Mr. Moore told us that you rarely come to the office."

"I work remotely."

"Are you compensated well?"

"Reasonably."

"You think you deserve more?"

"As a matter of fact, I do."

"Did you ever bring it up with Mr. King?"

"I did. Unfortunately, he passed away before he could take it up with the board."

"I understand that Y5K is a tough place to work."

"Working for a startup is demanding. For every Y5K, there are a thousand companies that fail within the first six months."

"I understand that Jeff wasn't always an easy guy to work for."

"He never asked anybody to do anything that he wouldn't have done himself."

"We've been told that many people at the company didn't like him."

"Jack Steele thought he talked too much and treated our employees poorly. Alejandro Sanchez resented the fact that Jeff got credit for code that Alejandro wrote. Tristan didn't think he got enough credit for building our customer base. Gopal got tired of smoothing things over with the investors."

"Sounds like he lacked judgment and self-control."

"I think they were jealous of Jeff's success. I could name a hundred other successful CEOs who had similar issues."

"Do you think anybody was angry enough that they might have been tempted to slip him a hot shot of heroin?"

He picked up his gym bag. "I could give you a thousand reasons why everybody had reason to be pissed off at Jeff. But nobody would have put the IPO at risk."

* * *

Big John placed a pint of Guinness down in front of me. "You don't look happy, Mikey."

Dunleavy's was quiet at midnight. "Long day, Big John."

He gave Pete a mug of Folgers. "You got this figured out, Petey?"

"Not yet."

My uncle turned back to me. "Anything useful from the 'Guy from Rye'?"

"Not much. We'll put him on the stand to testify that everybody at the party hated King."

"Sounds a bit thin."

"It is."

Pete set down his mug. "We're in serious trouble if that's the best that we can do."

"We have another week and a half until the trial starts," I said.

"Yeah." His iPhone vibrated. He read a text. "We need to get down to Chloe King's house in Palo Alto."

42
"DIDN'T SEE THAT COMING"

"Who's your source?" I asked.

Pete shook his head. "Can't talk about it, Mick."

"What's going on?"

"Maybe nothing."

At five-thirty on Thursday morning, he was hunkered down behind the wheel of his Crown Vic, a Giants cap pulled low. I was in the passenger seat. For the past four hours, we'd been parked across the street from Chloe's house in the quiet St. Claire Gardens neighborhood between El Camino Real and the 101 Freeway. Not a single car had driven by us.

Pete pointed at the cast-iron fence surrounding the McMansion that Jeff and Chloe had built after tearing down houses on four contiguous lots. The three-story, ten-thousand-square foot estate towered over the neighboring ranch houses. "I can't believe Palo Alto let them put up that monstrosity."

"Are you going to tell me why we're here?"

"My source told me to keep an eye on Chloe's house."

"We've been keeping an eye on it for the past four hours."

"Be patient." He pointed at the rear-view mirror. "That BMW M760i parked inside the gate cost almost two hundred grand."

"Chloe can afford it."

"I don't think it's hers."

"You didn't run the plate?"

"There is none, Mick. It's brand new."

"What about the VIN?"

"You want me to jump the gate of a house with security cameras and armed guards and snap a picture of the VIN with my iPhone?"

"I have a better plan. We wait to see who gets into the car."

"Good thinking, Mick."

"Does this mean that Chloe is having an affair?"

"Not sure if it qualifies as an affair since her husband is dead."

Technically, I guess that's true. We sat in silence for another hour.

The sky brightened at seven o'clock, and the sun peeked over the horizon at seven-twenty. A garbage truck rumbled by us. A Lexus pulled out of the driveway of the house next door to Chloe's. At seven-forty, the mechanical gates to the King compound finally opened.

Pete tensed. "Here we go."

The BMW backed out of the driveway, and the gate closed behind it. Pete used his iPhone to take video as the car sped by us. I couldn't see who was inside.

Pete ran the video in slow motion. "Didn't see that coming." He passed the phone over to me. "Look familiar?"

It was Tristan Moore. "This isn't going to play well at Y5K."

"Or at Patel Ventures. His fiancée is going to be unhappy. And you can add Moore's name to the list of options for your SODDI defense."

I looked at my younger brother. "This is good work, Pete."

"Thanks."

"So, who's your source?"

He turned on the ignition. "I told you that I can't talk about it."

"This stays between us. Nick the Dick?"

"No."

"Kaela Joy?"

"Maybe."

"She works for Chloe."

"Not anymore. They had a falling out."

"About what?"

"Overdue bills."

"Chloe has plenty of money."

"Evidently, she doesn't like to share it with her service providers."

"How'd you get Kaela Joy to talk?"

"Professional courtesy. I gave her information about another guy she's tailing. Want something, give something."

"Doesn't that violate some ethical obligation to keep her client's secrets confidential?"

"There's no privilege between a P.I. and an ex-client. Besides, you don't know Kaela Joy as well as I do. She cares more about the truth than collecting a fee."

"The same is true about you."

43
"IT DOESN'T GET A JURY TO REASONABLE DOUBT"

Rosie studied the video on my iPhone. "Moore is having a roll with King's widow?"

"So it seems."

Rosie, Nady, and I were meeting in Rosie's office at ten-thirty the same morning. I was operating without sleep. My head ached, my throat was sore, and my stomach was filled with acid. My foul mood was exacerbated by the fact that the heater was having one of its occasional spasms and blasting ninety-degree air. The City had promised to send over a team to tame the beast in a few days.

Rosie returned my phone. "How are you going to authenticate this in court?"

"Pete."

"Your brother is going to be your star witness?"

"His testimony will be brief."

"The jurors will connect the dots and conclude that Moore and Chloe were having an affair, which is interesting. It also fits nicely within your storyline that everybody at Y5K was engaged in sexual escapades—some more creative than others. But it doesn't prove that Moore spiked the heroin."

"It gives us another option. And it demonstrates that he's slime."

"So was everybody else at the party, including the victim, and, arguably, our client."

"He was cheating on his fiancée with his boss' widow. Jurors don't like cheaters."

"King and Chloe were already separated."

"Doesn't matter."

"It doesn't get a jury to reasonable doubt. Are you still planning to go to trial a week from Monday?"

"Yes. Our client has instructed us to move forward. Our pre-trial motions are submitted. We should receive the D.A.'s final witness list in the next day or two."

"Any new additions?"

"None. I've added Pete and Brian Holton to ours."

"The CEO of Mature Relations?"

"He's a straight shooter. And he can testify that King, Steele, Patel, and Pitt were all members of Mature Relations."

"Quite the exclusive club. Any chance of pleading this out for manslaughter?"

"At the moment, no. Ward has instructed Harper to go all-in on murder."

"Is the judge going to give instructions for manslaughter?"

"She hasn't decided."

In a first-degree murder case, the judge is obligated to instruct the jury that it may also convict for second-degree if the facts warrant. The judge is not required to instruct on manslaughter, but may elect to do so. It's a double-edged sword for the defense. Manslaughter carries a shorter sentence, but it gives the jury an easier route to a compromise conviction on the lesser charge.

Rosie considered our options. "Are you going to ask for a manslaughter instruction?"

"No."

"You're going all-or-nothing on murder, too?"

"For now. The judge doesn't have to make the final call until closing arguments."

"You'd get a substantially reduced sentence for manslaughter."

"I don't think Harper can prove murder beyond a reasonable doubt. If I'm right, Lexy will walk."

Rosie thought about it for a long moment. "I think I'd end up in the same place."

Good to know.

"What's the latest version of the narrative?" she asked.

"If there's no manslaughter instruction, we'll argue that there was no premeditation or malicious intent. In fact, King *asked* to be injected. Our medical expert will testify that King's heart condition made him susceptible to accidental death. If one juror buys it, we're done."

"And the SODDI defense?"

"That comes next. Everybody at the party detested King. And they seem willing to point fingers at everybody else. It's like *Game of*

Thrones—Silicon Valley."

"Do you have a favorite?"

"Moore was having an affair with King's wife. Patel comes in second because he's a jilted lover. Steele and Sanchez are next because King treated them like crap. Ben-Shalom is a wildcard. He couldn't stand King, either. The 'Guy from Rye' is a dark horse."

"You should ask him if he provided the heroin."

"I did. He denied it."

Rosie smiled. "Ask him again in court—just for fun."

At least somebody still has a sense of humor.

She asked, "How are you planning to handle the fact that Lexy bought heroin earlier that night?"

"I'll get Khalil Jones to admit that he's cutting a deal with the D.A. to get his sentence reduced. More important, the D.A. won't be able to prove that the heroin Jones sold to Lexy was the same stuff that she gave to King."

"And if that isn't enough?"

"We'll put Lexy on the stand to testify that King always provided the smack when they got together. And that King was her only source of support and it would have been crazy for her to have killed him—even by accident."

"You'd be playing with fire. How is she holding up?"

"Not great. You remember how it was with Theresa. It may be easier to get an acquittal than to get her off heroin."

"One day at a time."

I turned to Nady. "Could you ping Harper and ask him if he has any final additions to his witness list?"

"Yes. We're also meeting with our medical expert later today."

"Good. I want you to handle his direct exam."

"I'll be ready. Have you heard anything from Steele?"

"I've left more messages. He's ignoring me."

"How can we get his attention?"

"I'll send him another e-mail reminding him that he's on our witness list and he'll need to appear in court. I will also tell him that we've added his daughter to our witness list."

"We have?"

"As soon as you add her name. *That* will get his attention."

"Notifying her father isn't enough to compel her to testify. We'd still have to serve her with a subpoena—which means we'll have to find her."

"Pete will."

"How do you know?"

"Because he always does."

"I'll prepare a subpoena for her. Where are you off to now?"

"To talk to Jones's attorney."

44
"HIS TESTIMONY WILL NOT HELP YOUR CLIENT"

The veteran defense attorney smiled. "Kids okay, Mike?"

"Fine, Sandy. Yours?"

"All good."

Sandy Tran was a petite woman in her late forties who had started her career at the P.D.'s Office. Rosie always said she was the quickest study and the most tenacious attorney she'd ever known. After she was passed over for a promotion to head the Felony Division in an example of office politics run amuck and not-so-subtle misogyny, she opened her own firm. Nowadays, she was San Francisco's go-to attorney for accused drug dealers.

I looked around her cluttered office above a dry cleaner in the Tenderloin. Every inch of space was filled with file folders, trial exhibits, and storage boxes. "You still seeing the guy from the City Attorney's Office?" I asked.

"On occasion." She adjusted the sleeve of her flannel shirt. "Coordinating schedules of two single parents with five kids is complicated. You still okay working with Rosie?"

"We've always been good at working together."

"Why don't you drop the charade and get married again?"

"We're more married than most married people."

"You going to answer my question?"

"We get along better when we aren't married. We're trying not to jinx it."

"My daughter showed me Grace's app. How do you feel about the Love Goddess?"

"I'm not crazy about it, but I have little control over her."

"And Rosie?"

"Dealing with it."

"Kids are complicated."

"Life is complicated."

She leaned back and laughed heartily. "And how are things with

Sexy Lexy?"

"Challenging."

"For a guy who supposedly stopped trying cases two years ago, you seem to have picked up another heater. Jerry Edwards says she's going to be convicted of first-degree murder."

"He doesn't know what he's talking about."

"If you cut a deal for involuntary manslaughter, she'll be out before she's thirty."

"Nicole won't go for it."

"She's a TV lawyer. You need to talk to DeSean."

"I did. Nicole is calling the shots. It's an election year."

Her expression turned serious. "Why did you want to see me, Mike?"

"I need to talk to your client."

She pointed at a white board filled with a hand-printed list of five dozen active cases. "Take your pick."

"Khalil Jones."

"Pick again."

"I really need to talk to Jones."

"I can't let you do it."

"He's on our witness list."

"And the prosecution's. I'm not letting DeSean talk to him, either."

"Can I talk to him off the record?"

"No such thing."

"Professional courtesy?"

"Not this time."

I had to grovel. "Please?"

"No." She absent-mindedly twirled a few strands of her hair around her finger. "Come on, Mike. You've been to this movie more times than I have."

"You're in the middle of negotiating a plea bargain?"

"Possibly."

"And you don't want him to talk to anybody until the deal is in place?"

"Could be." She held up a hand. "We're at a delicate point in our discussions, so I'm doing all the talking."

"He's going to have to testify at Lexy's trial."

"He will. And he'll tell the truth. And if I can work out a deal, he'll be able to talk more freely because he won't have to worry about incriminating himself further. I can't tell you exactly what he'll say, but his testimony will not help your client."

"Is he credible?"

"In my judgment, yes. College educated. Intelligent. Practical."

"Why was he selling smack in front of the Sixteenth Street BART Station?"

"For the same reason that your client was sleeping with Jeff King: money."

"Will he testify that he sold heroin to Lexy?"

"It's the truth. And the cops have it on video."

"Will he testify that it was the same sort of high-end heroin that killed King?"

"He'll testify that it was good smack. That's also the truth. I don't see how he can offer any opinion as to whether it was the same stuff that killed King."

"Did he ever sell heroin to King?"

"You'll have to ask him in court." She arched an eyebrow. "If I were in your shoes, I'd talk to Harper again about cutting a deal for manslaughter."

* * *

Terrence the Terminator held up a hand as I was walking by his desk. He covered the mouthpiece of his phone. "Steele wants to talk to you. He sounds unhappy."

"I'll take it in my office." I walked inside, took off my jacket, and pressed the flashing button on my phone. "Michael Daley speaking."

"This is Jack Steele."

"Sorry that I missed you when you had to leave the country."

"Be at my office at eight o'clock tomorrow morning."

"I will. I trust you received my e-mail notifying you that we intend to call you as a witness at Ms. Low's trial next week?"

"I did. That's fine."

"I take it that you also saw that we plan to call your daughter?"

"I did. That isn't."

45
"NICE TO SEE YOU AGAIN"

Steele stood behind his immaculate desk, flashed an insincere smile, and tried to sound convincing. "Nice to see you again," he lied.

I did my best to feign sincerity. "Thank you for taking the time."

At eight o'clock the following morning, a Friday, the Y5K complex was already buzzing with midday energy. Steele had moved into King's office. His furnishings were minimal: an oak credenza, a leather love seat, and a round work table. His walls were lined with photos of himself with Silicon Valley players. The most prominent was a picture of a beaming Steele with a young Steve Jobs. There were no family photos.

The ever-present Yoav Ben-Shalom stood guard at the door. An imposing man standing next to him was sipping a Red Bull. He introduced himself as Robert "Don't Call Me Bob" Stumpf, Y5K's general counsel. Next to him was a hyperactive younger man who said his name was Lawrence "Don't Call Me Larry" Braun. He worked for the biggest law firm in Silicon Valley and was Y5K's lead outside counsel.

A towering man with a mane of silver hair, rugged features, and clear blue eyes was standing next to Steele. He handed me a card bearing the name of New York City's most prominent law firm. His voice had the intonation of a Boston Brahmin. "Chris Neils. I am Mr. Steele's personal attorney. I just flew in from the East Coast."

He had undoubtedly arrived in one of Y5K's private jets. "Mike Daley."

Steele sat down behind his desk, whereupon every member of his high-priced legal team dutifully took their seats. Ben-Shalom remained standing at the door—as if I was going to make a run for it.

Steele motioned me to the chair between the general counsel and the outside counsel. It wasn't easy to keep track of all the lawyers without a scorecard. "Please sit down, Mr. Daley."

"Perhaps we should move to a conference room."

"That won't be necessary. I thought it would be helpful to have our legal team here."

It was a heavy-handed attempt to try to intimidate me.

Steele pointed at Ben-Shalom, who shut the door. Then he templed his fingers in front of his face. "How can we help you, Mr. Daley?" He emphasized the word "we."

"I'd like to ask you a few questions about Jeff King."

"Happy to help. I have nothing to hide."

Maybe you do. "How are things here at work?"

"Busy. There's no Harvard Business School playbook for this situation. I am immensely proud of our people for their efforts after Jeff's untimely death."

And they're keeping your IPO on track. "It's fortuitous that you were available to step into Mr. King's role as chairman."

"There were several excellent options."

Your humble-brag needs work. "The IPO is still on?"

"Full speed ahead."

"Glad to hear it." *I couldn't care less.* "My client's trial starts a week from Monday."

"I'm well aware of that."

"Your name appears on the D.A.'s witness list."

"And yours."

True. "Has Mr. Harper talked to you about your testimony?"

"No. He simply asked me to be available. As I said, I have nothing to hide."

It's the second time you mentioned it.

His showed his first hint of impatience. "Why am I on *your* witness list?"

"Just a formality. We included everybody who was at Mr. King's house." *That's true.* "We probably won't need you to testify." *That's a white lie.* "If we do, it will take just a few minutes." *That's a real lie.* "Did you know that Mr. King and his wife had separated?"

"Yes."

"Did you know that he was seeing my client?"

"No."

I find that hard to believe. "Did you ever meet her?"

"No."

"Did you know that she was coming to Mr. King's house that night?"

"No."

"Did you see her?"

"I didn't even know what she looked like until I saw her picture in the paper."

"Did you know that Mr. King and Ms. Low met on a site called Mature Relations?"

"I do now."

"Do you know anybody else who has used that site?" *Other than you, Patel, and Pitt?*

"No."

His personal attorney finally spoke up. "Mr. Steele has given his statement to the police. He has nothing further to add at this time."

Sure he does. "If I can ask just a few more questions, we can probably remove Mr. Steele from our witness list." *That's a whopper.*

The dignified mouthpiece from the white-shoe firm nodded. "Please be brief."

"How was the party?" I asked Steele.

"Fine. It was low key. We had burritos and beer."

"Drugs?"

"Absolutely not."

"Did you know that Mr. King and Ms. Low always took heroin when they got together?"

"Jeff never mentioned it."

"Did Mr. King have an addiction issue?"

"Not as far as I could tell."

"Was Mr. King angry at Ms. Low? Or was she angry at Mr. King?"

"We never talked about it."

Deny. Deny. Deny. "Was anybody else angry at Mr. King?"

"Nothing out of the ordinary."

"I understand that Mr. King wasn't always easy to deal with."

"He was impatient at times."

"And his behavior toward women wasn't always exemplary."

The general counsel interjected. "It is against company policy for Mr. Steele to talk about personnel matters."

"Are *you* authorized?"

"Yes, but that information is privileged and strictly confidential."

We'll see. I pressed him for a moment, but he wouldn't budge. I turned back to Steele. "We understand that Mr. King and his wife had an open relationship."

"That's my understanding, too."

"At times, they were also involved in a multi-partner relationship known as polyfidelity."

He looked over at Neils, who answered for him. "I fail to see how this is even remotely relevant to your case."

"In a homicide investigation, everything about the decedent is relevant."

"The judge will never let you talk about it at trial."

We'll see about that, too. I turned back to Steele. "Were you aware that Mr. and Mrs. King were in a polyfidelitous relationship with Gopal Patel and his wife?"

His eyes darted toward his lawyer, then back to me. "What they did outside the office was none of my business and had no bearing on the company."

"The chairman and his wife were involved in a multi-party relationship with your venture capitalist and his wife. I would think that created some inherent conflicts of interest."

"It didn't."

"How did King and Patel get along?"

"They had a respectful and mutually beneficial business relationship."

"They never argued?"

"Jeff argued with everybody. This is a high-stress environment."

"Did you go upstairs during the party?"

"Briefly. To use the restroom."

"Did you see Ms. Low?"

"No." He stood up. "Anything else, Mr. Daley?

"We understand that your daughter interned at the company last summer."

"She did."

"We've tried to contact her, but we haven't been able to reach her."

"She's unavailable."

"We'd like to talk to her."

"She's skiing at Tahoe. And she has no relevant information."

She might. "She interacted with Mr. King."

"So did all of our interns."

"We'd really like to talk to her about her experience."

"No."

"It would be easier to do it informally than in court."

His eyes narrowed. "You have a daughter about the same age as Debbie, don't you?"

"Yes."

"How would you feel if a criminal defense attorney insisted on talking to her about something she knew nothing about?"

"Not great."

"Leave her alone."

"We included her on our witness list."

"Let me be absolutely clear. I will not allow her to testify."

Not your call. "We believe that she has relevant information about Mr. King."

Neils spoke up again. "You're crossing a line, Mr. Daley."

"You can't prevent us from talking to a legitimate witness."

"If this harassment doesn't stop immediately, we'll bring legal action. Mr. Ben-Shalom will show you out. This conversation is over."

It had lasted longer than I had expected.

* * *

I was driving past Serramonte Mall when I called Pete, who answered on the first ring. "How did it go with Steele?" he asked.

"About what you'd expect. I need you to find his daughter."

"I may need some help, Mick."

"Whatever it takes."

46
"WE NEED YOUR HELP"

"Are all of our exhibits loaded onto my laptop?" I asked.

"All set." Nady confirmed that our few items of low-tech evidence—charts, photos, and a diagram of King's house, were also ready to go.

"Any word on pretrial motions?"

"Judge McDaniel will let Jones testify about selling smack to Lexy, but she won't permit any testimony about Flynn's death."

It was what I had expected. "Any hint on whether she's inclined to give a manslaughter instruction?"

"Nothing."

A smart judge like Betsy McDaniel wouldn't show her cards until she had to. "Any final additions to Harper's witness list?"

"None."

I turned to Rosie, who was editing my opening statement. "Any update from your moles on the Flynn investigation?"

"If the D.A. had enough evidence to charge Lexy, they would have done so by now."

Another week had flown by. On Friday, February first, we were three days from the start of trial. Exhibits, file folders, police reports, and printouts covered the floor of our conference room. The white board was filled with the names of witnesses. The prosecution's list was on the left; ours on the right. Every few hours, we changed the order as we sharpened our story.

Rosie looked up again. "Is Harper still all-in on first-degree murder?"

"Yes."

"Have you reconsidered your decision not to ask for a manslaughter instruction?"

"No."

"Gutsy call, Mike."

"I learned it from you, Rosie."

Pete came inside, draped his bomber jacket over a chair, and took a seat. "You sure you want to do this, Mick?"

"Yeah. Is she here?"

"She's waiting outside."

Rosie took off her reading glasses. "Who?"

"Kaela Joy," I said. "We need more help." I quickly added, "I'm paying for it."

"I don't want to know."

"It's probably better that way." I turned back to Pete. "Please ask her to come inside."

* * *

Kaela Joy's golden locks were hidden by the same baseball cap that she was wearing when we had seen her at Red's. "You wanted to see me?"

"We want to hire you."

She pointed at Pete. "You already hired him."

"He's stretched a little thin. We need your help."

"You have competent investigators here in the office."

"We need somebody with intimate knowledge of Silicon Valley."

She folded her hands and waited.

"This is a short-term project," I said. "Lexy's trial starts Monday."

"Premium rates plus expenses."

"Fine. We need you to find Steele's daughter. Steele said that she's skiing at Tahoe, but Pete's people haven't been able to find her."

"She isn't skiing, and she isn't at Tahoe." Her eyes moved from me to Nady to Pete and then back to me. "In the Valley, 'skiing at Tahoe' is the current euphemism for rehab."

"Can you find her?"

"Do you have any idea how many rehab facilities are located in Northern California?"

"Dozens," I guessed.

"More. And it's possible that she has gone someplace out of the area." She turned to Pete. "We'll divide the list and start with high-end places."

"Sounds good."

She looked at me. "What do you want me to do if I find her?"

"Call me. And see if she'll talk to us."

"And if she won't?"

I hate my job. "I need you to serve her with a subpoena."

* * *

I was sitting in my office at ten o'clock on Friday night when my iPhone vibrated. I answered it and was greeted by Jerry Edwards' familiar smoker's hack.

"Evening, Mr. Daley."

"Evening, Jerry.

"My sources tell me that Khalil Jones has worked out a deal with the D.A. He'll plead guilty to one felony for sale of heroin in exchange for full cooperation on several other cases, including Sexy Lexy's. He will admit that he sold heroin to your client."

"That's news to me."

"I also have it on good authority that the D.A. is getting closer to charging Ms. Low with murder of Paul Flynn."

"I wasn't aware of that, either."

"I understand that you're working on a plea bargain for Sexy Lexy."

"I haven't heard a word about it from the D.A."

"If you can't work things out, I'll see you in court on Monday."

I ended the call and Nady came into my office.

"Harper wants to see us first thing tomorrow morning," she said.

47
"LAST CHANCE"

Harper was at his desk at nine o'clock the following morning. "Thanks for coming in on a Saturday."

Don't react. "Why did you want to see us, DeSean?"

His eyes shifted from me to Nady and then back to me. "Nicole has authorized me to make a final offer." He cleared his throat. "Second-degree murder with a recommendation of fifteen years. We won't pursue any drug or other charges." He waited a beat. "And we will not bring any charges in connection with the death of Paul Flynn."

"That's the same offer that you made before the prelim."

"It includes dropping all other charges."

"You would have done it anyway."

"And it includes my promise that we won't bring charges for Flynn."

Because you still don't have sufficient evidence. "You need to go down to manslaughter. I can't sell murder to my client."

"Can't do it."

"It isn't enough, DeSean. King exploited my client. He asked to be injected. You'll never get a jury to convict her of murder."

"Last chance. You have a legal obligation to take it back to your client. This offer will remain open until nine o'clock on Monday morning."

"Are you planning to request that the judge instruct the jury on manslaughter?"

"No."

Neither am I. "I'll take it to Lexy." *But I won't recommend it.*

* * *

Lexy responded to Harper's offer with an immediate and unequivocal, "No."

"Give it a little thought."

"No."

Her eyes were lifeless as she stared at me from across the metal table in a consultation on the fourth floor of the Glamour Slammer at noon on Saturday.

"We have until Monday morning," I said.

"It's the same offer as last time."

"It would eliminate any potential charges for Flynn."

"I didn't kill him, either. I didn't even inject him. And unless they're manufacturing evidence, there's no way that they can prove that I did."

"We can ask for a delay."

"At the prelim, the judge said that he wouldn't grant it."

"Judges always say that. If you aren't ready or you want to slow things down, we'll file papers tomorrow to ask for a continuance."

"I want to move forward and get this over with."

"Then that's how we'll proceed." I lowered my voice. "How are you feeling?"

"Better than a few weeks ago. The shakes have stopped. The cravings come and go."

"That's progress."

"I guess."

Nady took Lexy's hand. "It's going to be okay. We've got your back."

"I appreciate everything you've done." Lexy's eyes filled with resignation. "Even if we get an acquittal, then what? I have no money. I have no place to live. I have nobody to help me."

"We'll deal with it after the trial," Nady said.

As we headed back to the office, I felt as if we were going into battle with a client who had already surrendered.

* * *

Rosie's cobalt eyes reflected the light from the street lamp outside her bedroom window at eleven-thirty on Sunday night. "You ready?"

"Yes."

She leaned over and kissed me. "But?"

"Maybe I should have pushed DeSean harder for a deal for manslaughter."

"He's an excellent lawyer, but it was Nicole's call." She cupped my face with her hand. "You can get an acquittal on a murder charge. It would be harder on manslaughter."

"Harper still has time to ask for a manslaughter instruction. Judge McDaniel might still rule in his favor. Or she may decide unilaterally to instruct on manslaughter."

"Then you'll deal with it. At the end of the day, even if Lexy is convicted of manslaughter—voluntary or involuntary—it would be a better result than a murder conviction."

"It wouldn't be as good as an acquittal."

"Did Kaela Joy find Steele's daughter?"

"Not yet."

"Do you really think she knows anything?"

I answered her honestly. "I don't know."

"Get some rest, Mike. You have a busy day tomorrow."

"Thanks, Rosie." After all these years, I still never slept the night before trial.

48
"LET'S GET TO WORK"

The bailiff recited the traditional call to order in a world-weary voice. "All rise."

Showtime.

The stuffy courtroom came to life as Judge McDaniel emerged from her chambers and strode to her leather chair. She turned on her computer, put on her reading glasses, pretended to study her docket, and raised a hand. "Be seated."

I had appeared before her dozens of times. She had never picked up her gavel.

The heating and plumbing systems at the Hall were having a good day, so her courtroom was reasonably warm and smelled only of mildew instead of excrement. Lexy stood between Nady and me, eyes straight ahead. She was wearing a navy pantsuit and a silk blouse which Nady had selected for her from the donated clothing closet in the P.D.'s Office. Harper and a Deputy D.A. were standing at the prosecution table along with Inspector Lee, who was the only witness permitted to be in court before his testimony.

I leaned over and whispered to Lexy. "Stay calm, keep your head up, and make eye contact with the judge and the jurors."

The gallery was full, but Lexy had no rooting section. Rosie was sitting behind us in a seat usually reserved for family. I appreciated the show of support, and I always felt better when she was in court. Like many trial lawyers, I was superstitious, and Rosie was my lucky charm.

Pete couldn't sit in the gallery because he was on our witness list and he was looking for Debbie Steele. It was unfortunate because he had a knack for reading potential jurors. In his absence, and since we didn't have the resources to hire a jury consultant, Nady and I would have to rely on our instincts.

The second and third rows behind us were filled with members of the media, including Jerry Edwards, who was in his customary seat on the aisle. The last two rows were occupied by the usual rag-tag assortment of retirees, courtroom junkies, and hangers-on.

The prosecution side of the gallery was also filled with regulars. Ordinarily, family members of the deceased would be sitting in the front row, but Chloe wasn't coming to court. Members of Y5K's management team were also conspicuously absent. If anyone asked, they would say that they weren't allowed in court because they were on our witness list. In reality, they were busy with the IPO and trying to distance themselves from King.

Judge McDaniel nodded at her bailiff. "Please call our case."

"The People versus Alexa Susan Low."

"Counsel will state their names for the record."

"DeSean Harper and Andrew Erickson for the People."

"Michael Daley and Nadezhda Nikonova for the defense."

Judge McDaniel looked over my shoulder. "I see that our Public Defender is here today. Nice to see you, Ms. Fernandez."

"Thank you, Your Honor."

"Any last-minute issues, Mr. Daley?"

"No, Your Honor."

"Mr. Harper?"

"No."

"Let's get to work and pick a jury."

* * *

Three days later, on Thursday afternoon, our twelve jurors and four alternates were seated in the uncomfortable plastic chairs in the jury box. It wasn't a bad draw for us. Ten were college educated, which would have been unusual in many places, but not in San Francisco. Although it was risky to generalize, Nady and I were hoping that the nine female jurors might be more likely to give Lexy the benefit of the doubt.

Judge McDaniel addressed the jurors in a maternal tone. She thanked them for their service. She invited them to notify the bailiff if they had any problems. She admonished them not to talk about the case. "Do not do any research on your own or as a group. Do not use a dictionary or other reference materials, investigate the facts or law, conduct any experiments, or visit the scene of the events to be described at this trial. Do not look at anything involving this case in the press, on TV, or online."

She said it nicely, but she meant it.

She added the now-customary Twenty-first Century admonishment. “Finally, do not post anything about this case on Facebook, Twitter, Instagram, Snapchat, WhatsApp, or any other social media. If you tweet or text about this case, it will cost you money.”

The jurors nodded.

The judge looked at Harper. “Do you wish to make an opening statement?”

“Yes, Your Honor.” He stood, buttoned his charcoal suit jacket, walked purposefully to the lectern, and spoke directly to the jury. “My name is DeSean Harper. I am the head of the Felony Division of the San Francisco District Attorney’s Office. I know that jury duty isn’t everyone’s lifelong dream, but I am grateful for your service, and I appreciate your attention. I will attempt to keep my presentation brief because your time is valuable.”

No discernable reaction from the box.

“The facts of this case are not in dispute.”

I was tempted to point out that the facts of *every* case are *always* in dispute, but it’s bad form to interrupt during an opening—especially at the beginning.

“On December twenty-third of last year, there was a party at the house of the victim, Jeff King, a Silicon Valley entrepreneur and founder of a company called Y5K Technologies. Jeff wanted to thank his management team for their hard work on a forthcoming public offering. Tragically, by the end of the night, Jeff was dead.”

He pointed at Lexy. “The defendant is Alexa Low, who is sitting between her lawyers at the defense table. Jeff met the defendant on a dating website. He invited her to his house for a post-party rendezvous. The defendant took five thousand dollars from Jeff and then intentionally and with malice aforethought injected him with a lethal dose of highly potent heroin. He died a short time later.”

That’s enough. “Objection, Your Honor. Argumentative. I would ask you to instruct Mr. Harper to stick to the facts.”

“Please, Mr. Harper.” Judge McDaniel turned to the jury. “An opening statement should not be treated as fact. It merely constitutes a roadmap of what the anticipated evidence will show.”

It was a small point, but at least the jurors knew that I was paying attention.

Harper picked up where he had left off. "We will show you police video of the defendant purchasing heroin immediately before she went up to Jeff's house. And security video from the victim's house showing the defendant preparing a syringe. And video of the defendant injecting him with that heroin—which killed him almost instantly. And video of the defendant attempting to flee without providing help or calling nine-one-one. And video of the defendant accepting an envelope containing five thousand dollars in cash from the victim. We will show you a baggie containing traces of heroin—with the defendant's fingerprints."

Lexy turned to me, jaws clenched. "Can't you do something?" she whispered.

"Stay calm and be patient."

Harper spoke for another ten minutes about the "multitude of overwhelming evidence" that Lexy had given King a lethal hot shot. Finally, he moved directly in front of the jurors. "Ladies and gentlemen, it is your job to determine what happened. It is my job to present evidence to make yours as easy as possible. At the end of the day, I will provide more than enough evidence for you to find the defendant guilty of first-degree murder."

He returned to the prosecution table and sat down.

Judge McDaniel turned to me. "Opening statement, Mr. Daley?"

"Yes, Your Honor."

I could have deferred my opening until after Harper completed his case, but I wanted to connect with the jurors right away. I walked over to the lectern and worked without notes.

"Ladies and gentlemen, my client, Lexy Low, has been wrongly accused of a crime that she did not commit. Mr. King had a serious heart condition. He died of a heart attack that was exacerbated by his own reckless drug use, all of which was completely out of Ms. Low's control. She and Mr. King had a romantic and business relationship. They engaged in consensual sex and drug consumption, where Mr. King always provided the heroin and money. He was a billionaire who could afford it, and that's precisely what he did. He took advantage of Ms. Low, who is a victim in this case. Mr. King asked Lexy to inject him and offered no resistance when she did so." I lowered my voice. "Lexy isn't proud of her relationship with Mr. King, but she had no intention of killing him. Mr. King was her only source of support. In fact, she had a huge incentive *not* to kill him. There was no premeditation. Consequently, you cannot vote to convict her of first-degree murder."

The juror who worked at Salesforce was paying attention—or doing an excellent job of pretending to do so—but it didn't mean that she was buying everything I was selling.

"Our medical expert will testify that Mr. King had a heart condition making him susceptible to seizures and heart attacks. That condition combined with the stresses associated with an IPO, an evening of eating and drinking, and the consumption of heroin caused Mr. King to suffer a fatal heart attack. His death was a tragedy, but it doesn't mean that Lexy is responsible."

I moved closer to the jury. "Lexy has her own issues. She was once a rising star in the tech industry. Then she became addicted to narcotics. She lost her job. She lost her family. She lost her apartment. Mr. King was her sole source of support. Obviously, it wasn't an ideal situation, and it wasn't a fairy-tale relationship. On the other hand, she had no reason to kill him. In fact, she had every reason not to do so."

"We will provide video evidence that at least a half-dozen people had access to the bathroom where Ms. Low found the heroin. Every one of them had their own axes to grind against Mr. King. He was an entrepreneur, but he was also a liar, a cheater, and a misogynist."

I moved back to the lectern. "I know that you will use your best judgment, consider the evidence, and do your duty. At the end of the day, I am confident that you will conclude that Mr. Harper cannot prove Lexy's guilt beyond a reasonable doubt."

There was no discernable reaction from the jurors. I walked back to the defense table.

The judge spoke to Harper. "Please call your first witness."

"The People call Yoav Ben-Shalom."

49
"THAT'S CLASSIFIED"

Harper was at the lectern. "Please state your name and occupation for the record."

"Yoav Ben-Shalom. Director of Security at Y5K Technologies."

The jury was transfixed on the former Israeli commando, whose starched white shirt and matching pocket square dovetailed nicely with his charcoal suit and subdued necktie.

Harper moved about three feet from the stand and walked Ben-Shalom through his C.V. Ben-Shalom finessed his time with the Mossad by saying that he worked for the Israeli military.

Harper asked Ben-Shalom when he moved to the U.S.

"Three years ago. I worked for a company in the defense industry."

"Can you give us its name?"

"That's classified."

"What are your responsibilities at Y5K?"

"Securing our workplace. Cyber-security. Safety of employees and senior management."

Ben-Shalom confirmed that he was handling security at King's house on the night of the party. Harper introduced the guest list into evidence. Ben-Shalom identified everyone and confirmed their respective arrival and departure times.

"What time did the party end?" Harper asked.

"Twelve-ten a.m. Our CEO, Mr. Steele, was the last to leave."

"Was anyone in the house other than you and Mr. King?"

"Just the defendant, Ms. Low."

Harper had the first building block of his case: he had placed Lexy at the scene.

"Mr. Ben-Shalom, had you ever met the defendant prior to that evening?"

"I had never spoken to her, but I was aware of her relationship with Mr. King, and I was always nearby when they got together."

"In the same room?"

"In the same building."

"They had sex?"
"Correct."
"And took drugs?"
"Yes."
"Who brought the drugs?"
"Ms. Low."
"Every time?"
"Yes. That was their agreement."
"You knew that Mr. King and the defendant had arranged a rendezvous after the party?"
"Yes. I let the defendant into the house at eleven p.m. and instructed her to go upstairs and wait in the master bedroom. Mr. King went upstairs at twelve-fourteen a.m. I remained downstairs."
"When did you next see the defendant?"
"Twelve-thirty-two a.m. She came running down the stairs and attempted to leave. I asked her if anything was wrong. She said that Mr. King was fine, and then she tried to leave again. I insisted that she accompany me upstairs to check on Mr. King."
"What did you find?"
"Mr. King was on the floor. He wasn't breathing. He had no pulse. I called nine-one-one and administered CPR. The EMTs arrived within minutes, but they were unable to revive him."
It was another point for the prosecution: a body.
"Did Ms. Low offer any explanation?"
"She said that she didn't know what had happened."
"How was her demeanor?"
"Calm—as if she had expected something bad to happen."
"Move to strike," I said. "Mr. Ben-Shalom has no direct knowledge as to what was going on inside Ms. Low's head."
"The jury will disregard Mr. Ben-Shalom's last statement."
Sure they will.
Harper had what he needed. "No further questions."
"Your witness, Mr. Daley."
I walked across the courtroom and stood in front of Ben-Shalom. "Ms. Low was on the guest list, right?"
"Yes."
"You let her into the house?"
"Yes."

"Did she appear dangerous?"

"No."

"You didn't see heroin or other drugs in her possession, right?"

"Right."

"Did you search her?"

"No."

"You weren't concerned that she may have been carrying a weapon or illegal drugs?"

"Mr. King had instructed me not to search her."

"Did she show any anger toward you or Mr. King?"

"No."

"Did you talk to her?"

"Briefly. Other than instructing her to go upstairs, I didn't say anything to her until she came downstairs after she had murdered Mr. King."

Nice try. "Move to strike, Your Honor. The determination as to whether this case involves a 'murder' is up to the jury, not this witness."

"The jury will disregard the characterization as 'murder.'"

I asked Ben-Shalom how many times King and Lexy had been together.

"A few."

"How many is a few?"

"A dozen."

"Where did they meet?"

"At Mr. King's house, the Four Seasons in Palo Alto, and a resort in Carmel Valley."

"They had sex and took heroin each time?"

"Yes."

"Did Ms. Low ever force Mr. King to have sex or take drugs?"

"No."

"So their relationship was consensual, right?"

"Yes."

"And Mr. King compensated her for her services?"

"Five thousand dollars per visit."

I tried to catch him off-guard. "And he provided the drugs, right?"

"No, Mr. Daley. She provided the drugs."

"Seriously? A billionaire accepted heroin from a woman he met online?"

"Yes."

"A moment ago, you testified that you didn't see any drugs in her possession. How do you know that she brought heroin to the house?"

"I believe that it was in her purse."

"Did you open her purse?"

"No."

"Then how did you know that there was heroin inside?"

"Because Ms. Low always brought the heroin."

"But you didn't see it, right?"

"Objection," Harper said. "Asked and answered."

"Sustained."

I had made my point. "Mr. King was married, right?"

"Separated."

"Which means he was still married. Did it bother you that he was seeing Ms. Low?"

"It was none of my business."

"Weren't you concerned that he could have revealed trade secrets or been blackmailed?"

"Yes."

"Did you do anything about it?"

"I warned Mr. King about the risks and informed our board of directors. Our CEO, Mr. Steele, also advised Mr. King to use better judgment."

"That's it?"

"You'll have to ask Mr. Steele."

I will. "Did Ms. Low ever threaten Mr. King?"

"Not as far as I know."

"Did you monitor their activities in real time on the security video?"

"No."

"Why not?"

"Mr. King asked me not to do so, and I was trying to respect his privacy."

"Weren't you concerned when you left them alone in Mr. King's bedroom?"

"It wasn't the first time."

"Surely you would have intervened if you thought Mr. King's life was in danger?"

"Absolutely."

"But you didn't."

"I saw no evidence to that effect that night."

Until you found King's body. "You are aware that Mr. King and Ms. Low met through a dating app called Mature Relations, right?"

"Right."

"That's a so-called 'sugar daddy' site, which matches older men with younger women?"

"Yes."

"And you said that Mr. King was paying Ms. Low five thousand dollars per date, right?"

"Yes."

"Mr. King was her primary source of income, wasn't he?"

"I believe so."

"Why on earth would she have killed him?"

"Objection, Your Honor. Calls for speculation as to the defendant's state of mind. Assumes facts not in evidence. And this line of questioning is completely irrelevant to this case."

Absolutely true, mostly true, and somewhat true.

"Sustained."

"Mr. Ben-Shalom, are other members of the management of Y5K subscribers to Mature Relations?"

"Objection. Relevance."

Judge McDaniel raised an eyebrow. "Overruled."

I didn't think she'd give me that one.

"Not as far as I know, Mr. Daley."

"Have you checked?"

"No."

Really? "You aren't concerned that other members of management may be subject to embarrassment or blackmail?"

"No."

I find that hard to believe. Either way, we'll get to that later. "No further questions."

"Redirect, Mr. Harper?"

"No, Your Honor."

"Please call your next witness."

"The People call Dr. Joy Siu."

50
"HEROIN OVERDOSE"

Dr. Siu fingered the sleeve of her white lab coat and spoke with the precision of a world-class scientist. Her concise delivery combined the best elements of an experienced expert witness and a respected academic. "I have been the Chief Medical Examiner for three years. Prior to that time, I was the Chair of the M.D./Ph.D. Program in anatomic pathology at UCSF."

Harper was standing an appropriately deferential distance from her. "How many autopsies have you performed?"

"Hundreds."

I shot a glance at Rosie, who tugged her left ear, confirming my judgment that we had nothing to gain by letting Dr. Siu read her resumé into the record.

"Your Honor," I said, "we will stipulate that Dr. Siu is an expert in autopsy pathology."

"Thank you, Mr. Daley."

Harper introduced Siu's autopsy report into evidence and handed her a copy. "When did you perform the autopsy on Jeff King?"

"December twenty-fourth of last year. I issued my final report on January eighteenth."

"Why was there a gap?"

"I was waiting for final toxicology results."

"Did you pronounce the victim?"

"No, he was pronounced at the hospital. Time of death was officially set at one-forty a.m. on December twenty-fourth. However, based upon the condition of the body and evidence at the scene, I believe that it is likely that Mr. King died at his house."

"Cause of death?"

"Heroin overdose."

"Administered by injection?"

"Yes." Siu pretended to leaf through the document, which she could have recited by heart. "On page three, I describe a fresh needle mark on the victim's right arm. I found traces of heroin around it."

"Enough to analyze its quality?"

"Yes. Ninety-seven-percent pure. We also found traces of heroin in a baggie and two syringes in the defendant's purse. It was unquestionably toxic." She explained in clinical and layman's terms that a small amount of the super-powered heroin would have been enough to kill a man of King's size. "In my best medical judgment, Mr. King died of a heroin overdose."

"No further questions."

Judge McDaniel looked my way. "Your witness, Mr. Daley."

"Ms. Nikonova will be handling cross."

I had promised Nady a featured role. I wanted to get her in front of the jury right away.

She stood and buttoned her navy jacket. "May we approach the witness, Your Honor?"

"You may."

I looked on with pride as my latest protégé walked across the courtroom. Nady and Siu had different areas of expertise, but they were, in many respects, mirror images. Outstanding academic credentials. Always prepared. Comported themselves with professionalism and dignity. Never showboated.

Nady stopped a respectful distance from the stand. "Nice to see you again, Dr. Siu."

"Nice to see you, too, Ms. Nikonova."

"How much heroin does it take to kill someone?"

"Depends upon its potency and the decedent's height, weight, and overall health."

"Could it be a very small amount?"

"Yes."

"Could you tell how much heroin the decedent took?"

"It was impossible to determine precisely from the toxicology and my examination of the body. However, based upon video evidence of the defendant preparing two syringes, I believe that Mr. King was injected with approximately two hundred milligrams."

"Did you find evidence of other toxins in his system?"

"No."

Nady spent fifteen minutes chipping away at Siu's report: the state of the body; the collection of the samples; the procedures at the lab. She scored a few minor points, but we were still a long way from reasonable doubt.

"Dr. Siu, your report states that the decedent died because his heart was unable to pump sufficient blood to his body."

"Correct. Heroin slows your heartbeat and lowers your blood pressure, which can cause a pulmonary edema. In layman's terms, it means the heart is no longer capable of pumping enough blood through the body to sustain life."

"You said that an individual's reaction to heroin would depend upon his overall health?"

"Correct."

"Did you review the decedent's medical history?"

"Yes. He was in generally good health."

"Except for the fact that he was a heroin user, right?"

"Objection," Harper said. "Foundation."

"Sustained."

Nady didn't fluster. "The medical history indicated that he was a heroin user, right?"

"Yes."

"It also revealed that he had an arrhythmia, or irregular heartbeat, correct?"

"Yes."

"That's serious, isn't it?"

"Yes, but it can be controlled with medication."

"I trust that you wouldn't recommend using heroin to control it?"

Harper started to stand, then reconsidered.

"I wouldn't," Siu said.

"It isn't uncommon for people with arrhythmias to suffer heart attacks, is it?"

"It doesn't happen frequently, but it's certainly possible."

"And such heart attacks can occur without warning or symptoms, right?"

"Occasionally."

"And the chances increase if you are a heroin user, right?"

"I would think so, but I am not aware of any clinical studies showing any such link."

"It is possible that the decedent—a drug user with a heart condition—died of a heart attack unrelated to the injection of heroin, right?"

"Objection. Calls for speculation."

"Overruled."

Siu didn't fluster, either. "Anybody in this courtroom could have a heart attack at any moment. However, in my best medical judgment, Mr. King died of a pulmonary edema brought on by the injection of a massive dose of almost-pure heroin."

Our medical expert will express a different view.

Nady wasn't giving up. "A combination of a heart condition and any drug could reasonably result in a heart attack, correct?"

"Yes."

"And you therefore cannot rule out the medical possibility that such a combination caused Mr. King's death, right?"

"Right."

Nady returned to the lectern. "Do you know who provided the heroin?"

"No."

"It's possible that the decedent provided it himself, isn't it?"

"Objection. Calls for speculation."

"Sustained."

"And it is possible that somebody other than Ms. Low provided it, isn't it?"

"Objection. More speculation."

"Also sustained."

Nady glanced my way. She had planted a few seeds with the jury that we would harvest later. I closed my eyes—the signal to wrap up.

"No further questions."

Harper declined redirect.

"Please call your next witness, Mr. Harper."

"The People call Officer David Dito."

51
"I SOLD HIGH-END PRODUCT"

Officer Dito dutifully followed Harper's lead and reiterated his testimony from the prelim. "I was on patrol near the Sixteenth Street BART Station on the evening of December twenty-third. The defendant, Ms. Low, purchased heroin from a known dealer named Khalil Jones at approximately ten-thirty p.m. My partner and I placed Mr. Jones under arrest. We were unable to apprehend Ms. Low."

"That was about a half-hour before Ms. Low arrived at Mr. King's house?"

"Yes."

"Did you capture video of this encounter?"

"I recorded the transaction on my body cam."

Harper introduced the video into evidence and ran it for the jury while Dito provided commentary. The deftly choreographed testimony took less than thirty seconds.

Harper moved a little closer to Dito. "If you didn't arrest Ms. Low, how do you know that the baggie contained heroin?"

"Mr. Jones had two identical baggies in his possession. Each contained heroin."

"No further questions."

"Your witness, Mr. Daley."

I addressed Dito from my chair. "Did you confiscate the baggie from Ms. Low?"

"No."

"Did you handle it?"

"No."

"So you have no personal knowledge as to its contents, do you?"

"As I told Mr. Harper, Mr. Jones had two identical baggies containing heroin."

"How do you know that Mr. Jones didn't scam Ms. Low by giving her an empty baggie or one filled with another substance?"

"That's unlikely."

"But you can't rule out the possibility, can you?"

"That's unlikely."

That's unresponsive. "Just so we're clear, you have no hands-on evidence that Mr. Jones gave Ms. Low a baggie filled with heroin, right?"

"Right."

"And you have no hands-on evidence that Ms. Low had the same baggie in her possession when she entered Mr. King's house later that night, right?"

"Right."

"When you approached Mr. Jones and informed him that he was under arrest, he attempted to flee, right?"

"Yes."

"And you pursued him on foot to Mission Street?"

"Yes. That's where we placed him under arrest."

"As he was running down Mission, he emptied the two baggies in his possession into a puddle on the street, didn't he?"

"Yes. He was attempting to destroy evidence, but we were able to retrieve the baggies."

"Which were empty, right?"

"Our lab found traces of heroin."

"Which was contaminated by water and other elements, right?"

"Yes."

"So there was no way that the lab could have determined its purity or whether it contained any foreign substances, right?"

"Right."

"As a result, there was no way that the lab could have compared the heroin found in those baggies to the heroin found in Ms. Low's purse at Mr. King's house, right?"

He nodded. "Correct."

"So you have no proof that the heroin that Ms. Low allegedly purchased from Mr. Jones was the same heroin found in her purse, right?"

"Right."

"And it is also entirely possible that the heroin found in Ms. Low's purse was provided by the decedent, isn't it?"

"Objection. Speculation."

"Sustained."

"No further questions."

* * *

A short time later, a nervous Khalil Jones was sitting in the box, sporting an ill-fitting suit provided by Sandy Tran, who was in the front row of the gallery. The heroin dealer was gulping his third cup of water as Harper ran video from Officer Dito's body cam.

Harper pointed at the TV. "That's you and Ms. Low, right, Mr. Jones?"

"Right."

"What's happening here?"

"I sold her a bag of heroin."

"How much did she buy?"

"Fifty dollars' worth."

"Had you sold heroin to Ms. Low on other occasions?"

"A few times."

"Good quality?"

"Yes. Very pure. I sold high-end product."

"No further questions."

I glanced at Sandy. Then I walked to the front of the box. "Mr. Jones, you were arrested for selling heroin to Ms. Low, weren't you?"

"Yes."

"And you were also charged for other sales of heroin, right?"

"Right."

"You've entered into a plea bargain agreement with the District Attorney?"

"Yes."

"On what terms?"

"Objection," Harper said. "Relevance."

"Overruled."

Jones took another sip of water. "One count of sale of a controlled substance."

"That's a felony, right?"

"Right."

"How many counts were you originally charged with?"

"Ten."

"So your lawyer negotiated a deal for you to plead guilty to only one charge, right?"

"Right."

"And you got a reduced sentence, didn't you?"

"Yes."

"How long?"

"Three years."

Sandy cut him a good deal. It could have been up to nine. "You could have gotten nine years for each count, right?"

"Right."

"And you may get out earlier with good behavior, correct?"

"Correct."

"And you agreed to cooperate with Mr. Harper on this and other matters, right?"

"Right."

"So you agreed to say whatever he wants you to say, didn't you?"

"No."

"If you don't, you may lose your deal, right?"

"Yes. I mean no. I promised to tell the truth."

"You're lying now, aren't you, Mr. Jones?"

"No."

"You testified that you sold only what you described as 'high-end product,' right?"

"Yes. Very pure."

"Did it contain any substances other than heroin?"

"No."

"Are you a chemist?"

"No."

"Did you do any chemical tests on the heroin?"

"No."

"Then you can't possibly know that it was pure, can you?"

"I sampled it. In fact, I've sampled a lot of heroin."

"Let's be honest, Mr. Jones. You were selling cheap smack to tweakers on Mission Street, weren't you?"

"No."

"That's why you pleaded guilty, isn't it?"

"No." He looked at Sandy. "I mean yes. I mean that I was selling good stuff."

"You told your customers that it was pure, right?"

"It was."

"But you didn't really know, did you?"

"I'm not a scientist, Mr. Daley."

That much is true. "What did Ms. Low do with the heroin that you sold her?"

"I don't know."

"Do you have any evidence that she took it up to Jeff King's house?"

"No."

"Did you ever sell smack to Mr. King?"

"I don't know."

"Or anybody from a company called Y5K Technologies?"

"I don't know. I sold to a lot of people."

"No further questions."

"Redirect, Mr. Harper?"

"No, Your Honor. The People call Inspector Kenneth Lee."

52
"YOU CAN SEE IT ON THE VIDEO"

All eyes in the silent courtroom were fixed on Inspector Lee, who was standing next to the flat-screen TV which Harper had positioned for easy viewing by the judge, jury, and gallery. Rosie was sitting in the back row with Roosevelt Johnson, who was making an unannounced appearance. Perhaps my dad's old partner wanted to see how his one-time protégé fared in court. Or maybe he was checking on me.

Lee had already completed an hour of carefully rehearsed testimony to establish the timeline of the events at King's house. He and Harper were seasoned pros who had put on a textbook direct exam where I had little opportunity to interrupt or object.

Harper introduced the security video from the upstairs hallway. The HD color picture was much sharper than the grainy footage we used to see in videos from convenience stores.

Harper pointed at the screen. "When was this taken?"

"Eleven p.m."

"Who is in the video?"

"The defendant. She had just arrived at Mr. King's house. This shows her coming up the stairs."

Harper advanced the video and stopped it again. "Where did she go?"

"Into the master bath, which has a separate door leading into the master bedroom."

"What's in the defendant's hand?"

"A black purse."

Harper walked over to the evidence cart and picked up an item wrapped in a plastic evidence bag and tagged. "Is this the same purse?"

"Yes. I logged it in as evidence after we detained the defendant."

"Did you find anything inside?"

"In addition to various personal items, we found an envelope with five thousand dollars in cash, two syringes, a lighter, a spoon, some surgical hosing, and a baggie with traces of almost-pure heroin."

Harper introduced the items into evidence. I had no basis to object.

Lee remained next to the TV as Harper fast-forwarded the video. At twelve-fourteen a.m., King came upstairs and walked into the master bath.

"Who was in the house at this time?" Harper asked.

"The defendant, the victim, and Mr. Ben-Shalom."

Harper started another video and stopped it almost immediately. "Where was this taken?"

"Mr. King's bedroom."

"Could you please describe what's going on as I run the video?"

"At twelve-eighteen, the defendant entered the bedroom from the master bath. She's carrying a baggie of heroin along with a spoon, two syringes, surgical hosing, and a lighter."

"Did you find any identifiable fingerprints on the baggie?"

"Just the defendant's." Lee continued to narrate as Harper ran the video. "The defendant used the lighter to cook the heroin. She prepared two syringes. She accepted an envelope containing five thousand dollars from the victim and put it inside the purse."

"Move to strike," I said. "You can't see what's inside the envelope."

Harper kept his tone even. "Your Honor, we have already introduced the envelope and its contents into evidence."

"Overruled, Mr. Daley."

I was just trying to break up their flow.

Harper rolled the video and Lee kept talking. "The defendant and the victim began to disrobe. They embraced. The defendant injected the victim. You can see it on the video."

At first, King grinned. Then his smile disappeared. His face went blank. He began to have convulsions. Finally, he leaned forward and collapsed onto the floor.

Harper prompted Lee again. "Could you please describe what happened next?"

"Of course." Lee sounded like a sportscaster narrating football highlights.

Twelve-thirty. Lexy collected the drug paraphernalia and her belongings and headed into the hallway.

Twelve-thirty-five. She re-entered the bedroom followed by Ben-

Shalom, who called nine-one-one and administered CPR. King was unresponsive.

Twelve-forty-one. Two cops arrived.

Twelve-forty-two. The EMTs arrived and used paddles in a futile attempt to restart King's heart. One of the cops assisted them. The other stood next to Lexy, who was frozen in her chair.

Twelve-forty-eight. The EMTs and one cop hauled a lifeless King out of the room.

Twelve-fifty-five. The second cop escorted Lexy out of the room.

Harper stopped the video. "Could you please summarize what we just saw?"

Lee spoke with calm authority. "We know from Mr. Jones's testimony that the defendant purchased some pure heroin shortly before she went up to Mr. King's house. We believe that she brought it to Mr. King's house. She cooked the heroin, prepared two syringes, and injected Mr. King. When he experienced distress, she emptied the second syringe. Then she gathered her belongings, along with five thousand dollars in cash provided by the victim, the empty baggie, syringes, lighter, hosing, and spoon. She made no attempt to administer first aid or CPR, and she did not call nine-one-one. She attempted to flee, but Mr. Ben-Shalom stopped her."

"What did you conclude?"

"The defendant carefully planned to kill Mr. King and engaged in a cold-blooded act with a callous disregard for the victim's life."

In other words, Lexy committed first-degree murder.

"No further questions, Your Honor."

Judge McDaniel looked at the clock above the door. "It's after five, Mr. Daley. I am going to recess until nine a.m., when you may begin your cross-examination."

I glanced over at Harper, who was pleased with himself. He had timed Lee's testimony to coincide with the end of the court day. The jury would have all night to digest it.

53
"WE MAY NEED YOU TO TESTIFY"

A burly sheriff's deputy entered the consultation room and closed the door behind him. "I need to escort your client back to her cell in five minutes."

"We're almost finished," I said.

He let himself out.

At five-thirty on Thursday evening, Lexy's mood was grim as she stared at the cinder-block wall in the room down the hall from Judge McDaniel's courtroom. "That didn't go well."

"The prosecution always has the upper hand at the beginning."

"You said the same thing about the prelim."

"It was true then, and it's true now."

"Couldn't you have stopped them?"

"I objected when Harper asked inappropriate questions or tried to introduce inadmissible evidence. We'll lose credibility if I object to every question."

"Maybe we should have taken a plea bargain."

"I can raise it again."

She thought about it for a moment. "No."

Lexy was more engaged than two weeks earlier, but her mood swings were becoming more frequent and unpredictable. I was concerned that she might have an outburst in court, which would have been understandable, but not helpful.

Nady leaned over and touched Lexy's hand. "We need you to stay strong. We'll get you through this."

It was a kind sentiment. I cleared my throat and spoke to Lexy. "We may need you to testify."

Her eyes turned down. "I'm not sure that's a good idea."

Neither am I. "A forceful denial would impress the jury." *There's also a substantial risk that Harper will eat you up on cross.*

"I need to think about it."

So do I. "We don't need to decide now." *But we'll need to decide soon.*

* * *

Nady took off her reading glasses. "Do you think it was a good idea to mention the possibility of testifying to Lexy?"

"I want her to get used to the idea." *And I wanted to see how she would react.*

The P.D.'s Office was quiet at eight o'clock on Thursday night. I liked the quiet hours. It gave me time to think.

Nady lowered her voice. "Are you really planning to put her on the stand?"

"Maybe. We'll see how it goes and whether she's up to it."

"You've always taught me that a defendant shouldn't testify unless we're desperate."

"Correct."

"Are we?"

"Not yet."

* * *

Rosie touched my cheek. "You okay?"

"Fine."

"Really?"

I leaned over and kissed her. "No."

At eleven-thirty on Thursday night, I was dutifully giving a status report to my boss. Other than the fact that we were in bed, it was a standard de-briefing.

"I'll go after Lee in the morning," I told her.

"You won't be able to intimidate him. And you won't get an acquittal tomorrow, either."

I didn't always agree with her, but I appreciated her instincts and her honesty. "We'll have more arrows in our quiver when we start our defense. For one, King provided the heroin."

"Says Lexy. Jones said she bought it right before she went up to King's house."

"It doesn't prove that she brought it up to King's house. And it still seems unlikely to me that a billionaire didn't provide his own."

"They have video of Lexy giving him the shot."

"It proves that she injected him. It doesn't prove that she brought it. And it sure as hell doesn't prove that she intended to kill him."

It was Rosie's turn to kiss me. "You think it's enough?"

"Probably not. We'll tee up our SODDI defense and try to foist blame on everybody else at the party."

"Do you have any hard evidence to corroborate it?"

"Not yet."

"Or motive?"

"Working on it."

She pulled up the blanket. "Anything else, Mike?"

"I'm thinking of putting Lexy on the stand."

"Seriously?"

"Yes. I think the jury will respect her if she says that she didn't intend to kill King."

"It's up to the jury to decide whether she's telling the truth."

"We only need one to get to reasonable doubt."

My ex-wife, former law partner, and current boss flashed the smile that I still found seductive. "You'll find a way, Mike. You always do."

I wasn't as confident. "I hope so."

"Are you going to walk the steps in the morning?"

"Yes."

"Give my best to Zvi. How is he getting along?"

"Pretty well. His doctor won't let him do the steps every day, so he goes over to Safeway and walks the aisles. Some other seniors have joined him. He's the Pied Piper of Larkspur."

"He's my hero." Rosie leaned over and whispered into my ear. "The world will look brighter in the morning, Mike. It always does."

54
"IT'S IMPOSSIBLE TO PROVE A NEGATIVE"

Inspector Lee was sitting in the witness box at eleven-fifteen the following morning. For two hours, he had deftly parried my attempts to cast doubt upon the integrity of the crime scene, the handling of evidence, the process of interviewing witnesses, and the procurement of the security videos. To his credit, he had endured my onslaught of leading questions without taking a sip of water. Strong witnesses have strong constitutions.

I cued the video of Lexy coming up the stairs and froze it as she was about to enter the bathroom. "You testified yesterday that Ms. Low had heroin in her possession."

"Correct."

I stared at the screen for a long moment. "Would you please point it out for us?"

"You can't see it in the video. It was in her purse."

I picked up the purse from the evidence cart and showed it to him. "You can see through leather?"

"No, Mr. Daley."

"Neither can I, Inspector. Unless you have x-ray vision, you can't possibly know that there was heroin inside, can you?"

"She had purchased it from Mr. Jones a half-hour earlier."

"But she could have consumed it herself or disposed of it before she went up to Mr. King's house, right?"

A hesitation. "We found traces of heroin in the baggie inside her purse that matched the heroin in the syringe that she used to inject Mr. King."

"But we also watched video showing Ms. Low put the baggie, syringes, spoon, lighter, etc., into her purse right before she left the bedroom. It shows that she put the items inside her purse as she was leaving, but it doesn't prove that she brought the heroin into the house in the first place."

"Objection," Harper said. "There wasn't a question there."

No, there wasn't. "I'll rephrase. You don't have any physical or visual evidence that Ms. Low had heroin in her possession when she entered Mr. King's house, do you?"

"No."

Good. "And you don't have any physical or visual evidence that Mr. King did not leave the heroin in the bathroom for Ms. Low, right?"

"It's impossible to prove a negative, Mr. Daley."

Good answer. "But you would acknowledge that it's possible—and perhaps even likely—that Mr. King left some high-powered heroin in his own bathroom, right?"

"Objection. Calls for speculation."

Yes, it does.

"Sustained."

"Officer Dito testified that Mr. Jones was holding two baggies of heroin when he and his partner pursued him, didn't he?"

"Yes."

"He also testified that Mr. Jones had emptied those baggies into a puddle and dropped them onto the street, right?"

"Yes."

"Which means that any traces of heroin in those baggies were contaminated by water and other elements, weren't they?"

"Yes."

"So it was impossible to compare the traces of heroin in those baggies with the traces found in the baggie in Ms. Low's purse, right?"

Lee nodded. "Right."

Once more. "You can't possibly know that Mr. King did not leave a baggie of heroin inside his own bathroom, can you?"

Lee showed his first hint of impatience. "We're talking in circles, Mr. Daley."

That's the whole idea. "The fact remains that you have no proof that Ms. Low brought heroin into Mr. King's house, do you?"

Harper stood up. "Asked and answered, Your Honor."

"Please move along, Mr. Daley."

"The video showed several people other than Mr. King and Ms. Low entering the bathroom, didn't it?"

"Objection. Mr. Daley is asking Inspector Lee about matters not addressed during direct."

I fired back. "Mr. Harper showed the beginning of the video when

Ms. Low entered the bathroom, and the ending where Mr. King did so, too. He fast-forwarded through the period in-between because he didn't want us to see the other people who entered the bathroom—any one of whom could have left the heroin there. We should be allowed to show it in its entirety."

Harper responded from his seat. "This is an improper subject on cross, and Mr. Daley is testifying."

I'm definitely testifying, but it is an appropriate subject on cross. "Mr. Harper introduced the video during direct. I should be able to question the witness about it on cross."

"The objection is overruled. You may show the entire video and question Inspector Lee about it, Mr. Daley."

I started the video as Lexy entered the bathroom. Then I fast-forwarded to eleven-fifteen and froze it. "Can you identify the person entering the master bath?"

"The victim, Jeff King."

I ran it a little further, then stopped it again. "And now?"

"Mr. King exited the master bath and went back downstairs."

"Can you confirm that Mr. King did *not* have heroin in his possession?"

"We've already addressed this issue, Mr. Daley. I can't."

"It was his house. He could have left heroin in his own master bath at any time, right?"

"I found no evidence that he did so."

The woman from Salesforce looked skeptical. I forwarded the video to eleven-eighteen and stopped it again. "And who is this?"

"Gopal Patel."

"Did he have a baggie of heroin in his possession? Maybe in his pocket?"

"I have no evidence that he did, and you can't see it in the video. Moreover, when I asked him about it, he confirmed that he did not have heroin in his possession."

Big surprise. "You took his word for it?"

"I had no reason to disbelieve him, and I found no evidence that he did."

"Did you consider the possibility that he lied to you?"

"Yes. I had no reason to believe that he did so."

"Or he may be a very good liar. Either way, you can't rule out the possibility that he had a baggie in his pocket, can you?"

"Objection. Calls for speculation."

"Overruled."

Lee answered in a grudging voice. "I cannot rule out the possibility that Mr. Patel brought a hidden baggie into the bathroom, but I found no evidence that he did."

"What about the possibility that he tampered with a baggie that Mr. King had left there?"

"Once again, it's impossible to prove a negative, Mr. Daley."

"But you were willing to testify that Ms. Low brought a baggie of heroin into the house even though you have no evidence that she did, either."

"Objection. Mr. Daley is testifying again."

Yes, I am.

"Sustained."

It took me another hour to walk Lee through the rest of the video and identify everybody who entered the bathroom. Eleven-twenty: Ben-Shalom. Eleven-twenty-five: Sanchez. Eleven-forty-eight: the "Guy from Rye." Eleven-fifty-two: Steele. Eleven-fifty-five: Moore. Twelve-oh-one: Ben-Shalom again.

I stopped the video and the TV went black. "Inspector, based on what we just saw, isn't it true that between eleven p.m. when Ms. Low entered the bathroom, and twelve-fourteen a.m. when Mr. King returned upstairs, seven people—including Mr. King—entered the master bath?"

"Yes."

"Yet you concluded that the only person who could have left a baggie of heroin in the bathroom was Ms. Low?"

"She purchased heroin a short time before she arrived. We found her fingerprints on the baggie. We found no other identifiable prints, and we found no evidence that anybody else planted the heroin in the decedent's bathroom."

"What about the smudged prints? How could you rule out the possibility that the person whose prints were smudged brought the heroin into the bathroom?"

"I had no evidence in support of that conclusion."

"So you chose to believe everyone but Ms. Low, right?"

"We found her fingerprints on the baggie."

"She could have gotten her prints on the baggie as she was leaving the room, couldn't she?"

Harper was on his feet. "This subject has already been addressed."

"Please move on, Mr. Daley."

"Inspector, did you seriously consider the possibility that somebody other than Ms. Low put the heroin in the bathroom?"

"We considered everyone at Mr. King's house. We found no evidence that anyone else brought heroin into the master bath."

"Except for the video showing seven other people entering the bathroom."

"Objection. Argumentative."

"Withdrawn." I glanced at Rosie, who closed her eyes. "No further questions."

"Cross-exam, Mr. Harper?"

"No, Your Honor. We have no other witnesses. The prosecution rests."

"Did you wish to make a motion, Mr. Daley?"

"Yes, Your Honor." *Here goes.* "We move that all charges be dismissed on the grounds that the prosecution has failed to meet its burden of proving its case beyond a reasonable doubt."

"Denied." She looked at her watch. "We'll recess for lunch. Please be ready to call your first witness at one-thirty sharp."

* * *

I was standing in the stairwell down the hall from Judge McDaniel's courtroom when I punched Pete's number on my speed dial.

He answered on the first ring. "I trust you got Lee to break down on the stand?"

"Not quite."

"You're no Perry Mason, Mick."

I'm well aware of that. "I don't have a lot of time. Anything new that we can use?"

"Working on it."

"What about Debbie Steele?"

"Kaela Joy is checking rehabs south of the Golden Gate. I'm looking north."

"Can't you track her down using her phone?"

"She turned it off last week. Either she's going cold turkey, or she's using a burner."

"I'm due in court."

"Keep tap dancing, Mick. We'll come up with something."

55
"HE WAS A WALKING TIME BOMB"

The elf-like man with the trim beard and the John Lennon spectacles sported a double-breasted suit matching his styled gray hair. "My name is Dr. Gary Goldstein."

"You're a medical doctor?" Nady asked.

"I am. I've been practicing for forty-seven years."

He'd been a reliable paid-for-hire defense witness for almost as long.

Nady walked him through his C.V. Trained at Stanford and UCSF, the internist was a throwback to the days when doctors knew their patients by name. The fourth-generation native San Franciscan had opened an office across the street from Mount Zion Hospital decades before it was swallowed up by UCSF. He began supplementing his income with a lucrative side gig as an expert witness. When he started spending more time in court than with patients, he handed his practice over to his daughter and son-in-law (also UCSF-trained) and became a full-time hired gun. "Dr. G" was on the speed dial of every defense attorney in town. Juries loved the cherub-like man who dispensed earthy medical wisdom in easily digestible soundbites. More important, they believed him.

Nady handed him a copy of the autopsy report. "You're familiar with this document?"

"I have studied it very carefully."

For the better part of an hour.

"Dr. Siu concluded that the decedent died of a heroin overdose. In your best medical judgment, do you agree with her conclusion?"

He contorted his rubbery face in a manner suggesting that it gave him heartburn to disagree with the esteemed Chief Medical Examiner. "I have great respect for Dr. Siu, who taught at my alma mater, UCSF. However, in this instance, I'm afraid that she made an error."

Just the way they had rehearsed it.

"Could you please explain why?"

"It would help if I could refer to a copy of the decedent's medical chart."

Nady walked over to the evidence cart and picked up a manila folder. "Your Honor, we would like to introduce Mr. King's medical chart into evidence."

Harper spoke from his seat. "No objection."

Nady handed the file to Goldstein. "You've reviewed this document?"

"I have." He moved his glasses to the top of his head. "Mr. King had several ongoing health issues. In particular, he had high blood pressure and high cholesterol, which were treated with medication."

"Anything else?"

"He had an arrhythmia." He glanced at the jury. "In layman's terms, an irregular heartbeat."

"How irregular?"

"Very."

Nady turned to the judge. "We would like to introduce an electrocardiogram into evidence."

Harper nodded. "No objection."

Nady pressed a button on her laptop, and an EKG appeared on the TV. "Dr. Goldstein, are you familiar with this EKG?"

"Yes. It shows a normal heartbeat for a healthy and active seventy-four-year-old man."

"You know the patient?"

"Yes. Me."

Juror #2's icy demeanor showed the hint of a smile.

Harper stood up. "I fail to see the relevance."

Nady spoke in a reassuring tone. "We'll be there in a minute."

Judge McDaniel nodded. "Please proceed, Ms. Nikonova."

Nady lobbed another easy one to Dr. G. "Can you explain why this is a heathy heart?"

"Of course." Goldstein got out of the box and walked over to the TV. "A normal EKG shows what is known as a 'sinus rhythm.' To the untrained eye, it looks like a series of bumps, but each depicts an action in the heart. More important, the bumps are very consistent."

He explained that "P waves" represent the time when the atria—the upper chambers—squeeze blood through the heart. "Next come the 'QRS complex,' where the ventricles—the lower chambers—contract. This distributes blood throughout the body. Next is the so-called 'T wave,' which is the moment when the heart relaxes before starting to squeeze again."

The jurors were focused on the cheerful little man with the wiggly jowls.

Goldstein used a gold Cross pen as a pointer. "The high point is the 'R wave.' Notice that the waves are consistent." He flashed a reassuring smile to the jury. "This is the EKG of a normal, healthy heart." He waited a beat before adding, "I'm glad it's mine."

So am I.

Nady introduced a second EKG and put it up on the screen next to Goldstein's. "You've reviewed this EKG as well?"

"Yes. It's the most recent EKG in the decedent's medical record." This time he used his glasses to gesture. "This is a pattern known as an 'A-fib with RVR,' or rapid ventricular response. It means that Mr. King's heart was beating much faster than normal—from one-hundred twenty-five to one-hundred forty beats per minute. That's bad. The normal heart rate for a man of his age is between sixty and one hundred beats per minute." He smiled proudly. "For reference, mine is sixty-eight."

Impressive.

Goldstein kept talking. "Such a fast rate can weaken the heart and lead to failure—often without warning. The decedent's irregular beat was also inconsistent—it changed from time to time, unlike that of a healthy person."

Like you.

"How serious was this condition?" Nady asked.

"Very. Mr. King and his doctors had discussed various possible treatment options, including medication and, perhaps, a cardioversion, which is an electric shock administered to the heart, causing it to stop briefly. A moment later, the heart's activity restarts. Ideally, it will be in the normal sinus rhythm. It's a common practice where the side effects tend to be minimal."

"Did Mr. King elect to pursue such a treatment?"

"He did not."

"How would this irregular heartbeat have impacted his health?"

"He was a walking time bomb. He was at substantial risk of heart failure at any moment."

"Would he have been more susceptible to heart failure if he had been a heroin user?"

"Absolutely. Heroin slows the heart rate precipitously and causes drowsiness. In some cases, it causes your heart to stop."

"Is that what happened to Mr. King?"

"In my best medical judgment, it is more likely that his heart condition caused his heart to stop beating."

Nady's somber expression hadn't changed. "Are you being paid for your services today?"

It was better to raise this during direct than let Harper bring it up on cross.

Goldstein nodded. "Five thousand dollars."

"By whom?"

"The Public Defender's Office has a fund to handle such matters."

I'd put the arm on a few of my well-heeled pals to fund this program.

"No further questions."

"Cross-exam, Mr. Harper?"

"Yes, Your Honor." He spoke from his chair. "Dr. Goldstein, would you agree that taking a massive amount of pure heroin would likely exacerbate an existing heart condition?"

"Yes."

"Enough to kill someone?"

"Possibly."

"No further questions."

Judge McDaniel glanced at her computer. "I need to attend to some administrative matters this afternoon, so I am going to recess until ten o'clock on Monday morning."

56
"IT ISN'T ENOUGH"

Rosie's post-mortem combined succinctness with unvarnished realism. "It isn't enough."

"It might get us to reasonable doubt," I said.

"Not necessarily—especially if Judge McDaniel gives a manslaughter instruction."

"Harper hasn't asked for it."

"He may change his mind. Even if he doesn't, Betsy could still act unilaterally."

"It would be better than a murder conviction. I still think it was the right call to put Goldstein on the stand."

"You may think otherwise if the jury convicts for manslaughter."

I would. "At the moment, they won't have the opportunity."

Rosie's office was stuffy at four-thirty on Friday afternoon. Rosie, Nady, and I were sitting at the round table that doubled as her meeting area and campaign headquarters. The next election was still two years away, but fundraising never stopped.

I looked over at Nady. "Are we set on exhibits for Monday?"

"Yes. Who are you going to call first?"

"Jennifer Castle, the communications director."

Rosie gave me a sideways look. "Why are you calling the corporate shill?"

"To confirm that King had been accused of improper sexual advances multiple times."

"You think she'll admit it?"

"If I play my cards well enough."

"How does that prove that Lexy didn't kill him?"

"It doesn't. It shows that he was a bad guy who was disliked by everybody."

"Are you planning to call Chloe?"

"No. The jury will think we're trying to exploit the grieving widow."

"How are you going to discredit Castle?"

"Nick the Dick."

She grinned. "It won't get you an acquittal, but it will be entertaining. Who else?"

"Christina Chu. And everybody who went upstairs at King's house: Steele. Patel. Moore. Sanchez. The 'Guy from Rye.' Ben-Shalom."

"You're planning to accuse them of murder?"

"We're going to give the jury some options. We're going to put King, Y5K, and everybody on trial."

"It may be the best that you can do."

Not exactly a ringing endorsement, but a realistic summation of where we are.

Rosie stroked her chin. "Can you put somebody on the stand to break up the parade of deplorables and keep the jury's attention?"

"Kaela Joy for sure. Probably Pete. And we can always recall Nick if things get dull."

Nady grinned. "Can I handle his exam?"

"I called dibs."

Rosie turned serious. "Have you given any more thought to putting Lexy on the stand?"

"Too risky," I said. "Physically, she's okay. Mentally, it changes by the hour."

"Too bad. This is one of the rare instances where it might be helpful."

"I haven't ruled it out entirely. We'll see how things go."

* * *

Friday turned into Saturday, and then into Sunday. Nady and I spent the weekend doing trial prep. I took time off to walk the steps with Zvi and go to Tommy's basketball game. As always, I went to mass on Sunday morning. I've never been sure whether it's appropriate to ask for divine assistance when I'm preparing for a murder trial, but I figured that it couldn't hurt.

At seven o'clock on Sunday night, the aroma of Sylvia's chicken fajitas wafted through Rosie's house. Rosie and I were in the kitchen doing the dishes. Sylvia was in her customary spot in front of the TV and watching *60 Minutes*, her hands occupied with her knitting. Tommy was in his room—allegedly doing homework.

Sylvia looked up. "I'm surprised that you aren't still at the office,

Michael."

"I was there all afternoon with Nady."

"Rosita speaks very highly of her."

"With good reason."

Sylvia looked over at her daughter. "Maybe she can help you, too."

"She already does, Mama. So does Rolanda." She quickly added, "And Mike, of course."

Of course.

Sylvia's lightning-fast fingers never stopped. "I wasn't trying to be negative, Rosita."

Well, maybe a little. I'd been observing their dynamics for a quarter of a century, and there was rarely a clear winner. The discourse was always civil, but pointed. Neither was shy about expressing an opinion. Both insisted on having the final word. Most important, I knew to keep my mouth shut.

Sylvia wasn't finished. "Grace will be starting a new job in a few months. Tommy will be heading off to college in a couple of years. You're going to miss out."

"I'm doing the best that I can, Mama."

"How much longer are you planning to do this?"

"One more term."

Sylvia wasn't satisfied, but she left it there.

My iPhone vibrated, and I was grateful for the interruption. Pete's name appeared on the display. I excused myself and walked onto the front porch, where a cool breeze whipped through the oak tree in the middle of the lawn.

As always, his tone was terse. "You still planning to start the defense tomorrow?"

"Yes."

"You might want to slow-walk things. I may have something in the next couple of days." He cleared his throat. "What do you think of Brian Holton?"

"Except for the fact that he runs Mature Relations, he seems like a straight shooter."

"You think he might be willing to help us?"

"Maybe. What can we offer him?"

"An opportunity to thumb his nose at the Silicon Valley establishment and the venture capitalists who snubbed him."

"He might be interested. You aren't planning to do anything illegal, are you?"

"Absolutely not, Mick. That would be wrong."

Good to hear.

He cleared his throat. "Mind if I get in touch with him directly?"

It might be better that way. "Fine with me."

57
"THAT'S CONFIDENTIAL"

"Please state your name for the record," I said.

"Jennifer Castle."

At the office, you were "Jen." In court, you're "Jennifer." "Your occupation?"

"Senior Vice President of Corporate Messaging at Y5K Technologies."

She had ditched the Steve Jobs jeans and black top for a Hillary Clinton pantsuit and a cream-colored blouse. It's better to dress like a grown-up in court.

I moved from the lectern to the front of the box. "You knew Jeff King?"

"Yes." She turned slightly to face the jury. "I reported directly to him."

We're impressed. "Was he a good boss?"

"Yes. Demanding, but very smart and easy to work for."

Right. "Did the company ever receive any complaints from employees about Mr. King?"

Harper was on his feet. "Objection. Relevance."

I figured this was coming. "Your Honor, the decedent's character is relevant. He treated people poorly—including many who were at his house on the night that he died."

"Overruled."

"Thank you." I repeated the question.

Castle responded with a smirk. "Our personnel records are confidential."

Nice try. "Your Honor, the decedent's right to privacy terminated upon his death."

Castle spoke up before the judge could rule. "Privacy extends to other employees."

"I do not expect Ms. Castle to reveal names."

Judge McDaniel had heard enough. "Please answer the question, Ms. Castle."

The smirk disappeared. "Yes."

"How many employees complained?" I asked.

"I don't recall."

I find that hard to believe. "Can you give us a ballpark number?"

"I don't recall."

Not good enough. "Five? Ten? Twenty? Fifty?"

"Objection, Your Honor. Asked and answered."

"Asked," I said, "but not answered."

Judge McDaniel showed a hint of impatience. "Please answer the question to the best of your ability, Ms. Castle."

"I'd say about a dozen."

Was that so hard? "Did any of those cases go to trial?"

Harper tried again. "Objection. Relevance."

"Overruled."

Castle shook her head. "They settled out of court."

"Could you please tell us the nature of the claims?"

"That's confidential."

Judge McDaniel turned to her. "Please answer, Ms. Castle."

"Inappropriate comments," she said.

"Touching?" I asked.

"Unsubstantiated."

"Y5K entered into multiple confidential settlement agreements relating to these inappropriate sexual advances, didn't it?"

"Alleged," she said. "And I didn't say anything about *sexual* advances."

Is there any other kind? "Can you please describe the nature of the inappropriate touching if it did not involve sexual advances?"

"Mr. King liked to hug people. Some people misinterpreted his intentions."

"Perhaps they found it offensive that he grabbed them without permission."

"Objection."

"Withdrawn. It's your testimony that Y5K paid multiple settlements for misinterpretation?"

"Yes."

"Are you aware that the Medical Examiner determined that the decedent had taken heroin on the night that he died?"

"Yes."

"Was he addicted?"

"Objection. Assumes facts outside this witness's expertise."

"Sustained."

"Did the decedent ever take time off for treatment for substance abuse?"

"He *never* took time off."

I shot a look at the jury, then I turned back to Castle. "Did Mr. King ever hit on you?"

"Excuse me?"

"Did he ever make inappropriate advances to you?"

"Objection, Your Honor. Relevance."

"Your Honor, Ms. Castle testified that Mr. King was a serial sexual harasser. We should be allowed to inquire as to whether she was the victim of any such behavior."

"Overruled. Please answer the question, Ms. Castle."

King's enabler-in-chief squared her shoulders. "No, he did not."

"Are you subject to a confidentiality agreement regarding a settlement?"

"No."

"Did Mr. King ever go to a strip club?"

"Excuse me?"

"Did he ever go to a strip club?"

She fidgeted. "We received reports that some of our people entertained our customers at such establishments in Asia."

"Including Mr. King?"

More fidgeting. "Yes."

"Did the board of directors do anything about it?"

"They adopted a policy not to reimburse expenses incurred at such establishments."

You don't want to utter the word "strip club," do you? "Did they ban such activities?"

"They discouraged them."

"Did they discuss this policy with Mr. King?"

"Yes. He was instructed not to take customers to such places."

Or get caught. "Did he abide by that directive?"

"As far as I know."

We'll see. "No further questions, Your Honor."

Harper declined cross.

"Please call your next witness, Mr. Daley."

"The defense calls Christina Chu."

* * *

"You attended the party at Mr. King's house on December twenty-third of last year?"

Chu was sitting in the box, hands folded in her lap. "Yes, Mr. Daley."

"You had known Mr. King for a long time?"

She sported a conservative gray pantsuit with a beige blouse making her look more like a Wall Street executive than a Silicon Valley VC. "About ten years."

"And you recommended an investment in Y5K to Mr. Patel, didn't you?"

"Correct."

I was at the lectern. "You invited other women to the party?"

"Yes. They were business associates."

I pressed a button on my laptop and the TV came to life. I ran video from a security camera mounted outside the front door that Harper had shown to place Lexy at the scene. Chu identified each of the women as they entered the house.

I stopped the video. "How did you select them?"

"Jeff asked me to invite people who were successful and smart."

And young and pretty. "They all accepted your invitation?"

"It was an excellent opportunity to network."

I looked at the frozen video. "They were all wearing short black cocktail dresses, weren't they?"

Chu hesitated. "Yes."

"That's quite a coincidence."

"They're adults."

"You suggested that they dress provocatively, didn't you?"

"Of course not."

"And you suggested that they flirt with the men, right?"

"No."

"But it was okay if they did, right? Because Mr. King liked it?"

"Objection."

"Withdrawn. Did any of your business associates go home with the men?"

"I don't know, Mr. Daley."

I started another video. "Could you please describe what we're seeing here?"

"Mr. King's living room."

"How many people are here?"

She squinted. "Looks like about a half dozen."

"Can you describe what they're doing?"

She swallowed. "Some of them are kissing."

I stopped the video. "This is what's known as a 'cuddle puddle,' isn't it?"

She responded in a whisper. "Yes."

I teed up the video from outside the front door. "This was taken at eleven-fifty-five p.m. Can you please describe what we're seeing?"

She didn't answer.

I helped her. "Two of the women left with two of the male guests, right?"

"Yes."

"The men are Tristan Moore and Alejandro Sanchez, aren't they?"

"Yes."

"Mr. Moore is your fiancé, isn't he?"

"Yes."

"Does it trouble you that he left the party with somebody else?"

"Objection. I fail to see how this line of questioning has any possible relevance."

"Your Honor, I am attempting to demonstrate that this party was a cesspool of behavior typical of Y5K Technologies in general, and Mr. King in particular." *And Chu's fiancé.*

"You've made your point, Mr. Daley. Anything else for Ms. Chu?"

"One more item." I restarted the video and stopped it at eleven-forty-five. "Ms. Chu, can you identify the people in this video?"

"Mr. Patel and me."

"You were leaving the party with your boss?"

"Yes. We shared an Uber."

"You and Mr. Patel were holding hands, weren't you?"

"I don't recall."

"You can see it right there in the video."

"I don't recall."

"Were you and Mr. Patel in the habit of holding hands?"

"No."

"But you would acknowledge that you were doing so here, right?"

"Objection. Asked and answered."

"Sustained."

"No further questions, Your Honor."

"Cross exam, Mr. Harper?"

"No."

"Ms. Chu is excused. Please call your next witness, Mr. Daley."

"The defense calls Nicholas Hanson."

58
"INDEED I AM"

The diminutive P.I. adjusted the rose on his lapel. "My name is Nicholas Hanson."

I was standing at the lectern, and I wasn't going to move in any closer. "Are you the proprietor of the Hanson Investigative Agency in North Beach?"

"Indeed I am."

"How long has your agency been in business?"

"We will celebrate our diamond jubilee next year."

"That would be seventy-five years?"

"Indeed it would."

The gallery was packed, and a dozen people were standing against the back wall in blatant violation of the fire code. Word had spread that Nick the Dick was on the stand. At the Hall, this was like Christmas. Every courtroom junkie, reporter, cop, bailiff, security guard, and custodian within shouting distance tried to squeeze into Judge McDaniel's courtroom.

"Mr. Hanson," I continued, "how big is your agency?"

"We have over a hundred investigators."

I couldn't resist. "How many are related to you?"

"Including people who have married into my family?"

"Yes."

His voice filled with pride. "All of them."

This elicited a smile from the woman from Salesforce.

Harper decided to stop the love fest. "Your Honor, we will stipulate that Mr. Hanson is a well-known private investigator from a reputable agency."

Nick corrected him. "We're listed in the top ten in the country, Mr. Harper."

"I know, Mr. Hanson."

Judge McDaniel's poker face finally broke into a smile. "The record will show that Mr. Harper has stipulated to Mr. Hanson's national reputation. Please move along, Mr. Daley."

I was a bit disappointed that I wasn't able to give Nick a chance to plug his new novel. "Mr. Hanson, you've been hired by several tech firms to monitor their employees, right?"

"Yes, but I cannot reveal the names of my clients."

"Understood. Can you tell us if you have ever been hired by Y5K Technologies?"

"I have not."

"But you're familiar with the company?"

"Indeed I am."

"And Jeff King?"

"Everybody knew Mr. King."

"In the course of your investigations, have you ever been asked to conduct surveillance at a business called the Gold Club on Howard Street?"

"Indeed I have."

"Could you please describe the nature of that establishment?"

"It's a strip joint." He raised a bushy eyebrow. "And it has an excellent buffet lunch."

Laughter in the gallery. "How often do you go to the Gold Club?"

"Three or four times a week."

"Did you ever see Mr. King?"

"Three or four times a week."

More laughter. "When was the last time you saw him there?"

"About a week before he died."

"Can you describe his behavior?"

"He used to bring employees from Y5K for lunch, adult beverages, and, uh, the show."

"The strip show?"

"Yes. He also paid extra for adult services in the private areas behind the stage."

"What sort of services?"

He closed his eyes and grinned. "I think you know, Mr. Daley."

"I think I do, Mr. Hanson."

Harper got to his feet. "Your Honor, we're prepared to stipulate that Mr. Hanson saw Mr. King engage in adult activities at the Gold Club. While this is interesting and, for some, entertaining, it wasn't illegal behavior, and I fail to see any relevance."

"Anything else for this witness, Mr. Daley?"

"Just one more question. Mr. Hanson, a few minutes ago, we heard testimony from a witness named Jennifer Castle, who is the Vice President of Corporate Messaging at Y5K. She said that Mr. King discontinued visiting strip clubs at the request of the company's board of directors. Would you say that her testimony was accurate?"

"Indeed I would not."

"No further questions."

* * *

I was checking my texts in the corridor outside Judge McDaniel's courtroom during the morning break when I was approached by two men in matching charcoal suits. I recognized Yoav Ben-Shalom. It took me a moment to place Lawrence Braun, Y5K's outside counsel.

Braun acted as spokesman. "What the hell were you doing in there, Mr. Daley?"

"Excuse me?"

"You were trying to embarrass Jeff King, Jennifer Castle, and Christina Chu."

"Mr. King's behavior is relevant to our defense."

"It has nothing to do with your defense. You're just blowing smoke."

Well, that too. "His character is important to our case."

"Did you ever consider Mrs. King's feelings?"

"Yes." *Then again, she's having an affair with the company's acting CEO and was playing tennis a few days after her husband died.* "She wasn't in court."

"Do you think she won't find out?"

"I feel badly for her, Mr. Braun, but I need to do what's best for my client."

"Do you have any idea what's at stake here? You're destroying the company's reputation."

Actually, I'm only trying to destroy King's reputation. "I'm representing my client to the best of my abilities."

"You need to watch your step, Mr. Daley. Your client isn't the only person impacted by Jeff's death."

"Did you just threaten me?"

"Absolutely not." He tried to strike a more conciliatory tone. "I would ask you to be sensitive to the feelings of Mr. King's family and our employees."

And your venture capitalists, investment bankers, and lawyers who stand to lose millions if the IPO tanks. "I'll do the best that I can, Mr. Braun."

"Thank you. Will you be calling any other members of company management as witnesses?"

"All of them."

59
"HE HAD A VISION FOR THE FUTURE"

Steele sat ramrod straight in the box. "I am the chairman of the board of Y5K Technologies."

I was standing at the lectern. "You became chairman recently, right?"

"Correct." He adjusted the eighteen-karat-gold cufflinks under the sleeve of his ten-thousand-dollar Armani suit. "The board asked me to step in after Jeff King's untimely death."

"How long did you know Mr. King?"

"About five years. We had met at several Silicon Valley functions."

"When did you join Y5K?"

"About two years ago. The board wanted to bring in an experienced executive to assist Jeff in taking the company to the next level and eventually complete an IPO."

"You were also asked to deal with some of Mr. King's behavior issues, weren't you?"

"At times."

"He was accused of sexual harassment at several of his earlier companies, wasn't he?"

"There were some questions."

"Those issues carried over to Y5K, didn't they?"

"They were addressed."

"By paying multiple confidential settlements to women who accused Mr. King of sexual harassment, correct?"

"In some cases."

He was being more forthright than I had anticipated. Then again, King was dead, and he no longer had to cover for him. "What was he like?"

"He had a vision for the future."

Please. "How did you and Mr. King get along?"

"Fine."

"No disagreements?"

"Differences of opinion are inevitable."

"You must have been concerned that his behavior would have an adverse impact on the company, right?"

"No."

"Did it bother you that he took your employees to strip clubs several times a week?"

"We encouraged him to use better judgment."

"And the fact that he was a heroin user?"

"The board was aware of Mr. King's issues and spoke to him about it."

"Did the board consider replacing him?"

"No."

"Was the board also aware that Mr. King was picking up young women through a sugar daddy site called Mature Relations?"

"They are now."

"Were your investment bankers and venture capitalists aware of these issues?"

"They are now."

"Is the IPO moving forward?"

"Yes."

"You stand to make millions, right?"

Steele turned to the judge. "I cannot respond to Mr. Daley's question without violating the rules of the Securities and Exchange Commission."

"I'm not going to ask you to answer."

It was time to address more pressing issues. "Mr. Steele, you were at Mr. King's house on the evening of December twenty-third, weren't you?"

"Yes."

I spent twenty minutes walking him through a description of the party, which he tried to portray as similar to a ten-year-old's birthday party at Chuck E. Cheese's. Finally, I steered him to the matters at hand. "Did you know that Mr. King had planned a rendezvous with Ms. Low?"

"I knew that he had a date. I didn't know with whom."

Sure. "You used the upstairs bathroom at Mr. King's house, didn't you?"

"Yes."

"You left a baggie of high-powered heroin there, didn't you?"

"Absolutely not."

"Or did you tamper with a baggie of heroin that Mr. King left there?"

"Absolutely not."

"You were concerned that Mr. King's behavior was going to impact the company and delay the IPO, weren't you? And you wanted to send him a message, didn't you?"

"No, Mr. Daley."

"Do you know any other members of Y5K's management who are also subscribers to the Mature Relations site?"

"No."

We'll see. "No further questions."

* * *

Patel was next. We went through a similar exercise. He described the party as tame. He knew that King had scheduled a date, but claimed that he didn't know with whom. He was aware of King's behavior issues, and he believed that the board had addressed them adequately.

"Mr. Patel," I said, "in addition to investing in Mr. King's company, you had a personal relationship with him, didn't you?"

"I try to maintain distance from members of management of companies that we fund."

Especially after they're caught picking up women on a hookup site. "Your personal relationship was a little closer, wasn't it, Mr. Patel?"

"Excuse me?"

"Are you familiar with the term, 'polyamorous relationship?'"

"No."

"I think you are."

"Objection. Asked and answered. And I fail to see the relevance."

I kept my tone even. "It will become readily apparent in a moment, Your Honor."

"I'll give you a little leeway, Mr. Daley."

I turned back to Patel. "A 'polyamorous relationship' refers to a loving and committed relationship among more than two individuals, doesn't it?"

"So I've heard."

Here goes. "You and your wife were involved in such a

relationship with Mr. King and his wife, weren't you?"

He glared at me. "No."

"Our next witness will be the private investigator that Chloe King hired to monitor her husband's behavior. The P.I. is aware of the details of all of his relationships, including the one with you and your wife. I really don't want to ask Mrs. King to testify, Mr. Patel."

"Objection. There wasn't a question there."

"Let me repeat my original question and see if Mr. Patel wishes to change his answer. You and your wife were involved in a polyamorous relationship with Mr. King and his wife, weren't you?"

Patel swallowed. "It was complicated."

"I'm going to take that as a yes."

"Your description is too simplistic."

"Mr. King violated your agreement by sleeping with other women, didn't he?"

"Yes."

"One of those women was Ms. Low, wasn't it? Whom he met on a sugar daddy website called Mature Relations, right?"

"So I'm told."

"Do you know anybody else who is a subscriber to the Mature Relations site?"

"No."

We'll get back to that later. "Mr. King's behavior upset you and your wife, didn't it?"

"Yes."

"You attended Mr. King's party after he had cheated on you and your wife, right?"

"Yes."

"And you were still angry at him, weren't you?"

"Some time had passed."

"You knew that Mr. King had a heart condition and a heroin problem, didn't you?"

"Yes."

"You put a baggie of high-powered heroin in the drawer in Mr. King's bathroom where you knew that my client would find it, didn't you?"

"No."

"And you knew that she would inject Mr. King, didn't you?"

"No."

"And you knew that an injection of high-powered heroin into a man with a serious heart condition was likely to be fatal, didn't you?"

"Yes. I mean, no. If you're suggesting that I brought heroin to Mr. King's house, you're crazy, Mr. Daley."

"Am I, Mr. Patel?"

"Objection. Mr. Patel is not qualified to opine as to Mr. Daley's mental health."

"Sustained. Anything else, Mr. Daley?"

"One more item, Your Honor. Mr. Patel, you work with Ms. Chu, don't you?"

"Yes. She's a valuable member of our firm."

"You left the party with her, didn't you?"

"We shared an Uber."

I punched a button on my laptop and the video of Patel and Chu leaving King's house appeared on the screen. "Is it your practice to hold hands with your employees, Mr. Patel?"

"I was escorting her to the car."

"By the hand?"

"We had been drinking. It was dark."

"You and Ms. Chu are involved in a romantic relationship, aren't you?"

He swallowed. "No."

"No further questions."

"Cross-exam, Mr. Harper?"

"No, Your Honor."

"You can call your next witness after our lunch break, Mr. Daley."

The jury was in for a treat. They were about to meet Kaela Joy.

60
"THEY HAD AN UNCONVENTIONAL MARRIAGE"

All eyes in Judge McDaniel's courtroom were focused on the photogenic blonde sitting in the box. With perfect hair and makeup and sporting a Valentino blouse, Kaela Joy commanded attention.

I spoke to her from the lectern. "How long have you been a private investigator?"

"Almost twenty years."

"I understand that your business is very successful."

Kaela Joy's face transformed into the million-dollar smile that once graced the cover of *People Magazine*. "It is."

The jury was captivated as I walked her through her life story. Born and raised in Redding, the daughter of a cop and a high school teacher had built a thriving business after her ex-husband—a Niners lineman—had cheated on her and gambled away their money. Two decades later, she was running a multi-million-dollar security business, and her ex was working at the Cinnabon at SFO. Every so often, karma wins.

"Did you ever meet the decedent, Jeff King?"

"No, but I knew a lot about him. Mrs. King hired me to watch him. She believed that he was cheating on her and using heroin."

"Was he?"

"Yes."

That covers it. "Was he abusive?"

"Physically, no. Emotionally, yes. He didn't let her leave the house. He had people watching her because he thought she was cheating. He berated her in private and in public."

"How long was this going on?"

"From the day they met."

I stole a glance at the jury. The woman from Twitter was frowning. I asked, "What made Mrs. King think that her husband was cheating?"

"There were many late nights. He spent most of his time at their residence in San Francisco, while she was at their house in Palo Alto.

There were unusual text messages and charges on their credit cards. He had a burner phone. I found a listing for Mr. King on a hookup site called Mature Relations, where he met Ms. Low. He paid her over fifty thousand dollars."

"Was he seeing other women in addition to Ms. Low?"

"Yes."

"And patronizing strip clubs?"

"He went to an establishment called the Gold Club several times a week."

"Was he a sex addict?"

"Objection. Ms. Gullion is not qualified to provide medical expertise on that subject."

"Sustained."

"Did Mrs. King ever express unhappiness about the fact that her husband was having sex with other women?"

"Frequently." Kaela Joy frowned. "But it was a little more complicated, Mr. Daley. They had an unconventional marriage."

Finally the good stuff. "How so?"

"For a period of time, they had an open marriage in which they agreed that they would be allowed to see other people."

"How did that work out?"

"Not well. Mr. King had many more relationships than Mrs. King, so she decided that it wasn't an acceptable arrangement."

"Did they return to a more traditional monogamous relationship?"

"No. They entered into what is commonly known as a 'polyamorous' relationship with another couple. That didn't work out well, either. Mr. King continued to see women not in their polyamorous group, including Ms. Low, and other women he met on the Mature Relations site."

"Do you know the identity of the other couple?"

"Yes. Mr. and Mrs. Gopal Patel."

Murmurs in the gallery. "How do you know this information, Ms. Gullion?"

"Because I was at Mr. and Mrs. King's house on several occasions when Mr. and Mrs. Patel came over for the night."

"How long did this relationship last?"

"A few months."

"Who terminated this arrangement?"

"Mr. King."

"Was anybody upset?"

"Everybody. The Patels were especially angry after they found out that Mr. King had been seeing Ms. Low outside the scope of their multi-party agreement."

That's enough. "No further questions."

* * *

Brian Holton was up next.

"You're the founder and CEO of Mature Relations?" I said.

"I am." In his double-breasted suit and subdued necktie, Holton looked like the CEO of a media conglomerate. "We provide a legitimate service similar to Match or Tinder. We have over ten million members."

"What percentage are male?"

"About seventy-five percent."

"Was Jeff King a member?"

"Yes."

"Did he meet many women on your site?"

"About a dozen."

"Mr. Holton, are any other members of senior management of Y5K or related parties also subscribers to Mature Relations?"

"Yes, Mr. Daley."

"Would you mind giving us their names?"

"I'm really not supposed to."

"You're under oath, Mr. Holton."

"Jack Steele, Drew Pitt, and Gopal Patel."

"We raised this issue with Mr. Steele and Mr. Patel, who testified that they were not members of Mature Relations."

Holton flashed a wicked smile. "Let's give them the benefit of the doubt and say that they had memory lapses."

Sounds good to me. "No further questions."

* * *

There was a hint of optimism in the consultation room during the afternoon break. After Holton had testified, I had recalled Steele and Patel to ask them about their memberships on Mature Relations. There was raucous laughter in the gallery when Steele admitted that he was a member of the Premium Club.

For the first time since she was arrested, Lexy's eyes were a little brighter. "Did you see the look on Steele's face when you told him that Holton had confirmed that he was a member of Mature Relations?" she asked.

"Priceless."

Her expression turned serious. "Do you have enough for an acquittal?"

"Getting closer, but we still have work to do."

61
"HE NEVER THANKED ANYBODY"

"What is your position at Y5K?"

Sanchez took a sip of water. "Chief Technology Officer."

"You wrote the code for Y5K's products?"

"Most of it."

The gifted young geek had ditched his t-shirt and camouflage pants for an off-the-rack suit and a powder-blue dress shirt with no necktie. His shoulder-length hair was pulled into a ponytail.

"Did Jeff King write code?"

"No."

"The Silicon Valley press reported that he wrote the software for Y5K."

"He always took credit."

"How did you and Mr. King get along?"

"I wrote code. He paid me."

"You believe that you were underpaid, don't you?"

"A little."

"And underappreciated?"

"At times."

"That made you angry, didn't it?"

"I dealt with it."

Okay. "You were at the party at Mr. King's house on the night that he died?"

"Yes."

"Did you know that he was meeting Ms. Low?"

"No."

"Did he ever talk about her?"

"Not to me."

"Did Mr. King thank you for your hard work on the IPO?"

"He never thanked anybody."

"It bothered you, didn't it?"

"A little."

"You knew that he was planning to use heroin that night, didn't you?"

"No."

"You'd seen him take heroin at his parties, right?"

"Yes."

"Do you know where he got it?"

"No."

"The police think Ms. Low brought the heroin."

"I don't know."

"You really think a billionaire took smack from somebody he met online?"

"Objection. Speculation."

"Overruled."

Sanchez shrugged. "You never knew with Jeff. He was a quirky guy."

I might have used a more colloquial description. "Did you use the upstairs bathroom?"

"Yes."

"Did you see Mr. King put a baggie of heroin in the drawer in the bathroom?"

"No."

"Did you see Ms. Low bring a baggie of heroin into the house?"

"No."

"A few minutes ago, you expressed anger at Mr. King for slighting you. You brought a baggie of super-potent heroin into his house with the idea that he would take it and overdose, didn't you?"

"Whatever I thought about Jeff—and sometimes it wasn't much—I wasn't going to risk blowing up the IPO and losing millions just because he treated me like crap."

* * *

"How well did you know Jeff King?" I asked.

Tristan Moore was wearing a Calvin Klein suit and a Christian Dior necktie with a paisley design. "Very well."

"You liked him?"

He flashed a charismatic smile. "Of course."

"You knew that he was a regular heroin user, correct?"

The smile disappeared. "I had suspicions."

"After Mr. King's untimely death, you were promoted to acting CEO, weren't you?"

"Yes."

"That's a big promotion."

"And a big responsibility."

"I trust you're getting a raise?"

"We're working out terms."

"Seems you gained a lot from Mr. King's death, didn't you?"

"It's not the way I wanted things to happen."

"You knew that he and his wife had separated, right?"

"Yes. It was unfortunate."

Maybe not for you. "She's pretty."

"Yes, she is."

"You knew her well, didn't you?"

"We'd met on several occasions at the office and company events."

"Ever been to her house?"

"No."

"You're sure?"

"Yes."

I turned to the judge. "We would like to interrupt Mr. Moore's testimony for a few minutes to call another witness who has information relevant to Mr. Moore's testimony. We reserve the right to recall Mr. Moore after our next witness has completed his testimony."

"No objection," Harper said.

"The defense calls Peter Daley."

* * *

Pete was on the stand for less than two minutes. He summarized his credentials. I introduced the video of Moore leaving Chloe's house. He finished with a succinct conclusion.

"On January twenty-fourth of this year, Mr. Moore spent the night at Mrs. King's house."

"No further questions."

"Cross-exam, Mr. Harper?"

"Just a few questions." He walked up to Pete. "You're Mr. Daley's brother?"

"Yes."

"You embellished your testimony to assist your brother, didn't you?"

"No."

"You used to be a police officer, right?"

"Right."

"You were kicked off the force, weren't you?"

"My partner and I broke up a gang fight in the Mission. One of the criminals was drunk and belligerent. He was injured when we subdued him in self-defense. As part of a settlement with the City, my partner and I were terminated."

"The young man had a fractured skull, didn't he?"

"And I had a cracked rib."

"Please answer my question, Mr. Daley."

"Yes."

"No further questions."

* * *

Moore was back on the stand. I pressed a button on my laptop. Pete's video from in front of Chloe's house appeared on the screen. I ran it in slow motion and stopped it as the BMW was passing Pete's car.

"Do you recognize this vehicle?" I asked.

"No."

"Would it help you if I told you that it's a BMW registered in your name?"

"I'll take your word for it."

I zoomed in. "Do you recognize the driver?"

Moore's eyes darted. "Looks like me."

"Mr. Moore, the individual who shot this video just testified that he took it in front of Mrs. King's house on the morning of January twenty-fourth."

"I'll take your word for that, too."

"He also testified that you had spent the night at Mrs. King's house."

A hesitation. "I don't recall."

"Are you saying that the individual's testimony was inaccurate?"

"I'm saying that I don't recall."

"You're having an affair with Mrs. King, aren't you?"

"No."

"Do you want to reconsider your answer, Mr. Moore?"

He scowled. "We were attracted to each other. She was lonely. It just happened."

"And Mr. King's death meant that you were free to see his wife, right?"

"They were already separated."

"Mr. King's death meant you would also get a promotion and a substantial raise, right?"

"I didn't intend for things to happen that way."

"Come on, Mr. Moore. You're the only person who came out ahead. You were able to continue your relationship with Mrs. King and you got a promotion."

"That's absurd, Mr. Daley."

"You knew that Jeff King had a heroin problem. You knew that he was going to see Ms. Low that night. You knew that they always took smack when they got together. You knew that he had a heart condition susceptible to disaster if he took some pure heroin. So you planted some high-powered stuff in the bathroom upstairs and hoped that he would overdose. Isn't that what happened, Mr. Moore?"

"Absolutely not, Mr. Daley. Jeff King was my boss, my mentor, and my friend. I did not plant heroin in his bathroom. End of story."

I did my best to feign disbelief. "No further questions."

62
"I THINK HE WAS A SEX ADDICT"

"What is your position at Y5K?" I asked.

The "Guy from Rye" smirked. "Quality control."

"What does that entail?"

"Making sure our products work the way they're supposed to."

Gee, thanks. "You and Mr. King were friends for a long time, right?"

"Since high school."

"And you've worked at several companies that he started?"

"That *we* started."

Sure. "You also spent a lot of time together outside the office, didn't you?"

"Yes."

"You partied?"

"From time to time."

"Met women?"

"Occasionally."

"You knew that Mr. King had a substance issue, right?"

"I had suspicions."

"You were his best friend for forty years. You must have known."

"I was pretty sure."

Was that so hard? "You also knew that he and Mrs. King had separated?"

"I did. I tried to be supportive."

"You introduced him to women?"

"Periodically."

"And provided drugs?"

"No."

It was worth a shot. "He had issues with women, didn't he?"

"I'm not a therapist, Mr. Daley."

"I'm not asking for a professional opinion."

"I think he was a sex addict."

That got the jurors' attention. "You knew that he was meeting women on a site called Mature Relations, didn't you?"

"Yes."

"You're also a member of that site, right?"

"It isn't illegal."

"And you've met people through that site, haven't you?"

"That isn't illegal, either."

"You recently attempted to renegotiate your compensation with the company, didn't you?"

"Yes."

"And management was reluctant to give you a raise?"

"Just business."

"Did you discuss it with Mr. King?"

"Yes. He promised to see what he could do."

"You didn't get the raise, right?"

"He died before we could resolve the issue."

"I presume you were upset about it?"

"Just business, Mr. Daley."

"You were at the party at Mr. King's house on the night that he died?"

"Yes."

"You knew that he was planning to get together with Ms. Low, didn't you?"

"Yes."

"And you knew that they would engage in sex and take heroin?"

"That was usually the way it worked."

"Who provided the heroin?"

"Ms. Low."

"A billionaire accepted heroin from a woman he met on a pickup site?"

"Mr. King did some reckless things."

"Did you ever provide the heroin?"

"No."

"You're under oath, Mr. Pitt."

"No."

"Did you see Ms. Low that night?"

"No."

"Did you use the upstairs bathroom?"

"I believe so."

"You left some high-end heroin for your friend and his date, didn't you?"

"No."

"You let your best friend of forty years take cheap smack that a woman he met on a hookup site bought on the street?"

"Jeff didn't always use exemplary judgment."

"Let's be honest, Mr. Pitt. You slipped Mr. King some high-powered heroin to send him a little message about your disappointment, didn't you?"

"That isn't how I roll, Mr. Daley."

"Then perhaps you slipped your friend some high-end heroin to thank him for all of his hard work on the IPO, didn't you?"

"No, Mr. Daley."

"No further questions."

"Cross-exam, Mr. Harper?"

"No, Your Honor."

The judge looked at her computer. "I'm going to recess until tomorrow. How much longer will you need, Mr. Daley?"

"We should wrap up our defense in the morning."

"Very good. I want to see draft jury instructions from both sides first thing tomorrow morning. Once those are agreed-upon, we should be in a position to move forward to closing arguments."

63
"I JUST CAN'T"

Lexy's eyes were clear. "Are we almost done?"

"Close," I said. "I wanted to talk to you about tomorrow morning."

Lexy, Nady, and I were in the consultation room in the Glamour Slammer at seven-thirty on Monday night. We had developed a routine of meeting in the airless bunker every night after trial.

"How are you holding up?" I asked.

"Not great."

"We can ask the judge for a day off if you're hitting the wall."

"I want to finish."

"That's fine. I need to ask you something." *Here goes.* "Do you think you're up to testifying tomorrow?"

She swallowed hard. "I'm not sure, Mike."

"I want you to answer just a few questions. First, I'll ask if you ever brought the heroin when you got together with King. Second, I'll ask if you brought heroin up to King's house on the night that he died. Third, I'll ask if you intended to kill King. The correct answers, by the way, are no, no, and no."

This got the hint of a smile. "I figured."

"So?"

"So what?"

"Are you up for testifying in the morning?"

She waited a long moment. "I don't think so, Mike."

"I'll be right there. You just need to follow my lead."

"I can't."

"Would you be more comfortable if Nady asked you the questions?"

She thought about it for another interminable moment. "I just can't."

"You're sure?"

"Yes."

I reached over and touched her hand. "That's fine, Lexy."

"Is it enough?"

"It'll have to be."

* * *

At ten-fifteen on Monday night, Rosie and I were driving on Presidio Parkway toward the Golden Gate Bridge when Pete's name appeared on the display of my iPhone.

"Give me some good news," I said.

"How soon can you get down to Santa Cruz?"

"Tonight?"

"Yes. You got other plans?"

"I'll be there in two hours. What is it, Pete?"

"Kaela Joy found Debbie Steele."

64
"WE CAN DO THIS ANOTHER WAY"

Pete and Kaela Joy met Rosie and me in the lobby of an upscale treatment facility that resembled the Ahwahnee Hotel at Yosemite. Perched in the wooded hills above Santa Cruz, the aroma of pine needles filled the two-story atrium. At twelve-thirty a.m., it was too dark to see what I presumed was a panoramic view of the Pacific through the picture windows that opened onto a spacious veranda.

"How did you find this place?" I asked Kaela Joy.

"This is where the most affluent residents of Silicon Valley come to dry out."

"How much does it cost?"

"Ninety grand a month."

Wow. "You've been here before?"

"My ex- came here for treatment several times. I know the people who run it."

"I trust you were able to persuade them to let us talk to Steele's daughter?"

"Yes, but there are conditions." She lowered her voice. "First, we need to keep it short. Second, somebody from the facility will be present. Third, Debbie is having a rough time, so we'll need to be gentle. Fourth, she isn't leaving, so don't even ask. Fifth, she isn't going to give a statement or sign anything, so don't ask about that either. And sixth, she isn't going to testify, so don't go there. Got it?"

"Yes. Anything else?"

"If anybody asks, I wasn't here."

* * *

Rosie took a sip of tea. "Thank you for talking to us, Ms. Steele."

"Debbie."

"Rosie."

The young woman that Pete and I had met at Bird Dog looked pale and tired. Wearing jeans and a turtleneck, her soft features evoked a profound sadness. Debbie, Rosie, Kaela Joy, and I were sitting in a cheerful library with redwood bookcases. To avoid overwhelming her, we had decided that Pete would wait outside. A crackling fire in the stone fireplace provided warmth. The ambiance was soothing.

Rosie's eyes locked onto Debbie's. "How's your treatment coming along?"

"One day at a time."

"My sister went through the process for alcohol and coke. It's hard. And it takes time."

Debbie glanced at her counselor, who was sitting nearby. "That's what they tell me."

"We need to ask you about your time at Y5K last year. I know this is difficult."

Debbie's lips turned down. "It is."

"We won't take much of your time, and we're grateful for your help. If you want to stop and take a break, that's okay with us."

"I'm not leaving here, and I won't testify."

"That's fine, too. We can do this another way." Rosie took another sip of tea. "We understand that your experience at the company wasn't so good."

"It wasn't."

"Would you mind telling us why?"

"Jeff." A hesitation. Tears welled up. "He was a pig."

"So we understand." Rosie waited.

"He hit on the women—even the interns. He tried to get us drunk. He wanted us to do coke and heroin. He insisted that we go to strip clubs with him. He couldn't keep his hands to himself. And everybody at the company followed his lead. It was a boys' club. It was humiliating."

"Was there something in particular?"

The tears came freely now. "He tried to rape me."

"Where?"

"In his office. I fought him off and ran down the hall. It was horrific." She paused to regain her composure. "I took a couple of days off, then I came back to work. It was a huge mistake. I saw him in the hallway, and he pretended that nothing had happened."

"That's terrible, Debbie. Did you report it?"

"Are you serious? He was the Prince of Disruption. I was just an intern."

"Your father was an executive at the company."

"My father cheated on my mother. And my first stepmother. And my second stepmother. Do you think he was going to protect me?"

"Did you tell him what happened?"

"Not at the time."

Dear God.

"How did you deal with it?" Rosie asked.

"I stayed away from Jeff for the rest of the summer."

"What about the other interns?"

"Jeff kept hitting on them."

Rosie's lips formed a tight ball. She didn't say it aloud, but I knew that she was as appalled as I was.

She asked, "Anything else you might be willing to share with us?"

"I ran into Jeff at a restaurant about a week before he died. He pretended that nothing had happened. He said that he wanted to go out for coffee and talk about my career—as if I would ever work for him or ask him for advice. When I went out to my car, he was waiting for me. He told me that he wanted me to come back to the company so that we could get to know each other better. I was terrified."

"Did he touch you?"

"No. He just leered."

"I'm so sorry, Debbie. Did you tell your father this time?"

"Yes. I told him everything."

"Did he do anything about it?"

"He said that he was going to teach Jeff a lesson."

Rosie leaned forward. "Did you talk about this in person?"

"Mostly." Her eyes filled with panic. "I'm not going to testify."

"We won't ask you to do so. Are there any e-mails or texts between you and your father about this?"

"Maybe some texts."

"May we have permission to look at your phone?"

"I bought a new one."

"Did you transfer your texts to the new phone?"

"No."

"Any chance your messages are archived somewhere in the cloud?"

"Maybe."

"What about your father's phone?"

"Maybe." She thought about it for a moment. "We never called or texted on the phone that he used for company business."

"He had a second phone?"

"Yes. A burner."

"Do you happen to know the number?"

"I don't remember. It was programmed into my old phone."

"Is he still using the same burner?"

"No. He got a new one a few weeks ago. I'm sorry."

"You've been incredibly helpful. And very brave."

"Thank you."

"Good luck with your recovery, Debbie."

* * *

Pete, Rosie, Kaela Joy, and I were standing in the driveway of the treatment facility. I spoke to Kaela Joy. "I can't imagine what she went through."

"King was even more vile than I thought. I hope my daughter never works for somebody like him."

"I hope my daughter never knows anybody like him." I turned to Pete. "Can you track down Steele's burner?"

"Maybe."

"He may have used it when he set up his account with Mature Relations."

"I'll call your pal, Brian Holton."

65
"I PROMISED TO TALK TO HIM"

When I walked into my office at eight-fifteen the following morning, Pete was sitting behind my desk and sipping coffee. "Morning, Mick."

"Morning, Pete. You stay up all night?"

"Possibly."

Holton was sitting on the sofa. "Morning, Brian. All good at Mature Relations?"

"Couldn't be better. Did you ever sign up for a trial membership?"

"Not yet."

"Every day is a beautiful day for people to fall in love."

Uh, right. I turned back to Pete. "Anything I can use?"

He handed me a sheet of paper. "This is everything you'll need from King's old burner phone."

"Thank you, Pete."

"Don't thank me. Thank Brian."

* * *

An hour later, I spoke to Steele from the lectern. "You're still under oath."

He responded with an impatient, "Yes, Mr. Daley."

I moved in front of the box. "Your daughter worked as an intern at Y5K last summer, didn't she?"

His eyes narrowed. "I fail to see how her internship has any bearing on this case."

I turned to the judge. "Would you please instruct the witness to answer?"

"Please, Mr. Steele."

He pushed out a melodramatic sigh. "Yes, Mr. Daley."

"She had an unsatisfying experience, didn't she?"

"It was fine."

"No, it wasn't."

"Yes, it was."

"In fact, her experience was unsatisfying because Jeff King made numerous inappropriate sexual advances to her, didn't he?"

"There were some issues that were resolved."

"He assaulted your daughter."

"There was a misunderstanding."

"Why are you still protecting him?"

"I'm not."

"He made inappropriate advances and encouraged the interns to use illegal drugs, didn't he?"

"It wasn't reported to me at the time."

"He took your daughter and other interns to strip clubs, didn't he?"

His tone became grudging. "Yes."

"And when this was reported to you, you did nothing."

"I spoke to Mr. King. The practice stopped."

"Did it? We heard testimony yesterday from a private investigator who reported that Mr. King was still taking Y5K personnel to the Gold Club several times a week."

"I wasn't aware of it at the time, and nobody reported it to me."

"Except your daughter."

"I told you that I took appropriate steps to make sure that Mr. King modified his behavior."

"Seems he didn't listen."

"Objection. There wasn't a question there."

"Withdrawn. Mr. Steele, late last year, your daughter reported to you that she saw Mr. King at a restaurant in Palo Alto, didn't she?"

"Yes."

"And she told you that Mr. King had made inappropriate comments to her, right?"

"Yes."

"And she told you that Mr. King had made inappropriate sexual advances to her during her internship, didn't she?"

His face tightened. "Yes."

"Did you do anything about it?"

"I talked to Jeff. He promised to change his behavior."

"He assaulted your daughter and all you did was gently ask him to change his behavior?"

"I was very direct with him."

"Why didn't you fire him and report him to the police?"

"He acknowledged his inappropriate behavior. He was

remorseful."

"And he was your meal ticket."

"Objection."

"Withdrawn. Mr. Steele, isn't it true that when you daughter informed you of Mr. King's latest attempts at sexual harassment, you promised her that you would do something about it?"

"Yes. I promised to talk to him."

"You promised even more, didn't you?"

"I don't recall."

I walked back to the defense table, where Lexy handed me three copies of a printout showing texts from Steele's old burner phone. I introduced the document into evidence and handed copies to the judge, Harper, and Steele.

"Mr. Steele," I continued, "I trust that you're familiar with the messages that you sent to your daughter from your own throwaway phone?"

He speed-read the printout. "Where did you get this?"

Wikileaks. "Your Honor, would you please remind Mr. Steele that he isn't permitted to ask questions of counsel?"

"Please, Mr. Steele."

I flipped to page two. "On December twelfth of last year, your daughter sent you a text asking what you planned to do about Mr. King's latest sexual assault, didn't she?"

"Yes. And I wouldn't describe it as 'sexual assault.'"

Your daughter would. "Isn't it true that you sent your daughter a text indicating that you would talk to Mr. King and reprimand him for his behavior?"

"Yes."

"You also sent her a text noting that Mr. King was a regular heroin user, didn't you?"

"Yes."

"And you said that you would teach him a lesson, right?"

"Yes."

"You arranged to give Mr. King a substantial dose of pure heroin to send him a message, didn't you?"

"I didn't mean that I would actually give him enough heroin to cause an overdose. It was an expression. A metaphor."

"You're testifying under oath that your blatant threat was just a metaphor?"

"Yes."

"It sounded like a threat to me."

"You are misreading my intent, Mr. Daley."

"You aren't really going to tell us that it was all a misunderstanding, are you?"

"Yes, I am."

"You were at Mr. King's party a few days later. You knew that he was meeting with Ms. Low. You knew that Mr. King always left the heroin in the master bath. So you substituted a baggie of highly potent heroin, didn't you, Mr. Steele?"

"No."

"You knew that there was a substantial likelihood that he would overdose and become sick or even die, didn't you? That's what you meant by teaching him a lesson, right, Mr. Steele?"

"Absolutely not, Mr. Daley. That's utterly preposterous."

"Do you really think anybody in this courtroom believes you?"

"Objection."

"Withdrawn. No further questions. Your Honor. The defense rests."

Judge McDaniel looked at Harper. "Anything further from the prosecution?"

"No, Your Honor."

"I'd like to meet with counsel in chambers to discuss jury instructions and schedule closing arguments. We're in recess until nine o'clock tomorrow morning."

66
"YOU SHOULD HAVE ASKED SOONER"

Judge McDaniel put her reading glasses down on her desk. "I would like to hear closing arguments tomorrow morning and hand this case over to the jury. Does that work for you?"

Harper and I nodded.

"Good." She picked up Harper's draft jury instructions. "I see that you are now requesting a manslaughter instruction."

"It seems appropriate given the testimony and the evidence presented at trial."

I invoked a respectful tone. "Your Honor—,"

She stopped me with an upraised hand. "I'll get to you in a minute, Mr. Daley." She turned back to Harper. "You should have asked sooner."

"With hindsight, I would have."

"Here's my problem. We've empaneled a conscientious jury and conducted a trial under the assumption that you would not be asking for a manslaughter instruction. Mr. Daley has made certain strategic decisions based upon your choice. I am therefore reluctant to approve this request immediately before we begin closing arguments."

Harper frowned. "The jurors may decide the facts warrant a conviction for something less than murder. I think it is fair and just to give them the opportunity to apply suitable law in light of their determination of the facts."

"If you had asked for it earlier, I might have been more inclined." She turned to me. "How do you feel about this, Mr. Daley?"

Did we create enough doubt in the minds of the jurors to get an acquittal on the murder charge? Should I hedge my bets and ask for a manslaughter instruction to give the jury an easier route to a lighter sentence? Which is better for Lexy?

"Your Honor, we tried this case on the assumption that there would be no manslaughter instruction. We would have done things differently if manslaughter was on the table."

"You understand the risks if there is no such instruction? And you realize that your client would be subject to a shorter sentence—potentially much shorter—if she's convicted of manslaughter?"

"Yes."

Harper spoke up again. "Your Honor, you still have the authority to include a manslaughter instruction, even if Mr. Daley does not request it."

"I am well aware of that, Mr. Harper." She turned to me. "I am not inclined to act unilaterally and include a manslaughter instruction—especially since you've never asked for it, and Mr. Harper made his request so late in the process. However, if both you and Mr. Harper agree that such an instruction is warranted, I will abide by your unanimous decision. Mr. Harper has expressed his preference. So it's up to you, Mr. Daley. What say you?"

My mind raced to consider the possible ramifications. I thought about the things that I would have done differently. I flashed onto Lexy's face. Then I remembered Rosie's advice during our first trial together: sometimes it's necessary to make course corrections, but you should never second-guess yourself in the heat of battle.

"Your Honor," I said, "we are not going to request a manslaughter instruction."

"Then it's settled. There will be no such instruction to the jury."

Harper tried again. "But Your Honor—,"

"I've ruled, Mr. Harper. We'll begin closing arguments at nine-thirty tomorrow morning."

67
"MAYBE WE SHOULD HAVE TAKEN THE DEAL"

"They've been out too long," I said.

Rosie leaned back in her chair. "It's been three days, Mike. Stop second-guessing yourself. It's a waste of energy. And it makes everybody nervous."

On Friday, February fifteenth, the jury was in its third day of deliberations. Closing arguments had been a draw. Harper focused on the fact that Lexy had injected King. I emphasized the fact that King had asked for it and pointed out all the other people who could have planted the heroin in King's bathroom. I made an impassioned case for blaming Steele. The jurors were attentive and seemed equally skeptical about our respective presentations.

At three o'clock on Friday afternoon, there was nothing to do except wait.

Nady came into Rosie's office. "Anything?"

"Not yet," I said.

"How long do you think they'll go?"

"Maybe later this afternoon. They aren't going to want to come back on Monday."

"What do you think it means?"

"Hard to tell. Maybe we should have taken the deal for second-degree."

Rosie wasn't buying. "There's no way you should have pleaded this out for anything more than voluntary manslaughter."

"Then maybe I should have agreed to a manslaughter instruction. It would have improved our odds for a shorter sentence."

"Don't rule out an acquittal, Mike."

"I'm not as confident as you are, Rosie."

"Maybe you should be."

Nady smiled. "Is he always like this when a jury is out?"

Rosie closed her eyes and nodded. "Every time."

There was a knock on the door, and Terrence the Terminator came inside. "I just got a text from the bailiff. The jury is coming back."

* * *

"Will the defendant please rise?"

Lexy stood up between Nady and me.

The judge glanced at Lexy, then spoke to the foreman. "Have you reached a verdict?"

"We have, Your Honor."

My heart was pounding. Lexy tensed.

The gallery sat in silent anticipation as the foreman handed the verdict to the bailiff, who passed it to the clerk, who delivered it to Judge McDaniel. She studied it for a moment, then she handed the slip of paper back to the clerk.

Her tone was solemn. "Please read the verdict."

The clerk cleared his throat. "On the charge of murder in the first-degree, the jury finds the defendant not guilty. On the lesser charge of murder in the second-degree, the jury also finds the defendant not guilty."

Yes!

The courtroom exploded. Reporters headed out the door. I saw Rosie's smiling face in the gallery. I realized that Lexy was hugging me. She was sobbing as she turned around and hugged Nady.

Judge McDaniel asked for order, and the courtroom went silent. She addressed the foreman. "Is this a unanimous verdict?"

"Yes, Your Honor."

"We thank you for your service. You are now dismissed and free to leave."

After the jurors filed out of court, the judge spoke to Harper. "As always, the court thanks you for your professionalism and courtesy, Mr. Harper."

"Thank you, Your Honor."

She turned to Lexy. "Ms. Low, you are free to go. We wish you the best."

Lexy's voice was barely audible. "Thank you, Your Honor."

We all stood up and Judge McDaniel left the courtroom.

Lexy sat down and took a moment to get her bearings. Finally, she looked at me. "I don't know how I can possibly thank you and Nady."

"You're welcome, Lexy."

A look of panic crossed her tear-stained face. "Where am I going to go? I have no place to stay. I have nobody to call."

"They will assign a case worker when we get downstairs. She'll help you collect your belongings. She'll get you a hot meal and a place to stay tonight. Tomorrow, she'll help you find something more permanent."

68
"IT'S BETTER TO GET OUT A LITTLE EARLY THAN A LITTLE LATE"

Big John flashed his bartender's smile. "What'll it be, lad?"

"Just coffee tonight."

The evening crowd at Dunleavy's was thinning. I was dead tired, but I always seemed to end up at Big John's after finishing a trial.

My uncle put a fatherly hand on my shoulder. "You look like you could use a beer."

"Maybe I could. Is it too late to change my order?"

"I'll talk to the barkeep." He turned to Rosie, who was sitting across the table from me. "Can I get the distinguished Public Defender another beer?"

"Not tonight, Big John. I'm driving."

His gaze shifted to Grace, who was sitting next to Rosie. "Anything for the Love Goddess?"

"No thanks, Big John. By the way, I'm shutting down the Love Goddess."

"May I ask why?"

"These things have a short shelf life. We're losing users and gaining trolls. It's becoming more of a hassle than it's worth."

"Can you sell it to somebody?"

"I'm not for sale."

When Grace was born, I never figured that I would someday be immensely proud of her for declining a potentially lucrative payout for the rights to her sex-advice site.

Big John wasn't giving up. "This is going to be bad for my business, honey. I've gotten a lot of mileage out of telling everybody that my great-niece is the Love Goddess."

"Dunleavy's was here long before the Love Goddess, and it'll be here for a long time to come. Apps come and go. Classics are forever."

My last living uncle's wide face transformed into a broad smile. "Did I ever tell you that you're my favorite great-niece?"

"Every time I see you. You say that to all of your great-nieces, don't you?"

"Yes."

"Thought so."

"You're still the favorite of my favorites, Grace."

"And you're my favorite great-uncle, Big John."

"I'm your *only* great-uncle, honey." The greatest tight end in the history of St. Ignatius High School let out a throaty laugh and headed back to the bar.

I looked across the table at my ex-wife and daughter. Grace had come up from L.A. for the weekend to look for post-graduation housing. She now looked exactly like the Rosie I had fallen in love with a quarter of a century earlier. It made me feel old.

"Are you really shutting down the Love Goddess?" I asked.

"It's run its course. It's better to get out a little early than a little late. Besides, I want to make movies."

I wasn't heartbroken. "You still going over to Emeryville in the morning?"

"Yes. I'm looking at a condo a few blocks from Pixar."

"To rent?"

"To buy." She arched her eyebrow in the same manner that Rosie always did. "The Love Goddess is paying for it."

My daughter the sex-advice entrepreneur is becoming a real estate mogul. And I'm still living in the one-bedroom apartment behind the Larkspur fire station that I rented when Rosie and I got divorced. "You want company?"

"Sure."

"Do you need us to co-sign your mortgage?"

"Nope. I'm already pre-qualified."

Rosie and I exchanged a glance. Our twenty-year-old daughter was already light years ahead of us.

Grace stood up and put on her jacket. "I'll meet you at home. I want to see Tommy, and I need to be up early tomorrow."

I was filled with pride as I watched our ever-so-resourceful daughter say good-bye to Big John and leave through the back door, where her new car was parked in Big John's spot.

I squeezed the hand of my ex-wife, former law partner, current boss, mother of our children, and the first Latina Public Defender of the City and County of San Francisco. "I guess this means that she's launched."

"She was launched a couple of years ago."

"Let's not get cocky, Rosita. You're familiar with Daley's Rule Number One: When you think you have everything figured out, life has a way of reminding you that you don't."

"She'll be fine, Mike."

"She already is." I squeezed her hand more tightly. "Did you know that she was shutting down the Love Goddess?"

"She told me a couple of weeks ago. She didn't want me to mention it."

Rosie was better at keeping secrets than I was. "I'm not entirely disappointed."

"Neither am I. Is there a 'but' coming?"

"She was making a lot of money. It paid for that fancy SUV with the leather seats."

"You were okay with our daughter running a sex-advice site as long as it was profitable?"

"I must confess that the financial upside mitigated some of the moral downside."

"It's probably better that you aren't a priest anymore. I'm not bursting with pride about this, but I came down in the same place that you did."

"Does that make us terrible people?"

"Probably."

"How much do you think she made?"

"Enough to pay for her tuition, room, board, spending money, the new car, and a down payment on a condo."

"Not bad for a twenty-year-old," I said.

"I guess we did something right."

She left it there. While I knew that she was immensely proud of both of our kids, she thought it was unseemly to brag. In that respect, and many others, she was similar to her mother.

"Were you able to talk to any of the jurors?" she asked.

"Yes. They decided that there wasn't enough evidence to convict Lexy of murder."

"They got that much right."

"They also asked why she wasn't charged with manslaughter. I told them that it was the D.A.'s decision."

"Would they have convicted her for manslaughter?"

"Probably."

"Then you got an excellent result. Is Harper going to charge Lexy with possession or solicitation?"

"No. He decided that she's been through enough."

"What about Flynn's death?"

"Insufficient evidence."

Rosie pointed at the TV, which was tuned to the local news. "They're searching Steele's house for evidence relating to King's death. My moles tell me that he'll be in custody tomorrow, and likely to be charged with murder or manslaughter. Evidently, there was more information on Steele's burner phone."

"Did he intend to kill King?"

"Unclear. It is clear that he intended to arrange for him to get a massive shot of heroin to send him a message not to mess with his daughter—or anybody else—ever again."

"Message delivered."

"I'll say."

"Do your moles know where he got the heroin?"

"The 'Guy from Rye.' Pitt had a burner, too. There is communication from Steele to Pitt asking him to provide some high-end heroin to 'thank' King for his hard work on the IPO. Pitt was delighted to oblige."

"Is the D.A. going to charge Pitt, too?"

"Yes."

"For what?"

"Definitely for possession. Possibly as an accessory to murder or manslaughter." Her tone turned thoughtful. "All things considered, you and Nady got a fine result for our client."

"Thanks."

"Lawyering matters. Nady didn't want to come over for a celebratory drink?"

"I sent her home. She hasn't gotten much sleep lately. I told her that she needed to spend some time with Max and Luna."

"She's turning into a superb trial lawyer. It helps that she's learning from the best."

"Does that mean that I might be in line for a modest raise?"

"No."

"I also told her that she could bring Luna to the office."

"We're now a dog-friendly workplace?"

"I made an executive decision in my capacity as the co-head of the Felony Division. Besides, it's very trendy. All the tech companies are doing it."

"We aren't a tech company. It's a bad precedent, and it probably violates a dozen city regulations."

"You sound like a bureaucrat."

"I *am* a bureaucrat, Mike."

"Are you planning to report us?"

"Absolutely not." She grinned. "Besides, Luna is easier to deal with than some of our employees."

I hoped that she wasn't referring to me.

Rosie checked her iPhone for texts and e-mails. Then she put the phone into her pocket. "How did Kaela Joy find Steele's daughter?"

"She's very resourceful." I arched an eyebrow. "And she may have gotten a tip from Nick the Dick."

"How did Pete get Steele's burner phone number?"

"Brian Holton."

"You got an acquittal based on a tip from a guy who runs a sugar daddy site?"

"We don't ask our sources to sign a morality pledge."

"How did Pete manage to hack into Steele's burner phone?"

"A couple of Holton's cyber-security people used to be world-class hackers."

"You realize that may not have been technically legal?"

"We got to the truth, Rosie." *Or close enough to get the jury to reasonable doubt.*

"I could make a reasonable argument that you crossed the line. Please don't do it again."

"I won't." *At least I'll try.* "Is that the extent of my reprimand?"

"Yes. And we'll never talk about this again."

"Agreed. It also helped that Betsy McDaniel didn't allow a manslaughter instruction. We probably wouldn't be having a celebratory drink if she had decided the other way."

"She's a good judge."

"Yes, she is."

She smiled. "You did it."

"What?"

"Everything. You got an acquittal for Lexy. Steele is about to be arrested. So is Pitt. Y5K's IPO is on hold. You exposed King, Steele, Patel, Moore, Pitt, and the Y5K management team as a bunch of misogynist pigs."

"They did it to themselves."

"It wouldn't have been uncovered without you, Nady, and Pete. All things considered, I'd say we came pretty close to justice being served."

"Yeah."

Her lips turned down. "You don't seem happy about it."

"King is still dead. Lexy is still addicted and has no place to live. Steele's daughter is in rehab. Patel's marriage is blowing up. So is Chu's engagement to Moore. A bunch of people at Y5K will probably lose their jobs. And the rest of Silicon Valley will keep rolling as if nothing happened."

"We can't fix everything, Mike."

"We can keep trying."

Rosie finished her beer. "How is Lexy?"

"Grateful and scared. The case worker found her a spot in a halfway house near Alamo Square. It's good for a couple of weeks. There's a social worker on-site and a doctor on-call."

"It's a long process. And her mental state?"

"Relieved to be out of jail, but she understands that it's going to take some time before she'll get back to anything resembling normalcy."

"One step at a time."

"Yeah." I picked up my iPhone. "I need to show you something." I typed a few strokes, and the home page for Mature Relations came up.

Rosie looked at my phone. "Who's BigLaw714?"

"Me."

"You have an account at Mature Relations?"

"Pete helped me set it up."

"Is there something I need to know?"

"It's purely for research, Rosie. You'll note that I didn't post a photo. Besides, nobody would be interested in seeing me."

"I would."

"Good to know."

I hit a few more keystrokes. The homepage for the "Tech Princess" came up.

Rosie's eyes opened wide. "Lexy is already back up on Mature Relations?"

"Yup."

"That didn't take long."

"I'm not entirely surprised. It's going to be difficult for her to find a job. As a practical matter, she needs to figure out a way to pay her bills."

"There are other ways."

"This is more lucrative."

"Are you disappointed?"

"Yes."

"Are you planning to talk to her about it?"

"Yes."

Rosie lowered her voice. "Are you going to be okay?"

"I'll be fine."

"After all the hard work that you and Nady put in, Lexy is right back where she started."

"At least she isn't in jail. We take our clients as they come, Rosie. Just because we got an acquittal doesn't mean that we can fix the rest of her life."

Big John reappeared. "Anything else, kids?"

"We're good, Big John. Thanks for your hospitality."

"You're welcome. Why are you smiling?"

"You're the last guy on Planet Earth who still calls me 'kid.'"

"I was in the waiting room with your Daddy when you were born. You'll always be a kid to me, Mikey."

"Can I pay you for the drinks?"

"I don't take money from kids." The big bartender tossed his dish towel over his shoulder and headed back to the bar that my father had helped him build six decades earlier.

I looked across the worn wooden table where my dad and Roosevelt Johnson used to sit. The Public Defender of the City and County of San Francisco was looking at her iPhone again. She was more beautiful than the day I met her.

"How much longer do you want to do this?" I asked.

She looked up. "One more election cycle. That'll be enough."

"You can do this as long as you want. Nobody is going to beat you."

"Public officials shouldn't stay in office for life. Besides, I want to stop while I'm still young and healthy enough to travel. And I want to be around to enjoy our grandchildren."

What? "Is there something else that you haven't told me?"

"No. Grace isn't seeing anybody at the moment, and Tommy broke up with his latest girlfriend. This one lasted almost three weeks—a new record."

"He's only in high school, Rosie."

"It's always good to look ahead."

Good advice. "You really think you'll be able to give up being P.D. after one more term?"

"I do. It's better to get out a little early than a little late."

"I've heard the same thing."

She stood up and put on her jacket. "We should head home. We need to get up early to look at property with our tech-entrepreneur-turned-real-estate-mogul daughter."

We said good night to Big John, then we headed toward the back door. As we were leaving the bar, I squeezed Rosie's hand. "I love you, Rosie."

"I love you, too, Mike."

A NOTE TO THE READER

Dear Reader,

Thanks very much for reading this story. I hope you liked it. If you did, I hope you will check out my other books. In addition, I would appreciate it if you would let others know. In particular, I would be very grateful if you would tell your friends and help us spread the word by e-mail, Amazon, Facebook, Goodreads, Twitter, Linkedin, etc. In addition, if you are inclined (and I hope you are), I hope you will consider posting an honest review on Amazon and/or Goodreads.

Many people have asked to know more about Mike and Rosie's early history. As a thank you to my readers, I wrote **FIRST TRIAL**. It's a short story describing how they met years ago when they were starting out at the P.D.'s Office. The story is available exclusively for members of my mailing list. It's FREE and you can get your digital copy when you subscribe online at: www.sheldonsiegel.com/first-trial. I'm usually busy writing, but I do send out emails to the mailing list every few months with updates, book release information, special promotions, and of course pictures of our cat. Don't worry, I won't inundate you or sell your information, and you can get off the list at any time.

If you have a chance and would like to chat, please feel free to e-mail me at sheldon@sheldonsiegel.com. We lawyers don't get a lot of fan mail, so it's always nice to hear from my readers. Please bear with me if I don't respond immediately. I answer all of my e-mail myself, so sometimes it takes a little extra time.

Regards,

Sheldon

ACKNOWLEDGMENTS

Writing stories is a collaborative process. I would like to thank the many kind people who have been very generous with their time.

Thanks to my beautiful wife, Linda, who still reads my manuscripts, designs the covers for my books, and handles all things technological. You are a kind and wonderful soul.

Thanks to our twin sons, Alan and Stephen, for your support and encouragement for so many years. I am more proud of you than you can imagine.

Thanks to my teachers, Katherine Forrest and Michael Nava, who encouraged me to finish my first book. Thanks to the Every Other Thursday Night Writers Group: Bonnie DeClark, Meg Stiefvater, Anne Maczulak, Liz Hartka, Janet Wallace, and Priscilla Royal. Thanks to Bill and Elaine Petrocelli, Kathryn Petrocelli, and Karen West at Book Passage.

Thanks to my friends and colleagues at Sheppard, Mullin, Richter & Hampton (and your spouses and significant others). I can't mention everybody, but I'd like to note those of you with whom I've worked the longest: Randy and Mary Short, Cheryl Holmes, Chris and Debbie Neils, Joan Story and Robert Kidd, Donna Andrews, Phil and Wendy Atkins-Pattenson, Julie and Jim Ebert, Geri Freeman and David Nickerson, Ed and Valerie Lozowicki, Bill and Barbara Manierre, Betsy McDaniel, Ron and Rita Ryland, Bob Stumpf, Mike Wilmar, Mathilde Kapuano, Guy Halgren, Aline Pearl, Ed Graziani, Julie Penney, Mike Lewis, Christa Carter, Doug Bacon, Lorna Tanner, Larry Braun, Nady Nikonova, Joy Siu, Yolanda Hogan, and DeAnna Ouderkirk. A special thanks to our late colleague, mentor, and friend, the incomparable Bob Thompson.

A huge thanks to Jane Gorsi for your excellent editing skills.

Another huge thanks to Vilsaka Nguyen of the San Francisco Public Defender's Office for your thoughtful comments and terrific support.

A big thanks to Officer David Dito of the San Francisco Police Department for assistance on police matters.

Another big thanks to Bob Puts of SFPD (retired) for his help on the inner workings of SFPD.

Thanks to Tim Campbell for your superb narration of the audio version of this book (and many others in the series). You are terrific!

Thanks to Jerry and Dena Wald, Gary and Marla Goldstein, Ron and Betsy Rooth, Debbie and Seth Tanenbaum, Joan Lubamersky, Jill Hutchinson and Chuck Odenthal, Tom Bearrows and Holly Hirst, Julie Hart, Burt Rosenberg, Ted George, Phil Dito, Sister Karen Marie Franks, Brother Stan Sobczyk, Chuck and Nora Koslosky, Jack Goldthorpe, Peter and Cathy Busch, Bob Dugoni, and John Lescroart. Thanks to Lloyd and Joni Russell and Rich and Leslie Kramer. Thanks to Lauren, Gary and Debbie Fields. A special thanks to my late friend, Scott Pratt, who was a terrific writer and a generous soul.

Thanks to Tim and Kandi Durst, Bob and Cheryl Easter, and Larry DeBrock at the University of Illinois. Thanks to Kathleen Vanden Heuvel, Bob and Leslie Berring, and Jesse Choper at Boalt Law School.

Thanks to the incomparable Zvi Danenberg, who motivates me to walk the Larkspur steps.

Thanks as always to Ben, Michelle, Margie, and Andy Siegel, Joe, Jan, and Julia Garber, Roger and Sharon Fineberg, Scott, Michelle, Kim, and Sophie Harris, Stephanie, Stanley, and Will Coventry, Cathy, Richard, and Matthew Falco, and Julie Harris and Matthew, Aiden, and Ari Stewart. A huge thanks to Jan Harris (1934-2018), whom we miss every day.

ABOUT THE AUTHOR

Sheldon Siegel is the New York Times best-selling author of ten critically acclaimed legal thrillers featuring San Francisco criminal defense attorneys Mike Daley and Rosie Fernandez, two of the most beloved characters in contemporary crime fiction. He is also the author of the thriller novel The Terrorist Next Door featuring Chicago homicide detectives David Gold and A.C. Battle. His books have been translated into a dozen languages and sold millions of copies worldwide. A native of Chicago, Sheldon earned his undergraduate degree from the University of Illinois in Champaign in 1980, and his law degree from the Boalt Hall School of Law at the University of California-Berkeley in 1983. He specializes in corporate and securities law with the San Francisco office of the international law firm of Sheppard, Mullin, Richter & Hampton LLP.

Sheldon began writing his first book, Special Circumstances, on a laptop computer during his daily commute on the ferry from Marin County to San Francisco. A frequent speaker and sought-after teacher, Sheldon is a San Francisco Library Literary Laureate, a former member of the national Board of Directors and the former President of the Northern California chapter of the Mystery Writers of America, and an active member of the International Thriller Writers and Sisters in Crime. His work has been displayed at the Bancroft Library at the University of California at Berkeley, and he has been recognized as a Distinguished Alumnus of the University of Illinois and a Northern

California Super Lawyer.

Sheldon lives in the San Francisco area with his wife, Linda, and their twin sons, Alan and Stephen. He is a lifelong fan of the Chicago Bears, White Sox, Bulls and Blackhawks. He is currently working on his next novel.

Sheldon welcomes your comments and feedback. Please email him at sheldon@sheldonsiegel.com. For more information on Sheldon, book signings, the "making of" his books, and more, please visit his website at www.sheldonsiegel.com.

ACCLAIM FOR SHELDON SIEGEL'S NOVELS

Featuring Mike Daley and Rosie Fernandez

SPECIAL CIRCUMSTANCES

"An A+ first novel." *Philadelphia Inquirer.*

"A poignant, feisty tale. Characters so finely drawn you can almost smell their fear and desperation." *USA Today.*

"By the time the whole circus ends up in the courtroom, the hurtling plot threatens to rip paper cuts into the readers' hands." *San Francisco Chronicle.*

INCRIMINATING EVIDENCE

"Charm and strength. Mike Daley is an original and very appealing character in the overcrowded legal arena—a gentle soul who can fight hard when he has to, and a moral man who is repelled by the greed of many of his colleagues." *Publishers Weekly.*

"The story culminates with an outstanding courtroom sequence. Daley narrates with a kind of genial irony, the pace never slows, and every description of the city is as brightly burnished as the San Francisco sky when the fog lifts." *Newark Star-Ledger.*

"For those who love San Francisco, this is a dream of a novel that capitalizes on the city's festive and festering neighborhoods of old-line money and struggling immigrants. Siegel is an astute observer of the city and takes wry and witty jabs at lawyers and politicians." *USA Today.*

CRIMINAL INTENT

"Ingenious. A surprise ending that will keep readers yearning for more." *Booklist.*

"Siegel writes with style and humor. The people who populate his books are interesting. He's a guy who needs to keep that laptop popping." *Houston Chronicle.*

"Siegel does a nice job of blending humor and human interest. Daley and Fernandez are competent lawyers, not superhuman crime fighters featured in more commonplace legal thrillers. With great characters and realistic dialogue, this book provides enough intrigue and courtroom drama to please any fan of the genre." *Library Journal.*

FINAL VERDICT

"Daley's careful deliberations and ethical considerations are a refreshing contrast to the slapdash morality and breakneck speed of most legal thrillers. The detailed courtroom scenes are instructive and authentic, the resolution fair, dramatic and satisfying. Michael, Rosie, Grace and friends are characters worth rooting for. The verdict is clear: another win for Siegel." *Publishers Weekly.*

"An outstanding entry in an always reliable series. An ending that's full of surprises—both professional and personal—provides the perfect finale to a supremely entertaining legal thriller." *Booklist.*

"San Francisco law partners Mike Daley and Rosie Fernandez spar like Tracy and Hepburn. Final Verdict maintains a brisk pace, and there's genuine satisfaction when the bad guy gets his comeuppance." *San Francisco Chronicle.*

THE CONFESSION

"As Daley moves from the drug and prostitute-ridden underbelly of San Francisco, where auto parts and offers of legal aid are exchanged for cooperation, to the tension-filled courtroom and the hushed offices of the church, it gradually becomes apparent that Father Ramon isn't the only character with a lot at stake in this intelligent, timely thriller." *Publishers Weekly.*

"This enthralling novel keeps reader attention with one surprise after another. The relationship between Mike and Rosie adds an exotic dimension to this exciting courtroom drama in which the defense and the prosecutor interrogation of witnesses make for an authentic, terrific tale." *The Best Reviews.*

"Sheldon Siegel is to legal thrillers as Robin Cook is to medical thrillers." *Midwest Book Review.*

JUDGMENT DAY

"Drug dealers, wily lawyers, crooked businessmen, and conflicted cops populate the pages of this latest in a best-selling series from Sheldon Siegel. A compelling cast and plenty of suspense put this one right up there with the best of Lescroart and Turow." *Booklist Starred Review.*

"An exciting and suspenseful read—a thriller that succeeds both as a provocative courtroom drama and as a personal tale of courage and justice. With spine-tingling thrills and a mind-blowing finish, this novel is a must, must read." *New Mystery Reader.*

"It's a good year when Sheldon Siegel produces a novel. Siegel has written an adrenaline rush of a book. The usual fine mix from a top-notch author." *Shelf Awareness.*

PERFECT ALIBI

"Siegel, an attorney-author who deserves to be much more well-known than he is, has produced another tightly plotted, fluidly written legal thriller. Daley and Fernandez are as engaging as when we first met them in Special Circumstances, and the story is typically intricate and suspenseful. Siegel is a very talented writer, stylistically closer to Turow than Grisham, and this novel should be eagerly snapped up by fans of those giants (and also by readers of San Francisco-set legal thrillers of John Lescroart)." *Booklist.*

"Sheldon Siegel is a practicing attorney and the married father of twin sons. He knows the law and he knows the inner workings of a family. This knowledge has given him a great insight in the writing of Perfect Alibi, which for Siegel fans is his almost perfect book." *Huffington Post.*

FELONY MURDER RULE

"Outstanding! Siegel's talent shines in characters who are sharp, witty, and satirical, and in the intimate details of a San Francisco insider. Nobody writes dialogue better. The lightning quick pace is reminiscent of Elmore Leonard—Siegel only writes the good parts." *Robert Dugoni, New York Times and Amazon best-selling author of MY SISTER'S GRAVE.*

SERVE AND PROTECT

An Amazon rating of 4.5/5. Readers say: "A strong, thought-provoking novel. It is a page-turner and well worth the time and effort." "His stories are believable and entertaining. The main characters are written with human foibles. With everyday problems they reflect real life." "Sheldon keeps the reader involved, wondering and anxious to read the next line... And the real magic is the ability of the author to keep the reader involved up to and including the very last page."

HOT SHOT

With over 150 amazon reviews and an average of 4.7/5 stars. "The reader gets an inside view of Silicon Valley and is allowed us to see its very dark side. What a hornet's nest of cutthroat people only concerned for two things - themselves and money!"

"Sheldon Siegel is a great storyteller… One of my favourite parts of this series is reading what Mike thinks — I love his sense of humour!"

Featuring Detective Gold and Detective A.C. Battle

THE TERRORIST NEXT DOOR

"Chicago Detectives David Gold and A.C. Battle are strong entries in the police-thriller sweepstakes, with Sheldon Siegel's THE TERRORIST NEXT DOOR, a smart, surprising and bloody take on the world of Islamic terror." *New York Times* best-selling author Sheldon Siegel tells a story that is fast and furious and authentic." *John Sandford. New York Times Best Selling author of the Lucas Davenport Prey series.*

"Sheldon Siegel blows the doors off with his excellent new thriller, THE TERRORIST NEXT DOOR. Bombs, car chases, the shutdown of Chicago, plus Siegel's winning touch with character makes this one not to be missed!" *John Lescroart. New York Times Best Selling Author of the Dismas Hardy novels.*

"Sheldon Siegel knows how to make us root for the good guys in this heart-stopping terrorist thriller, and David Gold and A.C. Battle are a pair of very good guys." *Thomas Perry. New York Times Best Selling Author of POISON FLOWER.*

ALSO BY SHELDON SIEGEL

Mike Daley/Rosie Fernandez Novels
Special Circumstances
Incriminating Evidence
Criminal Intent
Final Verdict
The Confession
Judgment Day
Perfect Alibi
Felony Murder Rule
Serve and Protect
Hot Shot
The Dreamer

David Gold/A.C. Battle Novels
The Terrorist Next Door

Connect with Sheldon

Email: sheldon@sheldonsiegel.com
Website: www.sheldonsiegel.com
Amazon: amazon.com/author/sheldonsiegel
Facebook: sheldonsiegelauthor
Twitter: @SheldonSiegel
Goodreads: www.goodreads.com/author/show/69191.Sheldon_Siegel

Made in the USA
Monee, IL
07 December 2020

51203585R00174